MY LITTLE GIRL

BOOKS BY SHALINI BOLAND

The Secret Mother
The Child Next Door
The Millionaire's Wife
The Silent Sister
The Perfect Family
The Best Friend
The Girl from the Sea
The Marriage Betrayal
The Other Daughter
One of Us Is Lying
The Wife

MY LITTLE GIRL

SHALINI BOLAND

Bookouture

Published by Bookouture in 2021

An imprint of Storyfire Ltd.
Carmelite House
50 Victoria Embankment
London EC4Y 0DZ

www.bookouture.com

ISBN: 978-1-83888-148-1
eBook ISBN: 978-1-83888-147-4

For my family

DAY ONE

I spy her in her red dress, those dark waves tumbling down her back. What a happy child. Even against such a riotous backdrop of colour and sound and light, she shines.

I don't want to do this. I've never taken anything that wasn't mine to take. But there's no doubt in my mind this is what I have to do. It's the only way to balance the scales. The only way to make them pay. Why should they get the perfect family and the happy ending? It's my turn now...

CHAPTER ONE

JILL

Our faces have become stretched and distorted, our bodies thin and wavering in the glass. My seven-year-old granddaughter Beatrice and her best friend, Millie, are laughing so much, I worry they might make themselves sick. Especially after eating that enormous bag of sticky candy floss. My daughter-in-law Claire won't be happy that I've let them have so much sugar, but it's a special occasion, a treat. What's the point of being a grandparent if I can't spoil my only grandchild? I conveniently set aside the fact that it's actually my son, Oliver, who's treated them.

Oliver bought the fair tickets and gave me thirty pounds to spend on the girls, bless his heart. He was supposed to have brought Beatrice and Millie to the funfair this evening, but the poor boy has been so tired and stressed with work this week that I offered to do it for him. I know Claire has got it into her head that I can't mind my granddaughter responsibly, but I did raise my own child without any major mishaps, so I think I can just about cope. Oliver decided it would be best if we didn't actually tell Claire about it until afterwards. We'll say it was a last-minute work emergency. She's out with her friends this evening, so I'm sure she'll be nice and relaxed. She'll be fine.

She needn't have worried. Everything's going swimmingly. We're all having a wonderful time – me especially. Being here with the girls is making me feel young again. I remember Bob and I brought Oliver to this very same fair when he was a little boy. *My Bob.* I've been utterly lost without him these past four years. That heart attack was so sudden, so cruel. We should have had so much more time together. Tears prickle behind my eyes and I give a big sniff, tell myself not to be so maudlin. I'm here with my lovely Bea, having a rare fun evening. I can't spoil it with sad thoughts.

'Granny!' Beatrice takes my hand and pulls me into another of the little chambers in this labyrinthine hall of mirrors. Disconcertingly, the walls are jet black in this room, making it hard to gauge exactly how large the space is. Beatrice's mahogany hair is swinging, her dark eyes flashing. She looks like a little Spanish dancer in her red dress with frills around the hem, and her matching sparkly red sandals. Thankfully, she's always loved to wear swirly dresses and bright colours, unlike her friends who all seem to go for today's dreadfully boring fashion of jeans and leggings and those atrocious dark-coloured hoodies. *No*, my little Bea is gloriously extrovert and colourful, just like me.

I smooth my hands over my turquoise paisley wrap-dress and pat my long wavy hair, greying now, but still a hint of the glossy brunette I used to be. I glance up and join in the peal of Beatrice and Millie's laughter as we clown around in front of a mirror that takes up the whole of one wall. It's widened our bodies so that we appear to be almost square.

I'm thrilled the girls are having such a marvellous time. Maybe after this evening Claire will realise that I'm perfectly capable of looking after my own flesh and blood. I wish my daughter-in-law and I got along better. I really, genuinely do. I've tried and tried, but she's so spiky, so dismissive. I get the feeling that she just tolerates me.

'Granny, your phone's ringing.' Beatrice reaches into my handbag and pulls out my mobile phone, passing it to me.

'You've got good hearing,' I tell my granddaughter. 'I can't believe you heard that above all the noise in here.'

Beatrice and Millie giggle and race over to the mirror on the far wall. I peer at my phone screen to see a missed call from Laurel, my ex-daughter-in-law, Oliver's first wife. I'll call her back later.

'Wait for me, girls!' I hurry after them, my phone still in my hand, but it starts vibrating. It's Laurel again. I suppose it must be urgent if she's trying a second time. 'Girls,' I call, 'I'm just going to take this call. Stay where I can see you.'

'Don't worry, Granny!'

I slide the icon across the screen. 'Laurel?'

'Jill.'

'Hi, Laurel. Everything okay? You'll have to speak up. I'm at the fair with Beatrice. The music's too loud to hear anything properly.' I glance up to see the girls pulling silly faces at their wobbly reflections and I can't help smiling. A family with young children bustle past and I'm forced to move over so I don't lose sight of my two.

'Sorry, Jill. You're busy. I'll let you go.' Laurel's voice is steeped in gloom.

'No, it's fine,' I reassure, 'I can chat for a moment or two.'

'Are you sure?'

'Yes, of course.'

Beatrice beckons to me to follow them into the next chamber. I edge past the family and a gaggle of raucous teenagers, anxious not to lose sight of my young charges. The next chamber is as bright as the previous one was dark, with wide red-and-white-striped walls giving the impression we're inside a stick of rock or a candy cane. It's busier in here, and Beatrice is almost camouflaged, her scarlet dress the same shade of red as the walls.

'Did you say you're at the fair?' Laurel asks.

'Yes, with Beatrice and her friend. I thought I mentioned it to you yesterday.'

'Maybe. I can't remember. No Oliver?'

'No. Claire's out with friends and Oliver's tired, so I offered.'

'And Claire's okay with that? With you taking Beatrice?'

I hear the scepticism in Laurel's voice and I get a sudden urge to defend Claire.

'She doesn't know yet, but she'll be fine.' I do feel slightly guilty that Laurel knows my relationship with Claire isn't exactly the best in the world. I mean, I love my daughter-in-law, of course I do, she's Beatrice's mother. But I've always clicked more with Laurel. It's a personality thing. And I suppose I haven't quite come to terms with the fact that Laurel and Oliver are no longer together. Even though it's been over eight years since they divorced, Laurel and I stayed friends. 'Is everything okay?'

'I'm just feeling a bit... down. My flatmates are always out having fun, my art isn't selling enough to let me give up my shifts at the restaurant. I'm just calling to moan. Sorry. I'll go.'

'Oh, Laurel. You know you can have a moan whenever you like.' I feel sorry for her. She hasn't moved on from Oliver. Never met anyone new that she stuck with – or who's stuck with her. I feel it's the least I can do to be an ear for her when she needs it.

'Thanks, Jill. I don't know what I'd do without your friendship.'

I realise that I've lost sight of the girls for a moment. 'Hang on a sec, Laurel. I just need to...' I take the phone from my ear and glance around the room, the wavering reflections merging with the sudden crowd of visitors. I catch glimpses of red that make my heart skitter with relief, until I realise it's just the candy-striped wallpaper, or someone's T-shirt. Suddenly, I'm very hot and very cold all at once.

'Beatrice!' I cry, my voice tremulous and thin. 'Bea!'

A few people turn to stare, but I don't make eye contact. I'm too busy scanning the room. They've probably just gone into the next room. I need to calm down.

'Are you okay?' A young woman touches my arm, her brown eyes filled with worry.

'My... my granddaughter and her friend. They're only seven. I can't see where they are... Beatrice! Millie!'

'Oh. We'll help look. Don't worry. What do they look like?'

'Beatrice has dark hair, a red dress. Millie…' What does Millie look like? *Focus, Jill.* 'She's got dark-brown hair and she's wearing grey leggings and a T-shirt with a picture of a dog. You know, those little dogs with the squashed faces.'

'A pug?'

'Yes. Yes that's it.'

'Is that her?'

I look to where the woman is pointing, and feel my shoulders grow light with relief as I spot Millie pulling faces in one of the mirrors. 'Oh, thank goodness. That's her friend, Millie. Thank you.' I smile at the woman who says something comforting and gives a little laugh. If Millie's over there, then Beatrice can't be too far away.

I remember Laurel's still on the phone which I'm clutching tightly, my palm now slippery with sweat. I bring it back to my ear. 'Sorry, Laurel, I've got to go. I'll call you back, okay?'

'Is everything—' She's still speaking as I end the call. I'll apologise later, but right now I can't relax until I've laid eyes on my granddaughter. I stride over to Millie who glances up with a shy smile.

'Having fun?'

She nods.

'Where's Beatrice?'

'She's…' Millie frowns and looks to her left, and then to her right. She turns and scans the room. The hot and cold feeling returns, along with a loud and juddering heartbeat.

'Millie.' I take hold of her shoulders. 'Which way did she go?'

Her face pales. 'I don't know.'

I take the girl's hand and head to the next room of mirrors, the walls a kaleidoscope of colour. It's full of families and friends laughing, the music is pounding, the air stifling. There's no sign of Beatrice. Perhaps she went back to the previous room. I almost drag Millie with me and we push our way back through the crowded candy-striped room and into the black room once again. My worried, distorted reflections loom back at me.

'Beatrice!' I cry, my voice not powerful enough to cut through the laughter and the music. 'Beatrice! Where are you?' Maybe she went outside. It's so hot in here, she probably needed some fresh air.

'Still looking for your granddaughter?' I whirl around and see the face of the young woman I spoke to a moment ago.

'I can't find her!'

'Don't worry. She'll be here somewhere. Age seven, dark hair, red dress, right?'

I nod. *It'll be okay. She'll be fine.* I'm sure I'm panicking over nothing. I remember losing sight of Oliver when he was just a little younger than Beatrice. It was in a department store and he was hiding among a rack of winter coats. Little scamp. I got the store to put out an announcement over the tannoy. Scared me silly at the time. This will be the same thing. Of course it will.

Millie and I quickly scour each room in the hall of mirrors before stumbling outside into the warm evening sunshine. Millie is crying now, big gulping sobs and fat tears that slide down her face. I should comfort her, but I can barely see straight, barely breathe. I scan the area, but there's no sign of my granddaughter.

She's not in there.

She's not out here.

Where is she? She can't have just disappeared into thin air. I'm sure she must be somewhere nearby. She has to be.

How will I tell Oliver and Claire that I've lost our darling Beatrice? *They'll never, ever forgive me.*

CHAPTER TWO

CLAIRE

I stare back at my reflection in the mirror as I place my mobile phone on the oak dressing table with a gentle thunk. My makeup is immaculate, my straight black hair gleaming. One minute I'm getting ready to have a night out with my friends, the next minute I'm listening to my mother-in-law hysterically explain that she's lost Beatrice. *Lost* her. Why was Jill even *with* Beatrice? And where's Ollie? I don't think any of this is sinking in. It can't be real, can it? Things like this happen to other people. Careless people. Not people like me.

Don't get angry. Don't get angry. Don't panic. Stay calm. It will all be fine. It will be okay. Kids wander off all the time and their parents find them. She'll have been sidetracked by something or other. Although, in this case, it was probably Jill who wandered off or got distracted. Beatrice is probably looking for her absent-minded granny right this second. But Jill stressed on the phone that they'd looked everywhere – she and the fairground employees, the members of the public. They did a thorough search. She's already called my husband, Ollie, and he's heading over there now. The fairground manager has called the police. The *police*!

My vision blurs, my reflection distorting in the mirror. Why am I still sitting here? I need to move! I need to get to the fairground. I push myself to my feet, snatch up my phone and glance around the messy bedroom – clothes flung everywhere. I'd tried on numerous outfits for my evening out, opting for my favourite navy dress. I don't have time to change but I leave the new strappy brown sandals where they are and pull a pair of grubby white tennis pumps from the wardrobe, tug them over my feet – smudging my still-tacky toenail varnish – and lace them up with fumbling fingers.

Again, I try to tamp down the flare of anger at having Jill inform me that she was at the fair with my daughter and her friend instead of Oliver. He knows my feelings about his mother. It's nothing personal, but she's just too scatty to be trusted to look after Beatrice alone. She always has mishaps with her, and that's not an exaggeration. The final straw was around a year ago when Jill left Beatrice in her eighty-five-year-old neighbour's garden while she nipped to the shops to buy burgers for a barbecue. While she was out, Beatrice fell and hurt her wrist and had to be rushed to A & E. Her wrist was only sprained, thank goodness, but that's not the point.

Ollie and I both agreed that we wouldn't let Jill look after Beatrice on her own after that. And now look what's happened! What could have possessed my husband to change his mind and let her take them to the fair? What was so important that he had to call his mother to take them instead of him, as previously arranged? I grit my teeth in fury at the fact that the two of them have obviously concocted this behind my back because they knew I wouldn't approve. I hate being the bad guy, but it's not because I want to be mean, it's because I *dreaded* something like this happening.

Before going downstairs, I grab a tissue from the box on my dressing table and use it to wipe off my dark lipstick. I can't go to look for my missing daughter dressed up to the nines. It doesn't seem right. Surely the police will find Beatrice before I get there. Unless... what if someone took her? Someone from the fair? Or a random stranger. *No.* Don't think like that. My hands begin to shake, my knees buckle and a deep coldness rushes through me. I can't let my imagination get the better of me. I have to be positive.

Panicking won't help. I punch out a text to my best friend, Freya, to say I can't make it tonight. That Beatrice has gone missing at the fair but that I'm sure she'll turn up any minute.

I take a breath and hurry down the stairs into the dim hallway, the late summer light already fading. Snatching up the car keys from the hall table, I take a moment to call Oliver to see if there's any news. My call goes to voicemail. He must already be en route to the fair. I wait for the outgoing message to end before snapping.

'Ollie, what the hell happened? Why was your mum at the fair with the girls? Is there any news? Surely they've found Beatrice by now. I'm getting in the car but call me the second you hear anything.' My voice is sharp and shrill. I can't tell if what I'm feeling is fury or fear. Probably both.

Just before I head out the door, my gaze catches on a school photo of Beatrice on the wall. It was taken a couple of years ago. She's grinning at the camera, her eyes twinkling with mischief. My breath hitches and I blink back emotion. I have to get to my little girl.

My phone buzzes and my heart jumps at the thought of it being Oliver with news of our little daughter. But it's just Freya texting back, telling me to try not to worry, and to let her know if she can help in any way. I send back a quick text saying I'll keep her posted.

I close the door to our 1970s chalet bungalow that sits at the bottom of St Catherine's Hill. The summer air is warm and still. The birds are singing and I can hear children's laughter from the neighbours' gardens. It's a perfectly beautiful evening. But the dread in my stomach dips and roils. All I can do right now is drive to the fairground and hope that this feeling will end soon. That my bright and beautiful daughter will be home this evening and we can put this whole horrible episode behind us.

It'll be fine. Jill's so scatty, she's obviously just lost sight of her. It's happened before. This time won't be any different... will it?

CHAPTER THREE

JILL

'Is it my fault?' Millie asks through hiccupping sobs, her blue eyes swimming with tears. We're sitting on one of the wooden fairground benches, my arm around this little girl who isn't Beatrice, while Oliver speaks to the police. His face is grey with worry as he runs a hand through his brown wavy hair. I've already told the police what happened, and now they're letting me have a few minutes' break while they speak to my son. I haven't even had a proper chance to speak to Oliver myself yet, other than to give him a hug and say how sorry I am, how terrible I feel. My heart hurts that I'm the one who's brought this distress to his door.

I gaze down at Millie. 'Of course it's not your fault, Millie. Beatrice has just got lost, that's all. The police are going to find her any minute now, just you wait and see.' I'm trying to reassure myself as much as Millie.

She nods and puts her thumb in her mouth, even though she's not a baby any more. Must be a comfort thing. I feel like doing the same. I absolutely can't believe what's happened. One minute the three of us were all having a wonderful time, laughing and pulling silly faces in the mirrors, the next... well, it's all a terrible nightmare.

The police arrived quickly and set up a cordon around the whole fair, letting people out one at a time and asking them if they'd seen

Beatrice. I had to send them a photo of my granddaughter from my phone. Of course, they've had to close the fair temporarily. Right now, they're speaking to all the employees and asking to look in their vehicles and caravans. I was certain she'd have turned up by now. It's crazy. Where could she have got to? She wouldn't have run away, and I don't understand how she could have got lost – not when she was right next to Millie. Although, being in the hall of mirrors made it very confusing.

'Are you sure you didn't see where Beatrice went, Millie?' I ask again.

She shakes her head vehemently.

'Is Beatrice playing a joke, do you think? Did she tell you to keep it a secret?'

Millie unplugs her thumb. 'No. I want my mum.'

'Of course you do. She'll be here soon, pet. Don't worry.' I can't tell if Millie's being truthful, or if she's keeping something from me on purpose. The police questioned her very briefly, but they're waiting for her parents to arrive before they speak to her properly. Perhaps then she'll be more talkative. What a mess. How did this happen? Why did I take that call from Laurel? Is this really my fault? Surely not. Even when I was talking to Laurel on the phone, I still kept one eye on the girls. I literally lost concentration for the briefest of heartbeats.

I haven't mentioned to the police that I was on the phone at the time when Beatrice disappeared. It's not relevant and I know Claire would only hold it against me if she found out I was speaking to Laurel. Anyway, I'm almost certain Beatrice will turn up at any moment. The alternative is too unthinkable.

'Mummy!' Millie wriggles out from my arm and races across the grass towards a smartly dressed couple with blanched, worried faces. She throws herself at both parents, both of whom crouch down and bring her in for kisses and a hug. The woman looks over her daughter's head and locks eyes with me. I suppose I'd better go over there and explain what's happened. The thought makes me feel physically sick.

I suddenly feel my age. Earlier I was congratulating myself on feeling so energetic and vibrant. Being here at the fair with these sweet girls had reminded me of being a young parent again, but now... now I feel like a doddering old granny. Someone who's not to be relied upon. Not to be entrusted with the care of my own granddaughter. I make myself stand straighter, smooth down my dress and walk over to this family who are strangers to me.

They both stand. Millie's mother, an attractive blonde, holds her daughter in close, as though she's protecting her against *me*.

'Hello.' I hold out my hand. 'I'm Jill Nolan, Beatrice's grand-mother.' No one reaches to shake my hand so I let it fall back to my side.

'I'm Millie's dad, Paul Jensen. This is my wife, Tanya.' He's tall, intimidating, with short brown hair and a light tan. 'Can you tell us what's going on? Oliver called to say Beatrice is missing. He said he wasn't here when it happened. That you were here alone with the girls. With our daughter.' Paul Jensen's words are clipped; his eyes clouded and his face taut, a muscle in his cheek twitching.

Tanya puts a hand on his arm before turning back to me. 'Have they found her? Beatrice?'

'No.' I swallow. 'Not yet. The police are...' I gesture to the fairground. 'They're looking. Oliver's talking to them now. We're waiting for Claire to arrive.' I feel as though I'm in a bad dream. Everything is wobbling around me, like the distorted mirrors from earlier. I really don't feel good at all.

'What I don't understand,' Paul says, fixing me with a hard stare, 'is why you were looking after Millie. I mean, no offence, but we don't even know you. I thought Oliver was supposed to be bringing them.'

Oh dear, this isn't good at all. 'He was, but...' My hands are flapping around like demented crows and I can't seem to think straight.

'Go easy, Paul.' Tanya gives me a kind look while stroking Millie's hair. 'Her granddaughter's missing.'

'I understand that. But this could just as easily be Millie missing too. You're obviously not a fit person to be in charge of two young children, least of all my daughter.'

Tanya turns to him and pulls him back, whispering heatedly.

I'm mortified by his attack, but I don't have the emotional energy to stick up for myself. 'You're right. You're absolutely right,' I stammer. 'I'm so sorry.' My knees are giving way and I don't want to be rude to this couple but I have to get back to that bench before I keel over. 'I'm sorry,' I repeat before turning and walking away.

Tanya follows and puts a hand under my elbow to guide me. 'No, *I'm* sorry about my husband,' she whispers. 'He didn't mean to be so rude. He's just very protective of our youngest. He'll be mortified when he realises how he spoke to you.'

I nod, grateful for her help getting me back to the bench. I thank her as I sink down onto the wooden seat, the air whooshing out of my lungs. The evening is still so warm. I could really do with a nice cool breeze. I wish it were autumn already.

Tanya squeezes my hand. 'I'm sure they'll find Beatrice any minute now and we can all breathe a sigh of relief.'

'Tan!' Paul calls across the grass. 'The police want to speak to Millie in a minute. You coming?'

'Will you be okay sitting here on your own?' Her concern makes me feel older and frailer than ever. But she's sweet to worry. A really nice woman. Millie's lucky to have her as a mum.

'My son will be over any minute, and Claire's on her way. I'll be fine. Thank you.'

'Okay. Try not to worry. I'm sure Beatrice will be found before you know it.'

I nod, but somehow all my usual optimism has deserted me. All I can think about is my poor darling Beatrice frightened somewhere. Alone. Or worse.

CHAPTER FOUR

CLAIRE

I'm amazed I didn't crash the car on the short drive over to the fairground. I don't even remember the journey I was in such a daze. Before leaving, I received a text from Oliver asking me to bring a worn item of Beatrice's clothing for the sniffer dogs to use. That text almost made me vomit. It brought it home to me that this might not be one of those everyday family dramas. That it might be something more serious. With trembling fingers, I took Beatrice's rainbow nightshirt from under her pillow and inhaled the scent of her before folding it and putting it into my handbag.

I park in the supermarket car park opposite the fairground, buy a parking ticket from the machine and head to the pedestrian crossing where I wait for the lights to change. There's a steady stream of traffic; no chance of even the tiniest gap where I might dart across the road. A family standing next to me express their dismay at the CLOSED sign displayed at the entrance to the fair.

'I thought it was supposed to be open until ten,' the woman says.

'It is,' the man replies. 'I checked the website.'

'You sure you got the right day? It's not even eight and it looks pretty closed to me.'

'Look, there's police over there.' The man sighs. 'Something's obviously happened.' Their tween girls are interrupting their conversation, asking if they're still able to go to the fair, disappointment lacing their words. My heart stutters when I realise that their disappointment has been caused by my lost daughter. I want to tell this family to shut up, to stop being so insensitive. But it's not their fault. They don't know that my Beatrice has gone missing.

'Probably an accident,' the woman says. 'One of the rides might have broken. Maybe we had a lucky escape. That could have been us on there. Hope no one got hurt.'

'Let's ask if they're planning to open again tonight.'

The lights change and we all cross the road together. I tune out their speculative chatter and pull ahead, walking quickly. Focusing on the fairground, I scan the area, convinced that at any moment I'll spot Beatrice in her new red dress and everything will be right with the world again. I'll even go easy on Jill and Oliver for their part in this. Just please let my Beatrice be okay.

I head to the entrance gate where a uniformed police officer stands talking into his radio. It takes me a moment to catch his eye. He nods in the direction of the CLOSED sign. 'Sorry, fair's closed until further notice.'

'I need to speak to someone. My name's Claire Nolan. My daughter, Beatrice… she's the one who's…' I break off as my voice catches in my throat.

His eyes soften. 'You're Beatrice Nolan's mother?'

I nod. 'Have they found her?'

'Not yet.'

My stomach drops.

'Sorry to ask, but have you got any ID on you?'

I nod again, delve into my handbag and bring out my wallet with my driving licence. The officer speaks into his radio again, letting someone know I'm here.

He nods his acceptance at my ID. 'Come on through.'

I push at the turnstile and enter the temporary fairground. I feel the stares of the family who crossed the road with me. I glance over my shoulder and lock eyes with the mother. She quickly looks away and I dismiss her from my thoughts, turning my attention to the scene ahead. Straining my eyes, hoping desperately to spot Bea.

I see Oliver straight away, talking to a woman in a black suit, her raven hair streaked with white tied in a ponytail. Next to her, a younger, dark-haired tallish man in a grey suit is taking notes. I guess they must be police officers.

Ollie looks stressed, agitated, his eyes hooded, his palms constantly smoothing his hair in a self-soothing motion. There are sweat patches on his shirt, and his trousers are crumpled. Please don't let this be the beginning of a nightmare. Please let this be a short, stressful blip that will be resolved any minute now. One of those days that we'll look back on and gasp at how close we came to losing everything. Let us get our little Bea back safely and we'll hug her and laugh and cry and admonish her never to go wandering off again, and we'll treat ourselves to ice cream and it will all be okay. And we'll go home tired but relieved. Thankful.

I stride across the grass more purposefully than I feel. Ollie blanches as he spots me, no doubt wondering how he'll explain why his mother was looking after the kids instead of him. I can't let my anger at him overshadow what's important here. But at least my fury's distracting me from the sheer terror of the situation.

'Claire.' Despite his facial expression a moment ago, Ollie sounds relieved and he takes a step towards me. He halts after one step, unsure how to greet me. I make the decision for him and give him a brief hug which he returns before introducing me to the officers. 'This is my wife, Claire.'

'Hello, Claire.' The woman officer gives me a polite nod, a flash of sympathy in her smile. 'I'm the investigating officer, DI Meena Khatri, and this is DS Tim Garrett. We've been filling in your husband on what happened here, according to his mother, Jill Nolan.'

'Is there any news? Did anyone see anything?' I stare at DI Khatri, knowing the answer already.

'Not yet, but we're hopeful. It's only been an hour so she can't have got very far.'

'Unless she's in a car,' I add.

'We've spoken to almost everyone who was at the fair at the time, and we've taken the contact details of everyone who was in the immediate vicinity where she was last seen. CSIs are on their way to sweep the area.'

'What about CCTV cameras?' I ask, my brain racing forward to think of anything they may have missed. I know it's their job, but they'll never be as invested as me.

'We have instant access to local authority cameras. Private ones take a little longer. But we'll do everything we can to get you reunited with your daughter.'

'And Jill?' I ask, glancing at my husband. 'What does she have to say about it? What actually happened.'

'She's understandably very shaken,' Khatri says.

'I think she's in shock,' Oliver adds.

'Yes, but what actually happened?' I repeat.

'According to Mum, she was with them in the hall of mirrors and Beatrice just disappeared.'

I try not to sneer at my husband. 'How can she just disappear? What was Jill doing at the time? Was she with them, or did she wander off?'

'She said they were looking in the mirrors and having a good time, but it was crowded and she lost sight of the girls briefly. A woman helped her search for them and they spotted Millie but Beatrice wasn't with her. Millie doesn't know what happened either, so it wasn't just Mum.'

'Yes, but Millie's seven years old,' I snap. 'I wouldn't expect her to be keeping an eye on Bea.'

Oliver flushes. 'That's not what I meant. I didn't—'

'We've spoken to Millie,' DI Khatri interrupts.

'How is she?' I ask.

'A little shaken, but fine.' I open my mouth but Khatri anticipates my question before I can ask it. 'Millie says she didn't see anything or anyone suspicious. Did you manage to bring an item of Beatrice's clothing?'

I close my mouth and pull Beatrice's nightshirt out of my bag, reluctant to hand it over. The detective inspector reaches for it with a sympathetic smile.

'Thank you. This will help,' she says.

DS Garrett takes it from her and says he'll run it over to the dog handler.

The next few minutes are spent answering questions about Beatrice's mental health, her state of mind, was she happy, had we had any recent disagreements, was she on any medication.

I reply that she's a regular seven-year-old child, outgoing, friendly, happy, no medication, no issues as far as we're concerned. With each question we answer, Khatri's eyes lock onto ours, hard and probing.

'She didn't run away, if that's what you're getting at.'

'We're just trying to build up a picture,' the DI replies.

'Beatrice is a happy child,' Oliver adds. 'We're a close-knit family.'

Khatri gives a short nod, which makes me think that she's taking everything we say with a pinch of salt. That our word isn't good enough. I suppose I should be pleased that she's taking things seriously, but it's bad enough that our daughter's missing without being made to feel like it could be our fault. Even though Khatri is perfectly polite, it feels as though we're the ones who've done something wrong. As though we're responsible for Beatrice's disappearance. Like we're suspects.

'Does Beatrice have a mobile phone?' Khatri asks.

'No,' I reply. 'We thought she was too young.' Although, right now, I wish we'd let her have one. Maybe that way we could have used it to call or track her.

A juddering whirr overhead distracts Oliver and me from Khatri's questioning. 'That's a police helicopter,' Khatri confirms. 'It's nothing to be alarmed about. It'll be helpful in covering more ground more quickly. It's good that your daughter's wearing red – easier to spot from a distance.'

Police, helicopters, sniffer dogs… what is going on? How can this even be happening? An image of Beatrice in her red dress flashes into my mind like a photograph from a long time ago. I'm already leaping to the worst conclusions. Already imagining outcomes that I'd rather not. I have to stop this. Have to keep positive. She'll be found soon – I'm hopeful that this sharp-eyed inspector will see to that – and then we'll all make our way home. I'll tuck Beatrice up in bed and read her a bedtime story. The alternative doesn't bear thinking about.

CHAPTER FIVE

CLAIRE

The inspector leaves me and Oliver alone for the moment, telling us to stay put and that she'll be back soon. After she's gone, I find myself staring at my husband. I don't want to have an argument with him. We need to be united in our search for Beatrice. To support one another.

But I can't help asking, 'Why didn't you bring the girls to the fair? Why did your mum have them? I thought we agreed that she…' I want to say that she isn't responsible, that she's too scatty, but this is his mother. Being critical of her won't help. So I repeat myself instead. 'I thought that *you* were going to bring them?'

Oliver massages his forehead with his fingers, then pushes his dark waves back. 'I know. I'm sorry. I was feeling stressed with work, and I've got so much paperwork to catch up on.'

Oliver owns Priory Art Supplies, a local shop he set up over ten years ago, before we met. He also runs an online version which is just as successful due to a loyal customer base that he's built up over the years, along with group discounts offered to art classes and schools.

'Paperwork?' I think about my own mountains of paperwork. I'm an independent financial advisor so I always have a tonne of forms to fill in.

'Bills, tax forms, the usual,' he replies. 'I knew you were looking forward to your night out so I didn't want to bother you with it. Mum offered to take the girls and I said yes. I think she suspects we don't trust her to look after Bea. So she wanted to prove she can handle it.'

I clench my teeth to stop the various retorts flying to my lips. Oliver knows what I'm thinking. He's already beating himself up about it. It won't help if I add to his guilt. I look away and my gaze lands on a figure sitting at a picnic table wrapped in a blanket, sipping a disposable cup of tea – *Jill*.

Oliver follows my gaze. 'Go easy on her, Claire. She can't possibly feel any worse than she already does.'

I shake my head. 'Don't make me out to be the bad guy here.'

My husband sucks in a breath and follows me as I stride over to my mother-in-law trying to calm my pulsing veins and the white-hot simmering rage in my gut. I launch straight in.

'What happened, Jill?'

'Claire. I'm so sorry. I… I don't exactly know. One minute she was there, and the next…'

She makes to stand, but Oliver puts a hand on her shoulder.

'You're in shock, Mum. Stay sitting down.'

Jill does as her son says and I try to squash the resentment that my husband seems more concerned with his mother's well-being than with mine. I know it's not a competition and that I'm being unreasonable. Jill didn't lose Beatrice on purpose, but she's always so mellow and laid-back, silently judging me for my parenting style. For being too uptight.

I remember last summer when Oliver, Bea, Jill and I were walking along Christchurch Quay. It was a busy spring afternoon and the quay was packed with families like us out for an afternoon stroll. Beatrice was skipping ahead, feeding the ducks, and it was hard to keep sight of her. She was looking for her favourite duck – they all look the same to me, but she swore this particular duck was her friend. I called out for her to slow down, to stay where I could see her, and I could feel Jill's aura of disapproval, like I'm this stressed-out controlling mother who doesn't let her child breathe. That I should let her skip ahead and use her imagination more, loosen the reins. Well, Jill certainly loosened the reins tonight.

It's taking all my willpower not to scream at the woman. To tell her how incompetent she is. How she had no right to take my daughter to the fair. That she's not responsible enough, and *now* look what's happened! But I know it's not her fault. She didn't do it on purpose.

'Are you okay, Jill?' I ask instead.

She gives a slow nod and huddles over her tea, like a frightened rabbit.

I turn to Oliver. 'We should be looking for Beatrice, not standing around here talking.'

'I know, but the detective told us to stay put. Maybe we should tell her we want to help. Mum, will you be okay here for a while? Do you want me to call someone to sit with you or drive you home?'

'No, you go, I'll be fine. I'll drink this and then I'll join in the search with you. I just… I feel a little out of sorts. A bit shaky.'

'It's okay. You stay there, Jill,' I add, placing a hand on her arm, trying to be nice.

'Thanks, love.' Jill pats my hand distractedly, her eyes glazed. 'I'm sure they'll find her any minute. She probably got distracted and wandered off. Got herself lost.'

Not so distracted that she left the fair by herself. Beatrice would never do that. I squash down the fears that have begun shooting up like vines, twisting and squeezing out any optimism I may have had.

Oliver and I walk away from Jill, back towards the entrance, keeping an eye out for either DI Khatri or DS Garrett so we can tell them we're going to join in the search.

'Claire.'

I turn at a woman's voice. My heart plummets as fast as one of the fairground rides as I see Tanya, Paul and Millie Jensen coming up behind us. Oliver nods at them and I stutter out a hello. Millie's face is tear-streaked and her parents look drawn and stressed. Tanya has concern in her eyes but Paul's expression is hard, accusing.

'Any news?' Tanya asks.

'Not yet,' Oliver replies.

'I'm sure they'll find her soon.' Tanya turns to Paul as though seeking confirmation, but his eyes are trained on Oliver.

'I thought *you* were taking Millie to the fair,' he snaps to my husband. '*You* picked her up. You never mentioned your mother was bringing them.'

Oliver stiffens. 'It was a last-minute thing. I didn't think you'd mind.'

'Yeah, well, when it comes to who's looking after my kids, I always mind.'

Tanya mouths to me that she's sorry and I give her a discreet nod.

'Well, I apologise if I caused any upset.' Oliver's mouth tightens. My husband rarely gets angry. His laid-back attitude balances my tendency to worry. It's what attracted me to him in the first place. Well, that and his gorgeous looks. He's tall, and handsome in a dishevelled way. And he doesn't even know he's good-looking which only serves to make him even more lovely. But right now his easy-going nature is being stretched by Paul's accusation. To be fair, I can see Paul's point, but there's no way I'm going to let him make Oliver feel any worse than he already does. He has his daughter safe and sound. The man should show some compassion.

'I hope Millie's okay,' I cut in. 'And I really appreciate you being so concerned about our missing daughter while she's out their all alone with God knows who. So I'm sure you'll understand that right now we have to go and search for her.'

'Of course,' Tanya replies.

Paul grunts his acceptance. 'Good luck. I'm sure she'll turn up.'

'There's the DI.' Oliver pulls me away from the Jensens and back towards the entrance where the inspector's listening to a man who looks to be in his sixties with greying hair, a check shirt and chinos. The man is talking intensely, gesturing wildly.

As we draw closer, DI Meena Khatri cuts him off. 'I understand, but we have a child who's gone missing, so I'm afraid you'll just have to accept that your fair may not be reopening this evening.'

'Fine, but you do realise that children get separated from their parents all the time at fairs and parks and beaches and whatnot.' He has a Dorset accent and his face is growing redder with every word. 'Ninety-nine times out of a hundred the nipper shows up completely fine, meanwhile my fair's lost a whole evening's revenue and we'll be obliged to refund all the pre-ordered tickets. It's a bloody headache I can do without.'

I can't believe this man is more concerned with money than with my daughter's well-being. I glare at him before turning to Khatri. 'Hello, I just wanted to check – have you searched all the fair's caravans and Portakabins?'

'We have,' she confirms.

'I hope you're not accusing my staff of anything,' the man growls at me.

'These are Beatrice's parents,' Khatri tells the man.

He flushes and clears his throat. 'Oh. Well. Sorry about what's happened. I'm Monty Burridge, the manager here. Of course we'll do everything we can to help you find her.'

'Thank you,' Oliver replies more politely than I could at this moment in time.

Khatri dismisses Burridge with a curt thank you, and he stalks off, answering a call on his mobile.

'Claire and I want to help your officers in the search,' Oliver says to Khatri. 'We can't just stand around doing nothing. This is our daughter. We need to find her.'

'Of course,' Khatri replies, her dark eyes connecting with first him and then me. 'Before that, we'll need ask you a few more questions. It would also be helpful if we could come to your house and do a thorough search.'

'A search?' Oliver repeats. I'm as taken aback as he is. Why would they need to search our house? Surely they don't think we've got anything to do with this.

Khatri isn't fazed by our reticence. 'It's standard procedure.'

I can't help wondering if this really is standard procedure or whether Khatri believes we might be behind Bea's disappearance. I feel my cheeks grow warm under her gaze. It's as if I'm back at school in assembly where we're all being scrutinised by the head teacher for some misdemeanour and you still feel guilty even though you've done nothing wrong.

Khatri continues. 'We'll also take a look around Beatrice's bedroom. You said she doesn't have a mobile phone, what about a laptop? Or a tablet?'

'She's got an iPad,' I reply. 'But she's only allowed to use it occasionally.'

'Okay. I'll come with DS Garrett to your address. If you can meet us there in the next half hour, that would be great. It's the St Catherine's Hill address you gave me earlier, right?'

Oliver and I nod. I can't quite believe they still haven't located our daughter. That she's been missing for over an hour. My head swims for a moment as I try to comprehend what's happening. That there's a massive police search going on to find our little girl. That they're going to search our house and check her iPad. That at this moment in time I have absolutely no idea where our darling daughter is. It was only this morning that she was holding my hand, skipping back from the shops and singing silly songs.

Where are you, Bea? Where are you?

CHAPTER SIX

JILL

I ease myself out of my Nissan Micra and close the door, its light-blue metallic paint glinting under the street light. I'm home at last, but it all looks so different. Despite its painted white brickwork, my little terraced cottage in the centre of town appears darker somehow. Less welcoming. Its windows like hooded eyes. For the first time ever, I don't want to go inside. But what else am I going to do? Sleep in the car? Wander the streets?

I walk up to the blue front door. I don't have a driveway; the house sits right on the pavement. It can be irritating some days when I can't get a parking space outside my house, or even in my street. But tonight, there was a space large enough for two cars slap bang outside my front door. Not that I care about that right now.

The police were here earlier, doing a search of my house, in case Beatrice had made her way back here somehow. I told them it was highly unlikely as she doesn't have a key. But they asked to do a search nonetheless, and I told them they were welcome to do it.

After their search of my house, I spent two hours at the police station going over my statement, answering the same questions I answered back at the fair. I know the police have to be thorough, but it all felt so repetitive, and going over everything was so stressful. So upsetting. I'm absolutely exhausted and I can't stop thinking about Beatrice and where she is now. If she's okay. If she's scared.

If she's… I give myself a shake, take a breath and open my front door, turn on the hall light and walk into the narrow hallway. Its walls are adorned with framed artwork that I've gathered over the years by my former pupils, from when I was an art teacher at the local comprehensive, as well as works by local artists – Laurel's watercolours of the Dorset landscape are among my favourites.

As I loop my bag over the dark wood bannister, I realise my hands are still shaking. I need a drink. I march into the kitchen-diner and switch on the light. I love this room – cosy and perfectly formed with wooden sash windows and striped curtains, white-painted units with oak worktops, a square dining table, a squashy floral sofa and a green-and-white check armchair.

I reach for the gin on the side table, disappointed to note there's only a third of the bottle left. At least there's a full bottle of tonic water and I manage to locate a shrivelled lemon in the bottom of the fruit bowl. I plonk a couple of ice cubes into a cut-glass tumbler, its gold rim worn and scratched. Sinking into the armchair, I knock back half the glass and wait for the alcohol to numb my panic. To slow my heartbeats.

A nagging voice keeps insisting that it was my fault for taking Laurel's call. For not concentrating properly on the girls. I'm worried about the fact that I omitted to tell the police about the phone call. That I didn't own up to being a little distracted. Should I have told them? But that would have meant admitting that I'd left out that detail in the first place. They might think I left it out on purpose. That I lied. I take another gulp of my G & T, the warm silence of the room hanging heavy. The alcohol isn't erasing my utter distress, but at least it's taking the edge off. I shouldn't beat myself up about the call; it's irrelevant. The hall of mirrors was busy, I lost sight of the girls. That's the truth of the matter. That's all anyone needs to know.

I drain the rest of my drink and pour another generous one. What if Laurel says something? What if she mentions to someone that she was talking to me while I was at the fair? She'll realise that we were on the phone at the time Beatrice went missing. She'll know that I was distracted. No, it's okay, I'll just say that we were talking *before* I lost her. For goodness' sake, people chat on the phone all the time. It's not like I was doing anything wrong!

The events play over in my head. I try to remember how long it was between seeing Beatrice and then realising she was missing. But my brain is foggy. I can't quite remember the exact sequence of events. I think it was a few minutes at most. That's all. A few minutes between everything being wonderful and everything turning into the worst day of my life. My poor Beatrice. And Oliver. His face was… he was distraught, terrified. And I could tell Claire was furious with me, and with Oliver too. Even though she didn't specifically say so. I know she didn't mean to come across that way. It was simply her fear showing. Which is completely understandable.

I only wish I could have been more coherent. More comforting towards the two of them. Instead I did nothing but apologise over and over again, sitting there on that bench with my tea like a feeble old person, making no sense. No wonder Claire was frustrated. No wonder she didn't trust me to look after Bea. I realise now that the reason I never mentioned the phone call to them was because it would confirm Claire's low opinion of me, drive even more of a wedge between us. Not to mention that she'd wonder why I was talking to Oliver's ex-wife of all people.

But none of that is important. All that matters is Beatrice. Finding my granddaughter. That girl is my absolute joy. I adore her. From the moment I first clapped eyes on her swaddled in her soft white blanket after they brought her home from the hospital, I felt such a rush of love. As if she were my own child. With that dark mop of hair, and her precious face. Just like Oliver when he was a baby.

In those early days, Claire was only too happy to let Bob and I babysit. To take Beatrice off her hands while she had meetings with her clients. Claire's a financial advisor. She works from home and found it very difficult at first to separate her work and home life. Not surprising with a new baby. We revelled in our new roles as grandparents. We took her to the park, had messy craft sessions at home, showed her off to our friends. It was perfect. Until my wonderful Bob died suddenly from a massive heart attack and I felt as though the world had ended.

I continued to babysit Bea on my own – my darling grand-daughter gave me a reason to keep going after losing my husband. Beatrice was only three when Bob died so she was quite a handful, but I adored her energy and sweet disposition. Unfortunately, over the following couple of years, a few tiny mishaps meant that Claire became less trusting of me, and our relationship grew more tense. I mean, kids are always getting into scrapes, aren't they?

I tried my best to repair things between Claire and me, but every time I tried to prove that I was more than capable of babysitting my granddaughter, something small would happen that made me look like I couldn't cope. And now *this*. This will prove to Claire that she was right all along. I wish Bob were here to sort out this mess. He'd have found Beatrice straight away. He would know exactly what to do for the best.

I blink and sniff, trying to put these maudlin thoughts away. I've got enough to worry about without dredging up all that grief which can sometimes feel as raw today as it did four years ago.

I can't change what has happened this evening, but at least I can do something proactive. Instead of sitting here feeling sorry for myself, I can act. Make more of an effort to find my grand-daughter. I won't be the one who cries in the corner. I won't be the poor helpless widow.

I go to the loo, splash my face in the cloakroom sink until I feel clear-headed once again, and I leave the house. I'll drive around the local streets in case my darling Beatrice is trying to make her way back to my house. She could be wandering, lost and scared. Perhaps my efforts will prove fruitless, but at least I'll be doing something. Because there's no way I'll be able to sleep tonight. And I can't bear the thought of sitting around in my empty house, not with all these horrible thoughts whizzing around my head.

I ease myself into my car and head back towards the fairground, which is only a couple of minutes' drive away. The roads are quiet, despite it being a Saturday night. Christchurch isn't a big party town. There are a few nice little restaurants and bars, and one nightclub on the outskirts. Most of the younger people head into Bournemouth and Poole if they want a night out. Although my Oliver always preferred to stay local. He liked the relaxed atmosphere here rather than the frenetic energy of Bournemouth with its tourists and stag and hen dos.

There's no space to park on the main road by the fairground, so I cruise past, glancing to my left at the dark shapes of all the rides, still and silent now. I notice a police car parked on the grass outside the entrance gates. I'm glad to see they've posted someone there.

At least it's a warm August night. If Bea is out there somewhere, she won't be shivering with cold.

I try not to listen to the voice that's telling me Beatrice wouldn't be wandering around lost for this amount of time. If she were simply lost, she would have become visibly upset, and someone would have seen her and brought her to the police station by now. So if she's not lost, then what?

The fairground is already behind me and I'm coming up fast to the large roundabout that's always quite scary to pull out onto. I should have turned around before I got to it, but it's too late now. Hopefully it won't be too busy at this time of night. It's silly really, because I've lived here all my life, but I still get flustered about which lane I should be in. Other drivers get so short-tempered if I have to change lanes, as if I'm not allowed to make a mistake. I really do wish people would be kinder to one another.

I indicate right and wait until the roundabout's clear. They come whizzing around so quickly that you have to really put your foot down. Okay, it's clear. I pull out before realising that someone's already on my tail. They're too close. I speed up as they blast their horn and cut around me, music blaring from their car. I tell myself to pay them no attention. They're clearly driving too fast. They shoot off up the dual carriageway and I breathe a little easier. I'm going to double back, go past the fairground once more and then cruise up and down all the residential streets in the vicinity. Please just let me find her.

Finally, I'm around that hellish roundabout and back into familiar territory, keeping my eyes peeled for any movement. I put my headlights onto full beam to give me a better chance of spotting her. I wish Bob were here. He'd find Bea. He'd know what to do. Tears prick the back of my eyes, but I can't cry now. I have to reel in my emotions and stay focused. I must think positive. I'm going to find her. Any minute now, I'll see that swishy red dress, that dark hair. I'll stop the car and gather her into my arms, and everything will be okay.

Another car comes up behind me, its headlights shining too brightly into my rear-view mirror, making me squint. I check the dash and see I'm only driving fifteen miles per hour. I probably need to speed up, but if I do that, I might miss Beatrice. I should pull over to let them go past. The lights are blinding. I flick on my indicator and pull up onto the kerb, waiting for the car to overtake. Instead, it pulls up behind me. This is unsettling, perhaps I should drive off. But what if they follow me?

I can't sit here with whoever that is behind me. I check the driver's door and make sure it's locked. I remove my seatbelt and lean across to check the passenger side. I didn't check the back doors. I wish this car had central locking. I should definitely drive off. What if they're carjackers? My heart is knocking at my ribcage and my hands are shaking. I need to drive away *now*.

I suddenly realise that the light behind me is blue, not white. A blue light? I give a short little scream at the knock on my window. My hand flies to my chest as I see the man's face at the glass. His uniform. It's a police officer. The car behind me was a police car. Thank goodness for that. Suddenly I remember that I've had a drink – a gin and tonic. A *large* gin and tonic. Or was it two? I can't remember. This isn't good. This isn't good at all…

CHAPTER SEVEN

CLAIRE

This is a nightmare. An actual waking nightmare. Where's my daughter? I mean WHERE is she? I pull into the drive behind Oliver's navy VW Passat and get out of my silver Toyota Corolla just like a normal person. Like everything is still the same as it was. It seems like days since I was last home, not hours. I may look calm on the outside, but the reality of what's happened is squeezing my insides so hard I can barely breathe.

My phone buzzes. It's a voicemail from Freya, asking if there's any news about Bea yet, and letting me know that she cancelled the restaurant as my friends didn't think it was right to go out and socialise while I'm going through such a stressful situation. She tells me they'll rearrange once Beatrice is safely home. They all send their love and Freya says she wants to come over and help search. I'm grateful for her offer, but I have too much to deal with right now.

The police detectives will be here at any moment to search the house for possible clues to Bea's whereabouts. As far as I'm concerned, they'd be better off looking for Bea out there on the streets and questioning the fairground employees than wasting time in our house. But I suppose they have to follow procedure.

The front door opens and Oliver stands in the doorway as I bang out a text to Freya.

'What are you doing standing out here?' he asks.

'Nothing. Just texting Freya.'

'Do you want to come in before DI whatsername and the other guy get here?'

'I think her name's DI Khatri.' I climb the front steps to the porch. My phone buzzes with a reply from Freya letting me know she's here whenever we need her.

Back inside the house, Oliver is quiet. His face drawn. I can't tell if he's angry at himself or his mum or me or the situation. Probably all of it. The house feels different as we stagger through to the back lounge, shell-shocked. Ribbons of evening sunlight stream in through the sliding doors. I pull at the curtains, blocking out the glare.

So many questions and accusations bubble up from inside, hovering on my lips, but now is not the time to ask them. Not when I know they'll lead to a full-blown row. The last thing we need is to be in the middle of an argument when the police show up. Ollie and I don't normally *do* arguments. We're a team. We talk about stuff, we sometimes disagree, but we usually talk or tease our way out of any disagreements. But then again, our relationship hasn't really been put to the test before now. Our lives together have been pretty good.

We love one another's company, respect each other's space, we share the workload, share childcare. It's a partnership. And it helps that we also fancy the pants off each other. Our marriage has been almost *too* good. Maybe this is life trying to balance things out…

'Claire—'

'Let's leave our conversation until after the police have gone.' My voice sounds strange in the silent room. Harsh and out of place.

'Fine. What are you going to tell them?' he asks, patches of red mottling his neck.

'The truth. Same as before. That I was on my way out to meet friends. You were catching up on some work. And your mum took the girls to the fair. There's no point bringing up our disagreement about your mum looking after Beatrice.'

Oliver gives a curt nod. I suppose he's relieved that we won't be airing our dirty laundry in public. But this doesn't mean that I won't bring it up again later, after the detectives have gone. I know that blame won't help, but it's something I'll need to get off my chest. A way to relieve the fury still simmering inside me.

We both give a start and turn at the sound of a car revving up the steep drive followed by car doors slamming. I catch my husband's eye and despite the tension between us, we manage to convey some kind of silent solidarity before he goes to the front door to let them in.

I remain where I am, trying to breathe. To prepare for this invasion of our privacy. I remember the state of our bedroom; my clothes flung everywhere like a bazaar. I'm not naturally a messy person, but I was in a rush and didn't have time to tidy up after myself. I shake off the thought. Who cares about the state of the house? It's the least important thing at the moment. Anyway, there's no time left to race upstairs and sort things out.

The sound of voices filters in from the hallway. Oliver's bass notes and DI Meena Khatri's soft-but-firm tone layered over the top. My stomach lurches as they draw closer. The two detectives come into the living room before my husband and I nod at them both, not quite managing a smile.

'Any news?' I ask.

A quick shake of the head from Khatri. 'We're still searching.'

DS Garrett flashes me a sympathetic look, but I can't tell if it's genuine or not. Again, I have the uncomfortable feeling that they're treating us like suspects rather than victims. Even though they're being nice and polite, their gazes are flitting around the room, sizing up everything. Judging, assessing.

'Did no one see anything at the fair?' Oliver asks. 'She's wearing a bright-red dress. Someone must have seen something.'

'We're following all leads,' she replies.

'So you have some leads?' I want them to talk me through exactly what they know.

'Nothing concrete, but we'd like to search your home, if that's okay with you. It may turn up a clue about where she is.'

I take a steadying breath. 'She didn't run off, if that's what you're thinking.'

'We like to explore every avenue. That way we can be certain we don't miss anything.'

'Okay.' I realise they're going to want to do this whatever I say, so the quicker they start, the quicker they can leave and carry on coordinating the search.

The next two hours are spent with them going over every inch of the house. They even go up into the loft, although goodness knows what they expect to find up there. Oliver plies them with cups of tea and biscuits while I pace impatiently and bark out gruff replies to their questions.

After they've combed the place thoroughly, Khatri and Garrett follow us back into the kitchen. We all hover around the table. I don't ask them to take a seat as I'm anxious for them to be gone, to go out and search for our daughter. For Oliver and I to go out and do the same.

Khatri takes a sip of her tea. 'Whenever you're cross with Beatrice, or you argue, does she have a place where she goes, a place of comfort, that type of thing?'

I bristle at the question. '*What? No.* We don't argue.'

'You mean to tell me that you and your seven-year-old daughter never disagree?' Khatri raises an eyebrow.

'Yes, of course we disagree, but it never really gets to the arguing stage. If she's ever cross or upset, she usually just goes to her room.'

'I see.' Khatri looks thoughtful.

'What about a friend's house?' Garrett asks.

'We've already called them all,' Oliver says.

'And anyway, she never goes anywhere without us,' I add.

'She went to the fair with your mother-in-law,' Khatri says quietly.

I try to contain my temper. I don't want the police getting caught up in our family disagreements. If we start getting into Jill's unreliableness and my reluctance to let her look after Beatrice alone, then they might start drawing false conclusions about what happened tonight. I need them to stay focused on finding our daughter, not get bogged down by family drama.

'Yes, I know she went to the fair with Jill,' I reply, trying to keep my cool. 'What I meant to say was, she wouldn't be allowed to go out without adult supervision. So there's no place she would go without our knowledge.'

'You're certain of that?'

'For goodness' sake, yes!'

I know how I sound – like an ungrateful, angry child. This isn't me. This isn't how I am. But this whole searching-our-house thing is a gigantic waste of their time. Of course, it's not their fault; they don't know me or Ollie. They don't realise that we would never harm our child or hide her in the attic or whatever it is they think they might discover. To them, we're probably just as likely to be suspects as the fairground workers. Possibly even more so.

Khatri's eyes soften a little. 'I understand that these questions can be distressing, but we're just trying to—'

'Yes, I know. I'm sorry. I know you're just doing your job.' I bow my head, worried that I might start crying.

Oliver puts a hand on my arm for comfort, but I don't need kindness right now. I just need my daughter.

Finally, thankfully, they leave, taking Beatrice's iPad, along with her passwords and pin numbers. As Oliver sees them out and the front door clicks shut behind them, I exhale and sink into the sofa, pulling my legs up beneath me. I don't plan on relaxing for long, but I just need a moment to gather my thoughts and settle myself after such an invasion of our privacy. To try to get this whole situation straight in my mind. To consider if there's anything we might have missed.

Oliver doesn't return to the living room straight away, which is fine by me. Maybe he needs a moment, too. It's already dark out, a fact that terrifies the life out of me. If our daughter is out there lost and alone at night then goodness knows how she's feeling right now. But I would rather that than any number of alternatives.

Beatrice has never been a timid child. She's not afraid of spiders or thunderstorms. She loves to climb trees and leap off the top of slides instead of going down them in the normal way. She speaks her mind, wears bright colours and rarely gives in to peer pressure. To be honest, she can be quite a handful – a real bundle of energy. But I'm hoping that all these qualities will stand her in good stead when it comes to being brave about whatever she's going through right now. I'm praying she'll use her initiative and find her way back to us.

I notice my hands are shaking uncontrollably. I'd thought I was handling this okay, but the hard knot of fear in my chest is beginning to unravel, spreading its tendrils throughout my body. If I let it, it will disintegrate me completely. I get to my feet. No good will come of sitting here thinking.

'Ollie?'

I wait a moment but there's no reply.

'Oll?'

'Coming. Be there in a minute.'

I go out into the hall to see him. He's sitting on the staircase, massaging his head with his fingers.

'Ollie, are you okay?'

He doesn't reply.

'Shall I leave you alone? I think I'm going to go for a drive. See if I can spot her.'

My husband sniffs and looks up at me. 'Good idea. I'll come with you.'

'One of us should stay, just in case.'

'In case of what?'

'In case she turns up here, I suppose.'

'She won't have walked all the way home from the fair. She doesn't know the way.'

I know he's right. 'But what if she does?'

'I'm not staying here while she's out there.' He pulls himself up using the bannister, grunting like an old person. 'It's my fault, isn't it? It's my fault she's not home. If I hadn't left her with Mum. If I'd—'

'Don't beat yourself up, okay. Let's just go and find her.' I don't disagree with him though. I can't tell him it's not his fault, because the fact of the matter is that I knew his mother wasn't reliable enough to look after our child by herself. I wish with all my heart that I'd been wrong. It's not that I don't like Jill. She's a kind woman who adores her family, but I've noticed that she's become more and more absent-minded these past few years and I just don't trust her to be on the ball. Maybe that makes me a control freak. Maybe that makes me mean. Or unfair. Or whatever. But I wasn't about to risk our daughter's well-being for the sake of politeness. The fact that Ollie ignored my concerns feels like a betrayal. Like he took her side over mine. But no one wants to hear *I told you so*. And I don't want to say it.

Oliver and I grab our phones and head out the front door into the warm summer night. We take my car as it's blocking his in.

'Want me to drive?' he asks as we hurry down the stone steps.

My immediate thought is to say no, but I realise that I would actually like him to drive because that way I'll be able to do the looking. I'm desperate to search for Beatrice. Convinced I'll succeed in finding her where the police have not.

We set off into the dark night, merging with the sparse traffic on the main road that leads eastward, towards the fair on the outskirts of town. We drive around the backstreets that wrap around the fairground. We park up and search on foot, heading down back alleys and scouring patches of green space, peering alongside garage blocks and public buildings, looking in doorways and over garden fences. We're stopped a few times by disgruntled residents wanting to know what the hell we think we're doing on their property. But then we show them the photos on our phone of our sweet-faced daughter, and their anger melts away, replaced with concern. With subtle expressions of relief that it's not their child who's missing. With promises that they'll keep an eye out for her.

We keep this up for what seems like hours, until Oliver drifts and almost collides with a van on the opposite side of the road. Ollie swerves at the last minute and the van driver brakes and blasts his horn before rolling down his window, swearing loudly, his tyres screeching as he races off down the road. Ollie parks haphazardly and drops his head into his hands.

'We need to go home,' I say. 'We're exhausted. We need food.'

Oliver straightens up and gazes ahead. 'We can't leave her out here all night.'

'We won't. Let's just refuel. Eat something, grab a few hours' sleep, then we can come out again.' Every part of my body is screaming not to go home, to keep on searching, but I know that we're too tired to do any good out here. We'll end up causing an accident and that won't help Beatrice. 'Swap places with me. I'll drive.'

Ollie does as I say and stumbles out of the car. As we cross paths in the road, we end up hugging one another. Oliver kisses my hair and a single tear escapes from the corner of my eye. I want to say something reassuring, but I can't find the words.

It feels wrong to be heading home while Bea is still out here somewhere. She's just a child, she should be with us. But we have to be practical. We need to keep ourselves strong. Does this decision make me unfeeling? Make me a bad parent? Oliver and I break apart without eye contact and get back into the car. We'll keep scanning the roads as we head home. We won't stop looking. We'll find our daughter. We have to.

CHAPTER EIGHT

JILL

'Can you turn off the engine and step out of the vehicle please?' The officer's voice is muffled beyond the passenger window, but I can hear the official tone, the lack of warmth.

As if this day couldn't get any worse, I have the horrible feeling that I'm about to be arrested for drink-driving. Which would absolutely serve me right. I've never done anything so stupid and selfish before. But in my defence, I wasn't thinking straight. I'm still not. My head is all over the place. I realise the officer is still waiting so I do as he asks, unlock my door and climb out of the car, wishing I were at home in bed trying to sleep, instead of here.

'I'm sorry,' I stammer. 'Did I do something wrong?'

'You were driving very slowly and erratically. Have you been drinking?' The officer is young and stern.

Why are young people so serious these days? They always look as though they have the weight of the world on their shoulders. I'm sure we had a lot more fun when we were younger. Or perhaps that's just how I remember it – through rose-tinted spectacles.

I make my way around to the pavement until I'm standing next to the officer. 'I'm so sorry. I was looking for my granddaughter. She's lost.'

'Lost?' His brow constricts. 'Have you reported her missing?'

'Yes. Her name's Beatrice. Beatrice Nolan. She's only seven which is why we're so worried.'

'Ah, yes, okay. I'm sorry to hear that. We've been briefed and we're all on the lookout for Beatrice.' He throws me a sympathetic look and I'm hopeful that he might let me go on my way. My hopes are instantly dashed as his expression turns serious once more. 'I'm sorry about your granddaughter. But I have to ask again; have you been drinking?'

My breath hitches and I momentarily think about lying, but what if he doesn't believe me and I then have to take a breathalyser test anyway? That would look awful. 'I did have a drink earlier to calm me down.'

'Okay, in that case I'm going to ask you to take a breathalyser test.'

Oh no, oh no. What if I'm over the limit? I cast my mind back to earlier. I think I only had one gin and tonic, didn't I? Maybe two. I can't quite remember. I'm not entirely sure how large the measures were. Quite large I think. But maybe not. I really can't recall. This whole evening has just been one long nightmarish blur. My face heats up and sweat prickles under my arms. I'm so stupid. This is the last thing I need.

Swirling blue lights from his vehicle cast strange shadows over the two of us and I feel as though I'm in some TV police drama, not my real life. I notice another officer in the driver's seat. He gets out of the car and heads towards us.

This second officer seems just as young, maybe in his thirties, so not that young. It's simply that I'm older. A lot older. I suddenly feel light-headed and put a hand on the side of the car to steady myself. I hope they don't think it's because I've drunk too much. I quickly bring my hand back down to my side, try to take a deep calming breath without them seeing.

'Are you okay?' the first officer asks.

I nod. 'It's been a stressful evening.'

The second police officer gives his colleague a questioning look.

'This is Beatrice Nolan's grandmother. The girl who's gone missing.'

The second guy's eyes widen. He gives me a sympathetic glance. 'We're still looking.'

'Thank you,' I reply.

He nods and produces a small black contraption. The first officer takes it from him and turns back to me. 'I'm just going to get you to blow into this tube, okay?'

The next few minutes go by in a blur and then, to my horror, the officer tells me the proportion of alcohol in my breath exceeds the legal limit and he's arresting me on suspicion of drink-driving.

I blink, aware of my heart beating in my chest, in my ears, and in my throat. My vision blurs and I'm not sure if it's from shock or from blowing into the breathalyser for so long. 'Are you sure?' I quail. 'Could the test be wrong?'

'It's unlikely,' he counters, 'but we'll take you to the station for a second test. You'll have to get someone to collect your car for you.'

'What? The station? *Now?* How can this be happening on top of everything else? 'It's almost midnight,' I add uselessly.

The officers don't reply to that. They're brisk and detached. Not unkind, but not sympathetic either as they direct me to lock up my car and then guide me into the back of their vehicle. As I'm clambering in, a group of boisterous young lads walk past on the opposite side of the road.

'Naughty, naughty!' one of them calls out. 'What you been doing, grandma?'

Their delight in my situation makes me shrink into myself. Makes me squirm in embarrassment and mortification. Is this really happening? Of course my current predicament doesn't compare with Beatrice going missing, but what use will I be to her now? And these officers who were previously out searching for her are now going to have to deal with *my* situation instead. I'm taking up their precious time. Time that should have been spent locating my granddaughter and bringing her to safety.

The journey to the station is short. At least they didn't handcuff me. I don't think I could have coped with that. It suddenly hits me that if I'm disqualified from driving I won't be able to do anything to help with the search for Beatrice. I'll have to go everywhere on foot or by bus, which won't be anywhere near as effective. *Please let them find her tonight.* If they find her safe and well then I won't even care if they throw me in jail.

Before long, we're entering the police station, the same bright sterile place that I visited earlier this evening when I had to go over my statement about Beatrice. Now here I am again, except this time I'm under arrest! Both officers bring me to a desk where the custody sergeant introduces himself. As I stand there like a naughty child, the first two officers explain to him why I've been arrested. It's mortifying. I just want to curl up into a ball and die.

They ask if I'd prefer a blood test or urine test, but the thought of either feels even more invasive, so I opt for another breath test. The custody sergeant takes my details and then the arresting officer leads me down the corridor to another brightly lit room with a large machine in the corner. Apparently, it will tell just how far over the limit I am. As the machine starts humming, I look up and note the video camera. This is all being recorded. The officer explains the procedure to me. I stand up and move forward to blow into the tube, and in a short space of time it's all over.

I'm asked to wait while the machine calculates my readings. It continues to buzz and click until eventually it spits out a piece of paper that looks like a receipt. I thought I was already resigned to hearing the officer declare I'm over the limit, but a small part of me must have been hoping for a miracle, because when the officer finally confirms my worst fears, my whole body sags. It's official. I broke the law. I did something I've previously criticised others for doing. Something I never thought I'd do. If I'd caused an accident I would never have been able to forgive myself. I'm officially a bad person.

The officer asks me to sign a long printout. My fingers are still shaking and the scrawl looks nothing like my signature, but I guess it will have to do.

Now that's over, I'm taken back to the custody sergeant at the main desk. The arresting officer confirms once again that I'm over the limit and hands the printout to the sergeant.

But the nightmare isn't over, because right now they're taking me to a cell.

'Is this absolutely necessary? Can't I go home? Please won't you let me call my son to come and pick me up?'

'We'll do that, but I need to process your paperwork first. Someone will be back for you in a while. Would you like a cup of tea or coffee?' the officer asks.

I realise my throat is dry as sandpaper. 'Yes please. Tea would be lovely. No sugar, thank you.'

The officer nods and locks me inside. What am I doing here? I think back to my cosy kitchen. I should be there right now with Beatrice. Instead, I'm here in this godforsaken place and Bea is goodness knows where. When will this nightmare end?

CHAPTER NINE

JILL

The cell is basic and smells of disinfectant. There's a toilet, a wooden bench with a rubber mattress, a blanket and an unsavoury-looking pillow. I don't want to sit on any of it, but I have no choice. I don't think my legs will allow me to stand for much longer. I stagger over to the bench and collapse onto the blanket, the old mattress creaking beneath me. My skin is dry, my eyes scratchy and my mouth tastes sour. Even my hearing is strange, the blood whooshing in my head as though someone has pressed a seashell to my ear. I try to think calming, positive thoughts. Tell myself that this is a terrible day, but tomorrow will be better. Tomorrow the police will find my granddaughter and I'll be back at home.

I push out the voices that are telling me I may have to go to jail or pay a fine that I can't afford. Maybe even both. I've never done anything like this before. What do I do and who should I turn to for advice? I'm sure Oliver will find someone to represent me. I think I'm going to need an experienced solicitor who knows about these matters. How will I be able to afford it? *Don't think about that now…*

This cloud of worries is nothing compared to the whispers in my head saying that Beatrice has been snatched. That someone bad has her and she's never coming back.

'I'm just tired,' I say out loud. 'That's all. Tired and stressed. Come on, Jill, pull yourself together.' I just need to get through tonight. Everything will be sorted out tomorrow. *Please let it be sorted out.* Although, what in the world will Oliver and Claire think when they hear about my situation? This will only confirm Claire's opinion that I'm not to be trusted. Will she even let me see Bea again?

After what seems like forever, a female officer brings me a cup of tea. She's cheerful, thank goodness. I thank her but after she leaves I kick myself for not asking about that phone call. I should probably try to get some sleep, but I just can't bring myself to lay my head on that used pillow.

After an even longer wait the first officer visits me and I take another test on the device. It's negative. Now that I'm finally sober, to my shame and horror, I'm formally charged with drink-driving. I could sob. At least now that's out of the way, he tells me I can soon be released from custody.

'What's the time?' I ask, my voice hoarse.

He checks his watch. 'Half past one.'

I'm shocked. I thought it was only around midnight. 'Can I call my son to pick me up now?'

'Yes, sure. I'll be back soon.' Frustratingly, he leaves and I'm left to stew again. This time, I'm so tired I lie down with my head on the thin pillow and feel myself drifting off.

'Jill.'

A voice cuts into my slumber and I open my eyes, squinting against the unholy brightness.

'It's Sergeant Wilkes, time to go.'

'Who?' My mouth is dry and my bones are as stiff as iron bars.

'Come on. Up you get, Jill.'

It all comes rushing back. The fair, Beatrice, the drink-driving. This man is the arresting officer.

'Oh dear.' I heave myself up off the narrow bench and wobble to my feet, my hair plastered to my cheek, my dress twisted and wrinkled. I must look an absolute fright.

I follow him out of the awful cell, back to the front desk where I'm given some pieces of paper which, he informs me, are the charge sheet. I'm told that I'm on police bail to appear at the magistrates' court in a couple of weeks' time. Apparently, I'm allowed to drive until then but in court I'll be disqualified. He can't tell me how long the ban will last.

Finally, he returns my handbag which contains my mobile phone. Much as it pains me to add more trauma to my family, I sit in reception and call Oliver. I probably should have taken a taxi, but I really don't feel up to talking to another stranger. I need to see a friendly face. To hug my son.

But as soon as he answers the phone, I can tell it was a mistake to call.

'Mum? Is that you?' Oliver's voice is thick with sleep.

'Ollie, I'm so sorry to wake you.'

'Did you hear something about Bea?' His voice has snapped into wakefulness and I realise he thinks I'm calling with news. I berate myself for such thoughtlessness.

'No, nothing yet, sorry.'

'Oh.' His tone deflates. He's speaking to Claire now: 'No, it's just Mum. No, there's no news. Go back to sleep.'

'I shouldn't have called. I woke you both. Sorry.'

'Mum, It's two fifteen in the morning. What's the matter?'

I try to keep my voice even. 'I've done something silly.' He doesn't reply, so I keep going. I tell him of the night's events and how I got arrested. 'I'm still at the police station.'

'Drink-driving?' Oliver sounds incredulous. 'Mum, I can't believe this.'

'I know, I know. I'm so sorry. I hate to ask, but would you be able to pick me up and drop me home?'

'Now?'

'I know it's late.'

'It's not that. It's just… I can't leave Claire at the moment. We need to be together while this is going on. We've been out searching the streets, too. Only just managed to fall asleep. I'm… can you get a taxi home? You know that any other time I would come and get you like a shot, but—'

'Of course. I know you would.' I gulp down the lump in my throat.

'Look, I'll come over tomorrow, but right now… it's just…'

'Of course. Of course I'll get a cab. Look, don't give it a second thought. I'm so sorry for calling you, Olls.'

'You sure you'll be okay, Mum?'

'I'll be absolutely fine.' I inject firmness and capability into my voice so he won't feel any worse than he already does.

'Okay. See you tomorrow.'

'Night, darling.'

'Night, Mum.'

I end the call and take a deep breath, trying hard not to feel upset. I absolutely understand that it was terrible of me to wake him and Claire. To expect them to pick me up when they're so distraught about Bea. To add to their distress. I think tonight must be the night of bad decisions, because I'm messing up left, right and centre.

Before I can talk myself out of it, I call Laurel. She's always up late so I know she won't mind me ringing. I should have called her in the first place.

'Jill, is everything okay? I heard about Beatrice. I tried calling you at home and on your mobile but you didn't pick up.'

'How do you know what happened?'

'It's a small town. Everyone knows everything. How are you doing? How's Ollie… and Claire?' Her voice deadens on Claire's name. We try to avoid talking about her, Oliver's second wife.

'They're beside themselves. We all are. But listen, I need your help. Did I wake you?'

'I'm just reading in bed.'

I quickly explain what happened. That I need a lift home from the police station.

Laurel doesn't baulk at what I've done. Instead, she's furious. 'They breathalysed you after you told them about Beatrice!? That's so harsh. And how can you have been over the limit when you only had one drink? You should ask for a re-test.'

'I had another test at the station. Anyway, it's too late now, it's done.'

'Well, I'd be kicking up an absolute stink. Your granddaughter's just gone missing, for goodness' sake.'

But the more Laurel sticks up for me, the more I realise that I was in the wrong. That my carelessness and thoughtlessness are the cause of all this. Nothing more, nothing less. I let Laurel vent for a moment longer before gently cutting her off. 'So do you think you'd be able to come and pick me up? Drop me back home? Don't worry if it's too much of an imposition at this hour.'

'I'll be there in twenty minutes. And I'll be giving those police officers a piece of my mind, too. Are you hungry? Want me to bring you anything?'

'No, just your company and a lift would be wonderful.' I feel such relief at the thought of going home that I could cry. Guilt follows swiftly as I think about Beatrice. Where is she now? What's she doing? Is she sleeping? Frightened? Alone?

I would trade places with her in a heartbeat if I could.

DAY TWO

I don't know why I was so worried. The whole thing was far too easy. Not a single hiccup. The entire evening went perfectly to plan.

This is my time now. I'm finally getting what's owed. And if people have to suffer... well... that's not my problem.

CHAPTER TEN

CLAIRE

At the sound of the doorbell, I stagger from my bed and wrap my cotton dressing gown around me, fumbling to tie the belt. The shower thrums in the bathroom. Oliver must be in there. I barely slept last night; all thoughts consumed with Beatrice. And then when I finally managed to drift off in the early hours of the morning, there was Jill's ridiculous phone call waking us up and letting us know about her latest idiocy – arrested for drink-driving. I can't even let myself process that right now, not with this squirming feeling in the pit of my stomach.

As I head downstairs, I check the time on my phone – just before eight thirty. My inbox is rammed with messages from friends, but nothing from the police yet. No news about Beatrice. Perhaps this is them at the door. Perhaps they have her! I envisage opening the door and seeing my little Bea standing there before rushing forward and flinging her arms around me. I stuff my phone into my dressing-gown pocket and hurry to the front door.

It's a woman in her mid-thirties with chestnut hair to her shoulders and soft brown eyes. She's wearing smart black trousers and a patterned blouse, sunglasses pushed up onto her head.

'Hi. Claire Nolan?'

I nod, wondering who she is. *A client?* No, it's a Sunday. *Police?* Maybe. *Journalist?* Hope not. What do I say if she is? No comment, I suppose.

'Hi, I'm DS Gayle Hobart. DI Khatri asked me to come over to see you this morning. I'm the family liaison officer assigned to your case – FLO for short.'

'Uh, oh, hi. DS...'

'Call me Gayle. I'm here to help and support, and to keep you informed about what's happening in the search for Beatrice, and to answer any concerns you might have.' She gives me a gentle smile while I process what she's saying. I'm still not fully awake, but I feel like I'm operating on some other level. Detached, yet still taking it all in.

'So is there any news then? Any sightings or progress?' I peer over her shoulder to the road beyond. All is quiet – typical Sunday morning round here. An unfamiliar silver Polo glints in the sunlight at the bottom of the drive. I'm assuming it's Gayle's.

'Would it be okay to come inside and chat?' she asks.

'Um, okay.' I really hope she has some positive news and that she's not here to bombard us with more guilt-inducing questions.

'Thanks. I'd normally come with a colleague, but he's been unwell this week, so you just have me today.'

I step back to allow her into the hallway, fully expecting Beatrice to come skipping down the stairs for breakfast any second. The fresh realisation that she's not coming is a punch to the gullet. I try to catch my breath. 'Come through.'

Gayle follows me into the gloomy kitchen. I flick open the venetian blinds to let in some light and try not to feel too bad about the stack of dirty dishes on the side and the crumbs littering the counter. I don't even bother to excuse the mess.

'I need a coffee; do you want one?' I ask.

'That would be good. I can make it for you, if you like?'

I give her a sharp glance. 'Is that part of the job description?'

'Yep. Washer-upper, tea-and-coffee maker. I can do it all.' She tilts her head. 'Honestly, take a seat. I make a great cup of coffee.'

I don't think today could feel any stranger right now so I do as she suggests and take a seat at the pale wood table while she cleans out the cafetière and boils the kettle. 'Is your husband here?'

'He'll be down in a minute. He's just having a shower.'

She makes him a cup too and sits opposite me just as I hear Oliver's tread on the stairs.

'Was that someone at the door?' he calls out.

I wait for him to appear, his hair damp, dark circles beneath his eyes, before making the introductions. He's casually dressed in black cargo shorts and an olive-green T-shirt. I feel grotty – I haven't even brushed my teeth yet.

Oliver takes a seat and lifts the third mug. 'This my coffee?'

I nod while Gayle introduces herself.

'Has there been any news?' Oliver asks, taking a cautious sip of his drink.

I have a terrible feeling this is a question we're going to be asking a lot. I hope I'm wrong.

'Before I get to that,' Gayle replies, 'let me just explain to both of you who I am and why I'm here.' She goes on to tell us that she'll be the person who keeps us updated. Likewise, we need to tell her anything that comes to light at our end. 'Obviously, we're here to support, but also to investigate and act as a gateway to the incident room.'

I nod as she talks, trying to take it all in, to not let my mind wander. It's hard not to believe this isn't all some strange dream, or nightmare.

Like yesterday's detectives, Gayle asks all about Beatrice and her friends, and also about our family members as well as our own friends. She asks what we've been doing over the summer. Did we meet any new people? That kind of thing. Eventually, she gets around to answering our questions.

Oliver jumps right in, asking if there's been any news. But I don't get too excited. If there had been any big developments, surely she would have told us by now.

Gayle clears her throat. 'So, as you know, we had the search dogs out yesterday evening and they followed a trail which led to the far side of the park right up to the treeline. After that, the trail ends.'

'What does that mean?' Oliver sets his mug down on the table.

'It means the dogs lost the scent after that. We had a search helicopter scanning the area, but unfortunately there've been no sightings.'

My mind is racing. Someone led Beatrice over to the trees, and then what? They carried her the rest of the way? I scrape my chair back and rush from the room, throw open the door to the loo under the stairs, kneel and retch over the toilet bowl. Hardly anything comes up, but it's a shock. Everything is a shock.

Oliver has followed me and I reassure him that I'm fine. Even though I'm quite clearly not fine. My head is swimming and my temples pound with a sharp pain that spreads behind my eyes. I stand on wobbling legs and rinse my mouth in the sink. Splash my face and try not to look at myself in the mirror.

Now I have to return to the kitchen and talk to this Gayle woman about my daughter. Hear things that are hard to hear. Ask difficult questions. My stomach churns, acid burns in my throat. I hope I'm not going to throw up again.

As I walk back into the kitchen, Gayle hands me a glass of water. 'Drink that slowly.'

I do as she says, only taking the tiniest of sips.

'When did you last eat?' she asks. 'Can you manage some toast?'

I realise that I haven't had any food since yesterday lunchtime. I meant to eat last night, but I just wasn't able to force anything down. Despite my empty stomach, I don't feel at all hungry.

The family liaison officer makes herself at home in our kitchen, preparing Ollie some scrambled eggs on toast, while filling us in on the lack of progress they've made so far in locating Beatrice. But our daughter can't have vanished. She has to be somewhere.

We fire questions at Gayle, asking about security cameras and search plans, will they be questioning the fairground staff in greater detail and will they be going door to door? While Gayle makes breakfast, I sip my water and nibble a dry cracker, my stomach settling enough that I feel like I might be able to manage the toast now it's almost ready. It's surprising how unintrusive Gayle is, despite taking over our kitchen. I watch her as she bustles around and it occurs to me that rather than being here to look after us, perhaps she's here for the opposite reason – to keep an eye on us. To see if we might have something to do with Bea's disappearance. The cracker lodges in my throat and I try to swallow, suddenly feeling queasy again.

After our interviews with the detectives yesterday, it's obvious they haven't ruled me and Ollie out as suspects. So maybe sending Gayle here is their way of snooping. I clench my fists and walk out of the kitchen for a moment to compose myself. In the hall, I take a few deep breaths and consider telling Gayle to leave. But I guess she's only doing her job. She doesn't know us. She doesn't know that there's no way we'd do anything to hurt our child.

Fine. She can snoop away. We have absolutely nothing to hide.

As I return to the kitchen, Oliver's mobile rings.

'It's Mum.' He gives me a look that conveys everything.

I stop myself from rolling my eyes, still angry with Jill for her drink-driving episode on top of everything else. It's typical that, even with her granddaughter missing, Oliver's mother is still managing to demand all our attention.

'I'd better take it,' he says, leaving the kitchen. 'Won't be long.'

'Everything okay?' Gayle asks, nodding in Oliver's direction. 'His mum was the one with Beatrice when she went missing, right?'

The last thing I want is to talk about Jill's episode at the police station last night. But I guess Gayle will hear about it soon enough so I give her a brief recap of the situation. It turns out Gayle already knew. Of course she did.

'Jill isn't a big drinker,' I offer, wondering why I'm sticking up for her. 'I don't think she can have been thinking straight. Although I know there's absolutely no excuse for drink-driving,' I add.

Gayle doesn't offer an opinion either way. She just sets a plate of toast and perfectly scrambled egg before me. 'There, that should help settle your stomach.'

'Oh. Okay, thanks.' I take a tentative bite, listening to the faint murmur of Oliver's voice from the next room, and the banging of our next-door neighbour's hammer as he attempts whatever DIY project he's on to next.

Gayle sips her coffee and looks out the window onto our lawn with its steep terrace at the back. 'It's a lovely spot here.'

'Thanks. It would be even lovelier if our neighbour would stop drilling and banging at all hours.' I wonder how on earth I can be sitting in my kitchen making polite conversation with this stranger while my daughter is missing. I think I must still be in shock or something.

'It's a bit much on a Sunday morning,' she agrees.

'Oh!' My eyes suddenly fill with tears as I remember what Beatrice should be doing today. I push the plate of toast away and rest my face in my hands.

Gayle comes over. I feel her hovering next to me. 'What's wrong?'

'It's just… I need to call the dance studio…'

Gayle waits for me to continue, but I'm having trouble speaking. My throat is tight and I don't feel like I'm here. I swallow and take my hands away from my face.

Oliver returns to the kitchen. 'This looks amazing, Gayle. Aren't you having any…?' His voice trails away when he sees my face. 'What's happened?' His forehead creases. 'Did you get some news?'

'No.' I gulp. 'Nothing like that. I just remembered that it's Bea's dance recital today. At the Regent Centre.'

I'd been really resistant to the idea of her doing the summer dance school in the first place. It meant lots of rehearsing, making costumes, picking up, dropping off and – worst of all – getting her to practise her steps. Beatrice is enthusiastic about everything, but pinning her down to do such mundane things as practising and homework is a different matter. Oliver always says that Bea likes to work to her own timetable. Anyway, she begged me to let her do it, so I reluctantly agreed to her enrolling in the course, and today was the end-of-summer show. But now…

Oliver's face falls. 'The show's today?'

I nod, wishing I hadn't been such a stick in the mud about it. I should have been more enthusiastic. I could have made the practice sessions fun. I shouldn't have begrudged giving up my time.

'I'll call the organisers,' Oliver says. 'Tell them… what's happened. Text me the number.'

'Okay. Thanks,' I reply in a small voice.

Gayle has stepped back from our conversation, made herself unobtrusive. She's looking out the kitchen window again.

'How's your mum?' I ask Ollie, remembering that he's just been on the phone with her.

'Fine. She's home now. Still distraught about Beatrice, obviously. She wants to come over.'

I grind my teeth, trying to keep calm. The last thing I want is for my mother-in-law to come round and start apologising, looking for sympathy and forgiveness. I know that probably makes me a bitch, but I can't help it. I just can't do it. I don't have the energy for my mother-in-law right now, but there's another reason I'm so angry. A reason which has nothing to do with Jill, and everything to do with *me*. The fact of the matter is that I feel horribly guilty about wanting to go out with my friends rather than taking Bea to the fair. If I had put my daughter before myself… if I'd been a better mother…

Oliver interrupts my thoughts. 'Don't worry, I told Mum you didn't feel up to talking to anyone today.'

I blow out a breath. 'Thank you.' At least I don't have to have another argument with Ollie about his mother.

Meanwhile, Gayle has started tidying up the kitchen. Probably having a good old nose around while she's at it. I'm too wound up to tell her to stop. That she doesn't need to bother. That I don't care how messy the kitchen is. That I would happily take everything out of every cupboard and smash it all over the floor.

The only thing that matters right now is getting my daughter back.

CHAPTER ELEVEN

JILL

As I walk into the kitchen, Laurel looks up from her seat at the table, where she's sipping herbal tea and reading the free local paper, her scarlet hair tied into a complicated bun on top of her head, a powder-blue chiffon scarf at her throat and multicoloured bangles jangling.

'Laurel, thanks so much for picking me up last night. And for staying over. You're a gem. You really didn't have to.' True to her word, she was at the station within twenty minutes of my call, her battered red Peugeot 207 one of the most welcome sights I've ever seen.

She waves away my thanks. 'Don't be silly. I wanted to. Did you manage to get any shut-eye?'

'A bit. Maybe three or four hours. More than enough for me.' I make a beeline for the kettle, in need of a strong cup of tea. I'm already showered and dressed and ready to do whatever it takes to find Beatrice.

'Have you spoken to Oliver yet?' Laurel always manages to insert Oliver into our conversations. I think she's still a bit in love with him, even though she's accepted nothing will ever come of it. That part of her life is well and truly over. It's sad because they seemed to have the perfect marriage – she's a local artist and he runs an art supply store. They share the same taste in music, films, books, life. Whereas he and Claire are total opposites in almost every way. But don't get me wrong, Oliver seems happy with Claire, their dynamic seems to work. And, of course, without Claire there would be no Beatrice.

I never really got to the bottom of what happened between Oliver and Laurel to end their marriage. Oliver said she was unfaithful and yet Laurel flatly denies it; she always has done. I think he was a little harsh on her. Laurel loved Oliver. There's no way she would have jeopardised their marriage by being unfaithful.

I bring my tea over to the table. 'I actually just got off the phone with Oliver. There's a police officer with them at the house, some kind of liaison person he said. No news on Beatrice yet. I just… I can't believe it. Everything that's happened. It's like a bad dream.'

'I'm so sorry, Jill. Can I do anything else to help?' The thing about Laurel is that if she offers to help, you know she genuinely means it.

'Actually, yes you can. I've decided to arrange a local search party.'

She nods. 'Great idea.'

'I think time is of the essence. The more people we gather together, the more ground we can cover.' I woke up with the idea buzzing in my brain. I've already WhatsApped people from the local history museum where I volunteer, plus friends from my Pilates group and everyone else in my contacts who's local. All except for Claire and Oliver. He didn't sound very happy with me just now and he said he and Claire had a rough night, so I'll let them rest while we search. It's the least I can do. I've told everyone else to spread the word. We're meeting in just over an hour's time – 10.30 a.m. next to the fairground.

Laurel and I have a light breakfast and spend the remaining time photocopying a picture of Beatrice with my contact number, before leaving the house, although I also messaged an image of her to everyone's phones.

I already picked up my car last night on the way home from the police station as I was under the limit when they let me go. At least I'm allowed to drive for the moment – until I'm convicted. But we've decided to walk to the fair this morning as parking is either difficult to find or expensive, especially on a Sunday when the fairground is likely to be busy.

On our way to the meeting point, we bump into Leslie and Trina, friends from the museum. Leslie's my age, a small, quiet brunette, and we get on really well. Trina's around a decade younger than us, stocky with short ash-blonde hair. She's a little bossy, but I let her have her way most times as her issues aren't generally worth arguing over, and I prefer a peaceful life. I notice that Trina's carrying a megaphone. If this weren't such a dire situation, I'd have a giggle to myself about it.

I introduce them both to Laurel, then they give me a hug and ask how I'm doing.

'Shell-shocked. But glad to at least be doing something. I thought you were both scheduled to work today.'

'We've closed up the museum for the morning,' Leslie replies. 'Thought it was more important to be out here looking for the little one.'

Emotion bubbles up and I swallow it down before mumbling my thanks.

'We also put a picture of your granddaughter on the main entrance door with your contact details, telling people to join in the search party,' Trina adds. 'And I popped into town to pick up some whistles. So whoever finds her can use one to let everyone know.'

'I don't know what to say. Thank you.' I'm overcome by their thoughtfulness.

As we approach our destination, my heart sinks at the enormous crowd gathered on the playing field to the left of the fairground, some of them sporting high-vis sashes and jackets. There's already a heat haze rising off the patchy grass, making the crowds appear to merge and ripple. I stop walking for a moment. 'Oh dear.'

'What's the matter?' Laurel stops and turns, enveloped in a cloud of her cherry-scented vape steam.

'Over there on the field. I think there must be an event on, some kind of fun run or charity race. Look at all those people. I hope we can find our search volunteers in among all that lot.'

Trina gives me a friendly elbow in the side. 'Silly. Those *are* the search volunteers.'

I frown, sure she must be mistaken. 'There are so many of them. At least a hundred, maybe even two hundred. I only messaged about thirty or forty.'

'Brilliant.' Leslie gives me a smile. 'Word must have spread.'

As we draw closer, I spot friends and acquaintances, all of whom nod or wave or give kind smiles. But many of the volunteers are strangers to me. This is overwhelming. Almost too much to deal with. Once again, I have to gulp down my emotion. This isn't about me; this is about finding Beatrice.

Trina might be a touch annoying to work with, but here, in this situation, she's the sort of person you need around to take charge. Once we reach the swelling crowd of volunteers, she sets about organising everyone, using her megaphone to split people into different search parties and handing out whistles. I'm more than happy to let her get on with it. I can't imagine that we won't find my darling Bea, not with this many people searching.

In a rush of optimism, I picture myself calling Oliver to tell him that we've found her safe and well. Bringing Beatrice back home where Claire and Oliver will be overjoyed. We'll all go out to dinner to celebrate. Or maybe we'll stay in and I'll cook for everyone… But I'm getting ahead of myself. I can't let myself hope too much. First things first – find Beatrice.

'Jill!'

I turn at the sound of a woman's voice calling my name. She's tall and blonde, standing with a group of people in their thirties, all of whom I vaguely recognise. I give a guarded smile, trying to place them.

'Lucy Darraway,' she prompts. 'I went to school with Ollie.'

'Lucy! Of course. Forgive me.' I realise the group she's with are all Oliver's friends from school. I remember them crowding into our kitchen after lessons or lounging in the garden during summer holidays. Oliver went out with most of the girls at one time or another. But they were fleeting relationships, ultimately ending in friendship. As well as Lucy, I recognise Matthew Evans, Susanne, whose parents lived in a beautiful house at Mudeford Quay, and Freya Collins whose family owns a farm, and who's now firm friends with Claire.

They tell me how shocked they were to hear about Beatrice and assure me that they'll do their best to track her down. I hug them each in turn before moving off to greet other familiar faces and thank them for coming.

'All I'm saying is that I'd rather you didn't vape around me. It smells disgusting.' A deeply tanned couple in their forties are facing Laurel. The man's wearing jeans and a white shirt. The woman is dressed in jeans, a striped Breton top and gold jewellery, and she's currently having a go at my friend.

'Yes, well, I'm not keen on your face, darling, but you don't hear me complaining about it.' Laurel's high voice carries over the crowd.

'I'd rather you didn't speak to my wife like that.'

'I'd rather you didn't speak to me at all, but we can't always get what we want,' Laurel retorts.

'Hey, hey, let's calm down.' It's Freya, her shoulder-length chestnut hair tied back off her pretty freckled face. She glares at all three of them. 'This is about finding a lost child. If you're going to cause a scene then better to go home and leave the search to people who are serious about it.'

The couple glower and stomp off while Laurel blows steam in Freya's face.

'Very mature.' Freya shakes her head and turns away.

'I don't appreciate patronising busybodies,' Laurel calls after her.

But Freya walks back to her friends without responding.

I don't want to appear to be taking sides in this and now is certainly not the time to be drawn into any kind of altercation, so I turn away and pretend not to have seen anything. I decide to try to find Trina again and see where she suggests I search.

'Jill Nolan?' An attractive blonde-haired man in jeans and an open-neck shirt approaches. 'Someone pointed me in your direction and said you're Jill, grandmother of the missing seven-year-old, is that correct?'

I'm a little unnerved by his forthright manner so I glance around looking for a friendly face, but I can't seem to spot anyone I know nearby. All my friends seem to be dispersing across the field within their allocated groups, either towards the distant treeline or heading off to the side streets that snake away from the field. I don't think this man is here to help in the search and he doesn't look like a police officer.

'Hi. Sorry, who are you?'

'Giles Renton with the *Christchurch Daily Argus*.'

'A journalist.'

'That's right. We'd like to do our bit and put the word out. Help find little Beatrice.' He beckons over another man who's lurking beneath a leafy tree. Judging by the camera slung over his shoulder, he's the photographer. 'Can we get a photo of you?' Giles continues. 'Were you the one with her when she disappeared?'

I realise I'm gaping at the two of them, unsure what to do next. I wish I hadn't abandoned Laurel now. She'd know exactly what to say to these people. Unlike me. I'm completely out of my depth here.

'You want a photo of me? But I look an absolute fright.' I pat my hair self-consciously as the photographer's camera clicks. 'It would be better if you used a photo of Beatrice.'

'It must have felt awful when you lost her.' Giles's blue eyes are brimming with sympathy.

'It really did,' I reply, suddenly feeling close to tears again. 'It's been a dreadful time.'

'Well, let's see if we can find her for you.' He gives me an encouraging smile and I start to feel a little more optimistic.

CHAPTER TWELVE

CLAIRE

'Well, that was all quite strange.' Oliver comes back into the kitchen after seeing Gayle out.

I'm finally dressed, in linen shorts and a cotton strappy top, sitting at the kitchen table, the room now clean and sparkling after Gayle's visit. The family liaison officer didn't sit down the whole time she was here, which was basically all morning. She made tea, cleaned the kitchen and chatted virtually non-stop.

'At least she was nice,' I say.

'And easy to talk to.' Oliver joins me at the table. 'She said she'll be back tomorrow. Does that mean she's coming every day until we get Beatrice back?'

'Maybe.' I shrug and shake my head. 'I'm hoping and praying that they'll find Bea today. How can we just sit here, Ollie? While our daughter's God knows where? Honestly, I feel so useless!'

'Me too. But this wasn't exactly our plan. We said that this morning we were going to search the streets again. And then Gayle showed up. So we didn't really have a choice.'

'Now it's past lunchtime! I can't believe the police have no leads. How can they not have found her yet?'

'At least they're looking.' Oliver shakes his head. 'At least they're doing something. I mean, they had their search dogs and the helicopter and they questioned all the fairground staff...'

'But it's not enough. Questioning them isn't enough. They need to cross-reference things.' My brain suddenly clears, like wipers across a dirty windscreen. 'They need to look at whether any other kids have gone missing wherever the fair last set up, or the place before that. Are the police doing that?' My blood is heating up, my hands trembling. I just feel so helpless. I hate things being out of my control at the best of times, but this situation with Beatrice… it's torture. 'I just don't trust that they're doing everything in their power.'

'We'll ask Gayle,' Oliver replies. 'I'll call her. See if she knows.'

I finally get to my feet. 'Why didn't I ask her while she was here? I feel like I'm only just waking up. And I wish Phil would give it a bloody rest!' Our neighbour, Philip Aintree, is a DIY nut. He's in his forties and lives with his eighty-year-old mother, Sue. He's a nice enough guy but doesn't understand that people just might want a bit of peace and quiet at the weekend. His hammering has been intermittent all morning. The worst part is when he stops and you're on edge waiting for him to start up again. Sue's hard of hearing, so it doesn't bother her in the slightest.

'Want me to have a word with him?' Oliver's being particularly helpful today. Normally it's me calling people and sorting stuff out. Maybe he's feeling guilty.

'Ugh, don't worry about it now. We should grab some food and go out again. I checked online and the fair's only in town for another two days, so maybe we should go and have a snoop around.'

'You think she might be there?'

I grow cold just thinking about it. 'I don't know, but we can't rule out anything, can we?'

My husband's slate-green eyes fill with anxiety as the thought of where our daughter might be sinks in. 'I can't even… Right now I just want to punch the wall.' He gets to his feet and starts pacing, his fists bunched, the muscles in his jaw flexing.

'Are you going to ring Gayle, or do you want me to do it?'

He glares at me. 'I said I'll do it.'

He snatches up his phone as the doorbell rings. We lock eyes as hope softens our gazes for a moment. The mere fragment of possibility that Beatrice might be standing outside makes my heart stop.

I follow Oliver into the hall, towards the front door. I hold my breath as he opens it.

'Ollie!' A woman's voice. She throws her arms around my husband and holds him tight. 'How are you? How's Claire? God, I've been worried to death about you both. About Beatrice. What can I do to help?' It's Freya, and I realise that although I'm gutted it's not Beatrice at the door, I'm really, really relieved to see my friend. 'I bought some supplies in case you haven't had time.' We follow her through to the kitchen where she plonks two shopping bags on the table. 'Some eggs and milk from the farm, a homemade lasagne and some ready meals from M&S so you don't have to think about cooking for a couple of days.'

'You're an actual angel,' I say.

'Thanks, Freya.' Ollie's reception isn't as warm as mine. Although they went to school together, she's become more my friend than his, and he gets fed up with our chats about clothes, work, TV shows, local gossip and anything and everything else we talk about. Ollie is more of a listener and a thinker than a talker. He turns to me with a frown. 'Are we still going out?'

Freya tightens her chestnut ponytail and flicks a blue-eyed gaze from Ollie to me. 'Did I come at a bad time? Are you going out?'

'Yes, but have a seat for a minute.'

'I still can't believe what's happened.' Freya sits at the table and I slide in opposite her, watching Ollie shift impatiently. 'You two must be beside yourselves. I thought I'd see you down at the playing fields this morning.'

'Playing fields?' I don't know what she's talking about.

'You know, Jill's search party at the fair.'

I frown and glance up at Oliver, who stops fidgeting for the moment.

Freya continues. 'They're still all going strong down there, but I thought I'd nip up to see how you're both doing. I left messages, but…'

'Sorry, back up.' My frown deepens. 'What search party are you on about?'

'Your mum.' Freya looks up at Oliver. 'She got all her friends together to arrange a search party for Bea. This one friend of hers – a right mad bitch – you'd hate her, Claire, she's got a megaphone and a clipboard and all these whistles. It's like some kind of military operation down there. Honestly, they're covering some serious ground though, so I guess it's pretty good. I'm planning to head straight back down there.'

I feel my hackles rise at the thought of all this going on while I've been left here in the dark. I swing my gaze to Oliver. 'Did you know about this?'

'*What?* No, course not. Why would I have kept that from you?'

'Sorry, have I just put my foot in it?' Freya's tanned face reddens. 'Jill probably just wanted to leave you in peace. Maybe she thought you'd be too upset to join in.'

'Too upset to search for our missing daughter? Who, by the way, *she* lost.' I unclench my fists and exhale.

'Sorry.' Freya raises her hands. 'Don't shoot the messenger.' She lowers her hands again. 'On second thoughts, shoot away. You have every right to be angry with everyone today.'

'You're being a bit harsh on my mum, Claire,' Oliver interjects, a hurt expression that makes my chest pang with guilt clouding his face. 'I'm sure she's only trying to help, with this search party. She didn't lose Bea on purpose.'

'I'm sorry, Ollie. It's just… your mum seems to be dropping bombshell after bombshell this weekend.'

'I know it seems that way…'

'It *is* that way.'

'Well, I think Freya's right. Mum probably thought we had enough on our plate, especially after last night when I didn't pick her up.'

Freya raises a questioning eyebrow at me, but I just shake my head. I'll tell her about Jill's drink-driving debacle some other time when it's just the two of us.

She stands. 'I should get out of your hair, get back to the search. I won't stop until we've found her.'

'It's fine, you stay for a bit, Freya.' Ollie wipes the crumbs from the side of his mouth and turns to me. 'I may as well join in Mum's search party. Why don't you both catch me up in a while after you've had a chat.'

I give a half nod half shrug. There's no way I'm joining Jill's search party. I just can't face seeing her at the moment. In the meantime, I want to quiz Freya about it, find out who's there and how it's going. I want to hear if she's got any theories or suggestions. I also want to blow off some steam about my mother-in-law, and I obviously can't do that while Ollie's around. Besides, I wouldn't mind crying on my best friend's shoulder about Bea disappearing. Freya's a good listener.

Oliver's mad at me, and I can't blame him. Bea going missing seems to have removed my politeness filters. I'm spewing every thought that comes into my head without any consideration. I'm so stressed that I don't even care. I only hope I don't end up pissing off Freya too.

The stubborn, annoyed part of me doesn't want to join in Jill's search party, but more than that, I don't feel up to talking to people right now – especially not Jill and all her friends. Answering questions about what happened and how I'm doing. So I'll call Ollie a little later and tell him I've changed my mind. And then I'll go searching for Bea by myself. Perhaps I can cover the area around here and maybe even up St Catherine's Hill. I suppose there's the tiniest possibility that she may have tried to get home, but got lost, even though I know that's highly unlikely.

Oliver kisses me goodbye, which I'm hoping means we've made up after our embarrassing display of bickering. As the front door closes behind him, my body droops a little.

'You okay, chick?' Freya starts putting the groceries away, stacking the ready meals in the fridge. 'Silly question I know. You must be… I don't even know how you must be feeling. Anything you need, just tell me, okay? And I mean *anything*. Mum and Dad send their love too.'

I nod and murmur a quiet thank you. 'I don't even know what happened last night. Ollie was supposed to be taking the girls, not Jill. So when I found out she'd lost Bea, I was furious. Don't get me wrong, Jill's lovely and she absolutely adores Beatrice, but…' I throw up my hands, tired of repeating the same things over and over again.

'She's scatty,' Freya finishes for me. 'I get it.'

'I don't even think it's her age. It's more her personality. She thinks she's this free spirit and that Beatrice should have her freedom and not be micro-managed. I mean, in an ideal world, I agree with her. I'd love to live in a society where kids play out on their own and have as much freedom as we did when we were kids. But things aren't like that any more. Aside from the traffic, there are just too many bad people out there. Too many people who… if they got hold of Bea…' I stop talking because I can't bear to vocalise my fears.

Freya closes the fridge and comes around the table to take my hand. 'Hey, don't think like that. We'll find her. There are so many people out searching. We won't rest until she's home safe.'

'But she's obviously not just *lost*, right? Or they'd have found her by now. And she hasn't run away.' My voice cracks. 'So that really only leaves one possibility.' I realise I'm crying now, hot tears that sting my eyes.

'Oh, hon…' Freya enfolds me in her arms. 'Not necessarily. She could have wandered off, got lost and hurt herself. She might be lying somewhere with a twisted ankle, in which case Jill's search party is a great idea as it's the best chance of finding her.'

As I sob into my friend's shoulder, I really want to believe she's right. Because the alternative just doesn't bear thinking about. There's an ache in my gut, in my heart. Nothing else matters apart from getting Beatrice back. Nothing.

CHAPTER THIRTEEN

JILL

The journalist pins me with his gaze while the photographer fiddles with his camera.

I squirm under Giles's scrutiny, suddenly not at all sure that it's wise to be talking to a journalist, even a sympathetic one. 'Um, I don't really have time to talk right now. But if you want to help, you're welcome to join in the search and maybe we could talk at a later date when I've had a chance to think about it. Right now, I have to get back to the search.' I take a step backwards, eager to join my friends once more.

'Don't you think my time would be better spent getting the word out about your missing granddaughter straight away? We have a large local readership both online and in print. Think of all those people who'll see the photo of your granddaughter and may know something that would lead to her being found.'

The journalist has a point. But I'm still wary of talking to him. Fearful of doing anything that might make things worse.

He's not giving up. 'All I'd need are a few more quick photos of you, a recent image of Beatrice and a short account of the events leading up to her going missing. A piece like this in the paper could jog someone's memory.'

I swallow and tuck my hair behind my ears. I suppose that as he already knows about Beatrice, it would be best that I gave a true account, rather than allowing him to use guesswork to write his article. After a moment's silence, I give him my answer. 'Okay, so long as we're quick. I really want to get back to the search.'

I spend the next fifteen minutes going over the events leading up to Bea's disappearance. Giles Renton is gentler than DI Khatri. He says he has a daughter the same age as Bea and doesn't know what he'd do if anything happened to her. I feel reassured by his sympathetic attitude. Finally, the photographer has me standing by the fairground entrance as he snaps several pictures. All the while, I feel alternately hopeful that this could lead to Beatrice being found, and anxious that I've made a mistake by agreeing to the interview. But my discomfort at being photographed is overlaid by the thought that I'm doing this for my granddaughter.

Finally, Giles Renton shakes my hand and wishes me well. 'Hope she's found safe and well very soon.'

I nod my thanks before they leave just as Trina bustles over in my direction.

'There you are! I've been looking all over for you.'

'Sorry, I was just—'

Trina doesn't give me a chance to explain. 'So, the search-party groups have already headed off. I gave them each a specific area to cover, and they all have their whistles along with my mobile number in case anyone finds Beatrice, or anything else that might relate to her. I'm working with the local neighbour-hood sergeant who's allocated some special officers to go with each group, make sure we don't trample over any potential new crime scenes.'

'That's great, Trina. Thank you.' She's very businesslike, but at least she's getting things done. I'm distracted by a sudden breeze that ruffles Trina's short locks, giving her the appearance of a hedgehog. Giving myself an internal shake, I try to concentrate on what she's saying.

'I've told everyone to meet back here at one p.m. to break for lunch. And then I'll give them new routes for the afternoon. The sergeant seems quite pleased with my efforts so far.'

I get the feeling Trina could have had a shining career in the armed forces. Before she retired she was an office manager, so I guess she's used to taking charge.

'Thank you,' I offer again.

'It's not a problem, Jill. I'm pleased to help.'

'Shall we walk back?' I stick a hand out towards our original meeting spot.

Trina doesn't move, and instead continues talking as if she hasn't heard my question. 'Laurel, Leslie and myself have each chipped in a fiver.' She hands me three five-pound notes which I take, despite being bewildered by the offer. She continues, 'Are you able to nip to the supermarket to pick up some sandwiches and water?'

I'm taken aback. 'Oh, right. Shouldn't I go with one of the groups?' I'm a little put out that she's sending me off on a food run as I'd set my heart on being out there searching for Bea. I realise that I really want to be the one to find her. After all, that's why I organised today in the first place. I need to redeem myself.

'Well, it's a little late now.' Trina sucks air in through her teeth. 'The groups are all underway. And I need to stay here to plot this afternoon's routes. The thing is, Jill, lunch is super-important for everyone to keep their strength up. So you'd be really helping out.'

She's veering towards the patronising now, but I can't allow her tone to rile me. I couldn't have arranged such a good job this morning without her. And it shouldn't take long to pick up a few sandwiches.

I drop my shoulders. 'Okay, yes, sure, I'll go.'

'Wonderful.' She graces me with a perfunctory smile and strides back towards her makeshift headquarters like she's the queen of the world.

I watch her purposeful march across the grass and try to inject some of that briskness into my own body as I head for the pedestrian crossing which will take me into town. The sooner I buy lunch, the sooner I can get back to the search. As I cross the road and wind my way between the queuing cars in the already-full supermarket car park, I realise I never asked what sandwiches everyone wanted. Never mind, I'll buy a selection and let them choose. I'm not fussy so I'll just have whatever's left. I know Laurel likes egg mayo, so I'll get her one of those.

It's not quite midday, but the supermarket is already jammed. Probably due to the fact it's a baking hot Sunday in August so everyone's panic shopping for picnics and barbecues. Despite the crowds, it's blissfully cool in here and it feels like heaven to glide past the frigid air surrounding the chiller cabinets.

Thankfully, there are still a few packs of sandwiches left on the shelves, so I make my selections – an egg mayo for Laurel, a cheese ploughman's, a chicken salad and a BLT – adding four bottles of water and four packets of crisps to complete the meal deal that's on offer – sandwiches, crisps and a drink all for five pounds. Trina must have known about it. I also treat myself to a packet of fruit pastilles, my mouth watering at the thought of them. Guilt blindsides me as I remember that Beatrice loves fruit pastilles too. She always asks for them when she visits and of course I always indulge her. Her favourite flavours are the same as mine – lemon and lime.

I pay on my credit card and keep the cash that's already folded into my purse. My heart is pounding as I walk out of the automatic doors into the blinding heat of the morning. It's only as I reach the pedestrian crossing once more that I register the fact that the cashier only charged me five pounds for the four meal deals instead of twenty. I check the receipt just to make certain, and sure enough it shows five pounds. I realise that I must have put the other three lunches and the fruit pastilles straight into my bag before paying, instead of into the basket.

I should return to the checkout and admit what I've done. That would certainly be the ethical thing to do. It's what I would advise anyone else to do in my position. But my heartbeat is still thrashing in my ears, my skin prickling with sweat, my breathing shallow. I don't think I can do it. What if they don't believe it was an honest mistake? What if they call the police?

The green man flashes at the crossing and the beeps start up, as though urging me to get a move on and cross the road. They make the decision for me. I take a steadying breath and walk back towards the fairground. I don't have time to waste going back to the supermarket. My granddaughter needs me, and she's far more important than a silly oversight like this. And I can't deny that fifteen extra pounds in my purse is a weight off my mind.

CHAPTER FOURTEEN

CLAIRE

Freya stays for a quick cup of tea while I cry some more on her shoulder, and then she offers to drive me to the playing fields to join in the search.

'Thanks, but I don't think I'm up to talking to a bunch of strangers. I mean I'm grateful to them for being there...'

'Totally understand. It's probably for the best anyway.' She lowers her voice. 'Laurel's there.'

I freeze. 'Laurel? As in Oliver's ex?'

'Yep. She's in full confrontation mode. I had to break up an argument between her and this posh couple who were volunteering.'

'What the hell's she doing there?'

'I think she came with Jill.'

I take a breath, trying not to let this new piece of information bother me. I always knew that Jill had a soft spot for Oliver's ex-wife. That she probably wishes they never broke up. Laurel's an artist, another 'free spirit' like herself. I'm sure she thinks Laurel's better suited to her son than me. But right now I've got more important things to worry about. I shouldn't let Laurel's involvement in the search add to my stress.

'You should've seen her, Claire.' Freya rolls her eyes, trying to lighten the mood for my benefit. 'Swishing around in her hippy-dippy dress like she was queen bee, and then this couple in her search group asked her to stop vaping because they didn't like the smell.'

'Bet she loved that.'

Freya grins. 'She basically told them to get stuffed. I had to intervene. Told them all it wasn't the time or place.'

'Good for you. Thanks, Frey. So what happened after that?'

'Cheeky cow blew smoke in my face.'

I shake my head. Normally, if something like this happened, Freya and I would chat about it for ages over a glass of wine. But not today. I already feel guilty enough for the twenty-minute conversation we've just had. I can't sit around any longer.

As though she's read my mind, Freya gets to her feet. 'I'll go.' She wraps her arms around me, planting a kiss on my cheek. 'Stay positive, my lovely. We'll find her.'

'Thanks. And thanks for coming over.'

I'm grateful to Freya for letting me offload, especially as she's had troubles of her own. She split up with Joe, her boyfriend of two years, this May and she's been glum ever since. Last night's meal was supposed to be an evening out to cheer her up. I'll make it up to her once Beatrice is home.

After Freya leaves, the house feels even more forlorn, the air heavy and still as though it's holding its breath. I stay seated in the kitchen feeling inert and hopeless until my phone jolts me out of it. It's Jill. My first thought is to ignore her call. But then what if she's calling with news?

'Hello?'

'Claire. I just wanted to call to see how you're doing. Oliver said you're a bit upset about the search party.'

Good one, Ollie.

'About me not telling you both about it.'

'It's fine, Jill. I'm completely fine with it.' I lie because I don't have the energy to tell her how I really feel. 'Thanks for organising it.'

'Really? Oh, thank goodness. It's just, after yesterday, and then with what happened last night, I wasn't sure what to do for the best. Whether to call you or not. I didn't want you to feel obliged to join in the search. Not if you were exhausted, or just couldn't face it.'

'Honestly, don't worry. So how's it going? The search, I mean.'

'Well, we've had a terrific turnout. A couple of hundred people showed up first thing, and since then more and more people have come along as the day's gone on and the word's spread.'

'Sounds great.' I worry I'm sounding insincere. 'Is there any news about Bea? Did anyone find anything?'

'Not yet, but it's early days, isn't it?'

'Is it? She's been missing overnight. The longer she's missing, the less chance there is of finding her.' I need to end this call before I say something I regret. Before I lose my shit and start screaming down the phone at her about how she lost my daughter. About how she might be the person responsible for destroying my family.

'Let's think positive.' Jill's voice wavers in my ear, telling me she's not thinking positive at all. But I can't bring myself to feel sorry for Jill right now. And I don't want her telling me to think positive – not when she's the one who's caused all this. I suppose at least she's out there doing something, which is more than I can say about myself right now.

'How's Laurel?' I blurt out before I can stop myself.

There's a beat of silence. 'She's… uh… well, you know she and I still keep in touch. She wanted to help.'

'Of course she did.' I know I sound like a jealous witch, but I can't help myself. I feel as though my whole personality is unravelling. As though I can no longer control either my words or my emotions. Everything is bubbling up to the surface, boiling over.

'You always preferred Laurel anyway. I don't blame you. She's much easier to get along with than me.'

'Claire!'

Tears are spilling down my face now and it's nothing to do with Jill or Laurel or the search party, and everything to do with my missing baby. My daughter. What if I never see her again?

I suck in a breath and try to speak normally. 'Okay, Jill, well thanks for calling.'

'Claire, please, don't hang up yet. Are you all right?'

Of course I'm not fucking all right. 'Yep, yes, I'm fine. Sorry about that. Emotions are getting the better of me.'

'Of course, that's entirely understandable. I feel the same way. I'll send Ollie back home to be with you.'

'No, it's okay. I'm okay. Please don't worry.'

'Are you sure?'

'Absolutely.'

Jill spends another minute making sure I'm fine before I can finally end the call.

I'm not sure how much longer I can do this. This can't be my new reality. This can't be the way things are going to be. I need Beatrice back home. Her face flashes into my mind, and I hear her funny laugh and her constant bright stream of chatter. She's such a vibrant child. So alive. So much at the heart of our lives that there's no way we can live without her in it.

It's already lunchtime and I still haven't ventured out of the house. I realise that Jill being out there searching with half the town is the reason I don't want to join her search party. Is it sour grapes that's keeping me away? Maybe. On some deeper level I feel like the grief is mine alone. Like I'm the only one who has a right to it. Which is utter nonsense, I know. I'm behaving like a lunatic. I need to stop this right now.

I get up, fling open the back door and step out into the garden. I stand on the patio just out of the sun's reach. It's warm even in the shade. I close my eyes and take a deep breath, trying to gather strength, to steady my mind and my emotions. Lashing out isn't going to do me or Beatrice any good. I need to calm down and be more single-minded about what I need to do. I can't let myself get distracted by other people.

Thankfully, Phil from next door has stopped hammering and drilling for now. All I hear is the wind sighing through the trees and the faint hum of traffic from the main road. I breathe in and out, loosening my body, trying to ease the tension in my limbs, my back, my shoulders, my jaw.

As I stand there trying to centre myself, an idea comes to me. One that fires me up and gives me a tiny spark of hope.

CHAPTER FIFTEEN

CLAIRE

I leave the patio and head straight for my office at the front of the house. This room should really have been a dining or living room, and I could have used the third bedroom upstairs as my office. But, as an independent financial advisor, I often have clients visit the house, so having my office downstairs is more practical. Stops people traipsing up the stairs.

The room is square and functional with white blinds at the window and a grey desk, on which sits my laptop, a pile of pending paperwork and assorted stationery. Two straight-backed chairs face the desk, and my own chair is a comfortable red-leather number that Oliver bought me two Christmases ago. My professional certificates have been framed and hung on the wall beside my desk – another gift from my husband. He's always so thoughtful. Buying good gifts is a talent of his. The wall opposite is lined with grey cabinets where all my cases are meticulously filed.

Thought of work sets off feelings of guilt and panic. I have clients depending on me for mortgage applications, insurance policies and the rest. I'll have to call and apologise. I'll point them in the direction of other professional contacts who could take over for me while I'm going through this trauma. But I can't face doing any of that right now.

I sit at my desk and open my laptop, close down the files I'm currently working on and fire up Facebook instead. I'm not a big fan of social media. I rarely post anything because whenever I do, I feel like I'm either bragging or moaning. But it does have its uses. It's handy to catch up with old friends and also to share photos of Beatrice with my parents and other relations, all of whom live up in Scotland. Even though my parents are Scottish born and bred, I've never lived there myself. They moved down to the south of England thirty years ago when a job opportunity came up, but they always planned to return. They finally did just that nine years ago after Dad retired. Ollie, Bea and I usually visit them in the summer at their stone-built house on the outskirts of Aberdeen. They adore their only grandchild.

I haven't told them about Beatrice going missing yet. I'd rather have waited until we found her and everything was fine again. But I realise that right now I don't have any choice. Not if I'm going to create a public Facebook post about what's happened.

I spend the next half hour on the phone to my mum, her Scottish accent thick with worry. My parents are both pretty no-nonsense people, practical and straight-talking. But Mum is shocked and devastated by my news. After a few moments of silence where I know she's trying to get herself under control, she regroups. Mum tells me the Facebook post is a great idea. She tells me to get out there and search. To bug the hell out of the police, and don't let them slack off at all. She offers to get the next flight down with Dad, but I tell her to wait a while. I'll let them know if I need them, but right now I'd be too emotional if I saw my mum. She'd want to make everything better. She'd be warm and comforting, and I'd probably fall to pieces – even more than I'm already doing. I don't need kindness right now, I need action.

Speaking to her over the phone has given me the shot of energy and courage I need. Once I end the call, I get to work on the Facebook post. I upload a photo of Beatrice and write about what's happened, asking all my friends to share the post with locals and to keep a look out. Writing about it makes everything seem even more real. As soon as I hit *post* the first lot of reactions and comments start flying in. I can't face reading them just yet. I need a few minutes' break before engaging with everyone. Before accepting their sympathy and the suggestions I know will be forthcoming. Already I can see that I've had twenty-three reactions, four comments and sixteen shares. I just hope that between Jill's search party and my Facebook post, Beatrice will be found safe and well very soon.

I glance up at the sound of the front door.

'Claire?'

It's Ollie. I check the clock on the screen. It's only one fifteen. He's only been gone a couple of hours.

'In here!' I close my laptop and pinch the bridge of my nose.

The door opens and he comes in, his face a little sunburned.

'How did you get on? You're back early.'

'I came to see how you're doing. Mum said you were upset on the phone. She said you weren't happy about Laurel being there.' He pulls up a chair and gives me a look of concern. I've always been a little insecure about his ex-wife, even though they broke up before I came onto the scene. I think it's because we're such different people. I always feel like he must be comparing us, especially when I'm being uptight or angry. It doesn't help that his mum thinks the sun shines out of Laurel's behind.

'She shouldn't have said anything. I told her not to say anything.'

'She's worried about you.'

I click my tongue and try to calm my breathing. Try not to spiral into this irritating conversation – it just doesn't matter. 'So how's the search going?'

Oliver shakes his head and smiles. 'It's amazing. There are so many people there. Mum's friend Trina says there've been over five hundred volunteers so far. I mean, can you believe it? Surely with that many people out looking they'll find her.'

'Not if someone's driven away with her.'

Oliver's face darkens. 'We can't think like that.'

'Do you really feel that positive? I mean, genuinely? Do you think they're going to stumble across her walking down the road?'

'I don't know.' He throws up his hands.

'Because I don't think there's a hope that any of them will find her today. Not if I really think about it. It's almost been a whole day, Oll. A whole day of not knowing where she is.' My blood is heating up again, my emotions soaring. I want to lash out. To yell. My husband's forlorn expression makes me want to scream. Even though I know he's feeling just as bad. Probably worse, as it was his mother who lost her. 'Did your mum apologise for not involving us in the search?' I know it's a horrible thing to ask right now. Twisting the knife to make him feel even more guilty.

'Yes,' Ollie grunts. 'She feels awful about all of it. You know she does.'

I nod. 'I set up a Facebook page asking friends to look out for her. To share it with anyone else local.'

'Good idea.' His face reddens.

'What?'

He shakes his head.

'What is it?' I push.

'Mum did an interview with the *Argus*. They kind of ambushed her, but I think it's a good thing. Don't be mad at her.'

'I'm not this horrible person who's got it in for your mum, Ollie! Newspaper coverage is a good thing. The more people know about it, the better our chance at getting her back.'

'Good.'

'I feel like you're taking her side or something, against me. Like you think I'm being mean when all I'm doing...' I get to my feet and ball my fists at my side, take a breath. 'All I'm doing is trying to process everything. Trying to keep my shit together while everyone else is so organised and perfect. And I'm made out to be mean, horrible and unreasonable.' My voice goes shrill, and ironically all I can hear is this person who's being mean, horrible and unreasonable. This isn't me.

'Whoa!' Oliver gets to his feet too. 'I'm not taking sides, Claire. There are no sides. There's just all of us wanting to find Beatrice. That's it.'

It suddenly hits me that I know exactly why I'm behaving this way. Why I'm so mad. It's because I still haven't forgiven Oliver for not doing what he said. For not taking the girls to the fair last night. For going behind my back and asking his mother to do it instead. I want him to properly admit it's his fault. To say he's sorry. Even though I'd tell him that it's not his fault, that he doesn't need to apologise. I want him to say it anyway. Because right now I'm still feeling guilty.

'If I hadn't been going out, none of this would have happened.'

'Don't go down that road, Claire. You're allowed to go out. Just because we're parents, doesn't mean we're not allowed to have a social life. Come in the kitchen with me. I need a drink of water.' I follow him out of the office. 'Let's go and join Mum's search party. You'll feel better once we're doing something proactive.'

'I've just been doing something proactive – the Facebook page.'

'Yeah, I know, I just meant…' He gets himself a drink of water and downs it in one long draught.

'Can we just go out looking for her ourselves?' I ask. 'Just the two of us in the car?'

'I told Mum I'd go back.'

'Oh, well,' I snap. 'You better go back then.'

'Claire, don't be like that.'

'I'm not "like" anything.' I grip one of the chair backs, willing myself to calm down. 'Just go.'

'Come with me.'

'No. I already told you I don't want to.'

'Fine. See you later.' Oliver slams his glass down on the table and leaves the kitchen without even looking at me. The front door crashes shut and I hear the sound of his car engine start up.

Nausea swirls in my gut. Why did I push him away like that? What did I even hope to achieve? Nothing. A black fog descends, plunging me into a deep, regretful despair. After a few moments of paralysis, I stumble after him, down the hallway and out onto the front porch. But as I stand there in the blistering sun, mouth open ready to apologise, Oliver's car is already roaring away down the road.

DAY THREE

I stand outside the window watching her. Chestnut waves falling over her face as she scribbles on the paper. She's already started asking too many questions. I'm going to have to do something about that. But I'm not sure what. Not yet. I don't want to have to move to plan B. That would be a real shame.

I startle as she looks up from her drawing and stares directly at me through the glass, chewing the end of her pencil. As I gaze back, I realise she can't see me, not while I'm out here in the dark. All she'll be able to see is her own reflection.

CHAPTER SIXTEEN

JILL

I'm walking out the front door when a green florist's van pulls up outside the house and the driver waves at me to wait. She gets out of the van.

'That was good timing,' she puffs. 'I've got a delivery for you.' Walking round to the back of the van, she takes out a beautiful bouquet of yellow and white roses interspersed with various green leaves and sprays of white gypsophila.

'How gorgeous. Thank you.' I take the flowers inside and read the attached card. It's an apology from Millie's parents and an offer to help if I need it. That's so nice of them. I don't really blame Paul and Tanya for being cross on Saturday. The whole thing has been a terrible shock for everyone.

I was leaving the house to meet Laurel for a late coffee in town, but I think I'll pop these flowers in water first. I take a glass vase from the kitchen cabinet and start trimming the flower stalks with a kitchen knife. After Claire's outburst on the phone yesterday, Laurel is probably the last person I should be spending time with; it feels disloyal somehow. But who else do I have to confide in? Laurel has been a good friend to me. She's never too busy to listen. While Oliver and Claire are getting their support from one another, I'm getting my support from Laurel.

The final rose stem is tough and woody, but I finally manage to saw through it, piercing my thumb pad with a thorn in the process.

'Damn!'

Shoving the flowers into the vase with one hand, I suck my bleeding thumb and scrabble about in the odds-and-ends drawer. I can't locate any plasters, but I come across a battered tube of antiseptic cream so I squeeze a little of it onto the cut. That will have to do. I sweep the stalks, leaves and wrappings into the bin, wipe down the surface and leave the house.

It's already eleven thirty so I pick up my pace, walking briskly along the dusty pavement, a thin sheen of sweat coating my skin after only a few minutes beneath the baking August sun. I invited Laurel for lunch at home, but she asked if we could meet at the Bridge Street coffee shop as she's dying for one of their frappuccinos. I really don't have the money to be throwing it away on fancy drinks so I asked her to order me one too.

Thankfully, the café isn't far, and it's heaven to enter its cool interior. I spy Laurel halfway down in a booth, two tall glasses of iced coffee on the table in front of her. She looks up and gives me a wave, her red hair plaited today and draped over one shoulder. My own hair is in desperate need of a wash, but I woke up late and was in too much of a hurry to bother this morning. I run a hand down it self-consciously, wincing as I catch my sore thumb on a strand of hair.

'Hi, Jill. How are you doing this morning?' Laurel rises and I lean in for a hug before settling opposite her on the green leather bench seat.

'Is this for me?' I point at the drink.

'Yes. You look like you could do with it.'

I blow out a puff of air. 'You're not wrong. Thank you. I'll get the next lot.'

Laurel waves away my offer. She's not particularly well off, but she's always been generous. 'You sounded upset on the phone. What's been happening? Any news of Beatrice?'

I shake my head and bite the inside of my cheek to stem the emotion bubbling up inside. 'Nothing yet.' My voice is thin and brittle.

'Oh, Jill. I can't even imagine what you must be going through.'

I take a sip of my drink through a cardboard straw that's already turning soggy. The coffee is ice-cold and sweet. Reviving. I take another longer sip. 'It doesn't feel real. My poor Beatrice. I keep expecting to wake up and find it was all a horrid dream. I was so sure we'd find her yesterday with all those people out searching. How did we not find her?'

Laurel shakes her head. 'I know. Same here. It was such an unbelievable turnout. You did an amazing job organising it.'

'Claire wasn't happy though,' I mutter, feeling instantly disloyal. I really shouldn't be talking about my daughter-in-law to Laurel, but I can't help myself. I need to vent.

'How so? Why would Claire not be happy? I would have thought she'd be grateful.'

'Because I didn't involve her in the search party. But that was only because I wanted to let her and Oliver rest after the night they'd had. Especially after I'd called him from the police station, when I... you know.' I trail off, not wanting to articulate what happened that night.

'You mean the drink-driving thing?' Laurel finishes my sentence and I glance around the café, hoping no one heard.

'Yes, shh.'

'Sorry.' She winces and makes a zipping motion across her lips.

'It's okay. It's just, I can do without the extra drama of people finding out and gossiping.'

'What's happening with that, anyway?'

'With the driving thing?'

She nods.

'Nothing. Other than what they said at the station – I have to go to court next week.'

'Bummer,' Laurel drawls. 'I can come with you if you like.'

'Really?'

'Of course.'

'Thank you.' I reach across to squeeze her hand, which is freezing. 'You're a good friend, Laurel.'

'I try.' She smiles. 'So, Claire's mad at you?'

'Yes, sadly. She's a strange one. One minute I think we're getting on fine, the next she's yelling at me.'

'Blimey. Is she always like that?'

'No, well, not really. We've never been that close, but this has understandably sent her over the edge. It's sad, but I think she might be jealous of our friendship. Because I click with you a little better, that's all. I always try to spare her feelings and I never talk about you when I'm with her. But she got upset when she found out you were there yesterday.'

'Oh, for goodness' sake!' Laurel tosses her plait behind her back. 'She's already got my ex-husband, and now she wants to drive a wedge between you and me.'

'I don't think she wants to drive a wedge between us; she's just a little jealous of our friendship, that's all.'

'Of course she does. I love you, Jill, but you can be quite naive sometimes. Promise me you won't let Claire come between us. I consider you to be my best friend, you know.' She tilts her head and smiles at me.

I'm starting to think I shouldn't have offloaded on Laurel about Claire. I might be turning this into something bigger than it needs to be. 'Just ignore me. I'm definitely overthinking things. Claire's fine. She's upset about Beatrice so she's lashing out. Which is entirely understandable.'

'Maybe. But it's not fair on you. You're worried too. She should bear that in mind instead of using you as a punching bag.'

'I don't think it's quite that bad!' I frown at my friend's transparent attempt to turn me against my daughter-in-law.

'Hmm.' I can see Laurel's mind whirring. 'I don't understand how she and Ollie got together in the first place. They're nothing alike. She doesn't have a creative bone in her body. And Ollie is all about creativity and the arts.'

'I think it's an opposites-attract thing.' I realise I've opened up a new dynamic in our relationship. One where Laurel thinks it's okay to bash Oliver's wife. I should never have opened my mouth. I really need to nip this in the bud. I remember her trying to use this exact same tactic back when Ollie first met Claire, but I refused to be drawn in then and I refuse to be drawn in now. I'm going to have to cut off this conversation.

'But do they actually get on?' Laurel's eyes narrow with curiosity and a desire for me to spill the gossip.

I won't give her the satisfaction. Honestly, Laurel is really disappointing me today. I thought she was above this. I'm not enjoying the way she's pushing me to talk about Claire and Oliver's marriage. I should never have bad-mouthed Claire in front of her. It seems to have opened the floodgates to a side of my ex-daughter-in-law that I'd hoped I'd seen the last of. I sip my frappuccino, suddenly hungry for proper food. It is almost lunchtime after all, but I'll have to wait until I get home. I can't afford these coffee-shop prices.

'Of course Claire and Oliver get on,' I reply brightly. 'They love each other. How about you? Any new romances on the horizon?'

She shrugs. 'Nothing worth shouting about. I'd rather be on my own than with the wrong person.'

'I know what you mean. No one could replace my Bob.'

'He was one in a million, Jill.'

'He certainly was.'

'Oh, while I remember, you didn't come across my blue chiffon scarf yesterday, did you? It was so hot, I took it off, but it's not in my bag.'

'Sorry, no. That's a shame, it was pretty.'

She shrugs. 'Ah well.'

We sip our coffees in silence for a moment and I let the chatter and the clink of crockery swirl around me. I hope Laurel realises that I don't want to talk about Claire any more. That I made a mistake in criticising her.

'Jill…'

'Hm?' I look up to see Laurel looking serious, a little apprehensive even.

'I wasn't sure how to bring this up, or even whether I should mention it.'

'Mention what?' My pulse speeds up at the increasingly worried expression on her face. What is it that she wants to tell me? What *now*?

CHAPTER SEVENTEEN

CLAIRE

'I can't believe we're into day three and there's still no news.' Oliver pushes the tuna salad around his bowl with his fork before giving up any pretence of eating and sliding the bowl away.

We're having an early lunch, but I'm not hungry either, even though the hollow feeling in my stomach says otherwise. I chew my salad, but I may as well be eating cardboard for all the enjoyment I'm getting out of it. I'm too exhausted, upset and hot to eat. The back door is open, but there's not even the hint of a breeze coming through. Despite the light flooding in through the windows, the kitchen feels claustrophobic, stifling.

After yesterday's argument, Oliver came home for dinner and we barely spoke, aside from an apology from me. Despite the huge turnout, Jill's search party didn't turn up anything worthwhile. The only thing it did was show what a tight-knit community we live in. That there are people out there who genuinely care.

Oliver and I spent this morning searching the streets once again. And once again we turned up nothing. It's like our daughter has disappeared off the face of the earth.

'Have you checked the Facebook page recently?' Oliver's face is grey and drawn and there are purple smudges beneath his eyes. Neither of us slept well last night.

'I've been checking it constantly. Everyone's lovely, but no one's seen a thing. Did you speak to the police again?'

'Yeah. Nothing.'

We sit quietly for a few moments with nothing but the hum of the fridge and the ticking of the wall clock. The thought of going back onto the streets to search fills me with dread. Earlier, I was raring to go, convinced we'd find our daughter, but it's feeling more and more like a useless exercise, like we're killing time until the police can give us an answer. I made the mistake of googling 'missing children'. The statistics aren't good. Most children are found within forty-eight hours. After that, the chances of finding them safe and well decline drastically. We're fast approaching that deadline. We have to find her today.

Please let her be okay. Please don't let her be hurt or scared. Wherever she is, I need her not to be frightened. She's always been a fearless child, but she's never had to face anything truly awful. I couldn't bear it if she was traumatised by whatever's happening to her right now.

The doorbell shakes us from our thoughts. We stare at one another for a second before both getting up. I shouldn't allow myself to hope that this is some kind of good news because I can't face the disappointment, but that doesn't stop my speeding heart and lurching stomach as I follow Ollie to the front door.

'Flower delivery for Claire and Oliver Nolan.' The woman at the door is red-cheeked and flustered as she hands my husband a bouquet of yellow and white roses. He thanks her quietly.

I turn away and plod back into the kitchen. Seconds later, the front door closes and Ollie follows me, bouquet in hand.

'Who are they from?' I ask, even though I couldn't care less.

He lays the flowers on the table between our salad bowls and inspects the small white card. 'Says it's from Paul, Tanya and Millie.'

'The Jensens?'

'Yeah. It says they're sorry things got so heated and they're thinking about us. To let them know if they can help in any way.'

'That's nice.' Definitely Tanya's work. I doubt Paul had anything to do with the flowers or the apology.

We stare down at the bouquet. I should probably sort out a vase and some water, but the task seems beyond me at the moment. Oliver does the honours and I force myself not to say anything when he forgets to cut the stalks. It doesn't matter. None of it matters.

'I guess we should get back out there.' I start clearing away the lunch things.

'Definitely.' Oliver scratches his chin. 'Would you mind if I nipped to the shop first?'

I give him a look.

'I know. It's the last thing I want to do, but I have to finish my tax forms for the accountant. We'll get fined otherwise.'

'I suppose so, but surely they won't fine you if they know the circumstances.'

'I don't want to take the risk. If I just get it done, it'll be one less thing to think about.'

'Okay. Want me to come with you?'

'Don't worry, I shouldn't be long. Stay here and rest for a bit. We were out for hours this morning. You look tired, Claire.' He leans in and moves a strand of hair from my eyes. His fingers brush my cheek and I suddenly feel bad that the two of us are so out of tune right now. We should be supporting one another instead of bickering.

I dredge up a tired smile. 'Thanks, but I'm too antsy to rest.'

'I know what you mean. I'll be back soon, okay?' He rubs the top of my arm, a soothing gesture. I put my hand over his and we stay like that for a moment.

Oliver leaves and I'm back on my own again, the house mocking me with its silence. I decide that I'd rather be out looking for Bea than worrying at home alone. I make myself a coffee and take it with me into the office. I'll check my Facebook page before heading out. It's easier to check it on the laptop than on my phone.

Scrolling through the latest comments, I see that all kinds of friends and acquaintances are leaving messages of support and sympathy – some of whom I haven't seen or heard from in years – but no one has any news of Beatrice. I recognise names from school, college, old work places, friends of friends, ex-boyfriends, people I fell out with – they're all here on this page. And they're even having little sub-conversations; old friends catching up while my world is in freefall.

I notice that I also have several private messages. I click on the message icon and open up the first one, which is from an old school friend who's letting me know she was part of yesterday's search party and if there's anything else I need I should let her know. The next two messages are along similar lines. The last message is from a name I don't recognise – Faye Kerr. Could it be someone from my past who's changed their surname after getting married? But I don't know anyone, past or present, called Faye. A client? I don't think so. And then it hits me. I shake my head and curl my lip. I'm so stupid not to have twigged straight away. Faye Kerr = Faker. So it's a fake name. Probably spam. I open it anyway, steeling myself in case it's a dick pic or something equally gross.

It's a short message:

You deserve it.

I feel a spark of static as the hairs stand up on the back of my neck. Is this spam, or maybe some kind of advert? No. It feels more sinister. Threatening. I really hope this isn't to do with Beatrice going missing. Like they're saying that I deserve this to happen to me. That's just horrible. Sick. I click on their profile, but it was only made last week and they have no photos, no friends and no 'about' info. Their profile picture is a vase of red roses on a mantelpiece in front of a mirror. Wait a minute… a *mirror*.

Beatrice went missing in the hall of mirrors. This is too specific to be a coincidence. With trembling fingers I pick up my phone and call Gayle.

She answers after one ring. 'Hello, Claire, is that you?' It sounds like she's in a car.

'Hi, Gayle, can you talk?'

'I'm just on my way to you now.'

'Good timing. How far away are you?'

'Literally just turning into your road.'

I blow out a breath. 'Okay, see you in a sec.' I take a gulp of my almost-cold coffee, head to the front door and stand out on the porch, watching for her arrival. Within seconds, her silver Polo flashes into view and pulls into the driveway. She gives a quick wave through the windscreen before exiting the car and hurrying up the steps towards me.

'Something happen? You okay?'

'It's best if I show you.'

Gayle nods and follows me into the office where I sit and show her the awful message. 'Have you taken any screenshots?' She's looking over my shoulder at the offending message.

'No. Good idea.' I screenshot the message as well as the person's profile page. 'Did you notice their profile picture is a mirror? Do you think they might have done that on purpose because of where Beatrice went missing – the hall of mirrors?'

'Maybe. It's possible.' She shakes her head in disgust. 'Although it's not nice, I'd try not to worry. It's probably just an internet troll. Unfortunately, there are people who get off on this sort of thing. Some sad person hiding behind their keyboard trying to make other people's lives a misery.'

'Can you find out who's behind it?'

'We'll do our best.' She takes a few photos on her phone of the account and the message. 'Don't hold out too much hope though.

It'll probably be a fake account with a temporary email address. Like I said, try not to worry about it. We're better off spending our time looking for Beatrice.'

'What if this person's behind it? What if they took her?'

'Claire…'

I look up at Gayle. She's fixing me with a kind but firm stare. 'What?'

'Whoever's behind that message is hoping to cause this exact reaction. To make you feel even more scared and upset. Don't give them the satisfaction. Honestly, they're not worth spending a second more of your time on. We'll look into it, I promise. In the meantime, put them out of your head and try not to worry about them.'

'It's hard not to.' I know what Gayle's saying is true, but it's almost impossible to disentangle my emotions. 'It's such a personal attack. Another horrible shock, you know. On top of everything else, some bastard has to do this. I wish I'd never set up the page. Nothing helpful's come of it anyway. It's been a complete waste of time.'

'Why don't you change your settings so that no one can send you private messages. That should deter these types of trolls. If they're that persistent, they'll have to post their bile in front of everyone else and show the world how awful they are. Pretty sure they won't be up for that.'

'Good idea.' I do as she suggests and click onto my message settings. 'So no news from your end?'

'Not yet. The DI is working on a few things which is why I'm here. Is Oliver in?'

'No. He's had to go into work for a bit to sort out some forms and arrange cover while he's off. Can you tell me what these things are? I'll let him know when he gets back.'

'Okay.'

I finish updating my Facebook message settings and close my laptop.

'Do you mind if I sit?' She points to the chairs on the other side of the desk.

'Yes, of course. Sorry. Do you want a drink?'

'I'm fine.' She sits opposite me and I wait for her to tell me what they're planning. 'So we're going to be working with the National Crime Agency – NCA for short – to implement what's known as a Child Rescue Alert – CRA for short.'

'Child Rescue Alert? That sounds quite drastic. What is it exactly?' I feel as though I'm speaking from a long way away. Like I'm not even here. All these words and acronyms sound so official, like something out of a TV crime drama. Why are they now part of my real life?

'It's based on the US Amber Alert system, where we work with the media to get the public's help. Similar to what you've done with your Facebook page, but on a wider scale. We'll probably ask you to disable your own page at some stage so we can coordinate things from our end, but I'll let you know if that needs to happen.'

My mouth goes dry. 'I can't believe this is happening. Does this mean Beatrice will be all over the news and social media?'

'Possibly. Our absolute priority is to find your daughter. Of course, we'll always give consideration to the impact such a high-profile media alert might have on Beatrice's future.'

I try to absorb what she's telling me. Oliver and I are going to be like those couples you see on the news sometimes with their hollow-eyed stares and barely reined-in terror. The ones who have to stand there united giving a statement to the media amid camera flashes and shouted questions from the press. I feel ill at the thought.

'I know it's a lot to take in, Claire, but I'll be here with you both every step of the way, okay? You can speak to me about anything and ask any questions.'

I nod, my brain going blank, my body numb.

Gayle shifts in her seat. 'There's one other thing I have to tell you that you may or may not already know about.'

I wait for her to continue, still reeling from everything else and unsure if I can absorb yet more news.

'It appears that your mother-in-law gave an interview to the *Argus*.'

'Oh, yeah, Oliver told me about that. They accosted her yesterday while she was organising her search party.'

'Ah, okay. Well, the piece came out today and it's fair to say it's probably not what she had in mind.'

'What do you mean?' I don't understand how Jill has managed to cause so much chaos in such a short space of time.

'It's fine. The piece shouldn't interfere with our own media plan too much, but I doubt it will help either. From now on, we'll need you guys to run any media involvement through us first. We'll have a word with Jill and tell her the same thing.'

'Have you got a copy of the article?'

'No, but it's online. If I were you, I wouldn't bother reading it.'

'It's that bad?'

'Not really. Just not worth reading. That's my advice.'

'Okay. Thanks. I'm not sure I've got the mental energy to look at it right now anyway.' Not if it's as awful as I think it might be.

I slump down in my seat. This is all such a nightmare. Where is my daughter? Where *is* she? I miss her so much it feels as though someone has ripped out half of my soul. What if she's scared? Hurt? Beatrice is such a good girl. Such a bright, happy child. I wish I'd been a better mum. Less strict. More fun. More like Jill, I suppose. But then if it weren't for Jill, Beatrice would be here now...

CHAPTER EIGHTEEN

JILL

I shift in my seat, the leather pad creaking beneath me. Why is Laurel looking so nervous? What does she want to tell me? She reaches down by her side for something and I see that it's a folded newspaper. 'Is that… is that the *Argus*?'

'Mm.' She nods, placing the newspaper on the table.

If she's reticent about showing it to me, that must mean… 'Is that piece about Beatrice in there?'

'You could say that. It's on the front page.' She winces.

My heart is really thumping now. Yesterday, when I was all fired up about the search, it seemed only natural to give an interview. To make sure the net was cast as wide as possible, to leave no stone unturned. But today, after little sleep and two days of worry, I don't feel able to cope with it. With the attention this interview might shine on me.

'Have you read it?'

Laurel nods slowly.

'Is it okay?'

'Look, it's great in terms of getting the word out…'

'But…' I prompt.

Laurel winces yet again. 'The journalist was a bit mean.'

'Mean?' *Oh no.*

She slides the newspaper across the table. I take a breath, square my shoulders and unfold it. The main photograph isn't of Beatrice; it's of me. I look as though I'm posing for an old-fashioned postcard with my fingers touching my hair in an affected way, a half-smile on my face that makes it look as though I'm enjoying myself. Beatrice's picture is further down the page and is less than a quarter the size of mine. The huge headline reads: *Glamorous Granny Loses Granddaughter at the Fair!*

My mouth falls open. 'Oh, no. That's awful. It's just… awful.'

'Yep, they're bastards,' Laurel says. She seems relieved now that she's told me.

I shake my head and push the paper back towards her. 'I really don't want to read it, not after seeing that headline. I don't think I can handle any more awfulness. What's Ollie going to say?' *And I don't even want to think about Claire's reaction.*

'Do you want me to summarise it for you?' Laurel asks. I'm annoyed to see her mouth twitching as though she's trying to stifle a smile, even though her blue eyes are filled with concern.

'All right, Laurel, but please be gentle.'

'Okay, so…' She picks up the paper and clears her throat. 'It says that Beatrice went missing at the fair, but it makes you come across as a bit vain. It quotes you saying how Beatrice takes after you looks wise, and how beautiful she is. Basically it makes you sound like you're more concerned with your looks than with your granddaughter going missing. It also makes you sound a bit scatty. I mean, it's not as blatant as that, but that's the overall vibe of the piece. Do you want me to read the bad bits out? Or the non-bad bits?'

I feel nauseous. I taste milky coffee in the back of my throat, my skin has gone cold and my vision is blurring. This is horrible. 'I don't want you to read any of it out,' I squeak. 'Why would he do that? Why would that man write such terrible things about me? What did I ever do to him?'

'It's what they do, isn't it? They find an angle.'

'I was talking about how beautiful she is, not to blow my own trumpet, but because I love her and she's a beautiful child – inside and out. I'm sure any grandparent would say the same thing, wouldn't they?'

Laurel shrugs. 'I feel bad for telling you. I just didn't want you to find out from someone else.'

'He's twisted my words.' I feel like such an idiot. I thought Giles Renton and I were bonding. I'd felt sure he liked me and was going to write a sympathetic piece. I wonder if he actually does have a daughter the same age as Beatrice, or if he lied about that to get me to open up to him.

'I know it's rough, Jill, but you can't take it to heart.'

'It's hard not to!'

'At least it gets the word out about Beatrice. Maybe someone will recognise her.'

'From that tiny photo? I doubt it!'

'You should put it out of your head. In fact, if you look at it another way, it's actually a little bit funny.' Laurel tilts her head, trying to get me to smile.

I inhale and try to swallow down a surge of anger. 'I'm sure you wouldn't find it funny if it were your reputation smeared across the local paper. If someone had deliberately made you out to be something you're not.'

'I didn't mean that it was *funny* as in laugh-out-loud hilarious; I just mean it's not so important in the scheme of things. We need to rise above it. All that matters is finding Beatrice.'

I'm still too shocked by the piece to respond properly. I know for a fact that if it were Laurel being talked about that way in the paper, she would either be livid, or a blubbering mess. She wouldn't be brushing it off as unimportant and being all zen about it.

'I wonder what Claire's going to say when she sees it,' Laurel muses. 'Maybe you'd better lie low for a bit.'

I glare at Laurel across the table, but she's unaware of my displeasure with her. Instead she's focused on the article once more, with a strange expression on her face that's making me concerned she might actually be enjoying the situation. That she might not have my best interests at heart.

CHAPTER NINETEEN

CLAIRE

I'm sitting at the bottom of the stairs thinking about calling Oliver. He needs to know about the Child Rescue Alert system that Gayle explained earlier, and about his mother's disastrous newspaper interview – which I still haven't read. But it's all too much to relay over the phone. I'll wait until he gets back from work.

Is this the way it's going to be now? Am I about to spend the rest of my life waiting for my daughter to come home? With every hour that passes, I feel her slipping away from me, the thread that binds us stretching thinner. I can't sit here and allow myself to lose hope like this. To give up. A burst of anger at myself sparks a rush of adrenaline that propels me to my feet. I have to keep searching. I owe it to my daughter to go out there and find her. She's got to be somewhere. If anything bad had happened, surely I would feel it in my bones, in my heart. As long as there's a chance, I have to do everything I can to bring her home.

Just as I've decided to go out again, I hear the thud of footsteps coming up the drive. I don't remember hearing Ollie's car pull up so I'm pretty sure it's not him. The doorbell rings. Without giving myself a chance to speculate further, I open the door.

A tall man in his mid-forties, wearing a short-sleeved shirt and belted shorts, stands on the doorstep carrying a large brown envelope and the hugest bouquet of white lilies. He has messy ash-blonde hair and very red skin. It takes me a second to place him, and then it comes to me. It's Stephen Lang, one of my clients. I recognise his green Volvo parked at the bottom of the drive. I've been working on a new life insurance deal for him. He's a relatively newish client who discovered my IFA services via a Google search last year when he was looking for a mortgage. I managed to find him one which he was very happy with.

'Hi, Claire.'

'Oh, Stephen, hi. I'm so sorry but I'm not working this week. Didn't you get my email?'

'I did. But then I, uh, read the paper this morning and realised it was your daughter they were talking about. So I wanted to bring you these.' He passes me the flowers, their sweet scent overpowering. 'To let you know I've, uh, been thinking of you.'

'Well, that's very kind. Thanks.'

'You're welcome. Has there, uh, been any news?'

'Not yet, no.'

'Oh. I'm sure they'll find her soon.'

'Thanks.' I take a step back. 'Well, it was really good of you to think of us. I'd better get these in some water.'

'Oh, I also brought you this.' He passes me the brown envelope. 'It's those forms you asked me to fill in. I know you said you aren't working at the moment, but I'm not in any hurry. So if you could just hang on to them, we can resume once you, uh, get your daughter back.'

'Okay, great, thanks.'

I'm waiting for him to leave, but he's still on the doorstep, tapping his fingertips together. 'Would you mind if I just nipped in to use your loo?'

I'd really rather he didn't, but I can't exactly say no. 'Um, okay, yeah, that's fine. Come through.'

'You're very kind, sorry about that.'

'No problem.' I direct him to the downstairs cloakroom and take the lilies into the kitchen where I dump them into a patterned jug without cutting the stems.

Finally, I hear the flush of the toilet followed by the splash of the tap running. Stephen comes out of the loo and stands awkwardly in the hallway.

'How's your husband holding up?'

'Same as me really. Worried.'

'Of course, of course. Do you have friends and family helping out? Looking out for you, I mean? I read about the search party your mother-in-law organised.'

'I do, thanks.' I'm not about to tell him that my family's up in Scotland and my mother-in-law is the person who's responsible for this mess.

'Good. That's good.' I can see him casting around for something else to say. He's a sweet guy, but I don't have time for chit-chat right now – I need to be out searching for my daughter.

'Well, thanks again for the flowers. It was very thoughtful of you.' I glance pointedly at the front door feeling like a bit of a bitch.

'Oh, right, yes, I'll be off then. Let me know if there's anything I can do to help, won't you?'

'That's very kind. I will.'

'And, like I said, there's no rush with the insurance policy.'

'Thanks.'

Finally, he lumbers back down the hallway and leaves. Once his car has pulled away, I waste no more time, grab my bag, phone and keys and leave the house. In the car, I text Ollie to ask what time he'll be home. There's no immediate reply, so I send another text to let him know I'm going out.

The roads are busy with slow-driving holiday traffic. For some reason, the air con in my Toyota refuses to work and all I'm getting from the blasters is lukewarm air. I don't know where else to look, other than the area around the fairground which feels like a gigantic waste of time since Jill's search party turned up nothing. But where else can I go? I have no idea in which direction Bea went... or was taken.

Regardless of my frustration, I continue cruising the streets, looking for anything that might provide a clue to lead me to my daughter. Glimpses of long dark hair and flashes of red have me catching my breath and setting my heart jumping, but it's never Beatrice. I'll never find her out here. I feel as though I'm trying to run but my legs are stuck in mud. Like I'm expending all my energy on the wrong thing.

I find myself wondering if she might still be at the fair, in one of their caravans. The police assured me they searched all the vehicles and buildings on the site, but what if someone took Beatrice away during the police search and then brought her back afterwards? The fair was already back up and running yesterday, and it's there for a couple more days before it moves on to its next location.

I don't feel emotionally prepared enough to go in there right now, but I think I'm going to need to come back to the fair and have a snoop around. See if anyone knows anything. Maybe a member of staff will take pity on me. They'd be more likely to talk to a distraught mother than to a police officer, surely?

Back home, I text Oliver again, annoyed that he still hasn't answered my previous messages. I should probably call him, but there's no point interrupting him if he's working. The sooner he can get it done, the sooner he can come back home. I drag myself up the stairs and into the shower, letting the warm jets rinse off today's grime and sweat. Trying to wash away my fear and sadness. Trying to keep positive. Telling myself that we will find her. The police have a plan, and they wouldn't be implementing the CRA if they didn't think there was a chance of success. Plus, there's my new idea of revisiting the fair and seeing if that yields anything.

Once I'm dry and dressed in a clean vest top and shorts, I pad barefoot across the landing towards the stairs, pausing outside Beatrice's bedroom. My heart knocks in my chest. I shouldn't go in there again. It's too upsetting. I haven't been into her room since the police did their search on Saturday. I'm worried that if I'm surrounded by all her things, I'll dissolve into a puddle of tears. Despite this, I push open the door and walk inside.

I almost gasp at the normality of her room. So familiar, so ordinary, so *expected*. As our house is a chalet bungalow, the upstairs rooms are all in the roof, so from head height the walls slope inwards, making it feel cosy. Her furniture is all white – the bed, the wardrobe, the chest of drawers and the bookshelves. At her request, we painted each lower section of wall a different colour – blue, red, green and yellow. Beatrice adores her room, and is fairly tidy for a seven-year-old. There are a few clothes and toys on the floor, but if ever I nag her about tidying up, she's quick to insist that it's not as messy as some of her friends' rooms.

I sink onto her bed, pick up a discarded T-shirt and press it to my nose, inhaling its clean, soapy scent. Picturing my daughter wearing it, her smiling face, her infectious giggles. For a moment, I let myself believe that nothing's wrong. That she'll be along any minute, bursting through the door with something exciting or interesting to tell me. I'll listen, and then we'll sit and draw together, or I'll read her a story. I wish I'd done more fun stuff with her… I'll never take her for granted again.

Wallowing like this isn't helpful. It isn't good for me. But I need to feel her. To sense my little girl. To believe she's out there somewhere, waiting for me to come and get her. *Where are you, Bea?*

I jump as the front door slams. I've never been so on edge. I need to calm down. It'll be Ollie. I take a few steadying breaths and leave Bea's room, not wanting him to find me up here in such a state. We need to be strong for one another. I check the time on my phone and realise he's been gone for over four hours! It would have been nice if he'd let me know he was going to be so late. I tell myself to let it go. There's no point getting into an argument about it, even though I feel perfectly justified in being annoyed.

'Hey, Ollie, that you?' I hurry down the stairs and hear the sound of the tap running. As I enter the kitchen, my husband glances up briefly from the tap, before looking back down at the stream of water. 'How did it go? Did you get the tax forms finished?'

'Nope.' He makes an exaggerated popping sound on the 'p'.

'Oh.' I swear there's something strange about him. I take a couple of steps closer. 'So was it more work than you thought?'

'Yeah, it's a lot of work.'

I tense up as I realise he's slurring his words. I catch the faint odour of stale alcohol and realise he's *drunk*. A dark, angry heat flushes through my body and I grind my teeth. While I've been fending off abusive messages, talking to the police, and searching for our daughter, my husband has been out somewhere getting pissed.

'You've got to be fucking kidding me,' I mutter.

Oliver gulps down his glass of water and pours another. 'Thirsty,' he says, trying to smile, his eyes glazed.

In my head, I'm yelling at him, crying, screaming. Telling him not to be so bloody selfish. Spewing out every deserved expletive I can think of. Throwing insult after insult. In reality, all I say is, 'You're drunk.'

'Stopped off at the Red Lion on my way home.' He takes his water and sits at the table.

'I hope you didn't drive.'

'Got a cab. Left my car there.'

'That's something at least.'

'Don't start having a go, Claire.'

I let out a bitter laugh. 'This isn't "having a go", believe me.'

'I knew you'd be like this. It's why I didn't want to come home in the first place.'

I lean back against the countertop, arms crossed, gripping my shoulders. His words are a blow to the chest. He's acting like I'm the bad guy.

'So you're saying that I've driven you to drink?'

'No. I'm saying that I knew you'd be mad at me having a couple of drinks, so I didn't come home, I had more drinks instead.'

'Do you want to know what I've been doing while you've been in the pub?'

He waves an arm around. 'Oh, here we go...'

'I've been talking to the police about their upcoming media campaign, I've been out searching for our missing daughter, I've had to fend off a weirdo client of mine who gives me the creeps. Oh, and someone sent me a nasty message about Beatrice, saying that "I deserve it". So, sorry if I'm not exactly dancing around the kitchen when you come home half-cut after hiding away in the pub all afternoon.'

'Someone sent you a nasty message?' Ollie's eyes narrow. 'Who? Who did that? I'll sort them out.'

'Sort yourself out first.' I slam out of the kitchen, my whole body shaking in fury and disappointment. I can't do this alone. I need my husband to pull himself together. To give me some support. *Please.*

DAY FOUR

What an absolute joke. That online article in the local paper actually made me laugh out loud. If that piece is the best they can come up with, then there's nothing for me to worry about at all.

I should have guessed they'd set up a Facebook page. That everyone would be falling over themselves to offer their commiserations and good wishes. It's pathetic. No one actually cares. They're just being nosy. Or morbid. Or wanting to make themselves seem like Good Samaritans. They're all such hypocrites.

I know I shouldn't have risked sending that message… but I'm glad I did. Using a mirror as my profile pic was a stroke of genius. It's not blatant, but just enough to make them wonder whether it's from a crank or from the person they're after. Just enough to drive them crazy.

CHAPTER TWENTY

CLAIRE

Today feels different. Like something's changed inside me. I'm still terrified and anxious, but the shock has lessened and I'm somehow able to think more clearly instead of being pinned by that awful paralysis. I think that Oliver getting drunk must have knocked me out of my stupor. Made me realise that I can't rely on him to be there for me all the time. That he has his own demons to fight and I will have to take charge of things while I'm able to.

Yesterday, after our fight, Oliver admitted that he hadn't even gone to work, but instead had driven straight to the pub. Apparently, he hadn't intended to go there, it just happened. He said his mind went numb and he'd just wanted to blot everything out for a few hours. He apologised, and I forgave him. I agreed that the idea of getting blind drunk sounded tempting, but that we owed it to Beatrice to keep it together. At least for now. I didn't vocalise the thought that we might very well have to spend the rest of our lives falling apart.

So, I've come back to the fair and Oliver's gone back to work to do his tax forms. At least that's where he said he was going. I just have to pray he doesn't end up back in the Red Lion, like yesterday. It's not like him. He's not a daytime drinker. He's not one of those husbands who goes off to get drunk while I'm left at home worrying. He's more thoughtful than that. We're equal partners looking out for one another. His behaviour yesterday scared me. I've lost my daughter, I don't want to lose my husband too.

It's 10 a.m. and I've just read the opening hours on the board and discovered that the fair doesn't open until one. So I can either come back later or try to speak to a member of staff now. I'd pictured myself walking around the site while the fair was crowded and in full swing, peering in through windows and watching the buildings surreptitiously. With the fairground closed, I won't be able to blend in. So I guess I should probably leave it. Come back later. The thing is, I've geared myself up to do this. I've dredged up some courage which is likely to evaporate at any moment. I'm here now, so I should do something.

Before I can change my mind, I walk up to the deserted entrance gate and knock on the wall of the booth. 'Hello! Anyone there?' I wait for a few moments, but there's no response. 'Hello!' I call louder this time and knock again. Still nothing.

I skirt around the fair entrance and into the adjacent playing field, entering the fairground that way. The stalls and rides are all closed, each surrounded by a metal barrier to prevent entry, but the rest of the site is open to the public. I wander through the deserted fair until I finally spot someone by a closed-up food stand – a skinny teenage boy with an intricate sleeve tattoo. He's smoking a cigarette and watching a video on his phone.

'Excuse me,' I call out.

He looks up, expressionless for a moment before raising an eyebrow and sauntering over.

I clear my throat. 'Can I speak to the manager, please?'

He takes a drag on his cigarette. 'You want to speak to Monty?'

'Yes, please.'

'Can I take your name?'

'Claire Nolan.'

His brows knit together. 'You're the mum… of that little kid.'

'Yes.'

'That's rough. They found her yet?'

'No. That's why I'm here. I want to speak to the staff, see if anyone saw anything. Were you working here on Saturday evening when it happened?'

'Yeah, I was on the waltzers. We were all pretty cut up about it. Kind of felt like we were responsible, you know. Like we should've seen something.'

I blink, taken aback by his kindness, having assumed I'd encounter resistance or rudeness. 'Thank you. So you didn't see anything then? Or notice anyone acting suspiciously?'

'We spoke to the cops about this already.' He takes a long final drag of his cigarette before tossing it onto the grass and grinding out the butt with the toe of his trainer.

'I know, but maybe you remembered something since then.' I wrap my arms around myself, wondering at the strangeness of life and how I've found myself talking to a teenage fairground worker on a Tuesday morning. A stranger who might even hold my future happiness in his hand.

'I didn't see anything at all. Wish I did. Wish I could help.'

I'm not deterred by his insistence. 'She was wearing a red dress with frills around the hem, she's got long, dark hair, and she's about this tall.' I hold my hand out to indicate her height.

'Like I told the cops, it gets busy here, especially on a Saturday. There's kids all over the place. I don't remember seeing a girl like that. They showed me her photo, so I know what she looks like.' He scratches his arm. 'Sorry.'

My body wilts as I realise everyone here is going to say the same thing.

'I'd tell you if I'd seen her,' he assures me. 'I've got a little sister and I'd kill anyone who did anything to her. Sorry, not that anyone's done anything to your kid…' He turns scarlet.

'It's okay, I know what you mean.'

'I'm Kai, by the way.'

'Nice to meet you.'

'Anyway, I'll get Monty. Hope you find your kid.' He points behind me. 'Go down to the entrance, I'll get him to meet you there.'

Five minutes later, Monty Burridge comes striding up to the gate, wearing what looks like the same checked shirt and chinos as the last time I saw him. He sniffs and runs a hand over closely cropped grey hair without giving me any eye contact. He seems younger today than when I last saw him, I'd guess somewhere around his mid-fifties.

He sniffs again before finally looking at me. 'Kai said you wanted a word.'

'Yes please, I'm Claire Nolan. I was here on Satur—'

'I know who you are. So they haven't found her yet, your daughter?'

'Not yet, no. That's why I'm here.'

'I don't follow.' He frowns and puts his hands in his pockets, rocks back on his heels.

'I just wondered if I might talk to your staff – the ones who were here on Saturday. See if they might have remembered anything.'

He gives me an appraising look. 'I feel for you, Claire, I really do, but my workers have already spoken to the police several times. I've had them in to the office to speak to me too, and unfortunately none of them remembers seeing your daughter. I wish we could help.'

'Surely it couldn't hurt for me to have another word with them? If they remember the tiniest detail it could help.'

'I'd rather you leave it to the police. You should go back home and wait for her there. I'm sure she'll be found soon enough.'

'You obviously haven't got any children,' I snap, annoyed that he thinks I'd be content to sit around at home while my daughter's out here somewhere.

'I've got four of my own, plus two grandkids. So I do have the greatest sympathy for what you must be going through. But I stand by what I said – leave it to the police. Now, where are you parked? Do you want me to let you out through the front gate, save you walking all the way around?'

It's obvious he's desperate to get me to leave, but I'm not ready to go just yet. 'I don't suppose I could have a glass of water, could I? I'm not feeling too good.'

His jaw tightens, but he nods. 'I'll get Kai to bring you one.'

'Thanks,' I reply, faking weakness and heading over to a wooden picnic bench in front of a food stand. I sit and watch him walk off, soon losing sight of him beyond the rides. A youngish blonde woman comes out from one of the covered stalls carrying a black rubbish bag. She catches my eye and I give her a nod. She heads off towards the playing field, and I jump to my feet, catching up to her.

'Can I help you?' she mutters without turning to look at me.

'My name's Claire Nolan, I'm the mother of the girl who went missing.'

'Sorry about that.' Her voice is curt, emotionless.

'Just wondering if I could have a quick word with you about Saturday night.' I'm having to jog to keep up with her long strides.

'I already told the cops what I know, which is nothing.' She glances at me quickly. Her voice softens. 'I'd tell you if I saw anything, honestly.'

'Someone had to have seen something. Did none of your colleagues see anything, anything at all? Surely someone did.'

'Claire!' I turn at the sound of my name being called. It's Kai, back at the food stand waving a plastic cup of what I assume is water.

'Sorry,' the woman says. 'Monty'll get pissed off if he sees me talking to you. He doesn't want any trouble.'

I nod and pull one of my business cards from my purse. 'If you hear anything at all, please give me a call, any time of the day or night. Doesn't matter how trivial you think it is.'

She nods and puts the card in the back pocket of her jeans. 'Hope you find her.'

'Thanks.' I turn back and give Kai a wave. He's already started across the playing field to meet me.

'Monty said you wanted some water. Sorry, I've spilt half of it.'

'Thanks.' I don't make any move to take the cup.

'What were you doing going after Sam? She doesn't like talking to anyone, especially not strangers.'

'I was just asking if she'd seen my daughter.'

'Monty won't be happy. He told me to make sure you left. He'll get seriously annoyed with me if you don't go. Here…' He holds out the drink.

This time I take it and sip the lukewarm liquid, forcing myself to finish it. 'Thanks.'

He takes the empty cup and folds his arms across his chest.

I drop my shoulders. 'Okay, I'm going.'

Kai nods and stays where he is as I head back towards the car. I look over my shoulder once to see him still there, arms crossed like a skinny bouncer on a nightclub door.

Finally back at the car, I get in and sit for a moment before starting up the engine. What a waste of time that was. What do I do now? I don't feel like going back to my empty home. I'm too keyed up. I wish I had the nerve to sneak back to the fair and find some more employees to speak to, but I worry that Monty will spot me and get angry. That he'll call the police or maybe his own security. I'll have to be clever about this and maybe go back later once the fair's in full swing. When I'll have a better chance of blending in with the crowds.

For now, I've had an idea of exactly where I need to go.

CHAPTER TWENTY-ONE

CLAIRE

Twenty minutes later, I'm turning into the narrow country lane that leads to River Way Farm. Sitting just outside Christchurch in the little village of Hurn, it feels a world away from my life back in town. As my Toyota bumps down the farm track, the farm comes into view – a sprawling mass of white-painted buildings. The original house dates back to the seventeenth century, but it's had various additions over the years.

My arrival heralds a chorus of barking and as I step outside the car, I'm greeted by a pair of energetic border collies along with a much calmer golden retriever. 'Hello, Charlie, hi Timmy.' I stoop to stroke the two collies. 'And I haven't forgotten you, Bess.' I scratch behind the ancient golden retriever's ears. Freya's Land Rover isn't out front, so I'm hoping she's actually here. I should probably have called ahead. This is her family's farm and she lives here with her parents, who are just about the loveliest people on the planet.

I felt the urge to come over and chat things through with Freya. She'll know what to do for the best. Even if she doesn't, it will be nice to talk to someone other than Ollie. Someone who isn't as emotionally tangled up in it all. Of course Freya loves Beatrice, but not like Ollie and me, which means she can be more objective right now. That's what I need. Some clarity.

The kitchen door opens and Freya's mum steps outside, shading her eyes against the late-morning sun. 'Claire!' She shakes her head and holds out her arms. Lynn Collins is as un-farmer-like as you can imagine. Like her daughter, she's petite and dark-haired and looks as though she would snap in a strong breeze. The reality is that she's tough and incredibly hard-working and is the least breakable woman I know.

I straighten up from petting the dogs and walk over to give her a hug. 'Hi, Lynn.'

'Oh, love, we were absolutely devastated to hear about Beatrice. Is there any news?'

I shake my head, not trusting myself to speak in the glow of such warmth and comfort.

She steps back and holds my face, scrutinising me. 'You look peaky. Come inside. Trevor's just popped in for his mid-morning cuppa and I've taken a fresh batch of scones out of the oven. There's some lovely damson jam from last year that I've been saving. You need to keep your strength up. Come in, love, come on.'

Lynn ushers me into their bright kitchen where her husband is sitting at a cluttered table reading a farming magazine, a huge mug of tea in front of him. He looks up.

'Hello, Claire. How you holding up? Such a bad business with your little one. We've been thinking about you.' He sets his magazine down on the table.

In stark contrast to his wife, Trevor Collins is the stereotypical image of a farmer, with a broad frame, ruddy cheeks and shovel-like hands. River Way Farm has been in his family for six generations. Their two sons aren't remotely interested in River Way – Liam's in London doing something in IT and James is a perpetual traveller, currently working his way around the world as a deckhand on a luxury yacht. Freya, however, has farming running through her veins and is poised to take over the business once her dad retires, which he's been threatening to do for the past five years, but none of us believe he ever will.

Lynn starts transferring the scones from the baking tray onto a wire cooling rack. 'Freya's up in the top field. I'll give her a call to come down.'

I sit at the table and we make small talk while we wait. Neither of her parents asks any more questions about Beatrice or the search. Instead, they enquire after my parents and Oliver, and ask about my work, which is a nice, brief respite from my hellish new reality.

I tell Lynn and Trevor that my parents have been checking in with me several times a day, and are on standby to fly down from Scotland as soon as I say the word. I obviously don't tell them that my husband isn't coping at all. Instead, I mutter that he's as well as can be expected. Work feels like the safest topic, so I witter on about mortgages, pensions and life insurance for the next ten minutes or so – probably boring them senseless – until the door bursts open and Freya comes in, her eyes wide, her usual shiny brown bob scraped back into a short ponytail. 'Any news?'

'Hi, Frey. Not yet.'

Her shoulders sag. 'Oh, well it's lovely to see you. How are you doing?'

'Oh, you know.' I shrug. 'The same really. I went back to the fair today to see if I could find out anything else about what might have happened, talked to some people who work there.'

'And?' Freya goes over to the sink and starts washing her hands.

I tell them all about my morning while Lynn doles out the warm scones and sets pots of jam and thick clotted cream on the table.

'What about that Holloway fella?' Trevor asks.

'Who?' I cut my scone in half and spread on some cream and a smear of jam.

'Alfie, one of our labourers, mentioned him this morning.' Trevor takes a gulp of his tea. 'Can't remember the man's first name.'

Freya shakes her head. 'Dad, Claire doesn't want to hear any gossip or rumours about all this.'

My senses sharpen. Rumours always originate from somewhere. Could this be the information I've been waiting for? 'No, that's okay, Freya, I'd like to know what people are saying.'

Freya gives her dad a glare, but he shrugs. '*What?* I'm only saying what I heard.'

'So what did you hear?' I'm tense as a bowstring, my heart racing.

Trevor takes a sip of tea and leans back in his chair. 'Well, Alfie said that apparently this Holloway chap was at the fair at the same time your Beatrice went missing.'

'So? Who is he? Why would that matter?'

'He used to be the choirmaster at one of the local churches.'

I frown. 'Used to be?'

'He resigned last year under a cloud of suspicion. It was on the local news.'

'Nothing was ever proven,' Lynn adds, finally joining us at the table.

'Proven? Why? What did he do? I've never heard of him. How do you know he was at the fair?' I realise my voice is sharp and brittle. I need to breathe.

'Like I said, I don't know for certain, I heard it from Alfie,' Trevor replies. 'Alfie heard it from someone else.'

'Yes, so there's no concrete evidence,' Freya adds. 'Even if he *was* there, it's probably just one of those things where people put two things together even though they're completely unrelated.'

'Exactly.' Trevor wipes his mouth with a napkin. 'Like I said, it's just a rumour, but worth checking out, just the same.'

'So why exactly did Holloway resign as choirmaster?' I ask, not really wanting to hear where this is going. My stomach is already clenching, my appetite diminishing.

'Dad, I really don't think Claire wants to—'

I hold up a hand to stop Freya. 'It's fine. I want to hear.'

Trevor shifts in his seat and his eyes drop to the table. 'Well, you know the sort of thing. Allegations about inappropriate behaviour…' His voice trails off.

Lynn tuts. 'It's all speculation. Probably nothing in any of it.' She turns to me with a kindly smile. 'You know what people are like, love.'

They all change the subject and start talking about life on the farm and other, safer subjects, but I can't take any of it in. I'm too fixated on this choirmaster and whether or not there's any truth to the rumour, my mind conjuring up all kinds of awful scenarios. After ten minutes or so of pretending to eat my scone, I make my excuses and get up to leave. If there's any truth in this rumour, I'm going to have to speak to Gayle about it. Get them to go straight round to this Holloway person's house.

I hug everyone goodbye and Freya walks me out. 'Sorry about Mum and Dad, I think they were trying to help, but…' She throws up her hands. 'Try not to think about that side of it.'

'It's fine.'

'No it's not. I'm going to kill Dad for upsetting you.'

'No, please. It might be important information. I'm going to follow it up with the police. If it leads to us finding Beatrice sooner then it's a good thing.'

'Okay, if you're sure. I think he was trying to help in a clumsy kind of way. I'll let him live for another day.'

I muster a pathetic smile. 'Thank them again for the tea and scones.'

'Drop by any time. You know we always love to see you. How's Ollie holding up?'

I don't have the energy to talk about what's going on with him right now, so again I mumble something about him being as well as can be expected.

Once I'm in the car again, driving back towards Christchurch, I can't stop thinking about Holloway. A strange buzzing has started up in my ears, and my chest is so constricted I can barely breathe. I unclick my seatbelt and open the window to let in some fresh air, but it's no good, I need to pull over. I can barely see straight, let alone drive safely. The road isn't that wide, so I pull up onto the kerb and click on my hazard lights.

I inhale warm air and close my eyes, trying to let my mind go blank, but I can't do it. I snap open my eyes and pull my phone out of my bag, letting out a silent prayer of thanks that there's signal here. I google 'choirmaster' and 'Holloway' and wait for the results. It takes a while for the blue line to cross the page and I'm about to give up and continue on my way home, when the screen suddenly fills with news stories from last May.

His name is Gavin Holloway and he was a choirmaster and pianist who ran a youth group at his local church. The photo shows a good-looking man in his early thirties with mid-brown hair, wearing an open-neck shirt. It seems there were several allegations by young teenagers about inappropriate behaviour and, while nothing was ever proven or taken to court, he resigned from the job.

As I read the articles, I try not to let my mind create awful scenarios, telling myself to be logical and realistic. First, there's no proof that he did anything wrong. Second, I don't even know for sure if he was at the fair at the same time as Beatrice. Third, even if the first two points are true, that doesn't mean he has my daughter.

If that's the case, why do I feel sick? The thought of that man with Beatrice sends my heart slamming to the floor. With trembling fingers, I call Gayle and tell her about the rumour. She listens carefully and tells me she'll follow it up immediately.

So now all I can do is go home and wait.

CHAPTER TWENTY-TWO

JILL

I wipe down the surfaces in the kitchen, even though they're already clean. After the past few days of trauma, I'm letting myself have a few hours home alone to try to get myself straight. What with the humiliation of the newspaper article – which I still haven't plucked up the courage to read, and don't think I ever will – and Laurel's disappointing attitude to everything, I think it will do me good to try to rest and gather my strength so I can be of use somewhere.

I'm still not sleeping well at night. Just dozing a little, in between getting up to make tea and trying to read or watch television. I can't settle to anything. I keep feeling like I should be doing something useful. Even though I have no idea what. On top of all this, I feel so alone. Claire and Oliver have each other to lean on. And, according to Oliver, they also have their police officer who's keeping them up to date with everything. I haven't met her, but he says she's nice and approachable. Meanwhile, I'm left here to stew.

Laurel isn't proving as good of a friend as I thought she'd be. I'm grateful to her for picking me up from the police station and for coming to the search party, of course I am, but it's her attitude that baffles me. I've never noticed that side to her personality before. It's as though she's enjoying the drama that's unfolding. Like she's almost excited by it. So I think it's better if I keep her at arm's length for a while.

It's almost lunchtime and I'm still in my dressing gown. I really should shower and dress but I'm not sure there's much point. Why haven't the police found Beatrice yet? Surely she should be home by now. It's Tuesday already and she's been gone since Saturday. Where is she? I'm aching to see her – a hollow yet heavy feeling in my stomach that won't go away.

I'd give anything to be able to give her a cuddle and hear one of her funny stories. It's a thing we used to do when she was with me – she'd pretend to be someone famous or important or clever – a film star, or an explorer or a queen – and she would make up these silly, crazy stories about it. We'd dress up and turn the house into a pretend palace or a film set, or we'd make believe we were on a safari or in space or on some other exciting adventure.

I pull out a photo album from the sideboard. It's one that Bob and I put together during a particularly wet and dreary February several years ago when Bea was little more than a toddler. I take it over to the kitchen armchair and sit, pulling my feet up under me, like I used to do when I was a girl. On opening the album, my heart fills up at the sight of us all with smiles on our faces. Especially the pictures of Beatrice with her chubby face and her hair in little bunches. And then there are the rest of us – me, Bob, Oliver and Claire. There are also a few snaps of Claire's parents, Doug and Sheena Mitchell; such a nice couple.

Sheena actually called me yesterday and we had a long chat. It sounds like they're keeping optimistic. I could tell she was trying to gee me up, making it clear that she didn't think Bea's disappearance was in any way my fault, which was really lovely of her. She said that it's impossible to keep an eye on them every single second. Her kind words brought a lump to my throat, but I managed not to cry down the phone.

My pulse jumps at the sound of my phone pinging. It could be news. Please let it be something good. I glance around the room, searching for my phone before realising it's in my dressing-gown pocket. I pull it out to see that I've received a text. I open it and frown as I read the few short words:

How could you lose your own granddaughter?

I re-scan the words, thinking I must have read it wrong. That no one would be so nasty as to send such a vile message. There's no mistaking what it says or the meaning behind it. My mouth goes dry and my heart speeds up. Someone is blaming me for Bea's disappearance. Someone anonymous. The mobile number isn't from any of my contacts. So who sent it?

My first thought is to call Laurel. But then I remember our talk yesterday where it seemed like she was enjoying my discomfort over the newspaper story. I have the awful feeling that if I told her about this text message, she might have the same reaction. I absolutely couldn't bear that. Besides, I'd have thought she might have called me after we left things yesterday on such an awkward note, but I haven't heard a peep out of her. Not so much as a text... unless... no, don't be silly. Laurel would never do anything as terrible as this. I push the thought from my head. I'll call the police and let them handle it.

The phone wobbles in my fingers as I try to steady my hands enough to find the DI's number. I've already entered it into my contact list, but I can't remember her name. My mind has gone blank. I stare at the screen, willing myself to concentrate and get control of my emotions, but my eyes are pooling with tears. Why is everything so hateful right now?

Bea, where are you?

I take a breath and wipe my eyes, trying to be sensible about this. Whoever sent that message is a nasty individual and they don't deserve my tears or my worry. They won't reduce me to a blubbering mess. I try to think about what Bob would say right now if he were here. He'd put a comforting arm around me and say, *Come on now, Jilly, you can do this.* And so I shall.

The fog in my brain clears, and I remember that the DI's name is Meena Khatri. Scrolling through my contacts, I find her listed under 'D' for DI. Even if I hadn't remembered, all I would need to do is call the station and tell them who I am. I must stop getting into a flap all the time. If I just take a moment to calm myself, I usually manage just fine.

I call the number, tell them who I am and ask to speak to the DI. I don't have to wait long before being put through. I calmly tell her about the horrible text message and give her the number it originated from. Meena Khatri is very sympathetic and patient, assuring me that she'll look into it as soon as she's able. She asks if I'm all right and suggests that I should call a friend or member of the family as it must have been a shock. I thank her and tell her I'm fine, but after ending the call, I realise that I *would* actually like to be with someone right now. Someone who understands what I'm going through.

I'm going to visit Claire.

It's time to put this bad feeling behind us. I'll go over there, apologise again, grovel if I have to. I just can't bear this hostility hanging between us. Especially not at a time when we should all be pulling together. Not to mention the fact that it makes things awkward for Oliver. He shouldn't have to be caught between us, having to choose sides. It's not fair on him. And it makes no sense. He rang me earlier from the shop to check in on how I was doing, but he didn't sound like his usual warm, caring self. He was detached, like he was calling out of a sense of duty.

I decide not to call ahead, even though I know that Claire isn't a fan of people showing up unannounced on the doorstep. But if I call, that will give her the opportunity to fob me off. I suppose

I'm taking the risk that she won't even be in, but if that's the case, I'll sit on her doorstep and wait.

I quickly dress in plain linen trousers and a floaty patterned top that will hopefully be nice and cool, and leave the house. I don't feel up to driving, so I decide to take the bus instead. As a pensioner I have a free bus pass so it's daft not to take advantage of that. It'll be good practice for when my licence gets revoked next week. Part of me doesn't even mind losing my licence. I live so close to town that I can walk most places anyway. I may even get rid of the car altogether. It could be quite liberating in a strange kind of way, and at least I won't have the exorbitant running expenses.

The only downside to taking public transport is the time it takes – I have to walk to the bus stop, then wait for the bus, then there are the endless stops it makes. What would have been a ten-minute drive takes forty minutes. But that's fine, I'm not on any deadline. As I approach the St Catherine's Hill stop, I ring the bell, make my way to the exit, thank the driver and finally step down onto the pavement. The bus lurches away and I start to feel a little nervous. It's all very well having good intentions, but what if Claire slams the door in my face? What if Oliver is back home from the shop already and is cold towards me?

No sense in worrying and wondering; I'll find out soon enough. I walk along to the pedestrian crossing and wait for the green man to flash. As I stand here, I can't help looking out for Beatrice. I did the same on the bus. Every time I saw a dark-haired child through the window, my heart did a little flip. But it was never her.

I head along the main road a short way, turn into their road and start walking up the hill. I cross over the street to be in the shade, but the early afternoon air is warm and heavy and my breath is laboured by the time I reach their property – a boring-looking yellow-brick 1970s chalet bungalow with no character whatsoever. And yet the location of the house is wonderful, set at the base of

St Catherine's Hill, a stunning nature reserve that forms part of a ridge between the Avon and Stour valleys.

I note that Claire's Toyota is parked on the sloping drive, but Oliver's car is nowhere to be seen. Pausing to rest against their wall for a minute, I tell myself it's so I can get my breath back, but I know it's also to steel my nerves and calm the ebb and swell in my stomach before braving the steep steps that lead to their front door. Before I come face to face again with my daughter-in-law.

Back before they bought the house, Oliver invited Bob and I round for a viewing. Bob warned him against buying it because of these very steps. Claire was pregnant at the time and he worried about her having to lug the pram up and down in all weathers, not to mention the fear of her or a toddler tumbling down. I told him not to be such a stick in the mud, that they were young and fit and it would be fine, especially with all that wonderful nature on their doorstep – perfect for bringing up children. Oliver had looked at me gratefully, and Bob hadn't mentioned it again. In hindsight, he was probably right. Claire did take a nasty tumble one icy winter, banging her coccyx on one of the steps. But Bob was never one to say I told you so.

Once my breath is back, I climb the steps and ring the doorbell, the blood pumping through my veins and whooshing in my ears. I really need to calm down. I'm here to try to make amends, to build bridges and be nice. A loud hammering rings out from one of the neighbouring properties. The sound goes straight through my brain. I hope I'm not getting a headache.

I hear footsteps beyond the door, the jangle of keys and then Claire's standing there, squinting as the sun hits her face. 'Jill? I wasn't expecting you. Is everything okay? Have you got news?' Her words are staccato bullets, fast and sharp. Her expression is harsh and drawn.

'No news, I'm afraid. Can I… would you mind if I came in?'

'Oh. Well, sure, but Oliver isn't here. I can get him to call round to your place when he gets home if you like?' She makes no move to step back and allow me in.

'It's actually you I've come to see, Claire, not Oliver.' I try to make my expression as soft and friendly as I can, but my face hurts with the effort. This isn't going to be a pleasant visit. Maybe I shouldn't have come.

CHAPTER TWENTY-THREE

JILL

I stand on the doorstep waiting for my daughter-in-law to let me into her house. Surely she won't refuse me entry.

'Oh, right.' Claire blinks furiously and moves to the side. 'Sorry, come in.'

Finally, I step into the blissfully cool hall and we give one another an awkward peck on the cheek.

'Would you like a drink?' she asks as I follow her through to the kitchen.

'A glass of water would be lovely.'

'I've got orange juice if you prefer?'

'Actually, that sounds perfect.' My gaze alights on a jug of white lilies on the kitchen table. 'Who gave you those?'

Claire waves her hand dismissively. 'Just a client.' She opens the fridge and pulls out a bottle of what appears to be fresh orange juice. It looks heavenly.

'Strange choice of flowers,' I muse. 'White lilies are supposed to signify death.'

She gives me a funny look. 'They're just flowers, Jill.'

I bite my lower lip, annoyed with myself for sounding judgy. 'Of course.' Then I spot a vase of yellow roses on the windowsill. 'Are those from Paul and Tanya Jensen?'

Claire pours two glasses of orange juice. 'How did you know?'

'They sent me the same bouquet.'

She passes me one of the glasses. 'Was Paul rude to you as well?'

I give her a knowing look and, for a second, it almost feels like we're bonding. 'Yes, but I think it was just the stress of the situation. I'm sure he didn't mean to be so snappy.'

Claire mutters something under her breath.

'Sorry, did you say something?'

'Nothing. I'm just up to here with Phil next door and his incessant hammering.'

'Oh, yes, I noticed it when I was standing outside. It gave me a headache after two minutes so goodness knows how you're putting up with it.'

'It's never-ending. I think he's addicted to DIY.' Claire sighs and sips her drink. I take a sip of mine too. It's ice-cold, sweet and sharp and gives me just the zing of energy I need. Claire sits at the table and gestures to me to sit opposite. She moves the lilies to the side so we can see one another. Her lips are pressed together and her brow is ridged with stress lines. 'So, did you come over for a reason, Jill?'

My mind is suddenly blank, but I open my mouth hoping something sensible and conciliatory will emerge. 'I just… I wanted to say that I'm so, so very sorry about everything. I'm sure Beatrice will be found, but in the meantime, I'm here for you. I'm… I know you and I haven't got along so well these past few years and I know it's my fault that Bea's missing. I love you and Oliver and Bea – truth be told, you're my world. I just…' The words tumble out quickly, but now there's a lump in my throat and I don't think I can continue, not without crying. And if I do that, then this will become all about me, and not about supporting Claire.

Claire doesn't say anything for a moment. There's just a heavy silence. Even next door's hammering has paused. She finally exhales. 'I appreciate that, Jill. Thanks.'

I nod, unsure what to say next. We sip our drinks. Then I say something stupid. 'I should probably tell you something else…'

Her eyes sharpen and her body tenses. 'Tell me *what*?'

Shut up, Jill. Shut up. 'The thing is, it's irrelevant, and it wouldn't have made any difference anyway...'

'What wouldn't have made any difference?' Claire's voice is like rusty nails.

'At the time Bea went missing, I was on my mobile phone. I mean, I was still with the girls, still looking out for them, but I answered a call.' I hear the quaver in my voice. *Why didn't you just keep your mouth shut, Jill?*

'Did you tell the police?' Her eyes don't leave mine. I almost feel as though she's inside my head.

'I'm afraid I forgot. At the time, everything was so muddled.'

'I don't believe you.' Claire shakes her head in disgust. 'You wouldn't have forgotten that. Who were you talking to?'

I cringe. 'Laurel.'

'You were chatting to Ollie's ex-wife while my seven-year-old daughter was being abducted?' Claire rises to her feet, folding her arms across her chest.

'We don't know she was abducted.'

'No, and we didn't know you were on the phone either. Does Ollie know about this?'

'What? No. No one knows. Like I said, I didn't think it was important.'

Claire gives a disbelieving grunt. 'What were you talking about with *Laurel*?' She says her name like it's a dirty word.

'What? Oh, I don't know. Nothing really. She was just calling to have a chat.'

'You've always preferred her, haven't you?'

I feel my cheeks redden as I deny it.

Claire pours the rest of her juice down the sink and rinses the glass. She stands with her back to me and I feel wretched. I've utterly messed this up. I came here to make my daughter-in-law feel better, not worse. I need to think carefully before I open my mouth again.

I take another sip of my drink and try to explain. 'It's not even a matter of who I prefer. There's no contest – you're my son's wife, my daughter-in-law, Beatrice's mum. The fact is, I feel sorry for Laurel. Oliver treated her badly when they broke up. He accused her of having an affair, but I don't think she did. She worshipped him too much to do anything like that. Anyway, things didn't work out and they parted ways. That's all in the past and of course I'm happy that you're with Oliver now. The three of you are my world and I feel terrible about my part in this nightmare. I will never forgive myself if anything's happened to that precious child.' My voice is cracking now and I can't stop the tears escaping. 'I came here to apologise, because I feel dreadful about everything. I want to support you and Oliver. I want to be here for you both.'

Claire sniffs and puts the glass on the drainer. 'You'll have to tell the police... about the phone call.'

'Of course.' I rummage in my bag for a tissue and dab at my eyes. 'I'll call them today.' I think about the other call I made to them earlier, about the nasty message I received. But I can't bring myself to tell Claire about that. I don't want to frighten her unnecessarily.

When she turns around, it looks like she might have been crying too. She comes and sits back down, takes a breath. 'I'm not particularly happy about what you've just told me, Jill, but I can't concentrate on that right now. Not after what I discovered this morning.'

I give her an enquiring look.

She leans back in her seat. 'Firstly, I went back to the fair earlier today and spoke to a couple of the workers there.'

'Oh?' I wait for her to continue.

'I didn't learn anything new, but I'd made up my mind to go back there this afternoon and do some more digging.'

'I don't think that's such a good idea,' I interrupt. 'You should really let the police handle that side of things. It could be dangerous.'

'Hang on, let me finish. I said I'd planned to go back, but then I went to see Freya and her family and learned some new information.' Her face pales and she runs her tongue over her teeth, trying to stop herself from crying.

'What is it. What's the matter?'

She swallows. 'There's a rumour that this choirmaster, called Gavin Holloway, was at the fair the evening Bea went missing.'

I frown, trying to remember where I've heard that name before.

'He was forced to resign from his job last year because...' her voice trails off and she covers her mouth with her hand.

Now I remember where I heard his name. It was on the local six o'clock news. 'Oh no.' A dark knot of terror tightens in my chest. 'Surely not.'

She nods, tears streaming down her face. I reach across the table to take her hand as she gulps and heaves. 'I called the police earlier and told them about the rumour. They're looking into it.'

'Okay,' I soothe, trying not to let panic overwhelm me. 'Well, I'm sure they'll investigate as soon as possible. So let's not jump to any awful conclusions. It's a rumour, that's all, okay?'

'Okay,' Claire whispers, looking more frightened than I've ever seen her. Her eyes wide and her teeth grazing her upper lip, looking the image of Beatrice when she's scared.

Our eyes lock together in horror at the possibility of what all this might mean.

CHAPTER TWENTY-FOUR

CLAIRE

As the front door closes on my mother-in-law, my mind whirls with all the new information I've been bombarded with today. First this new Gavin Holloway suspect, and now the phone call between Jill and Laurel on the night Bea went missing! I don't even know what to make of that piece of information. Jill's probably right that it had nothing to do with Bea's disappearance, but then again, maybe it did. Her concentration can't have been fully on the girls, not if she was on the phone. Then I think about all the times I've been on the phone or talking to friends while I've been with Beatrice.

In my heart of hearts, I know it's not fair to blame Jill for what happened. It's Oliver I'm mad at, for letting his mother take the girls in the first place when we'd already agreed she wasn't up to it. Or maybe I'm just mad at everyone and everything. Not least of all myself for agreeing to go on that girls' night out when I'd already arranged to take my daughter and her friend to the fair. But Oliver said he was happy to take them… I bunch my fists in frustration. I can't keep playing this blame game with myself. The same guilt trip over and over again. It's no use to anyone. I can't change what's already happened.

I'm still standing in the hall, motionless, as an outrageous theory suddenly pops into my head. One that I dismiss straight away as far too extreme to entertain. Nevertheless, I can't stop my brain making instant connections. What if Laurel called Jill at the fair as a distraction? What if she planned the whole thing? But what would her motive be? Revenge? Much as Laurel has never been my favourite person, for obvious reasons, I can't believe she could be responsible for something so evil. Surely not.

I shake off the thought and head back into the kitchen, the cloying scent of Stephen Lang's lilies making me nauseous, especially when I remember that Jill said they were supposed to signify death. I reach down beneath the blooms for the stems and lift the whole bunch out of the jug, not caring that I'm dripping water over the table and across the kitchen floor as I head out the back door and march around the side of the house to where the bins are kept. I dump the lot into the almost full garden-waste bin, letting the lid fall with a satisfying clunk.

Back inside, I call Gayle to see if there are any further developments about Holloway. I know it's probably too soon for any news, but I won't be able to concentrate on anything until I hear back. As predicted, there's nothing concrete she can tell me about Holloway, but she said they're also dealing with a few leads from the Child Rescue Alert. She promises to let me and Oliver know the minute they find anything important to the case.

Gayle's mention of my husband has my whole body crumpling. I sit at the kitchen table and let my head fall onto my arms. It's already mid-afternoon, so why isn't Oliver home yet? According to him, the shop paperwork wasn't supposed to take very long, but he's already been gone for hours. What if he's ended up in the pub again? I don't think I can handle things if he gets smashed every day. I'm barely clinging on as it is.

I ease my body upright and check my mobile phone again, but there are no texts or voice messages from him. I grit my teeth and call his number, ending the call angrily as it goes to voicemail after two rings. I don't trust myself to leave a message, not without screaming and swearing into the phone. I try the shop's landline next, but it transfers to an answerphone message which says to go to the website.

So what should I do? Sit around waiting here as the minutes drag on? *No.* I push myself up off the chair, grab my phone and bag and leave the house. I spend the ten-minute drive trying to calm down so that I don't burst into the shop in a furious rage. Perhaps there's a good explanation for why my husband isn't answering my calls. For why he's avoiding me. I'd thought that after yesterday's drunken debacle, we'd patched things up. I obviously thought wrong.

As the traffic crawls along towards town, I try to be objective. Am I overreacting? I honestly don't think so. It really comes to something when my mother-in-law is being more supportive than my husband. That's never happened before, ever. When Ollie and I met eight years ago, she was less than enthusiastic. I think Bob had to talk her around to the idea of Oliver being with me rather than Laurel.

Between Ollie and me there had been this instant, zinging connection. One of those moments when you see someone and your stomach flips over with butterflies, your skin tingles and you can't breathe properly. He said it was the same for him. We met at the Larmer Tree, an outdoor music festival in North Dorset. It wasn't my sort of thing, but I'd been dragged along by a group of friends, one of whom had a boyfriend who knew Oliver. Our two groups mingled and Ollie came and sat next to me. We spent the next twenty-four hours talking non-stop about everything and when we finally kissed, it was like fireworks going off. And that was it. We never looked back. So for us to be in this dark place right now... it's not us. It's not who we are.

There's no parking outside Ollie's shop, so I find a space in one of the backstreets and walk towards the main road. A distant noise makes me look up and I see a V formation of ducks flying overhead towards the river. Beatrice would have loved to see that. We often feed the ducks and swans on the quayside, or along the Mill Stream which runs around the back of the priory. It's one of our favourite things to do.

Ollie's shop, Priory Art Supplies, is situated just off the main high street where the rents are a lot cheaper and the square-footage is more generous. He's usually in there six days a week, but he also has a couple of part-timers who help out over busy weekends and cover for him when he's on holiday. Otherwise, Jill pitches in and so do I if he gets really stuck. But today, the shop is dark, closed.

I let myself in, disable the alarm and make my way through to the spacious office at the back of the property. It's empty. Oliver's desk is uncluttered and clear of paperwork. It feels like it's been undisturbed for a while. I run my finger over the desk immediately in front of his chair to reveal a very light film of dust around my finger mark. I don't think he's been in here today. I don't know what to think. If he's not here and not answering his phone, then there's not a lot I can do. I'm not driving around searching for my husband as well as my daughter.

I try calling his mobile once more, but yet again it goes straight to voicemail. I guess I could go into the Red Lion, see if he's drinking himself into a stupor. But I don't want to argue with a drunk. I don't want to go in there and see my suspicions confirmed. I edge around the desk to sit on Ollie's office chair. I close my eyes and try to keep calm. To stop myself spiralling into a panic. I can't allow myself to plummet into despair. But it feels as though my family is disintegrating. As though I'm losing everything. How much further can there be to fall?

CHAPTER TWENTY-FIVE

CLAIRE

I'm sitting in the back lounge watching the shadows change and lengthen, my empty stomach grinding with a potent cocktail of anger and anxiety. My heart is thumping louder than our next-door neighbour's hammer as Oliver walks through the front door at 6 p.m. I'm so furious with him that my whole body is shaking and I can barely trust myself to speak.

Where the hell has he been? This is the second day in a row he's gone off by himself. That he's lied to me. I want to see how far he takes the lie.

The front door closes quietly. I hear Ollie's footsteps as he crosses the hall and goes into the kitchen. My heart pumps faster as I wait for him to come into the lounge, but instead I hear him pad up the stairs. What the hell is he doing? I should follow him up there, confront him. But I can't seem to move. His footsteps sound steady and controlled. They aren't the lumbering gait of a drunk person. At least I don't think so.

After what seems like an age, he pads back down. The door to the lounge creaks open and he walks in. I look up, unable to plaster any kind of expression on my face. His skin is pallid, his green eyes muddy with an emotion I can't place.

'How did you get on with your paperwork?' My voice sounds as though it belongs to someone else, someone from another time and place.

'Fine.'

'You got it all done?'

'Yeah. How are you?'

'So you were at the shop?' I press for an answer. 'You were working there all day?'

He sits on the arm of the sofa without replying.

'Ollie?' I stare at him, but he doesn't catch my eye.

He shakes his head. 'You obviously know I wasn't there, so why are you asking?'

My chest tightens with grief that we've come to this place where we can't even talk to one another honestly. 'What's going on, Oll?' This isn't the yelling match I've been envisioning all afternoon. This is far worse.

'There's no urgent paperwork for the accountant,' he admits, rubbing his forehead with his fingertips. 'There aren't any tax forms. I'm sorry.'

'So where were you? You look pretty sober, so I guess you weren't in the Red Lion all day.'

'I just needed to be alone. Away from everyone and everything. I couldn't deal with it all – the police, the worry, the questions, the fear. So I just drove and drove, and then I walked. I'm really sorry, Claire. I think I've managed to clear my head a bit. I'm here for you now, okay?'

'Well, good for you. I'm really pleased you were able to go and clear your head. How fucking nice for you.' Oh, here it comes. Here's the tempest I envisioned. It was simply biding its time. There's no slowing it down now, the blood is roaring in my ears.

'Claire, I'm sorry.' Oliver holds up his hands as though I'll be placated by this. As though his palms are enough to ward off my fury. As though our shared history will cancel out his callous, selfish abandonment of me.

'You're sorry?' I scrape my teeth over my bottom lip in a grimace. 'You've basically pissed off for two days during the most stressful time in our lives, when I needed you the most, and all you can say is you're "sorry". I don't even know what to say right now.'

'I know, I know. Claire, you have to believe me—'

'Believe you!' I spit. 'When all you've done is lie? When you've left me to deal with all this shit on my own?' I get up and lurch out of the room, slamming the door behind me so hard that the house shakes and my arm judders with the impact. Do I storm out? March upstairs? I honestly don't know what to do with myself. I want to know exactly where he's been and what he's been doing. I want a better explanation than the one he's just given me.

The lounge door opens. 'Claire…'

'What!?' I back up against the hall bannister rail.

'Please. *Please* forgive me. Just listen to me.'

I gaze at this man. My husband. 'I feel like I don't even know who you are.' My voice fades to a whisper. I try to get the words out. 'The Ollie I know wouldn't drink to escape his problems. He wouldn't abandon his wife to go off for hours at a time to clear his head. He just wouldn't. This isn't you.'

'I know. I know.' He's crying now, choking down the tears. A tiny part of me feels sympathy, but I can't forgive him for putting his own needs above mine and Beatrice's.

'What about your daughter? How does you going off for a pity party help *her*?'

His fists bunch by his sides and his whole body tenses. I've riled something in him now.

I keep going. 'You haven't even asked what's been going on here while you've been gone. You don't know about the new suspects and new investigations, about your mum coming over. You probably don't even *want* to know, do you? You're just burying your head in the sand. Hiding from reality so you don't have to deal with it. But that's fine, because good old sensible Claire will sort it out. She'll do it all. And then, when it's all done and dusted and Bea's back home, and the stress is out of the way, we can pick up where we left off. *The fuck we can!*

Oliver's eyes narrow and he shakes his head. But he's not disputing any of it. Is this what he really wants?

'This isn't you!' I cry. Is he truly this much of a coward? I never ever thought he was. To me, he's always been fun-loving and brave, someone who pushes the boundaries. 'Oliver, tell me you're not going to be like this from now on.'

'I don't want to be,' he says quietly. 'I promise you I don't want to be like this.' He looks down at the floor for a moment before looking up again, this time staring directly at me. 'Will you at least tell me what's been happening today?' He gazes at me from under his lids, like he's nervous of my reaction. As well he should be.

I realise I'm tired of being angry and upset. The best thing right now is for us to be united in our search for Beatrice. If we're at one another's throats, we won't be as effective as if we're supporting each other. All the emotion rushes out of me like a deflating tyre. 'I'm starving,' I reply quietly.

He exhales. 'I'll make you something. Come in the kitchen. Tell me what's been going on while I cook.'

There's so much more I could say to him. So much more to be angry about. But I'm suddenly so weak with exhaustion I can barely stand.

As Oliver heats up one of Freya's homemade lasagnes in the oven, I sit at the table and tell him about my day, trying to keep the bitterness from my voice. The resentment that I had to deal with all of it on my own.

As soon as I tell Ollie about Holloway, he stops what he's doing and starts googling the news story from last year. He's white and shaking and I can't tell if it's from anger or fear.

'Is this him?' He holds out the phone and shows me the image of the man that's been seared into my brain all day.

'Yes.'

Oliver's pacing around the kitchen now, muttering and staring at his phone. 'What did the police say? Did they pull him in for questioning? Do we know where he lives?'

'Gayle said they're dealing with it, but she didn't elaborate.'

'I'm calling her.' Oliver starts tapping and swiping at his screen before putting the phone to his ear. 'Hi, Gayle. Yep, it's Oliver here. Fine thanks, well, you know. Anyway, I'm just calling about Gavin Holloway. Is there any news?' I hear the faint, tinny sound of Gayle speaking, but I can't make the words. 'Okay, and do they believe him?' … 'They did?' … 'Do you have an address?' … 'I understand that, but—' … 'Yes, but this is my daughter we're talking about.' … 'Fine. But will you keep me posted? Yeah, because, this seems to be the biggest breakthrough we've had so far.' … 'I know, but—' … 'Okay.' … '*Okay.*' … 'Thanks, Gayle. I understand.' … 'Really?' … 'That's disappointing.' … 'Okay, will do.' Oliver finally ends the call and takes a seat at the table. The aroma of Freya's lasagne wafts through the kitchen.

'Well?' I prompt.

He blinks and shakes his head. 'So they interviewed Holloway today, but he denied being at the fair that evening. Apparently he has an alibi, which they're checking, and they're also going through the CCTV footage again.'

I take it all in, wondering if his alibi will hold up. 'Did they search his house or flat or whatever?'

'Yes, with his permission. No sign of Bea or that he's had someone there.'

'Do you think he lives alone?'

'I don't know,' Oliver grinds out.

I pull at my fingernails, flicking and scraping them. 'I know the police do this for a living, but do you think they searched his place properly? Do you think they looked in the attic? I mean, what if he has a hidden room or basement? You hear about these things, don't you? I know it sounds overly dramatic, but—'

'No, I agree.' Oliver brings his interlocked hands to his mouth, pressing them against his lips over and over again. 'I wish I knew where he lived. I'd go over there right now and beat the living shit out of him.'

'I'd help you.'

'Do you think it was him?' Oliver asks.

'I honestly don't know. If it *was* him, then there's a chance we'll get Bea home soon. Unless…' Neither of us want to say what we're both dreading. 'If it isn't him, then we're no nearer to finding out what happened and where she is.' We let a moment of silence hang over us. 'What else did Gayle say?'

Oliver leans back in his seat. 'They've examined the fair's CCTV cameras and they managed to spot Beatrice and Millie going into the fair with Jill, but there was no trace of Bea leaving. Problem is, the funfair works with wristbands, so they don't need a perimeter fence. They only have a camera at the entrance, where the money's taken. So Beatrice could have easily left the fair undetected via the playing field or through the woods at the rear of the site.'

'Shit.' I exhale. 'So there's no chance of seeing where she went?'

'Doesn't look like it, no. Unless they pick something up on the road cameras.'

The oven beeps and Oliver takes the food out. He dishes it up, while I wash a few salad leaves. Oliver opens a bottle of red and pours us each a large glass. I'm about to refuse it, but maybe it will be a small relief, take the edge off my torment.

We eat in the kitchen as the light fades outside, a lone blackbird warbling on the roof of next door's shed. I see Philip heading up his garden path with a drill in his hand. He'd better not start making a racket at this hour. I'm in no mood to be polite.

Supper is nourishing but hard to swallow and I barely taste it as my mind jumps from one terrifying thought to another. I stop drinking after one glass, but Oliver's going hard at the bottle, pouring himself a second glass and then a third.

'Maybe you should slow down a bit.'

'It's just a couple of glasses of wine.'

'I know, but…' I trail off. I was going to say we should keep our heads clear in case we're needed at the station or something, but I don't have the energy for another argument. 'Never mind.'

He drains his glass and pushes his plate away. 'I needed that. I hadn't eaten all day.'

'Want anything else?'

'I'm good thanks.' Oliver gets up and starts rinsing our plates, then loads them into the dishwasher.

'I was planning to put some posters of Beatrice up around the neighbourhood. Do you want to come?'

'What, *now?*'

'Yeah.'

He stretches and yawns. 'Okay. It's a good idea.'

I nip into the office to get the posters I printed out earlier, along with some tape. Oliver gets the staple gun from the shed. We spend the next two hours flyering trees and lamp posts, and posting leaflets through doors. It's difficult seeing Beatrice's smiling face on each sheet of paper. In the end, I have to turn the stack over so she's face down.

When we eventually arrive back home, footsore and weary, the sun is almost past the horizon and the security light flicks on as we trudge up the steps towards the house. Once inside, Oliver turns to me and cups my face in his hands, then leans down and kisses me deeply. A brief reprieve from the nightmare. When I finally pull away, he studies my face and strokes his fingers through my hair.

'How are you doing, Claire Bear?'

I give him a small, sad smile and stroke his cheek without replying. I'm more than ready to collapse into bed and forget today ever existed. I have to hope that tomorrow yields some positive news. Our house just doesn't feel like a home right now. It's nothing more than a building with walls and a roof. A place to eat and sleep. There's no comfort here at all. Not without the sound of Bea's laughter filling the rooms.

DAY FIVE

I wonder how Claire is taking Oliver's daytime disappearances. Is she upset? Angry? Bewildered? I hope so. Because I'm enjoying sending him running around, thinking he'll get his daughter back if he does exactly what I say. I mean, he won't. Everything he's doing is purely for my entertainment – and I'm SO enjoying being the anonymous abductor. Enjoying the fact that, for once in my life, things are going my way.

I want it so that neither of them are there for the other. So that the wedge I drive between them will splinter their relationship apart. For good. I instructed Oliver to explain to Claire that he needed time on his own, away from her. That will really piss her off, I'm sure of it. It's all too perfect I can hardly stand it.

CHAPTER TWENTY-SIX

JILL

I nip into M&S to get a couple of pre-prepared salads. It's a total extravagance but I've already done my main shop down the road at the cut-price supermarket, so I don't feel quite so guilty about this. And things are so hellish at the moment that I can't think about cooking right now. I justify the expense by telling myself that I need to eat healthily in order to keep my strength up for whatever comes next. I came out early to avoid the crowds, but it's already stupidly busy.

I make my way down the aisle, marvelling at the people who can afford to pile their trolleys high with so much luxury food. Even when Bob was alive and earning good money in his sales job, shopping here was always seen as a special treat. I come to a stop at one of the salad chiller cabinets and run my eyes across the shelves, finally selecting a feta and avocado salad that's big enough to last two or three days, along with a smaller pasta salad. I can bulk them up a bit by adding some cheaper chopped-up veggies. That will do. I pop them into my basket along with a small bottle of fresh orange juice – I've got a taste for it after visiting Claire yesterday.

I wander down the next aisle, trying not to dwell on what she told me while I was there – the rumour about the choirmaster. I barely slept last night with it all whizzing around in my head, and when I finally did nod off, I had the most terrible nightmares that I can't even bear to think about. I wonder if I should visit Dr Lazeby and ask for something to help me sleep. He prescribed the most wonderful tablets after Bob died that let me drift off into a haze of nothing. The only downside was that I felt awfully groggy during the day, so perhaps that's not the best idea at the moment.

I stand in front of the health and medicine section and see if I can find any herbal sleeping remedies. There are a few here that look as though they might do the job. I finally settle on the mildest looking one.

'Jill? What are you *doing*?'

I almost jump out of my skin at the sound of my daughter-in-law's voice. She's standing right next to me, her black hair pulled back into a messy ponytail, her skin puffy, eyes red-rimmed, dressed casually in denim shorts and a crumpled white top.

'Oh, Claire, hello. I didn't hear you creeping up on me. How are you? I'm just doing a little shop.' I'm gabbling. My heart is going like the clappers and sweat is prickling on my lower back.

'*Jill*,' she hisses. 'I *saw* you!'

'Sorry, what?' I crumple my brow and give her a bemused look. 'I don't follow what you mean. Saw me where?'

'Just now.' She comes closer and lowers her voice even further so I can barely hear it. 'I saw you put that pot of pills into your handbag.'

I give a small laugh of disbelief, holding myself straighter. 'I can assure you I did not. I put them into my basket. Here…' I rummage in the almost empty basket for the sleeping tablets, but they're blatantly not there. I flush and shake my head.

'Look in your handbag,' Claire insists. 'That's where you put them.'

I huff. 'Well, this is just ridiculous.' My fingers start shaking, but I make no attempt to open the large leather bag slung over my shoulder.

Claire gives me a hard stare. 'Look, Jill, I'm not saying you did it on purpose or anything, but if you walk out of here with something you haven't paid for in your bag, you might get stopped by security.'

'Fine.' I slip my fingers into my handbag, but I can't seem to locate the pot of pills, not without opening up the whole bag. Claire leans in and pulls the edges apart. She gasps before taking her hand away and giving me a look of disbelief. I purse my lips together to stop myself from crying. Because crammed into my handbag, plain for us both to see, are a tube of M&S luxury chocolates, an avocado, a small tub of feta olives and a packet of salted-caramel Florentines. The only thing that's not immediately visible is the pot of sleeping pills, which must have slipped down to the bottom of the bag.

'Oh, Jill,' Claire breathes. 'What have you done?'

I quickly reach into my bag and scoop all the items into my shopping basket. There's no point in making excuses or denying it. I know very well what I was doing and so does she. The question is what's she going to do about it. Claire takes the shopping from my hand and places it on the floor next to her own abandoned basket.

'Come on,' she says, taking my arm. 'Leave all that and come with me.'

I don't have the courage to tell her that the sleeping pills are still in my bag.

Claire leads me out of the store and we walk up the road a little way until we reach the faded wooden bench by the bus stop, which is currently unoccupied. There's a ringing in my ears and my legs have suddenly gone very wobbly.

'That's right,' she says, 'sit down next to me and take a few deep breaths.'

I do as she says, but I'm finding it hard to draw in enough oxygen and I'm suddenly feeling extremely light-headed. My breathing is raspy and laboured. Claire takes my cold hand in her warm one and breathes along with me, telling me to inhale through my nose and out through my mouth. I want to tell her that I know how to breathe. I've done yoga and meditation, visualisation, all of that. But I must admit that hearing Claire's voice gently guiding me through it is starting to make me feel better.

Finally, the tingling in my body subsides and I'm back in the present, the noise of the high street and the brightly dressed shoppers coming back into sharp relief.

'Feeling better?' Claire asks, giving my hand a pat.

'Yes, thank you.'

She pulls a water bottle from her bag, flips the lid open and passes it to me. I take a few small sips of the cool water, wondering what she must think of me. How will I ever hold my head up around her again? What if she tells Oliver about what she saw? I'm absolutely mortified. I can't have my son think so badly of me. Especially not after everything else.

'Do you want to tell me what's going on?' Claire looks directly at me, but her eyes are filled with compassion rather than the scorn I was expecting.

I press my tongue against my teeth, not sure I'll be able to speak without breaking down. 'What must you think of me?'

'I don't think anything, Jill. You know you were shoplifting back there, right?'

I nod several times, wincing at the same time. 'I do. I know. I've been doing it for a while. Not all the time. Just now and again. I'm afraid I'm struggling a little, financially – and I know that doesn't excuse what I did, but I'd somehow justified it to myself.' Admitting that out loud makes it sound so much worse than when it was just in my head.

'You're having money worries?' Claire's face darkens and I can't tell if she's upset with me or for me.

'My pension doesn't quite cover the bills, so there's not an awful lot left over for food, and my savings ran out last year.'

'Oh, Jill!' Claire leans in and gives me a hug. An actual, genuine hug. 'Why didn't you say anything to me or to Ollie? You know we would have helped you out.'

'Well, it's embarrassing, isn't it? A mother having to admit to her son that she can't manage her money.' I don't mention the shoplifting part again. I still can't quite believe I've been doing it.

'Of course it isn't embarrassing. Look, Jill, did you not think to come to me? I'm a financial advisor, for goodness' sake. Helping people with their money is what I do.'

'Yes, well, when you put it like that…'

'Ollie and I are one hundred per cent here for you. Just promise me you won't do anything like that again.'

'I won't. I promise. If you must know, I think I'm still in a bit of shock. I can't believe I did it in the first place. Please, you won't tell Oliver, will you? I couldn't bear for him to be disappointed in me, *embarrassed* by me.'

She takes a breath at the same time as I do. 'I won't tell him about the shoplifting, as long as you tell him about your money worries, okay?'

I nod, relieved. I feel as though I'm skating along on the surface of everything. Like I'm no longer in control of my life. It reminds me of when I was a teenager and had just passed my driving test. Careering madly along the road without really knowing how the gears worked, or even how to stop.

We're interrupted by Claire's mobile. 'I'd better get this,' she says, pulling her phone from her bag, 'just in case…'

I tell her to go ahead and she stares at the screen before mouthing at me that it's the police. My pulse instantly speeds up. Claire stands and answers the call.

'Gayle, hi.'

She paces up and down the pavement in front of me while she listens to what the officer says. Claire's expression is neutral, verging on serious. There are no shocked or hopeful noises from her, so I doubt the news is good or bad. I slump back into the bench, mulling over my shameful morning. Hoping to goodness that Claire keeps her word not to tell my son about his disaster of a mother. What would Bob think of all this? He'd be horrified. I correct myself: *No, he wouldn't.* He'd be sympathetic and lovely.

Claire wanders back looking grim.

'What is it?' I ask, wishing I had the strength to stand, but not wanting to chance it yet.

'Holloway's alibi checked out. They don't think he was at the fair that evening. Although it was his mother who vouched for him, so I'm not exactly sure how reliable that alibi can be.'

'Holloway? You mean the choirmaster? I didn't realise the police had been questioning him.'

Claire nods and sits back down, slipping her phone back into her bag. 'They searched his flat but didn't find anything to suggest that Bea was there.'

'Have they arrested him?'

'No. They don't have any grounds – they were only able to search his property because he gave them permission.' Claire gives a frustrated growl. 'He could be holding her anywhere. He wouldn't be stupid enough to keep her in his flat.'

'I'm sure the police know what they're doing,' I say, trying to soothe her, hoping that Beatrice's disappearance has nothing to do with Holloway. Praying that my precious granddaughter isn't anywhere near the man, if the rumours about him are true.

Claire crosses her arms and scuffs at the pavement with the heel of her sandal. 'I'm tempted to question him myself!'

'Please don't do that, Claire. He might be dangerous. Not to mention, you might jeopardise the case.'

'If there even is one,' she snaps. Claire stares off into the distance, her eyes like chips of flint, her jaw tense.

'Claire, promise me you won't do anything stupid.'

'It's not stupid to want to find my daughter.'

'I know, I didn't mean—'

'It's fine, don't panic, I won't do anything.' Her face droops and it looks like she might be finally listening to reason. I'm still worried she might do something reckless. Something that could end badly. For all of us. I try not to dwell on the fact that up until now it isn't my daughter-in-law who's been reckless.

CHAPTER TWENTY-SEVEN

CLAIRE

What the hell is Lang doing here again? I'm in the car, about to leave the house, when my client's Volvo pulls up outside. I'm tempted to pretend I haven't seen him and just drive off, but he's already out of the car and headed up the drive. If I reverse now, I'll end up knocking him over. After my morning with Jill and her supermarket incident, I could do without having to deal with Stephen Lang right now, harmless though he may be.

I take a breath and buzz down the window. 'Stephen, hi. How are you? I'm actually just off out.'

'Oh.' His face falls. He's wearing a similar outfit to the last time he called round – belted shorts, a short-sleeved shirt that still has the creases from when it was in the packet, and canvas deck shoes. 'I, uh, just wondered if there was anything I could do to help. It occurred to me, after I left the last time, that you may need manpower, either to search for your daughter or to run errands or, uh, some such thing and I thought I might be of use to you.'

His face flushes beetroot and I realise that Lang might have a crush on me. The thought is disconcerting and I hope it isn't true. Although I can't deny that it's very generous of him to offer his time like this.

'That's so nice of you, Stephen, thanks. I'm in a bit of a rush right now, but I'll chat it over with my husband and if we need any help, I'll certainly give you a call.' I hope I'm being polite and grateful enough. I don't want to offend him, but at the same time, I can't deal with any weirdness. Offers of help are one thing, but Stephen Lang gives off a decidedly creepy vibe.

'Oh, yes, of course. I'll, uh, I'll get out of your way, Claire.'

The polite part of me wants to say that any other time I'd invite him in for a cuppa, but I don't want to encourage his visits. I feel like a total cow, brushing him off like this when he's being so thoughtful. 'Thanks so much, again. It really is very kind of you.'

Lang steps back from the car and gives me a little wave as I reverse out into the road. He's parked so close to our driveway that the turn is tight and for a moment I think I'm going to scrape his wing. I glance up to see him watching me intently before I straighten up the car and drive off. As soon as I'm on my way, I push Lang from my thoughts.

I've come to the conclusion that I need to give Ollie a bit of space each day, so that he doesn't feel overwhelmed. I also realise that a little time apart will do *me* some good as well. We both need to protect our mental health. To deal with this in our individual ways. We don't know how long it will take the police to find our daughter, so we need to pace ourselves, and be kind to ourselves and to each other. I know that's easier said than done and that we'll inevitably take things out on one another from time to time. But at least we're both trying. To this end, Oliver's gone to visit his mum today – my suggestion.

Before I left, I told Ollie that I'd bumped into Jill in town this morning. True to my word, I didn't mention a thing to him about her shoplifting debacle. I'm not sure if that was the right call or not, as I don't make a habit of keeping secrets from my husband. But I gave my word to Jill that I wouldn't tell him, so I'll try to honour her wishes.

Thank goodness I caught her in the act before she tried to leave the store. The last thing any of us need is for Ollie's mother to be arrested for shoplifting, on top of everything else. I think the two of us may have reached a bit of a truce. I feel like maybe I've been a little hard on her these past couple of years. I never realised she was so stressed about money.

I'll give Jill time and space to explain to Oliver about her precarious financial situation. It's probably not something she'll want to blurt out right now, especially with Beatrice missing. No, the best thing I can do at the moment is put Jill's financial situation right out of my head. We'll all deal with it later.

For a brief moment, I have the crazy idea that Jill and Laurel might have kidnapped Bea for the money. But that's just my mind running away with itself. There's been no ransom demand, no request for any cash. We're not exactly rich, anyway. I almost wish it were true – at least then I'd know Beatrice would be safe. But I must be losing the plot to even think such a thing. There's no way Jill would do anything like that. Unless… maybe Laurel was working on her own…

Was it a coincidence that Laurel called Jill at the very moment Beatrice went missing? Maybe she called to distract her? They say that things like this are usually carried out by people you know. Should I mention my suspicions to Gayle? Jill and Oliver would be outraged if I did that. They'd be incredulous that I was even thinking this way. They'd assume it was jealousy talking. That I had it in for my husband's ex-wife.

The car's air con is taking its sweet time to get going. I'm tempted to open all the windows and start some kind of breeze circulating. I resist, instead cranking up the air con to its max setting. I wish I'd remembered to bring a bottle of water.

While Ollie goes to visit his mum, I'm driving over to see Freya. She's my sanity right now. This time she knows I'm coming, and has offered to make brunch. Even thinking about going to my friend's for brunch while Beatrice is still out there missing brings up intense feelings of guilt. How can I be doing something so normal while my little girl is lost?

I don't think I've taken it in yet. Not properly. Part of me doesn't even believe it's real. That it's not all some horrible dream. If I allowed myself to truly think about what's happened, to project forward all the possible scenarios and outcomes, I don't think I'd be able to function. Instead, I'm refusing to think about things too deeply. I'm simply focusing on the practicalities. On doing whatever it takes to save my daughter. That's all that matters.

When I reach Freya's, I'm greeted once more by a volley of barks as Charlie, Tim and Bessie come to say hello. Freya opens the door with a smile, her shiny caramel bob sleek and swinging today, unlike my ratty ponytail. I follow her inside.

'Hey, you.' She gives me a hug.

'Hey.'

'You hungry yet?'

The kitchen is warm with the aroma of something delicious and my stomach rumbles. 'If I wasn't before, I am now. What's cooking?'

'I put some croissants in the oven. They should be done any minute. Thought we could eat in the courtyard. It's a bit cooler out the back.'

'Sounds perfect. Are your mum and dad not around?'

'They've gone to the auction today. Won't be back till later, but they send their love. How's Ollie?'

'Gone to see his mum.' I don't say anything more about him. Freya and I are good friends, but I wouldn't feel right complaining to her about my husband. It would feel disloyal.

Soon, we're both sitting beneath the wisteria-covered pergola on the ancient wrought-iron patio set that manages to somehow look elegant in this beautiful setting. Thankfully, the chairs are furnished with comfy seat cushions. Bees buzz and butterflies flit and for a brief second, as I sip my iced coffee and pick at the plate of fresh fruit, it feels as though everything is good. Until I remember that, actually, nothing is good.

'Sorry about Dad yesterday.' Freya winces at the memory. 'He thought he was helping by mentioning that choir guy.'

'Don't apologise. I'm glad he did mention it. I reported him to the police and they've been following it up.'

'Really?' She proffers the plate of croissants. I take one; it's warm and flaky.

'Yeah. Gavin Holloway. They've been interviewing him. Checking out his so-called alibi.'

'So-called?' Freya tilts her head.

'His mother.' I roll my eyes.

'Well that's rubbish.' Freya starts spreading jam on her pastry, batting away a wasp which buzzes angrily towards me instead. I tilt my head back and wait for it to move away. 'How can you have your mum as an alibi? Course she's going to lie for him.'

I shake my head in disgust. 'It's obvious, isn't it? I was thinking that I might pay him a visit myself.'

'What!?' Freya puts her knife down and looks at me in horror. 'You can't do that. He might be dangerous.'

'I thought you didn't believe he did it.'

'I didn't say that. It's just, we don't know either way. It was just a rumour that he was at the fair. Whether he's involved or not, I don't think it's a good idea to confront a total stranger. Especially not one with such a dodgy past. Anyway, I don't think the police would be too happy about you talking to him. I don't want you getting into trouble.'

'I don't care about that. He could be our best bet at finding Beatrice. Ollie said he wanted to beat the shit out of him.'

'Hah! Doesn't surprise me. He always was a bit of a hothead at school. Got into more than a few fights back then did our Oliver.'

'*Really?*' I frown. How come I never knew that about him? '*Ollie* did? Are you sure?'

'Probably teenage hormones,' Freya drawls. 'He grew out of it. But he's definitely capable of doing some damage. You should ask Jill about his suspension from school when he was... I think he was about fourteen, maybe fifteen.'

'Bloody hell, Frey. Why did I never know about this?' I can't help thinking that if I didn't know about this side of my husband, what else might I not know about him? The thought unsettles me.

'He'll probably kill me for telling you. Forget I said anything.' She gives a little laugh and shakes her head to let me know she's not really worried. 'Back to Holloway though, don't do anything stupid. Promise me.'

'Maybe I'll just follow him, rather than a direct confrontation. He might lead me to her. They didn't find any trace at his property. But that doesn't mean he didn't take her.' Just saying those words out loud curdles my stomach.

'I really don't think you should be doing anything like that, Claire.'

Freya gives me a long, hard stare, until I soften my gaze.

'I can't do nothing.'

'Well at least promise me you won't do anything without letting me know first – so that I can rescue you if you get into trouble.'

'Fine.'

She nods, satisfied, and gets back to her croissant.

I can't be bothered with butter or jam, so I just break off small pieces and start popping them into my mouth, chewing without really tasting, like all my meals at the moment.

'There's another person I've been thinking about, who may or may not have been involved.' I want to get my friend's take on my recent theory. I need to hear if she thinks it's a possibility or if I'm way off base.

Freya squints. 'What do you mean?'

'Okay, so hear me out.' I feel a bit silly even telling her. 'I wondered about Laurel.'

'Ollie's ex-wife?' The look on Freya's face tells me I'm crazy for even thinking it.

'Just listen before you say anything.'

She raises her hands and nods. 'I'm all ears.'

I tell her about Laurel calling Jill's mobile at the exact moment Beatrice went missing. And about how Laurel is still very much in Jill's life. How Jill feels sorry for her and thinks that she never really got over Oliver.

Freya taps her lips, thinking for a moment. 'That's weird, that she's still friends with Jill. You'd think it would be awkward with Ollie.'

'I know, right. But that's the thing – I don't even think Ollie knows how close they are.' I push away the thought that he might know, but has chosen not to tell me, which would really piss me off.

Freya gives a thoughtful *hmm* sound as she pushes her hair off her face with both hands. 'Even if Laurel does still have a thing for Ollie, it doesn't necessarily mean she'd do something as drastic as taking Beatrice. I mean, what would be the endgame? What's her motivation, other than being a total psycho?'

'Revenge? Jealousy? To put a strain on our marriage?' When I put it like that, it doesn't sound quite so outlandish after all.

'Come on... *Laurel*? She's so wishy-washy, so peace and lentils. She'd never be able to carry off something like that. I know she can be annoying, but I honestly don't think she's behind it.'

'I know what you mean. But to ring Jill at the exact moment Bea went missing... surely that's no coincidence.'

Freya looks sceptical. 'Maybe that phone call was the reason Jill took her eye off Bea. Maybe it was simply the catalyst for Bea's disappearance. Just a horrible coincidence. Honestly, I'm sure Laurel wouldn't have done something like that. Think about it. Think about *her*. Would she really do that?'

'You're probably right.' I sigh. I love Freya, but sometimes I wish she'd be a bit less trusting. She's always so keen to see the good in everybody, which is probably why she ends up getting hurt by men all the time. Always going for the wrong guys and believing their bullshit.

'So what are you going to do?' Freya takes the last few sips of her coffee, stirring the ice with her straw.

'Jill said she'll contact the police about Laurel's call, so we'll see what they make of it.'

'You mean she hasn't told them yet?'

'Apparently she didn't think it was important. Well, if she doesn't tell them soon, then I will.'

'Careful you don't get Jill in trouble,' Freya replies.

'Oh. Yeah. Good point. I'll tell them that Jill asked me to report it. So they don't think she's keeping information from them.'

Freya gives a heavy nod. 'You poor thing. I wish I could do more to help.'

'Oh, Frey. You're already doing loads by just listening. And by feeding me!' I gesture to the spread on the table just as that persistent wasp makes a reappearance and stings me on the wrist. 'Shit!'

'What is it? *Claire*, are you okay?'

'I'm fine. That wasp just stung me.'

'You okay?'

I nod, examining the angry red dot on my skin that's now starting to swell.

'Stay there. I'll get some bite cream.'

I sink back into my chair, thinking that this is just typical. I know it's just a wasp sting, but it feels somehow personal. Like the universe is against me. Tears prick at the corner of my eyes and I have to blink and take a breath to stop them falling. I can't let something as tiny as an insect unravel me. Not now.

CHAPTER TWENTY-EIGHT

JILL

I'm finally back home, resting with my feet up on the sofa. Bless Claire's heart; earlier this morning, after the M&S situation, she left me seated on the wooden bench by the bus stop while she returned to the supermarket and paid for everything that I'd left in my basket, plus a few extras. She also told me that sometime soon, we'd have a confidential meeting, just the two of us, where she'd help me sort out my finances. I can't believe that she's being so lovely. I think I might have misjudged her all these years. Which was possibly due to my closeness to Laurel.

Aside from this morning's drama, I'm a little disappointed right now. Oliver was supposed to come over to see me later, but he left a message to say that he doesn't want to leave Claire so he'll visit tomorrow instead. I'd really been looking forward to having my boy all to myself. I wanted to support him. To find out how he's bearing up. To make him tea and feed him biscuits and pamper him with a fancy lunch. But I can't begrudge Claire his attention. Not after what she did for me this morning. Not after what she's been through, and is still enduring. I just hope she doesn't spill the beans to Oliver about what she saw earlier in the supermarket. Or about my money worries. I know I promised Claire I'd tell Oliver, and I will. Just... not yet.

I'm pulled from my thoughts by the doorbell. Normally, I love the chime of my doorbell and the ringing of my phone – they usually signify friends and family who are thinking of me – but these past few days those sounds have invoked deep feelings of dread. Of fear that it will be more bad news.

I drag myself upright and walk towards the front door with a swooping feeling in my belly. So much so that I put a hand to it, to try to calm the jitters. I open the door, surprised and quite relieved to see that it's Claire. 'Hello, I wasn't expecting to see you so soon.' I peer beyond her shoulder hopefully to see if Oliver's here too, but the space behind her is empty.

She gives what looks like a nervous smile, and my anxiety returns. 'Hi, Jill. Can I come in for a sec?'

'Of course.' I step aside and follow her through to the kitchen. 'Thank you so much for your help this morning – and your understanding.'

'What? Oh, yes, of course. Not a problem.' She seems distracted.

'Have a seat.' I gesture to the sofa while I take one of the dining chairs before immediately standing again. 'Sorry, would you like a drink?'

'No, I'm fine thanks.'

I sit again, waiting, with no small amount of trepidation, for her to explain why she's come. I also wonder why she's not with Oliver. He said he didn't want to leave her this morning and yet here she is, alone.

She takes a breath as though she's building up to whatever it is she wants to say. 'I just wanted to let you know that I've spoken to Gayle, our police family liaison officer – remember, I told you about her?'

I nod. 'Okay. What were you speaking to her about?'

'Well, after the conversation you and I had this morning, I told Gayle about Laurel's phone call to you at the fair. I hope you don't mind, but I didn't want to wait. We have to tell them anything that might help find Beatrice, right?'

My heart is suddenly pounding. What must the police think of me keeping back that piece of information? What if they think I'm negligent? That I was distracted while I was supposed to be looking after my granddaughter and her friend.

'Don't worry.' Claire leans over and puts a hand on my knee. 'I told them that you'd just remembered and were about to tell them yourself, but that I said I'd do it for you.'

'Oh, okay.' Nausea swirls up from my gut and I have to swallow it back down. 'I understand why you told them, Claire, but it does paint me in rather a bad light, don't you think? It should really have come from *me*.' My voice is weak and quivery.

'No, honestly, it doesn't. Gayle was fine about it. She thanked me for letting her know and said she was glad you'd told me.'

Despite Claire's reassurances, my skin is clammy and my breathing is becoming shallow again. It just seems to be one blow after another at the moment. I know Claire doesn't think there's a problem with what she's done, but I hope the police don't think that I was trying to hide the call. Although, if I'm honest with myself, I *was* trying to forget about it. I wish I'd never answered my mobile that evening. Maybe then we wouldn't be in this dreadful situation.

'I did have the craziest theory,' Claire says, pulling me out of my thoughts.

'Theory?'

'It's probably a little far-fetched. But I couldn't stop it popping into my head.' She pauses for a moment. 'I worried that Laurel might have made the call on purpose to distract you.'

'Distract me?' All I seem to be doing is repeating everything Claire says. My mind is all over the place right now.

'You know, while she… I dunno, took Beatrice? I know that's probably a ridiculous and awful thing to say.'

'You think Laurel might have taken Bea?' I know I sound shocked by Claire's theory, but didn't I have the exact same thought myself? Although, the difference is, I dismissed it as soon as it flew into my brain.

'I know it sounds crazy, but right now I'm willing to explore any possibility no matter how slim.'

I straighten up in my chair and nod. 'You're right. We need to look at every single option and follow it through. Just like the police would. This is Beatrice we're talking about, and we have to do everything we possibly can to get her home.'

'Thank you, Jill. Yes! This is what I'm talking about. I'm so glad you agree.'

'I'm not necessarily agreeing that it was Laurel, you understand. Just that I'm not ruling it out.'

'Exactly.'

I worry that Claire will want us to confront Laurel and I'm really not up to that right this second. 'At the same time, I don't think we should go flinging accusations around. Let's wait and see what the police do about her phone call. Maybe they'll bring her in for questioning and come to the same conclusion.'

Claire gives me a dubious look. 'I think it would be better if we told them our theory. We don't have time to waste.'

'What if we're wrong though? And we get an innocent woman into trouble?'

Claire scowls. 'What if we're not wrong? Don't you want to find Bea?'

I try to keep calm. Remember that Claire is frightened for her daughter's safety. As am I, but we can't go around accusing everybody.

'Sorry,' she says. 'Of course you do. I was just lashing out. I don't seem to be able to keep my temper at the moment.'

'Don't worry. It's understandable.' Now it's my turn to reassure. 'Let's wait a day or so. See what happens.'

She scrapes a hand through her hair and finally relaxes her shoulders. 'Okay. Oh, I forgot to ask, did you have a nice time with Oliver today?'

'With Oliver?'

'Yes.' She falters. 'Did he not come over to see you?'

'Not today, no.'

'Oh.' Claire's brow wrinkles. 'Maybe I got that wrong.'

'Maybe he'll pop over later?' I brighten at the thought.

'Yes, maybe.' She looks distracted.

I was going to ask her how he's doing, but her darkening expression tells me that's probably not the best idea right now. Maybe they've had a row.

After this, there doesn't seem to be much left to say. My daughter-in-law politely declines my offer to stay for lunch and we give one another a brief hug before she leaves.

It hasn't been ten minutes since Claire left, before the doorbell chimes again. Maybe it's Oliver. Perhaps he's changed his mind and decided to come over after all. I answer the door hopefully, only to be disappointed, the swooping in my stomach returning with a vengeance. Standing on the pavement are a man and a woman both wearing suits – DI Meena Khatri and DS Tim Garrett.

'Hello, Jill. May we come in?' DI Khatri looks serious and I'm sure I must be in deep trouble over my failure to report Laurel's phone call. I knew Claire should have left it to me to tell them. Now they obviously think I was trying to hide something.

I take a step back. 'Of course. Come through.'

They follow me into the kitchen and accept my offer of a cup of tea. I busy myself making it, while they sit on the floral sofa and make small talk for a moment, chatting about the warm weather and admiring my pretty garden through the back window. I bring their drinks and a plate of biscuits over and sit on the armchair, waiting for them to get to the point. They each help themselves to a custard cream and compliment me on my tea-making ability.

Finally, DI Khatri clears her throat. 'Would you mind if we record our conversation?'

I can hardly say no. 'Um, yes, that's fine.'

She states the day and our names and sets a small recording device on the coffee table. 'We're here to ask about the phone call your ex-daughter-in-law, Laurel Palmer, made to you while you were at the fair on Saturday.'

Neither of them take their eyes from my face as I feel myself flushing. I can already tell that I've turned a deep shade of beetroot, making it look as though I'm guilty of something.

I take a breath and decide to be completely honest. 'I told Claire about Laurel's call this morning and was planning to come and see you next.'

'We were wondering why you failed to mention it on the night in question, when you gave your statement. It seems like quite a big thing to omit.'

'I know.' I pause before ploughing into my explanation. 'I'd convinced myself the call wouldn't have made any difference to the outcome of Bea going missing. The hall of mirrors had become so crowded that, even without Laurel's phone call, it was hard to keep an eye on the girls. They were flitting about from one mirror to another.'

I wait for them to comment, but they just continue looking at me so I press on, my fingers twisting in my lap. 'I did actually ignore her first call, but when she called again, I thought it might be important, which is why I eventually picked up. Since that night, I haven't been able to stop thinking that if I hadn't answered it, I might never have lost sight of Beatrice. The truth is, I feel guilty for taking the call…'

'Laurel called twice?' Khatri's eyes narrow ever so slightly. 'Must have been something important. So what was the reason for her phone call?'

'I think she just needed cheering up.'

'What makes you think that?' Khatri pushes.

'Just by what she was saying. She said she was feeling down because she isn't making enough money from her art to give up her shifts at the restaurant where she works. Let me see, she also said that her flatmates are always going out and having fun, while she's either at home or working.'

'And do you regularly speak to Ms Palmer?'

'Um, yes, I suppose I do. She was married to my son and we always got along well. So we stayed friends even after they divorced. I feel a bit sorry for her.'

'Did your son and daughter-in-law know about your continued friendship with Ms Palmer?'

'I'm not sure how that's relevant,' I reply, instantly regretting my sharp tone.

'In these types of investigations, we like to get a full picture.'

'I haven't kept our friendship a secret, but I haven't exactly shouted about it either. I didn't want to wave it in Claire's face. Nobody wants to hear about their husband's ex, do they?'

'So would you say you get on better with Laurel Palmer, than you do with Claire?'

Goodness, I would never have expected for the police to be so… probing in their enquiries. I can't even see what this would have to do with Beatrice's disappearance.

'Jill?' Khatri interrupts my thoughts.

'I don't really know. I suppose so. Laurel and I have more in common – she's an artist and I used to be an art teacher.'

'How would you characterise your relationship with Claire Nolan?'

'How do you mean?'

'Are you on good terms?'

I think back to this morning. 'Yes.'

'Have you always been on good terms?'

'I'd say this business with Beatrice has brought us closer.'

'And before that?'

'We've never been on bad terms, I just...' I realise that I don't want to start getting into mine and Claire's differences over Beatrice. That Claire wasn't happy about me looking after my granddaughter. I worry that the police might start thinking that our shaky relationship has something to do with Bea's disappearance. That they might even start suspecting *me*.

'You just what?' Khatri prompts.

I've forgotten what I was even saying. 'I don't know. My mind's all over the place.' I realise that I need to calm down. I need to concentrate on what I'm saying, but I've already started panicking. I can't seem to think straight.

'I was asking about yours and Claire's relationship. About how well you got on before Beatrice went missing.'

I try to slow my thoughts. 'We got along fine, but I wouldn't say we were the best of friends.'

'Did you ever argue?'

'No.' I don't tell them that I used to complain to Oliver about her. That I would ask why on earth he let her get away with not allowing me to look after my one and only grandchild. Things might have improved drastically between us since this morning's incident, but I'll never truly forgive her for denying me proper access to my darling Bea.

I take a breath and fix them both with a steady gaze. 'Do you have any news about Gavin Holloway?' I ask, proud of myself for regaining control of my emotions.

'We're still exploring all avenues of enquiry,' DS Garrett replies.

It doesn't seem as though they're willing to expand any further and I don't want to prolong their stay. Thankfully, they end the interview and finish their tea, taking a biscuit each for the road. Thank goodness Claire didn't report my shoplifting incident. I was paranoid that I was going to accidentally mention it myself. As I close the door behind them, I almost collapse with the stress of it all. What a day it's been.

CHAPTER TWENTY-NINE

CLAIRE

I can't sleep. The air is as heavy and thick as unstirred treacle. This evening's argument with Oliver replays in my head over and over like a bad gif. I'm having déjà vu. I can't believe he got drunk again after everything we talked about. After he promised he would do everything he could to help find Bea. He admitted that he didn't go to his mum's today. He just drove around and then ended up in the pub again in a repeat performance of Monday. What's happened to my husband? I really didn't believe he was the sort of person to crumble like this. I thought he'd put up more of a fight for our child. But no. Instead he's chosen to check out.

With Oliver passed out downstairs on the sofa, I feel as though I'm the only person left in the world. The only one left to cope with the darkness that's pressing in on my head and crushing my chest. I'm suddenly aware of my bedside clock ticking, and it's strange because I've never noticed it before. The sound seems to expand, filling the emptiness until I can't think of anything else. It's driving me crazy. I sit up and scrabble for the bedside light, knocking over my glass of water in the process and swearing aloud. Eventually I find the light switch and click it on.

Taking a moment to breathe, I lean back against the headboard. The ticking sound has shrunk a little, but it's still there, still too intrusive. I lunge for the alarm clock and pry off the back cover, using my one decent-length nail to flick out the batteries, dropping them onto my bedside table and giving a sigh of temporary relief. It's 3.20 a.m.

A fox cries outside, the sound sinister and eerie, befitting my current state of mind. All I need now is a howling wolf and a crow tapping on the window pane. I throw off the bed sheet and get up, pad across to the window that overlooks the garden, trying to see if I can spot the fox. Earlier in the summer we had cubs playing on the garden terraces, rolling around and looking so cute that Beatrice wanted to try to tame them. I haven't seen the little creatures for a while. Maybe if I spot them now it will be a sign that we'll find my daughter soon. That Bea's coming home.

I throw the window wide open and peer into the darkness, straining my eyes for any movement, for their small dark shapes, their glinting eyes, or the white brush of a tail. But all is silent and still.

I breathe in the warm night air, a faint breeze whispering across my arms. I wish it were morning already. How am I going to pass the time between now and then? Because there's no way I'll be falling back to sleep. My brain is spooling backwards and projecting forwards, worrying and imagining everything and anything. I lift my gaze upwards towards the dark hill behind the house, to the deep velvet sky above. A couple of stars wink down at me, their cold light uncaring. I glare at them, envious of their lack of feeling, wishing I could be so still and stoic.

As I bring my gaze back down, movement catches my eye. A dark shape. A person in next door's garden! Could it be an intruder? My heart pounds as I step back behind the curtain and watch the figure walk along the path towards the end of the garden. By their height and stature, I'm pretty sure it's a man. Did he break into the garden through the hedge at the back? Or maybe he's already broken into the house and now he's leaving. I should call 999. He turns briefly to look up at Philip and his mother Sue's house and I see that it's not an intruder after all.

It's Philip.

What's he doing out there at this hour? He'd better not start hammering. Although it's not as though I was getting any sleep anyway. He's heading towards the shed and it looks like… yes… now that I look again, there's a faint glow of light in the shed… a silhouette at the window. Someone's in there! From their outline, it looks as though it's someone with long hair – a woman, or… a *girl*.

With a creeping sense of unease and a booming heartbeat, I wonder if it might be my daughter in there. After all, how well do I know Philip? He's in his mid-forties, lives with his mother, doesn't speak much, never seems to have any friends over. My God, what if Beatrice is in that shed?

Forgetting any quarrel I may have with my husband, I hurry downstairs to the living room to where Oliver is sprawled on the sofa, snoring lightly, his mouth open. It smells like a brewery in here. I pull at his shoulder. 'Ollie, wake up.' I shake his arm. 'Oliver… Ollie, get up.' He's absolutely blotto. There's no way he's waking up right now, and even if he did, he'd be no good to me or Beatrice. I seriously feel like punching him. Instead I settle for pushing his shoulder angrily and letting out a frustrated growl. 'Idiot!' He gives a loud snore in response.

I shake my head in disgust and rush back upstairs to the window. Philip's no longer in the garden, but I can see his outline through the shed window. The person with him is a similar height… so not Beatrice then, but a *woman*. I put a hand to my heart and lower my head taking a few deep breaths. For a few moments, I really thought it might have been her in there.

So what's Philip doing out in his shed at three thirty in the morning? I cross the bedroom and bring the stool from my dressing table over to the window where I sit and watch. They've disappeared from the window, but they can't stay in there forever. I'll wait until one or the other of them leaves before deciding what to do.

The fact that Philip is meeting a woman in his garden shed should really be none of my business, but with everything else going on, I can't dismiss it as nothing. As I can't sleep anyway, I may as well try to work out what's going on. Maybe Philip has a girlfriend, or maybe it's just a hook-up, or it could be something else entirely. Hopefully, time will tell.

As the minutes drag by, my eyes grow heavy and I find myself stifling yawns. Why am I growing sleepy now all of a sudden? Where was this tiredness hours ago when I needed it? If only it weren't so warm in here. If only my bed wasn't two steps away begging me to climb back into it. I give myself a shake and pat my cheeks, resting my arms on the windowsill for a while. Eventually, my patience pays off.

I shift the stool back from the window as the door to the shed opens and Philip emerges, followed by the woman. I can't make out her features, but she has long hair and she's wearing a long flowing dress. According to the time on my phone, they've been in there for a little over two hours. As they tiptoe through the garden towards the house, I draw back even further, hoping the curtains and the darkness of the room will shield me from view if they should happen to look up.

The quiet hum of their murmured conversation floats up to me. The woman's voice is low and somehow familiar. She looks over towards our garden and I almost cry out in surprise. It's *Laurel*! What's she doing with my neighbour? Surely she and Philip aren't... are they?

They soon move out of view and I hear the clank and scrape of Philip's side gate opening and then closing, followed by the dull thud of Philip's back door closing. I rush to Beatrice's room to look out over the front of the house. A minute later, I make out the shape of Laurel sashaying down the road, her red hair illuminated by the street lamp, her green maxi-dress swirling around her slim body. She must have parked further away, not wanting to risk me or Oliver seeing her car.

This is all really weird. Laurel and Philip? I would never in a month of Sundays have put those two together. And it's a bit strange that she's visiting her ex-husband's neighbour. That doesn't feel like it's a coincidence. I wish I could talk to Oliver about it, but I don't want to talk to a drunk, hungover Oliver; I want the sober, sensible Oliver. The Ollie I know and love. No time for self-pity, I need to act before the sun comes up. Which will probably be any minute. I already sense a faint lightening in the sky.

I rush downstairs and pull the torch from one of the cupboards in the utility room, slip my toes into a pair of old trainers and step outside in my nightdress. I hope to goodness Philip isn't looking out of his window, but I can't worry about that right now. I have to get a look inside that shed. I make my way up the steps in our terraced garden, thinking about the damaged fence panel that I've been asking Ollie to replace all summer. Thank goodness he never got around to it. The edging baton has come away from the slats and I'm able to pull them back and squeeze through the gap into Philip and Sue's garden.

It feels different now that I'm on the other side of the fence. Unfamiliar and dangerous. Despite the hour, it's still so warm out here. My pulse is racing and there's sweat forming under my arms, running down my back. I traverse a flower bed, heading for the crazy-paved path that leads to the shed. I glance back at Philip's house with a shiver of fear, but the windows are all dark and still, the curtains all drawn tight, apart from in the opaque bathroom window which is also dark. I'm hoping he's gone back to bed.

I turn back to the path and pick my way up it, grimacing as I step on something soft and squishy, gagging at the thought that it might have been a slug. Finally, I reach the shed. My heart is thumping now, the blood whooshing in my ears as I peer through the window, suddenly worrying that there might be another person inside, or people, plural. Pausing, I cock my ears, listening… but all is silent. I switch on the torch and shine it through the glass. On first look, the shed appears to be deserted, but the interior is not at all what I expected.

Despite its shabby exterior, the inside has been done out like a cosy den. The walls are half-panelled wood, painted sage green, with artwork hanging on them. There's a sofa in there, with a folded quilt and cushions – looks like it's a sofa bed. I angle the beam around some more and note a sink, a fridge, and a small table and chairs. There's a pad and paper on the table with a pot of colouring pens and pencils. But Philip doesn't have children. Neither does Laurel. A chill slithers along my veins. I've got a bad feeling about this…

DAY SIX

Things are really ramping up now. So many theories. So much distrust and blame. And Oliver is doing a wonderful job of imploding his marriage. Going missing all day would have been enough, but getting smashed every evening is a nail in the coffin for his relationship.

They all think that searching the streets and interviewing suspects is edging them closer to Beatrice. They think that social media campaigns and putting up posters will bring them success. They have no idea how far off the mark they are. No idea at all.

CHAPTER THIRTY

CLAIRE

Back in the house, Oliver's still crashed out on the sofa, his face awash with a faint dawn light that's creeping over St Catherine's Hill and in through the lounge window. According to my phone it's a little after 6 a.m. I'm clammy with sweat and beyond exhausted. What does all this mean? Philip and *Laurel*, of all people. And what about the paper and coloured pencils in the shed? Does that mean they've had a child in there? Should I go back and break in? Call the police? Could they have Beatrice?

I lean over my husband. 'Ollie.' My voice sounds too loud in the silent living room. He doesn't stir, so I give his arm a shake. 'Ollie, wake up.'

He mumbles, flinging his arm up over his face. I pull it away and tap his cheek with the tips of my fingers. 'Oliver! I need you to get up. Come on, wake up. Ollie. Please.'

I try a different tack, taking his hands in mine and trying to pull him upright, but he's resisting me, his eyes still closed. I debate getting a jug of water and tipping it over his head, but I want him to listen to me, not yell at me.

'What?' he groans.

'Finally! Come on, open your eyes and sit up. Something's happened. I need to talk to you.'

'What?' he mumbles. 'What is it?' My words seem to be sinking in and I now have his attention. His eyes are half open and he's squinting at me, confusion and worry drawn across his face, his hair plastered down on one side and sticking up on the other. 'Ugh. Feel like crap. Give me two minutes, 'kay?'

I wait while he goes to the loo and then to the kitchen to fetch himself a glass of water. He sits heavily on the sofa and takes a few sips before washing down a couple of paracetamol. I'm too focused on what I saw next door to bring up last night's argument. Right now, I need my husband's opinion on what to do for the best.

'What's the time?' he asks, still bleary eyed. His phone is on the coffee table, but he makes no move to get it.

'I dunno, just after six.'

'Why did you wake me up, Claire? Is it something to do with Bea?'

'Just listen. Last night, I couldn't sleep, so I was looking out the window for the fox cubs. You remember we used to watch them—'

'With Beatrice, yeah I know.'

Ollie and I look at one another for a moment, our eyes bright with emotion.

I sniff. 'Anyway, I saw Philip from next door going into his shed and you'll never guess who was with him.'

Ollie shrugs. 'Who?'

'Laurel.'

The faintest flicker of surprise crosses his face. 'Laurel as in—'

'Yeah, Laurel Palmer. Your ex-wife.'

'So she and Philip were…' He raises his eyebrows and then frowns. 'That's weird. Good on Phil for getting himself a woman.' Oliver nods to himself before switching his attention back to me. 'I would have thought you'd be pleased Laurel's found herself someone at last. But couldn't you have waited until I woke up to tell me this?'

'I don't care about Laurel's love life. Or Philip's. This isn't about that.'

'Oh, so, what *is* this about?'

'So, like I said, I saw Philip walking up the path towards his shed. I thought it was odd to be going out there so late at night. And then I saw someone else through the shed window. Someone with long hair. For a minute, I thought...' I swallow. 'I thought it was Beatrice.'

'Beatrice! It wasn't—'

I shake my head 'No, it wasn't her, but—'

'That must have been a shock,' he finishes.

'Yeah, it was, I was ready to scream out the window at them. I came downstairs and tried to wake you up, but you were completely out of it. So I went back up and carried on watching out the window and that's when I realised it wasn't Bea, it was Laurel. She and Philip were in there for ages doing whatever, but I couldn't shake the feeling that this was somehow related to Bea. I mean, did you know about the phone call Laurel made to your mum at the fair, at the exact moment Beatrice went missing?'

'What!' Oliver straightens, his eyes sharp for the first time since waking up.

'Yeah, if you'd been sober last night I would have told you everything that's been going on.'

He looks down at the glass in his hands. 'I'm sorry... What's the deal with the phone call?'

I give him a brief rundown of yesterday's events. Of Jill omitting to tell the police about the call from Laurel, and about me subsequently reporting it. 'So you can see that with what I found out about Laurel's call, and then seeing her in next door's garden in the middle of the night, it made me a bit suspicious.'

'I dunno, it's probably just a coincidence.'

'Maybe, but I was freaked out last night so once Laurel left and Philip had gone back inside the house, I snuck into his garden and looked through his shed window.'

'You didn't.'

'He's done it out like a little den. It's all painted and cosy. The thing that freaked me out the most was that I could see a colouring pad and pencils on a little table in there. And snacks. It looks like they might have had a child in there.'

'Are you sure?'

'About the child? No. But why else would they have that drawing stuff?'

Oliver's phone buzzes. He reaches over to the table and picks it up. He swipes the screen and his face drops.

'What is it? Who's that?'

He huffs. 'It's Mum. She wants me to go over.'

'Oh, right. Well we need to deal with this first.'

He gets to his feet. 'There's nothing to deal with. Phil's shagging Laurel, end of story.'

I stand up too, annoyed that he's not seeing what I'm seeing. 'What about the snacks and the paper and coloured pencils?'

'Laurel's an artist. They're probably hers.'

'Yes but—'

'I'm sorry, Claire, I have to go.'

'Go? You're not going out again. You're not leaving me to deal with all this on my own for the fourth day in a row.'

'Mum needs to speak to me.'

'So do I. I need to speak to you. Me. Your wife. *The mother of your missing child.* I need you here.'

'I'm sorry.'

'You're sorry?'

'Just know that I'm not doing this on purpose. I'm not…' He growls in frustration.

'You're not what? Speak to me, Ollie. Tell me what the hell's going on with you. Because from where I'm standing, it looks like you've already checked out. Like you're running away.'

'I promise you I'm not. But right now I have to go.'

I feel helpless as my husband runs upstairs to change and then comes back down still with the intention of leaving me to go to his mum's instead of staying here and deciding what to do about next door. He leans in to kiss me on the lips, but I don't reciprocate, turning my head so his lips graze the side of my head instead.

'Sorry,' he mutters.

'Yeah, so am I,' I reply pointedly.

He pauses, and it looks as if he might say something. As if he might even change his mind and stay. But then he walks away, the front door closing firmly behind him, and I realise I've never felt so alone as I do right now.

CHAPTER THIRTY-ONE

JILL

The kettle is on and I'm preparing toast with scrambled eggs. Oliver's on his way over to see me. He sounded quite grumpy on the phone when he called to say he was stopping by, but I'm hoping that a home-cooked breakfast might help. I bet he's been eating rubbish – crisps and pot noodles, most likely. He can't function properly if he doesn't keep his strength up. I must admit his phone call woke me up from the deepest sleep, but it's worth the rude awakening to have a rare breakfast with my boy.

'Hello?' Oliver's voice wafts into the kitchen.

I peer down the hall to see that he's already let himself in. I'm so lucky to have him living such a short distance away. Some of my friends have children who have emigrated to the other side of the world; that must be so hard. Oliver says that Claire misses her parents terribly since they moved back to Scotland. I thank God every day that Oliver decided to stay in Christchurch.

'Hi, Ollie, darling, come through. It's so lovely to have you come over, even if it is rather early.'

'Hi, Mum, I can't stay long.'

We hug and, despite his stubbled jaw and a faint sour smell that tells me he didn't shower this morning, I don't want to let him go. I want to squeeze him tight and kiss his cheeks like I used to when he was a boy. Like I do with my little Bea. He follows me into the kitchen where I get a better look at him, and I absolutely don't like what I see. His face is blotchy, his eyes bloodshot and he definitely looks like he's lost weight. 'Oh, Ollie, you look so tired. Are you getting enough sleep?'

'I'm fine. Don't fuss, Mum.' His phone buzzes. He pulls it out of his pocket and frowns at the screen.

'Would you like tea or coffee?'

'Just a quick coffee would be great. One sugar, no milk.'

'That's not how you normally have it.' I spoon coffee into two mugs and pour on boiling water.

'I need the sugar, and I can't face the milk – had a bit too much to drink last night.'

'Oh, Ollie.' I stop myself from saying any more. I don't want him to think I'm nagging. I want to be here to support him.

He holds his hands up as he sinks into the armchair. 'Yeah, I know.'

I bring our coffees over and head back to the kitchen area to finish making breakfast. 'I'm doing us some toast and scrambled egg, unless you'd prefer something else?'

'Sorry, Mum, but I won't be able to stay that long.'

Disappointment tugs at my chest. 'It will only take two ticks.'

He glances at his phone again.

'Are you waiting for a call?'

'What? No,' he snaps in irritation before softening his expression. 'Sorry. No, I'm just checking in case of, you know, any news about Bea.'

'Of course, I understand. It's just unbelievable that we haven't got her back yet.' My voice catches and I try to mask my emotion by clearing my throat.

'You okay, Mum?' Oliver shoots me a worried look.

I need to be strong for my son. The last thing he needs is for me to start crying all over him. I blink and give him what I hope is a bright smile. 'I'm fine, darling. I'm sure the police are doing everything they can. Darling Bea will be home before we know it.'

Oliver mutters something under his breath. I try to recover my equilibrium. I'm desperate to be strong and supportive, to say something wise and soothing that will comfort him. But all I seem to be able to do is worry, irritate or nag him. I can't find a way to connect. Have I lost my son as well as my granddaughter?

'Are you sure you can't stay for breakfast? Just fifteen minutes or so to catch your breath and rest. We don't even have to talk, if you like. You can sit and eat in peace.'

'Mum, please.' He sucks air in through his teeth and I notice his fists are clenched. It's torture to not be able to fix things for him. To be the one who caused this in the first place.

Ollie's phone buzzes again and he almost jumps out of the chair. He checks the screen and gets to his feet. 'Mum, I have to go.'

'What is it? Have you had some news?'

'No, I… I just have to go, okay.'

'What about your coffee?' He hasn't even taken so much as a sip.

'Sorry.' He leans down and plants a swift kiss on my cheek. 'I'll call you.'

I get up, not understanding what's going on, why he's leaving already. I have to stop myself from begging him to stay. 'But you only just got here. Let me put your drink in a flask at least. That way you can take it with you.'

'Sorry, no time. Got to go, Mum. Bye.' He can't even manage a smile as he heads back down the hall. The front door closes behind him and I'm left standing in an empty room.

CHAPTER THIRTY-TWO

CLAIRE

I seriously consider crawling upstairs to bed and refusing to engage with anyone or anything else. After experiencing Oliver's total disregard for me and the whereabouts of our daughter, all I feel like doing is sleeping for the rest of the day. I can't make excuses for him any more. Yes, it's a nightmare situation that is pushing us both to our limits. But we can't simply run away and pretend it isn't happening. Our daughter deserves more than that.

An image of Beatrice's face floats into my brain – her infectious smile and bright eyes – and I know I could never give up on her. The thought that she might have been trapped in next door's shed the whole time, that she might even be in Philip's house right now, spurs me on. So, I drag myself upstairs and into the shower, get myself dressed and call Gayle, while making a strong, hot cafetière of coffee.

Gayle listens on the phone while I tell her about my visit to next door's shed. She doesn't pass comment on my admission that I crept onto Philip and Sue's property without permission. She simply says she'll pass the information to the DI and that they'll probably want to come over.

While I'm waiting for DI Khatri to make an appearance, I drink my coffee and make myself some Marmite on toast and wolf it down, surprised by how hungry I am. Everything in my body is screaming to rush next door and demand they let me in so I can search for my daughter. Reason tells me this would be a bad move. That I should wait a little longer for Khatri to arrive so they can go in there to do a proper search.

The wait is killing me. It's now 7.15 a.m. I tell myself I'll wait until eight, and if the inspector hasn't arrived by then, I'll go round there myself. If there's a chance my daughter is there, then I can't just sit here waiting. No parent would be expected to do that. I almost wish I smoked, just to give me something to do. You see people in TV dramas smoking, sucking in nicotine and puffing out plumes of smoke. It looks satisfying, relaxing, instead of this tense grinding of teeth and digging my nails into my fingers. I suppose I could make myself another coffee, but I've already been to the bathroom three times.

Instead, I lurch into my office and stare out the front window. The couple opposite are getting into their respective cars to go to work, a guy cycles past on a racing bike, freewheeling down the hill. A woman with two cocker spaniels walks up the road towards the footpath which leads onto the heathland. Beatrice is always going on at me to get a puppy, but I've so far managed to resist her and Oliver's pleas. I chastise myself for being so sensible. So mean. Once we get Beatrice home, I'll get her a whole litter of puppies. I don't even know why I said no in the first place. I mean, I work from home, we live at the bottom of a nature reserve, for goodness' sake. It's a dog-walker's paradise.

Thankfully, I only have to wait twenty more minutes for the police to show up. My heart thumps as a grey Volvo pulls into the drive behind my Toyota. Two officers get out. I recognise one as DS Tim Garrett, but the other isn't a face I've seen before – he's young and, unlike Garrett, is in uniform. I'd hoped to be dealing with Gayle or Khatri. I'm suddenly nervous that these guys won't take my concerns seriously. That they'll think I'm an irrational parent who's clutching at straws. I wish Ollie had stayed to back me up.

I move away from the window as the officers climb the steep front steps. After the doorbell sounds I wait a beat and take a breath before going to answer the door.

'Hello, Claire.' Garrett stands on the doorstep next to his colleague. 'Sorry DS Hobart or the DI couldn't come this morning. You're stuck with me and PC Morgan today.'

'That's fine. Thanks for coming round so quickly. Please, come in.' At the last minute I decide to usher them into my office rather than the kitchen. My office is a place where I feel in control. Where I usually know what I'm talking about. Maybe it will give me some confidence. I sit behind my desk and gesture to the officers to take the other two chairs. Garret takes a relaxed seat, his broad frame filling the space. Morgan is stiffer in his slightly-too-big uniform. I don't offer them a drink as I'm desperate for them to go next door to see what they can find.

Garrett clears his throat. 'I spoke to DS Hobart earlier, and she says you saw some children's colouring things in your neighbour's garden shed. His name's Philip Aintree, is that correct?'

'Yes.'

'She also said that he was in there with your husband's ex-wife, Laurel Palmer. Is that also right?'

I nod, thankful they haven't brought up the fact that I was trespassing over there. 'It just felt a bit suspicious, after hearing that Laurel called Jill at the exact moment my daughter went missing.'

'Does Mr Aintree have any children or grandchildren?'

'Not that I'm aware.'

'Does he live alone?'

'No, it's his mum's house – Sue Aintree. She's in her seventies. Are you going to go over there? Ask to have a look round? I'm concerned he might have Beatrice in the house.' I'm making myself speak calmly and professionally, not wanting to come across like an irrational crazy person, but it's so hard not to ask them what they're waiting for, to tell them to rip Philip's house apart until they find my daughter.

The officers glance at one another before Garrett replies in a soothing voice. 'Let's not jump the gun. We'll go and have a word next door.'

'Should I come with you?'

'That won't be necessary. Stay here and we'll pop back afterwards, okay?'

'Okay.' I nod, wishing for the millionth time that Oliver was by my side. That he was here to calm me down. Keep me from spiralling. We've always been there for one another. Apart from now, when it really matters.

Somehow, I get to my feet and see the two officers out of the front door. I watch through the office window as they traipse down the steps and along the pavement, their mouths moving as they talk in low voices – hopefully about their plan of action. They stop and talk for a while longer before trudging up next door's sloping driveway.

Through the window, I hear the muffled ring of Philip and Sue's bell. A pause, and then the door opening, voices, followed by the thud of their front door closing. My heart is beating so fast. I daren't hope that they'll find Bea there. That this nightmare might soon be over.

I rush upstairs to our bedroom and partially close the curtains, leaving a gap for me to peer out. I should have asked them to make sure they looked in the shed. I don't want to give Philip the chance to clear out any evidence. I needn't have worried. Minutes later, Philip appears in his back garden and starts marching up the path, his body rigid and awkward. Following him are the two officers. They stand and wait while Philip unlocks the shed door and stands to the side ushering them in with what looks like an angry sweep of his arm.

They're not in there for long. Thirty seconds at most before they step outside again and thank Philip. *Thank* him. Why did they spend such a short time in there? Surely they should have gone through the place with a fine-tooth comb. Unless they're going to call in the specialists – CSI, or whatever they're called.

Philip glances up at my window with a scowl and I step further back into the room. Although I don't know why I'm skulking about in the shadows. I've got nothing to hide. I sit on the bed and try to think positive. Hopefully, the police will search the house next. Although surely they'd need a warrant to do that. Would they have one ready prepared? I should have asked them when they were here.

Minutes later, the doorbell rings. I quickly glance out of Beatrice's bedroom window to see the tops of the officers' heads. No child with them. No Beatrice. Deep disappointment lands in my gut, a heavy pull of hopelessness and despair. What's the point in opening the door to hear them tell me she's not there? That I got it wrong. That my overactive imagination has been wasting police time.

But then I reason that just because she's not with them, doesn't mean they didn't find something. I leave Bea's room and hurry down the stairs to open the front door and invite them back in. We stand in the hallway while I listen to Garrett explain that Philip Aintree offered to let them search his house and the shed.

'Did you find anything?'

'Mr Aintree was very cooperative and understanding.'

Understanding! I can't even formulate a reply to that.

Garrett continues talking. 'He wasn't happy that you've been spying on him and trespassing on his property, but he knows what you've been going through and is sympathetic.'

'What about the sofa bed, and the colouring pad and pencils, the snacks? It looks like he's had a child in there.'

'I know you're disappointed we didn't find your daughter there, but it's not illegal to have a sofa bed and, if his girlfriend is visiting… well… The man lives in his mother's house. I'd say he was just looking for some privacy.'

'Fine.' I rub my forehead.

'We took a good look around. The pad is an artists' sketch book, and the pencils are watercolour pencils. Mr Aintree showed us some of the drawings – they're landscapes done by his girlfriend, not the work of a seven-year-old.'

So, Ollie was right. That's what he said they'd be. I feel so stupid. But I still think that something's off with Laurel. I'm about to voice my doubts to Garrett, but I stop myself. Rather than throwing out accusations based on gut feelings and intuition, I'd be better off trying to gather some evidence. Otherwise, the police might stop taking me seriously.

I breathe deeply, trying to disperse the excess adrenaline coursing through my body. 'Okay,' I reply. 'Thank you for looking into it. I really appreciate your time.'

Garrett's shoulders relax. I think he was expecting more resistance. 'You're welcome. It's always worth letting us know about any suspicions. Only next time, maybe leave out the trespassing, okay? You were lucky he was so understanding.'

Lucky. Yeah, right. 'Sure. I'm sorry.'

The officers leave and I remain where I am in the hall. I can't shake the feeling that I'm missing something obvious. That if only I could get my brain to work properly, I'd be able to see what's going on. It feels like one of those pictures where you have to blur your eyes in order to see the image, but it takes a while. What am I not seeing? I sit on the stairs, rubbing my jaw as I try to let my mind come up with an answer.

Earlier, I'd been convinced that Laurel and Philip had taken Beatrice. Now I'm not sure what to think. I run through all the suspects and possibilities in my head, not discounting any of them – Holloway, Philip, Laurel, someone from the fair, a random stranger, an accident. Why is it that the list of possibilities is expanding rather than narrowing? Why aren't we any closer to getting Beatrice back?

Eventually, I heave myself up from the stairs and go into the kitchen to get a glass of water. I gaze out the window at Philip's shed, wondering if Beatrice was ever in there, or if I let myself believe it because I wanted it to be true. Because I wanted it to be that simple. My mind turns to Oliver. What was the reason he had to rush over to his mother's this morning? Did she need him for something? Or was it an excuse to get out of the house? I can't be worrying about him right now. He's a grown man; he doesn't need me. Beatrice does.

I sit at the table sipping my glass of water, trying to decide whether I should go out searching the streets again, or have a power nap first to restore some of my energy. I'm starting to feel the effects of a night with no sleep. My eyes are heavy and my thoughts are becoming erratic and strange. I rest my head on my arms and close my eyes for a moment, letting my mind drift off. It feels so nice to just let everything fade out for a short while.

I'm startled awake by a chiming sound. I sit up and wipe a line of drool from my chin. My back and neck are stiff, my face sweaty and gross. How long was I asleep for? The chime sounds again. It's the doorbell. I groan as I'm brought back to my surroundings, to my hideous situation. And now I have to face someone while I'm still half asleep and feeling slightly nauseous.

Wiping my mouth and chin again, I stand and stagger through the kitchen towards the front door. It could be anyone. I'm not even going to try to guess who it is. I decide that unless it's someone with news of Beatrice, I'm going to tell them to go away.

I open the door and immediately wish I hadn't. Standing on the doorstep is Oliver's ex-wife Laurel. And she doesn't look happy.

CHAPTER THIRTY-THREE

CLAIRE

'How *could* you?' The hurt and outrage on Laurel's face looks fake. As though she's auditioning for a really bad movie.

'Do you want to come in?' I stand back and she glides past, her Indian-print skirt swishing, her purple sandals creaking, the bangles on her arm jangling, all of it setting my teeth on edge. 'Go through,' I say somewhat redundantly as she's already in the kitchen, turning to face me, a deep scowl settling onto her delicate features.

'How could you ever think I would take Beatrice? What sort of person do you think I am?' She takes a breath, but doesn't pause long enough for me to answer her rhetorical questions. 'I can't believe you told the police there was something dodgy about my phone call to Jill while she was at the fair. Jill and I call one another all the time! There's nothing unusual or sinister about it.'

'So I've recently been hearing.'

'What's that supposed to mean?' She puts a hand on her hip.

'Nothing. Just that a friend recently told me she saw you with Jill.'

'Who?'

'Freya. She ran into you at the playing fields last Sunday. Said you blew smoke in her face when she tried to stick up for you.'

'Freya wasn't sticking up for me. That cow has always had it in for me. I bet she's the one who put my name in your head, turned you against me.'

'Actually no. She stuck up for you. I told her my suspicions and she defended you. Said you wouldn't have done anything like that.'

'Hmph,' Laurel folds her arms across her chest. 'Well that's something I suppose. Does Ollie know you reported me and Phil to the police? I bet he doesn't! Where is he anyway?' She glances around the room then goes over to the window to peer into the garden. 'Not out there. Is he upstairs?'

'He's not here,' I reply, trying to marshal my thoughts.

'Are you sure?'

'Why would I lie?' Laurel has swept into my home like an unpredictable force of nature so I wouldn't be at all surprised if she raced upstairs to search for him. 'His car's not here, in case you didn't notice.'

'Fine.' She starts playing with one of the many silver rings on her fingers, twisting it around. 'Phil rang me. He's furious and his poor mum is completely mortified. You've embarrassed both me *and* Phil. What possessed you to call the police? You could have just gone round there and spoken to him. Or called me. I mean, I know we don't really know each other that well, or necessarily have anything to do with one another, but I did used to be Ollie's wife, so I'd have thought you could have done me the courtesy of—'

I need to stop her monolithic rant. Right now, Laurel's voice is on a register that could cut through double glazing. It's making my head throb. 'Laurel, do you have any idea what it's like to lose a child? How terrified it makes you? How utterly desperate I am to get her back? If you felt one tenth of what I'm feeling right now, you'd know that I would do literally anything to make this pain and fear go away. To know that she's safe and well. To know that she's not...' I don't finish my sentence.

Laurel's mouth is still open, her jaw dropping lower with each second.

I take a breath and continue. 'If I have good reason to think Beatrice might be in the neighbour's shed then I am going to act.

I'm not going to stop and think how embarrassing it might be for you, or Phil's mum, or how awkward it might make you feel. So I'm sorry, but I'm not sorry, okay? I had to know for certain that Beatrice wasn't next door.'

Finally, Laurel's mouth snaps shut and she clears her throat. 'I suppose I get that… but still. It was a shock.' She blinks and nods, toying with a silver chain at her throat.

'Of course,' I concede.

Her shoulders droop and she tosses her dyed red hair over her shoulder. She points to one of the chairs. 'May I?'

I shrug as she sits, although I remain standing. I'm not about to sit at the table with Ollie's ex-wife like everything's hunky-dory and civilised after she's barged into my house to have a go at me. I need her to realise that this isn't all about her.

She sighs. 'Look, I was as upset as anyone to hear your news. If you must know, I've been supporting Jill through all of this. I picked her up from the police station the night she was drinking, I helped organise the search party. It's all been just awful. So stressful.'

As I stand here listening to Laurel's attempts to make herself sound great, I wonder how Oliver could ever have married this self-absorbed woman. I'm still not sure whether or not she might have had something to do with Beatrice's disappearance. This whole situation with her and Philip feels like too much of a coincidence. As if it's been engineered.

'How did you and Philip even meet?'

Laurel clears her throat and looks up at me from under her lashes. 'Well, he used to come into the restaurant where I work, and after a while we got chatting and he asked me out. I couldn't believe it when I found out where he lives. I mean, what are the odds of my new boyfriend living next door to my ex-husband?'

What are the odds indeed? I decide to keep questioning her – who knows when I might get this chance again?

'Why were you meeting in his shed in the early hours of the morning? Why not his house, or your place?'

'Not that it's any of your business,' she snaps, 'but the reason we meet there is because… well, it just feels weird being in his mother's house. Although I did tell him to fix the shed up nicely or I wouldn't be coming over again. I had to design the whole interior for him. He wouldn't have had a clue otherwise.'

'Hence the DIY obsession,' I mutter.

'What?'

'Nothing. Go on.'

'Well, there's absolutely no privacy at my place because I have annoying and very nosy housemates. Then of course there's the most obvious reason we've had to sneak around…' She gives me a pointed look.

I shake my head and hold out my hands. 'I give up. What reason?'

'I didn't want you or Oliver to know I'm seeing your neighbour, of course. Of all people! It's like this weird, annoying coincidence. It's not the best situation in the world, is it?'

'I suppose not.'

Eventually, Laurel and I run out of things to say to one another. She gets up from my kitchen table and gives me a withering stare. 'Well, I'm still not happy about what you did, but I suppose I can understand why you did it. I do hope Beatrice is found soon.'

'Thanks.'

'Right, well, I'll be off then. Say hello to Ollie from me.'

I won't be doing that. 'Sure.'

'Bye then.'

'Goodbye, Laurel.'

I walk down the hall to see her out. From the office window I see her march straight next door to Philip's. God, what did I do to deserve all this? If she's going to be round at my neighbour's all the time, I might seriously have to consider moving house.

Everything is a jumble in my head. Beatrice is gone. My husband may as well be gone. My neighbour hates me. Laurel hates me. And I can't think straight. So I've decided to stop thinking and start acting. Time for me to stop moping and worrying and pull out all the stops. I grab my bag and phone, scoop my keys up from the hall table and head out. I've already spoken to Laurel. Now I'm going to get some more answers.

CHAPTER THIRTY-FOUR

CLAIRE

The drive to Wimborne is frustratingly slow, the summer afternoon traffic clogging up every route in Dorset. I try not to let it stress me out and instead use the journey to plan this afternoon's strategy. Of course, trying to plan anything is close to useless as I've learned that nothing ever works out the way you expect. But going over the details in my head helps me stay calm, keeps my mind occupied and, most importantly, stops me from spinning out at the thought of what might go wrong.

Thankfully, the fair's new site is on the outskirts of Wimborne, so I don't have to join the growing tailback of traffic across the bridge into town. Instead, I head to the showground where they're setting up, ready for tomorrow.

I don't know this area too well, so I let the satnav on my phone guide me. Once I'm close enough to spot the big wheel, I drive a way down the road and park up in a lay-by just along from a busy burger van.

After locking the car, I stroll back down the road towards the fair, trying to keep hold of the determination I felt earlier. To not let it give way to the nerves starting to bubble up, and to the voice in my head telling me this is a bad idea.

The birds in the hedgerows chirp and flutter as the occasional car zooms past, exhaust fumes hanging in the humid air. I'm wearing a pair of nondescript denim shorts, a plain black T-shirt, dark sunglasses and a navy baseball cap with my hair tied back in a low ponytail. Hopefully, none of the fair staff will pay attention to me. Hopefully, I'll blend in with the fair workers who are setting up the rides. That's the aim anyway.

The showground is on the opposite side of the road. I walk along, glancing across at the jewel-green grass, at the clusters of teenagers lounging or kicking a ball around, at the dog walkers, at the parents with young children, and finally at the temporary fairground site up ahead, the sound of metal on metal, of hammering and scraping as they build up the fair.

I stay on the opposite side of the road, walking past, taking in the layout. There are large lorries ranged around in a kind of semi-circle, facing outwards, and various other vehicles, trailers and caravans parked behind them. The whole area is a hive of activity, with people – mainly shirtless men – carrying poles and shouting orders. But thankfully, I've spotted a few women too, and my bland clothes should help me blend in. The main obstacle I can see is the temporary metal fencing right the way around the fair site. They didn't have that in Christchurch. Maybe it's just needed while they're setting up. While the vehicles are all open and vulnerable. This convinces me that it's the perfect time to snoop around. I just need to get inside those barriers.

I stop in line with the end of the fairground, pull out my phone and pretend to be talking into it as I scan the area again, considering my best plan of action. Most of the rides are still in the process of being built, but they've already assembled the spotted teacup ride and the carousel with all its brightly painted horses – Bea's favourite. To the left of the carousel, I spy the hoopla stand with all its tacky stuffed toys swinging from the rafters. Whenever we visit the fair, Oliver's mission is always to win the biggest teddy, but he usually ends up spending more than three times what it's worth before he either wins it, the stallholder takes pity on him, or he has to part with more money to buy the thing.

I turn and walk back the way I came. Once I return to where the fencing starts, I cross the road onto the open part of the grass and start walking around the barrier. I stay several feet away, so it doesn't look like I'm scoping out the place. Thankfully, the lorries are blocking me from view. There's absolutely no gap in the fencing. It's over head height and I really don't want to attempt to climb it. There has to be another way in.

Despite my trembling hands, I don't feel nervous, or anxious. What I'm feeling is more like fury and determination. I'm angry at everyone. At Jill for losing Beatrice, at Laurel for being a self-obsessed moron, at Oliver for abandoning me and giving up on our daughter, at the police for not having found her yet, and at Monty Burridge the fairground manager for not being more understanding. He should be letting me in and throwing his vehicles wide open for me to see that my daughter isn't in one of them. And the fact that he isn't doing it makes me doubly suspicious.

I decide that I have nothing to lose. If they catch me, they'll throw me out, but I'm hoping I'll get to do some snooping first. Maybe I'll stumble across some kind of clue to Bea's whereabouts, or find someone who'll tell me something useful. I stride around the fair's perimeter, no longer looking for gaps in the fence, but instead heading for the opening by the road that's being manned by security.

I'm hot and sweaty by the time I reach the entrance, which is just wide enough to let a vehicle through. A man stands inside to the left. He's looking at his mobile phone and sipping from a coke can. I walk through the gap as purposefully as possible, looking straight ahead. I'm almost certain I'm getting away with it, until the man calls after me.

'Oi, can I help you?'

I turn around and point to my chest. 'Me?'

'Yeah.'

'Oh, right, I'm here to help Sam. She's not feeling too good. Kai told me to go straight over to the stall. Is that okay?' I give him a hesitant smile.

'Kai knows you're here?'

'Yeah. I'm his cousin.' I hope I haven't gone too far. What if this man's related to Kai too? But I needn't have worried.

'Cool, yeah, sure, go through. Sam's setting up opposite the ghost train.' He points to a spot in the distance on the right.

'Cheers.' I walk off confidently, my heart hammering at how spectacularly wrong that could have gone.

Once I'm a few hundred yards away, I step behind a hoopla stall and try to calm down. That's one hurdle over with. Now I have to focus on what I came here for and check as many of these vehicles and trailers as possible, before they realise who I am and why I'm here.

I head out towards the metal fencing to where most of the trucks are parked, keeping my phone to my ear so it looks like I'm occupied. I slip alongside a massive red lorry. The cab is empty and the rear door is shuttered. I move on to the next truck, which is open at the rear but completely empty, aside from a few metal poles. As I keep going, I realise that Beatrice is less likely to be in one of these trucks – they're all either empty or full of fairground equipment. If she's being held at the fair, she's more likely to be in one of the caravans or trailers. I should search those first.

Skirting close to the fence, I make my way around the site until I spot what I'm looking for – a cluster of cars and caravans parked between two huge trailers. There doesn't seem to be anyone around here at the moment; I guess they're all busy setting up the rides. I keep my phone clamped to my ear as I walk up to the closest caravan. The curtains are all closed. I try the door handle, but of course it's locked. One of the windows has been left open a crack, probably because it's such a hot day. I crouch down and try to peer through, but the interior is dark.

'Beatrice,' I hiss. 'Bea, are you in there?' There's no reply. I glance around to check that no one's about, before sliding my fingers in through the gap and dislodging the window catches. This allows me to open the window fully. I can't believe it was that easy. I poke my head inside the caravan. It's neat and tidy, quiet and still. 'Beatrice?'

Unless she's been shut in the toilet, she's not here.

I need to move quickly if I'm to check all the caravans. A couple of them are locked up tight with no means of seeing inside, but most have left their windows open and I'm able to take a look. I'm guessing they don't keep anything of value in them – they probably lock their valuables in their cars. Even so, I'm surprised at the lax security and at the fact I was able to get onto the site so easily.

Male voices coming my way have me skirting around a pickup truck and walking towards the fence. I lurk behind a camper van until the voices die away. I must have checked eight or nine caravans so far and there's no trace of my daughter. I don't know what I expected to find – Beatrice tied up in a van? Or unconscious? Drugged? If someone took her would they then be so stupid as to keep her here at a busy fairground? Although, I suppose she could be locked in one of the bedrooms, out of sight. I can't deny that I'm starting to feel completely disheartened. But I'm here now; I may as well finish checking the other caravans.

The next three are all locked, windows closed, with no way of seeing in, but as I approach a large silver camper van, I stiffen in shock as I hear a child crying inside. My whole body goes on alert. Chills lift the fine hairs on my arms and on the back of my neck. I start shaking in anticipation. I want to cry out, shout her name, but I can't alert anyone that I'm here, that I may well have found my daughter. If whoever took her knows I'm standing right outside the camper, I could end up endangering us both.

The thing is, I don't know if she's in there alone, or if she's being guarded. I have no idea what to do for the best. From this side, I can see that the curtained window at the rear is open, but can I risk peering in? It's dark in there and bright out here, so if there are other people inside the van, they'll see me straight away. The sunlight glints off the silver exterior. This isn't like the other basic caravans. This is a top-of-the-range motorhome.

Now I can hear another set of voices getting closer. I edge back around the van and stay still, hoping whoever it is goes away.

'Well I didn't know. She said she was Kai's cousin.'

This isn't good. It's the guy from the main gate. They must be looking for me.

'I don't care if she said she was the Queen of England; you don't let anyone in without a pass. Idiot.' That sounds a lot like Monty Burridge.

I don't know what to do. If they find me before I've had a chance to check the camper van, then I might miss my opportunity. If Monty is behind her abduction, then I'm in serious trouble right now. Especially as I didn't tell anyone where I am. I quickly open WhatsApp on my phone and take a picture of the camper van, making sure to get the number plate. I send it to Oliver with the caption 'Wimborne fair'.

'Hello, Claire.' I almost cry out in shock as Monty comes striding around the camper.

I shove my phone into my bag. 'Hi, Monty.' My heart is hammering against my ribcage. 'I just have to…' and then before he comes any closer, I leg it back around the camper to the rear window and yank it fully open before hoisting myself up into the interior of the van where I land on a table with a thump.

A youngish woman jumps to her feet. 'What the hell! Who are you?' She shoves a child behind her. It's so dark in here after the brightness of outside, I feel almost blind.

'Beatrice!' I cry. 'Bea, is that you? It's Mummy, I'm here, Bea. I'm here.' I lunge for the woman, but she dodges me.

'Get the fuck away from me, you crazy bitch.'

'Is that my daughter? Did you take her?'

'You come any closer, I'll punch your lights out.'

The door to the camper crashes open and three figures burst in, throwing a shaft of light across the interior. I recognise all three men – the security guard, Monty and Kai.

'You okay, Jen?' Monty puts a hand on the woman's shoulder.

'Yeah.' She nods without taking her eyes off me. 'Who's this psycho?'

'Claire Nolan,' Monty replies. 'You know. The mother of the girl.' He looks at me. 'Claire, you need to calm down and step outside. You're scaring the little one.'

The child peers out from behind the woman, her brown, tear-filled eyes wide with fright, dark hair tied into an unfamiliar bun on the top of her head. I blink once, twice. She's young. Too young to be Beatrice. It's not my daughter.

I feel my jaw slacken, my body slump, my brain computing the awfulness of what I've just done. 'Oh, no, I... I'm so sorry.' I put a hand out as though to stroke the child's cheek, even though she's several paces out of reach. I let my hand fall back to my side and bow my head.

When I finally look up again, everyone's staring at me like I'm a bomb about to blow them all to smithereens. 'Come on, Claire,' Monty says, calmly. He comes and stands beside me, ushers me out of the dark camper and back into the glare of the sun.

I don't even know what to say. It's obvious they know why I went in there, so there's no point explaining. The three of them escort me back across the fairground where I stare straight ahead at the gates, ignoring the dozens of fair workers who are giving me sideways glances as word spreads of what's happened.

'Are you going to call the police?' I ask, my voice sounding foreign to my ears.

'I should,' Monty replies. 'But no. As long as you promise not to come back again. You scared the daylights out of Jen and Sia.'

'I'm so sorry. Will you apologise to them for me?'

Monty gives a terse nod. 'They're my daughter and grand-daughter, you know.'

'I didn't know. I really am very sorry.' I swallow the lump in my throat, mortified that I've put him and his family through such trauma. The colours and shapes of the fairground rides merge in my peripheral vision, swimming in and out of view as we walk – the dodgems, the chair ride, the ghost train… it's all supposed to be such good fun. Instead, this fair has become my nightmare.

We finally reach the entrance gates and everyone comes to a halt. Monty turns to face me. 'You can't go around breaking into private property. I know this must be awful for you. But your daughter isn't here at my fair. Like I said, the police checked, and I checked. She's not here. Do you understand?'

I nod, unblinking, barely breathing, my hands hanging loose at my sides as I stare at my feet.

'Good. Now I hope you find your little one, but right now, you need to go home. And if I see you at my fairground again, I will be calling the police.'

I leave the fairground as though in a dream, putting one foot in front of the other, I reach the pavement and have to take a few deep breaths to work out where I am and which way I need to go in order to get back to the car. My legs feel soft as marshmallow and I wish I could take the time to sit and recover, but I'm sure Monty, Kai and the others are watching me. I need to get out of here.

There's a gap in the traffic so I start walking across the road just as a dark-green car pulls away. There's something familiar about that vehicle. I snap up my head and stare at its receding shape. That's… it's… a green Volvo. And the driver… I recognised his face as he drove off, that messy ash-blonde hair. It's my client – Stephen Lang! What the hell was he doing parked across the road from the fair? This is all too much to process. My head is spinning. It's just one thing after another.

CHAPTER THIRTY-FIVE

JILL

Against all my good intentions to keep Laurel at arm's length, I find myself walking into town late this afternoon to meet her. Her phone call came at a weak moment after Oliver left my house this morning. I couldn't believe he didn't even stay long enough to have a cup of coffee with his own mother. What was the point in him even coming around if he was just going to leave again? Although I have to remind myself that my poor boy is hardly thinking straight at the moment. Nobody is. So when Laurel called and asked me to meet her at the Bridge Street coffee shop, I foolishly said yes.

Now that I'm on my way over, I'm starting to realise that this might not be the best idea. Especially since I told Claire about Laurel calling me at the fair, and then Claire reported it to the police. I have a feeling that Laurel might want to meet me so she can tell me off. I could really do without the drama and accusations. I need support, not aggravation.

But here I am, heading to meet her anyway. I wish I were better at saying no. Never mind – I'll go for half an hour, listen to what she has to say, then make my excuses and leave.

Town is busy, the pavement thick with shoppers and tourists, the main road choked with crawling traffic. So many people. I wonder if any of them know what's happened to my granddaughter. I gaze at the cars, at their occupants. Any one of those people might have seen Beatrice and not know it. Or perhaps one of them is responsible for her disappearance. How would I ever know?

I shake away these useless thoughts. It's not like me to speculate like this. There's really no point. It won't do any good. I simply have to trust that the police will do their job and find Beatrice. They have to. There's no acceptable alternative. I take a breath to stop the tears that are suddenly threatening to fall. I can't break down in the middle of town. Despite all attempts, a lone tear escapes. I bow my head and brush it away with a no-nonsense swipe from the back of my hand.

At least with the traffic at a virtual standstill it's easy enough to cross the road. I weave through the cars and almost trip up the kerb on the other side. These sandals are a menace, I should have worn less hazardous footwear. As I walk down Bridge Street, I try to steady my breathing and stifle my emotions. Part of me wants to turn tail and run home, but I keep going until I'm entering the coffee shop, the bell above the door sounding decidedly too cheerful.

I glance around, but there's no sign of my ex-daughter-in-law. The café's full so I hover at the counter, gazing longingly at the overpriced cakes while throwing glances over my shoulder to check on the table situation.

A few moments later, an elderly couple at a window seat start making a move to stand up. I dart over and ask them if they're leaving. They are. I stake my claim by laying my handbag on the table and do the polite thing by holding open the door for them as they shuffle out – one with a walking stick, the other with a walking frame. As they're attempting to walk out through the door, Laurel appears and rudely sidles past them with an exasperated huff. Oh dear. She does not look happy.

'Hello, Jill,' she manages through thin lips.

'Hi, Laurel.' My throat constricts at the thought of another confrontation. Once again, I wish I'd stayed home.

Laurel's aloofness doesn't last long. 'Ugh, it's so busy everywhere, I couldn't get parked, and now it looks like it's full in here too.' She proclaims this loud enough that several customers look up.

'It's fine,' I hiss, not wanting her to make a scene. 'I got us a table.' I point to the prime spot in the window.

'Oh, thank goodness.' Laurel sinks into the chair facing the street, leaving me to edge around the table and wedge myself into the seat opposite. She raises a hand and waves over a waitress. 'A pot of tea please, and a glass of tap water.'

'Make that two of each please,' I add.

'Anything to eat?' The waitress asks.

'No thanks.' I shake my head regretfully.

'I'll have a toasted teacake,' Laurel replies. 'Could you make sure they spread the butter on while it's still warm, so it melts.'

'We usually bring the butter out separately,' the waitress says with a hesitant smile.

'Fine, okay, thanks.'

The waitress wipes our table down and leaves.

Laurel picks up a menu, using it to fan herself. 'I'm so hot and sticky I could die.'

'Everything okay, Laurel? You seem a bit flustered.'

'Yes, well that would be down to your new daughter-in-law.'

'She's hardly new, Laurel. Eight years is a while.'

'You know what I mean.' She flaps a hand dismissively.

'What's happened?' I ask, bracing myself.

'Did you know that Claire reported the call I made to you at the fair, as though there was something suspicious about it? As though I'd done it on purpose to distract you or something?'

I wince.

'You *did* know!'

'I told her to leave it to me to sort out, but you can't blame her. She's beside herself about Beatrice. We all are.'

'I know! But for her to think that I could be responsible for such a thing… I'm really hurt. Does Ollie know about this? What's his take on it? Have you seen him recently? He wasn't at home today.'

'You went round there?' Claire and Laurel don't have any kind of relationship, so I'm surprised Laurel showed up at their house.

'Of course I went round there! I'm not going to let someone smear my name and then not give my side of the story.'

'It's hardly smearing your name.'

'Since when did you start taking her side?'

'Oh, Laurel, it's not about taking sides. It's about my missing granddaughter. You really have to stop taking this personally.'

'I'll stop taking this personally when she stops getting personal.' Laurel leans forward and lowers her voice. 'Do you know what she did?'

'Who, Claire?'

'She broke into her neighbour's shed because she thought he might be hiding Beatrice in there.'

I frown. 'You mean the DIY neighbour?'

'He's not a DIY neighbour!' Laurel seems overly upset for something that doesn't relate to her.

'Yes he is,' I insist. 'You know, always hammering and drilling. He's been driving Claire and Ollie mad with all the noise. So she thought he had Bea? What made her think that? Is it true? Oh my goodness!' I clap a hand over my mouth at the thought of it.

'No it isn't true!' Laurel snaps, her eyes narrowing.

'Sorry, I was only asking.' I stare at Laurel for a moment. She looks tired, her forehead is creased and dark shadows sit beneath her eyes. She's fiddling with her rings, twisting them around her fingers, a thing she always does when she's worried. 'What's happened, Laurel?'

Her face flushes and she glances up at me quickly before looking away.

'You know you can tell me anything. How long have we been friends? I'm not going to judge or blame you.'

She lets out a sigh. 'Oh, Jill, it was awful.'

'A pot of tea for two, two waters and a toasted teacake.' The waitress puts our order on the table and leaves us to it.

'I don't know why I ordered this teacake now, I'm not hungry.' Laurel pushes it towards me. 'Do you want it?'

'Thanks, I'll have half.' I pour our teas while Laurel launches into her story.

'Claire and Ollie's "DIY neighbour" as you call him, is actually my boyfriend.'

I put down the teapot. 'What? You have a boyfriend? Why didn't I know about this?'

'His name's Philip, and we've been seeing one another for a few months now. It's not that serious. He lives with his mother and he's not even my type really. He used to come into the restaurant on his own and would always chat me up. He'd been asking me out for ages, but I'd always knock him back. Then one day he came in when I was feeling particularly low and I thought, what the hell, why don't I go on a date with him, nothing to lose.

'Anyway, we ended up having quite a nice time. He was so attentive and he worships me. I mean it's almost embarrassing how much he likes me. It makes a nice change to have someone like me more than I like them. So we carried on seeing one another.'

'Well that sounds nice.' I start buttering the teacake, a little hurt that she never told me about him. That she let me believe she was lonely and without a partner. 'But what does this have to do with Philip's garden shed, and why Claire might think Beatrice was in it?'

'I don't even want to say. It's totally embarrassing.'

'Laurel, I'm a sixty-five-year-old widow who's going to court next week for drink-driving. I've also been humiliated on the front page of the local paper. I think we're past the embarrassment stage of our friendship.'

'Fine.' She shifts in her seat and takes a sip of tea. 'Because Philip lives with his mother, we meet in his garden shed.'

I raise an eyebrow, but don't comment. She looks at me for any sign of judginess so I school my face into a neutral expression.

'It's nice in there, he's transformed it into this really lovely lounge area. Anyway, last night, Claire looked out of her bedroom window and saw him walking up to the shed to meet me. For some reason, Claire waited until we'd gone and then she went up there to have a nose around. She basically went into his garden without permission. The thing is, I sometimes draw and paint up there, so when she looked through the window she saw what she thought was a child's colouring pad and pencils.'

I join the dots. 'So she thought a child had been in there, and assumed it was Beatrice.'

'Exactly. And then she called the police.' Laurel throws her hands up in the air and leans back in her seat. 'It was so humiliating. First I felt like a criminal, and then I felt like I was nothing more than a sordid little joke. I bet the police thought it was hilarious – this couple shagging in the garden shed to hide from his mother.'

'I'm sure they didn't think anything of the sort.'

Laurel starts viciously buttering her half of the teacake. 'Bloody butter's so hard it won't melt.' She tosses her knife down and bursts into tears. 'It's been such a horrid morning, Jill.'

'I'm sure it has.' I reach a hand out and place it over hers. 'So have the police now cleared you and Philip?'

She sniffs and draws an old tissue from her bag, wiping her eyes and blowing her nose. 'Yes. Thankfully it was all dealt with quite quickly. The police could obviously tell that we'd been wrongly accused. Although the damage has already been done – Phil was quite cross, and his mum looked at me as though I was something she found on her shoe.'

'Things will settle down. You've all had a shock, that's all.'

'I suppose.' She crams a piece of mangled teacake into her mouth and starts chewing. 'This tastes awful. I think it's burnt on the bottom.'

'Well I think it's nice that you found someone. This Philip sounds like he's a good person.'

She shrugs. 'Yes, I suppose so.'

'Why didn't you ever tell me about him?'

Laurel stares out the window. 'I don't know really. I suppose I never thought of it as a real relationship. We never told anyone we were seeing each other. Like I said before, he's not my usual type. He's older for a start. With him living next door to Oliver, I didn't want to make it official because it would have been awkward. I mean, what would they have thought? Ollie's ex-wife suddenly going out with his neighbour. It's too weird.'

I can't disagree with her so I give a sympathetic smile instead. 'Do you want more tea?'

She nods so I turn to catch the waitress's eye, and point to the teapot. As I turn back, my phone pings. I look at the screen to see that I have a new message. It's from an unknown number. The same unknown number that sent me that awful text asking how I could lose my own granddaughter. As I read this new message, I'm unable to stifle a gasp. My mouth goes dry and my heart starts racing. Can what it says be true? If so, I have to leave right now.

CHAPTER THIRTY-SIX

CLAIRE

Why on earth was Stephen Lang parked opposite the fairground? He's a single guy with no family that I'm aware of. Did he follow me to Wimborne? Or was he here for another reason? I caught his eye for a split second as he drove off and he looked decidedly guilty about something. Maybe he arrived before me, but I don't remember seeing his car when I got here. No, I walked along that stretch of pavement and he definitely wasn't there then. So why here? Why now?

Should I call the police? Probably not a great idea, because then I'd have to explain what I'm doing here. And I really don't want to get into all that. I grow cold at the thought of what I've just done – breaking into someone's camper van and scaring a young child. I feel ashamed of myself, even though I did it for my daughter. I know I said I'd do anything to get her back, but when does it become too much? When do my actions start crossing the line? I know the police have to follow the rules for a reason, but would anyone blame me for bending those rules if it meant saving my child?

I realise I'm still standing on the edge of the road. What must Monty and the other fairground workers think, seeing me frozen to the spot like this. I daren't turn around to see if they're still there, watching. I force myself to move. To walk away, back towards my car parked further up the road. As I walk, I draw my mind back to Lang. I'm sick of speculating about things. There's only one way to solve this. I'm going to ring him.

As a client of mine, his number is already in my contacts. I press call but it goes through to voicemail. Hopefully, he'll pick up the message once he stops driving.

'Hi, Stephen, it's Claire here. Claire Nolan. Look, I might be mistaken, but did I just see you opposite the showground in Wimborne? Can you give me a call back once you get this message? Thanks.'

I finally reach my car and slide into the driver's seat, my hot sweaty body crumpling against the black cloth. *What a day.* Is this what my life is going to be like now? Suspicion, disappointment and despair? A rollercoaster of emotions with no resolution at the end of it.

I try to recall what day of the week it is... pretty sure it's Thursday, but I wouldn't swear to it. That means it's almost a week since Beatrice went missing. I'm not sure how much more of this I can take. Not that I have a choice.

I'm not ready to throw in the towel. Unlike my husband, I'm still prepared to do whatever it takes to find my little girl. He hasn't even called or messaged to see how I am today. I think I'm done with him right now. Sickening though it is, I can't worry about his apparent lack of interest. I come to the realisation that, even if Oliver has given up, I have not. I will break into houses, lie, steal and crawl over broken glass to get my baby back.

First, I need to sort myself out. I'm not remotely hungry, but I have zero energy, my throat is dry and my stomach is hollow. I start up the car and begin the drive back to Christchurch.

My grocery trip yesterday was derailed by Jill's shoplifting debacle, so I decide to head back there now. The journey takes a little over half an hour and I zone out through most of it, my brain too exhausted to think.

The supermarket car park is off Soper's Lane, which will be gridlocked at this hour, so I try my luck along the high street. I shouldn't have bothered. There isn't a single parking spot to be had. Maybe I should give up and try to cobble something together from the leftovers at home. I'll give it one last shot and try Bridge Street car park before calling it a day.

My luck returns and I finally manage to get parked, although it's quite a walk back to M&S. The pavement is narrow, and the air is close. I'm absolutely dying for a drink of something cold. I'm dreaming of ice cubes clinking in a glass. I glance over the road to the café, wondering if I should nip in for a quick juice, when I spot Laurel in the window seat. I stop walking for a moment. It looks as though she's crying. The person opposite has her back to the window, but I'd recognise that stiff-backed posture anywhere – it's Jill.

Why do I get the feeling Laurel has met up with my mother-in-law to bitch about me? Probably because it's not hard to work out. Oh well, I'll leave them to it. Pity about the juice, but there's no way I'm going in there right now. I've had enough of Laurel to last the rest of the year.

I'm about to continue on my way when Jill gets abruptly to her feet and turns away from Laurel. She's clutching her phone and is staring at it with her mouth open. Laurel looks taken aback and starts speaking urgently to Jill. But my mother-in-law slings her bag over her shoulder and edges around the table. It looks like she's leaving.

I'm not sure what to do. I don't want either of them to see me, but I can't exactly run off down the road as that will only draw more attention. Instead, I turn around so my back is to the café and I pretend to be looking down at my phone. After thirty seconds or so, I throw a glance over my shoulder to see Jill hurrying off towards the high street. Why is she in such a rush? Did she get some news from Ollie? From the police? I would hope that if she's found out something about Beatrice, she would let me know.

With an anxious tug at my chest, I realise I have no choice but to follow her. If it's nothing, then it doesn't matter, but if it's something important then I need to know what it is. And right now I don't trust anyone, including Jill, to tell me the truth about anything.

When she reaches the end of Bridge Street, she turns left, heading towards the priory. Maybe she's going home. Maybe Laurel said something to upset Jill and she simply walked out on her, but that doesn't explain the look of shock on her face while she was staring at her phone. No. She definitely received some news. Something that's got her spooked.

I keep a good distance away, but I'm pretty sure Jill is too flustered to see me. And if she does, so what? I live in the same town, walk the same streets. If she spots me, I'll act innocent and just say hi. She enters the priory grounds and makes her way through the ancient graveyard, the thousand-year-old grey stone building untroubled by our fleeting lives.

Jill rounds the corner and walks down the narrow strip of road beyond the graveyard. It's darker down here beneath the press of the old buildings and the thickly leaved trees. I tense as Jill trips over her sandals and nearly goes flying. But she manages to steady herself on a lamp post. She stops for a moment, her hand on her chest, and I almost think about catching up to her to ask if she's okay. But what if she chooses not to confide in me? What if she and Laurel really are working together? I have to keep following her to see where she's going. To see if she actually might lead me to Beatrice.

My mind races forwards, thinking of possible scenarios that could have led to this. Maybe Jill was angry with me for not allowing her to spend time on her own with Beatrice. Maybe she enlisted Laurel's help to steal our little girl away. What if Oliver knows and that's why he's been funny with me? My skin tingles with dread at the thought. My theories all sound outlandish, but

I'm willing to entertain any possibility right now. Everything I've googled about children going missing seems to point to it nearly always being someone close to the child who's responsible – either a friend, an acquaintance or a family member.

So I steel myself against going to Jill's aid. Instead, I hang back and wait for her to recover her equilibrium. Still gripping her phone, she brings it up to stare at the screen before swiping it and bringing it to her ear. She waits and then starts speaking, but she's too far away for me to hear what she's saying. I take a few steps closer, but she's already ended the call and has started walking again. Instead of turning right to head towards her house, she walks into the busy car park. I hope she didn't leave her car here. My own car is all the way over in Bridge Street, so if she drives off, I'll lose her.

I needn't have worried. She strides along, her pace quickening once again as she aims for the pedestrian exit at the other end of the car park. And now she's turning right again, walking past Place Mill art gallery towards the quay and along the wide concrete path by the River Stour. The quomps, a huge grassy area alongside the footpath, is busy with people enjoying the weather. But they're all irrelevant, just a backdrop to what's going on here with Jill. Something is telling me that she's leading me towards something important. I feel it in my gut.

The brisk walk is making me sweat even more, and I'm so thirsty now that I'm almost tempted to ask a group of picnickers if they'll sell me a bottle of water. I don't, of course. There's no time for that. I swallow and try to think about something other than my thirst and light-headedness.

Where is it exactly that Jill's headed? She continues marching west, alongside the children's splash park and on past the rowing club where they're hauling boats out of the water and hosing them down on the shingle. As she passes the rowing club's car park, she starts to slow her pace. Maybe she's heading to the riverfront hotel?

I guess she could be meeting someone there. She stops before she reaches it, bearing left towards the jetty and joining the short queue for the Wick Ferry, the little boat that takes foot passengers across the River Stour between Wick village and Christchurch.

I stop where I am, just past the rowing clubhouse. This is tricky. If I want to keep following Jill without being seen, I obviously can't board the boat at the same time as she does. But if I wait for the next one, then I'll lose her. There's only one other option, and that's to race ahead to Tuckton Bridge, cross the river that way and double back. The thought makes me dizzy with exhaustion. I don't want to take my eye off Jill but need to get some energy from somewhere. I realise that I have a while as the Wick Ferry is still on the opposite bank.

I used to visit the rowing club with an ex-boyfriend when I was in my early twenties. I duck into the car park and head towards the clubhouse entrance, slipping in through the open door and puffing up the stairs. I almost cry with relief when I find that the bar is open.

The barman smiles. 'What can I get you?'

'An orange juice with ice, please, and do you have any chocolate?'

'I can do you the orange juice, but you'll have to get your chocolate from the machine.' He nods to a shiny vending machine in the corner.

'Amazing. Thanks so much.'

I pay for the juice and chug the whole glass in under thirty seconds. My body instantly perks up. I use the change to buy a Snickers bar which I cram into my mouth in huge bites, and a can of Tango and a bottle of water which I shove into my handbag. Fuelled up, I make my way back outside. I scan the ferry queue and see that Jill is still waiting there. My gamble paid off, so I start jogging towards Tuckton Bridge. The distance isn't too far, but the juice and chocolate in my gullet are not exactly enjoying themselves. Plus, I'm not that fit, and the sun is still lasering down.

Thank goodness for my baseball cap. I'm soon across the bridge and onto the opposite river bank, coming up behind the Wick Ferry just as it reaches the dock, disgorging its five passengers, one of whom is Jill.

Instead of continuing west towards Tuckton, Jill walks away from the river towards Wick village. It's trickier to follow her here as the path is narrow and twisty, overhung with trees. I can't lose her now. Not after making it this far. I catch my breath as I spot her again, heading back towards the river. She's on the path, heading east this time. Where on earth is she going? This is more than strange. My heart hammers in my ears. Is she going to lead me to my daughter?

She keeps up the pace and I pray she doesn't turn around because this riverbank is far quieter than the Christchurch side. I've only seen a couple of other people walk by. The smell of the river is stronger here too – a warm, loamy, earthy scent of water and reeds that makes me think of oily depths and white-eyed fish. I shudder. While Jill stays on the path, I stick close to the treeline, so that I can duck behind some foliage if I need to.

Suddenly she stops and shoots a glance behind her. Thankfully, the path is empty as I'm now skulking beneath the trees. Seconds later, she looks down at her phone before sidling over to a ratty old boat that looks as though it's been moored on this quiet bend in the river for decades. It's cream and brown with a mossy canopy and low windows which hint at dark cabins below.

I edge closer along the bank, only a few feet away from Jill now. My heart is in my throat as I watch her approach the boat. Wait to see what she does next.

I daren't allow myself to hope that Beatrice might be inside.

CHAPTER THIRTY-SEVEN

JILL

Through the green-slimed canopy window, I can see that the cockpit area of the boat is empty. It looks abandoned, like no one has tended to it for years. That text message scared the life out of me. One minute I was sitting in the café listening to Laurel's woes, the next, I'm hurrying along the riverbank to reach... this old boat, and whatever lies inside. I should rush in there and go down into the cabins, but I'm absolutely terrified at what I might find.

Whoever sent me that text did so to scare me. To taunt me. To lead me here. They sent me a photograph of this boat with the caption:

> *Want to know where Beatrice has been? Come right now. On the river, opposite the rowing club. Take the Wick Ferry. Don't tell ANYONE. Make sure you come alone. From a friend.*

Reading it sent actual shivers down my spine. Now that I'm here, I don't know what I'm supposed to do. I can't see through the murky cabin windows and I have no idea who, if anyone, is inside. What if the abductor is down there waiting to do me harm? But my Bea could be down there, in any state. I need to be brave. *Can I be brave?* I wish I at least had some kind of weapon; a stick or a rock or something. Even if I did, being realistic, anyone could probably overpower me. I'll just have to go in there and hope for the best.

My pulse is racing so fast I'm scared I may have a heart attack. *Come on, Jill, you can do this.* I reach forward and unzip the canvas door. The plastic teeth of the zip are in surprisingly good condition, and the flap opens easily. I hold onto the wooden mooring post and step onto the lip of the boat, hoping to goodness I don't lose my balance and end up in the water.

'Hello!' I call out as I step into the boiling hot interior. The air in here smells stale, of old fish and rotting wood. The blood pumps through my veins and my ears feel as though they need to pop. 'Beatrice, darling, are you in here? It's Granny!'

'Jill!'

I turn at the sound of my name being called, and I'm confused to see a woman coming down the riverbank towards me. She's dressed in denim shorts, a black T-shirt, baseball cap and dark glasses. Could this be the abductor? Should I step back onto the path? Or continue on down to the cabin to search for my granddaughter?

'Jill, it's me.' The woman removes her sunglasses and I see that it's my daughter-in-law!

'Claire! I didn't recognise you in that hat and glasses. What are you doing here?'

'What? I should ask you the same question. Why are *you* here? Who's boat is this? Is it yours?' Claire jabs her sunglasses at me. 'Is Beatrice here? What have you done with her Jill?'

I step off the boat for a minute, back onto the pathway. '*What?* I haven't done anything with her!'

'Right. So why did I just hear you calling out her name?' Claire folds her arms over her chest for a second before pushing past me and pulling back the flap of the cockpit. 'Is she down there? You better not have harmed a hair on her head!' My daughter-in-law's face is white with fury, her hands shaking. I can't believe she thinks I might have had anything to do with my granddaughter's abduction.

'Claire, hold on a minute, let me explain.'

'Explain?' she spits. 'There's nothing that can explain this.' She turns away and stoops to open the inner door that leads down below deck.

'Claire!' I follow her on board. 'Just listen to me!'

She's panting and trembling. 'Beatrice!' she cries, pulling at the door handle which is miraculously unlocked. 'Bea, it's Mummy, I'm coming!' Claire doesn't wait for my explanation, but rushes down the few stairs into a dank-smelling, dark galley area with a fake-wood table and grey velour banquette seats. There are two old sandwich packets on the table and a couple of small empty plastic water bottles lying on their side.

'Don't touch anything!' I cry.

'What do you mean?' she asks, continuing on through the kitchenette to what appear to be the sleeping quarters. 'Beatrice! Bea, it's Mum. It's me!'

'No, I mean you really can't.' I follow her. 'Don't you watch crime dramas? You'll contaminate the scene. If Beatrice is in there, or was in there at some time, it needs to stay exactly how it is, so the police will have a better chance of finding who took her.' I grab her arm. 'Claire! Stop, and listen to me.' My daughter-in-law's arrival has kick-started something in me. Instead of the nervous wreck I was a few minutes ago, I'm suddenly determined to be the one who's sensible and does the right thing for a change. Instead of being scatty and messing things up.

Claire shrugs me off and goes into first one cabin and then the other, finally wrenching opening the bathroom door, using her mobile phone torch to see in the gloom. 'She's not here! Tell me where she is, Jill! Why isn't she here?' Her hands press on her stomach and she stares at me with desperation in her eyes. 'Are there any cupboards or other places she could be hidden?'

'I don't know, like I'm trying to tell you, I've never been here before. Look!' I thrust my phone into her hands and she looks down at the captioned photo of the boat. Maybe now she'll listen to me. 'That message is the reason I'm here. I was having a chat with Laurel when someone sent me this. That's the only reason I'm here, Claire. I know as much as you do about this boat.'

'So why did they send you this message if she's not even here?' Claire glances wildly around and I retrieve my phone from her. 'Who sent it? It says, "a friend". What friend?'

'I don't know. I don't recognise the number.' A thought strikes me. 'How did you know I was here?'

'What? Oh. I saw you come out of the café and I followed you.'

'Why would you follow me?'

Claire sidles past me back into the galley shining her phone light around the dingy room. 'Because you looked like you were going somewhere in a hurry, and I wondered—' She breaks off. 'What's that?' She points to something on the floor tucked under the banquette, her torch beam highlighting it. 'Looks like a scrap of material.' She stoops down and reaches out.

'Don't touch it,' I advise.

Thankfully, she listens this time and withdraws her hand. I stare at the item in question and my fingers fly to my mouth as I realise that I recognise the gauzy blue material.

'Laurel's scarf,' I murmur.

'What did you say?' Claire snaps her head around to look at me.

'That's Laurel's scarf. She said she misplaced it. Asked me if I'd seen it.'

'Shit. Do you think…'

But I don't hear what Claire is saying as my gaze has travelled to the area beneath the table, where I spy something that makes my blood freeze in my veins. This time I use my own phone torch to highlight the area. There, on the floor, sitting in a puddle of light, are a pair of glittery red sandals. The same red sandals that Beatrice was wearing on the evening she disappeared.

CHAPTER THIRTY-EIGHT

CLAIRE

I follow Jill's eyeline to see just what it is that has caused her mouth to fall open. As I take in the familiar sight of my daughter's favourite red sandals, a dark chill snakes its way down my spine. 'Are those…?'

Jill turns to look at me. 'Bea's sandals,' she whispers.

The sound of an engine thrums outside. Water slaps against the side of the boat. Is my mother-in-law to be trusted? The anonymous text she received corroborates her story, but, then again, couldn't that have been contrived to throw me off the scent? I honestly don't know what to think any more.

I'm aching to snatch up Bea's glittery sandals and cradle them in my arms, but I know I must leave them exactly where they are. Like Jill said, the police won't want us to touch anything. 'She was here.' I exhale. 'Beatrice was here, on this horrible boat.'

'It looks that way,' Jill replies. The two of us are still rooted to the spot. 'And if that's Laurel's scarf, then…'

We turn to stare at one another, conclusions forming.

'The sandwich packets!' Jill cries.

'What are you talking about?'

'There are a couple of empty sandwich packets on the table.' She shines her phone over the water bottles and the empty cartons. 'What were the fillings in the sandwiches?'

We shift around to get a better view. I read one of them. 'Plain cheese on white bread – sounds like something Bea would pick.'

'The other one's egg mayo on wholemeal – Laurel's favourite.' Jill shakes her head.

Laurel's scarf and Beatrice's sandals... the empty sandwich cartons... there's only one conclusion to be drawn from that.

'We need to find Laurel.' I turn to leave, ducking my head to make my way up the stairs and onto the deck. I'm desperate to be off this boat, to breathe in fresh air, rather than the stagnant stench of the cabin.

'No,' Jill cries. 'You can't tip off Laurel. If she knows we're on to her, she might do something stupid. She could hide Beatrice or try to flee.'

I push my way out of the cockpit, through the canvas door and back onto the footpath once more, squinting into the brightness, gulping down the warm but fresh air. Jill follows close behind.

'Did you hear what I said?' Jill's face is screwed up against the sun's evening rays.

'Yes, don't worry.' My mind is whirring. In among the panic and shock, I can't believe that Jill is being the sensible one right now. The one with the clear head. 'Do you think Bea's been here this whole time, in that horrible dark boat? I can't bear to think of my daughter shut up down there.'

Jill pulls at the skin on her neck. 'I don't know.'

'So where is she now?' Something else suddenly occurs to me. 'I still don't understand that text.'

'What do you mean?' Jill's face is ashen. She puts a hand on one of the wooden posts to steady herself. She's in shock with everything that's happening. We both are.

'I mean, who sent it? Who tipped you off, and why?'

Jill swallows. 'I don't know. Maybe Laurel's been working with someone else. Philip maybe?'

'Show me the text again.'

Jill swipes her screen and holds it out for me to see:

Want to know where Beatrice has been? Come right now. On the river, opposite the rowing club. Take the Wick Ferry. Don't tell ANYONE. Make sure you come alone. From a friend.

I think for a second, trying to make sense of it. 'So the texter wanted you to come here alone. Did they know her sandals would be here? And Laurel's scarf, or were they left there by mistake?'

'And the sandwich wrappers,' Jill adds, rubbing her forehead. 'We have to call the police. Perhaps they'll be able to make sense of it.'

'Someone was definitely trying to help us by sending you the text, right?'

'Not necessarily.' Jill shakes her head and swipes at her phone. She shows me the screen. 'This was sent to me by the same person.'

I read the text:

How could you lose your own granddaughter?

'That's horrible!'

Jill nods as the phone begins to shake in her trembling hands. 'I told the police about the first text, but they said these types of messages are par for the course. Apparently, there are a lot of nasty people out there. The fact they've sent me this new, specific message must mean that they really are something to do with Bea's disappearance.'

I nod in agreement. 'I wonder who owns the boat. Maybe that will shed some light.' I let my shoulders relax for a second and rub my collarbone, trying not to get my hopes up. Could this be the breakthrough we've been waiting for? I also have the unwelcome thought that this could simply be the abductor playing sick games, trying to mislead us.

Jill makes a call to the police and, from then on, everything seems to move at lightning speed, as though we're in a movie on fast forward. DI Khatri and DS Garrett are first on the scene. They take a brief look inside the boat before taking Jill's phone, saying that they'll need it to try to trace the origin of the text. They interview us here, going over everything from the moment Jill met Laurel at the coffee shop earlier. We also tell them that the empty sandwich cartons once contained both Bea and Laurel's favourite sandwiches.

Finally, they let us take a breather and the two of us walk back towards the bridge and sit on the grassy riverbank a short distance away from the boat. Meanwhile, the officers set up a cordon blocking off the area around the boat. Apparently CSI are on their way to do a thorough search, while other officers try to locate the boat's owner.

Jill clears her throat. 'We should let Oliver know what's happening.'

The mention of my husband's name makes my stomach drop. I don't want to admit to her that Ollie and I are barely speaking at the moment. That I can't even think about him right now because if I do I'll either cry or scream. I'm also nervous to find out if he's been drinking again.

'Do you want to call him?'

Jill nods and reaches into her bag for her phone, but comes up empty-handed. 'The police took my mobile, remember?'

I call his number and hand my phone to my mother-in-law. She looks surprised, but takes it from me.

'I'll tell him to come here, shall I?' She interprets my silence as a yes and puts my phone to her ear. After a moment's pause, she starts talking. He's obviously not picking up because she leaves a message. 'Oliver, it's Mum. Claire and I think we've found who took Bea. You need to come here as soon as you get this message. We're at the river on the Wick side almost opposite the rowing club. You can't miss us. The police are here. Okay, Ollie, hopefully see you soon.'

She ends the call and passes back my phone, giving me an appraising look which I ignore. 'What's going on with you two?'

'Our daughter's missing,' I reply bluntly.

'You know what I mean. Why aren't you together, supporting one another? It's not like you, or him, to be so… separate.'

'You'll have to ask Oliver about that.' I get to my feet. 'Will you excuse me; I'm just going to stretch my legs. I need to get away, from here' – I gesture to the boat and the increasing number of officers – 'for a few moments.'

Jill doesn't reply and I don't look at her face for a reaction. Instead, I head up the bank, away from the river. After a couple of minutes, I find myself in the tiny village of Wick with its pretty cottages and well-tended gardens. There's no pavement, so I hug the verge and try to avoid eye contact with the families and couples out for an early evening stroll. I shouldn't have walked this way. It's too unsettling to be surrounded by such happy normality. After fifteen minutes, I give up and turn around.

When I return to the river, Jill is standing on the footpath talking to DI Khatri. Jill catches my eye. 'Oh, here she is. Claire, the inspector says we can go home, but to stay close to a phone in case they need to talk to us.'

'Okay.' I turn to DI Khatri. 'Are you going to speak to Laurel?'

'We're bringing her into the station. I'm on my way over there now. In light of what we've found in the boat pertaining to Laurel Palmer, we'll also bring your neighbour Philip Aintree in for questioning and will get CSI to do a proper sweep of his house. In the meantime, you head home and have a rest. You both look done in.'

I feel reassured by what she's telling me, but I won't be able to rest until I'm holding my little girl in my arms again. 'Please find her,' I beg.

'We'll do everything we can,' Khatri replies kindly but non-committally.

'Surely this is a breakthrough,' Jill adds. 'Finding Beatrice's shoes here, and Laurel's scarf?'

'It's progress.' Khatri looks over to her right. 'If you'll excuse me, looks like CSI has arrived. DS Hobart or I will call you if there's any news.' That's basically us dismissed. Khatri walks towards the approaching officers, but I don't pay too much attention because behind them, I spot Oliver jogging along the path, his face flushed, brow creased. He nods to the DI but heads straight for me and Jill. He looks sober, but I'll find out soon enough.

'I got your message,' he pants, stopping in front of us. 'Came straight away. What's happened? Did they find Bea? Is she here? She okay?'

I'm so relieved that Oliver isn't slurring his words, that his breath doesn't reek of alcohol. 'They haven't found her yet.'

His face falls. 'But they know who did it?'

We move up onto the grass again, out of the way of the police activity. Jill and I spend the next few minutes filling in Oliver on what's happened. We have to go over it several times, but I understand that. I'd be the same; wanting every tiny detail.

'I can't believe it's Laurel,' he keeps repeating over and over. 'I thought I knew her. I was married to her for over five years, for goodness' sake. How can she have done this? It can't be her, surely.'

'I might have to go home,' Jill says, sitting down heavily on the grass. 'I don't feel too good.'

'Oh, Mum, I'm not surprised.' Oliver crouches down next to her.

'I don't think I'll be able to walk all the way home. I'm a bit dizzy.'

Remembering the can of Tango I bought earlier, I reach into my bag and pull it out. 'Your blood sugar's probably low and you might be a bit dehydrated. Sip this.'

'You're an angel.' Jill takes the can from me with trembling hands. I've never seen her look so frail. Over the top of her head,

Ollie gives me a grateful smile. I'm not quite ready to smile back at him, but I manage a small nod. 'That's better,' Jill says, holding out the can. 'Does anyone else want some?'

Oliver and I both decline.

'Do you think you're up to walking a short way, Mum? I'm parked in the village so it's only a minute's walk.'

'Oh, that's music to my ears. Yes, let's go. Drop me home, will you, darling?'

'Of course.' Oliver helps her to her feet.

We give a short wave to Khatri and Garrett before heading through the trees to Oliver's Passat. I'm already dreading the moment we drop Jill off at her house and I'm left alone in the car with my husband. How can I be civil to the man who's supposed to be my partner in life, my best friend, the one I love, yet who abandoned me when I needed him the most? Who also abandoned the search for his seven-year-old daughter? The short answer is: I can't.

CHAPTER THIRTY-NINE

CLAIRE

After driving his mother home, Oliver takes me to the Bridge Street car park to pick up my Toyota. The journey there is all kinds of uncomfortable. Dusk is falling, which only adds to the dark, sullen atmosphere. Oliver says he'll meet me back at home, but I'm finding it hard to believe he'll be there when I get back; he's lied so many times this week. However, when I finally turn into our road, the first thing I see is Oliver's car parked in the drive. I'm dreading going into the house. I don't have the energy for an argument. Maybe I should check into a hotel for the night, avoid the confrontation.

Muscle memory kicks in, and I find myself turning into our driveway and trudging up the steps. I stand outside the front door for a moment while I locate the key. Before I have the opportunity to slot it into the lock, the door swings open. Oliver stands in front of me.

'I wasn't sure you'd come home,' he says.

'I nearly didn't.'

He steps back to give me room.

I walk past him. 'I need a shower.'

'Are you hungry? I'll make food.'

I shrug. 'There's not a lot in the fridge.' I realise that I never made it to the supermarket.

'I picked up some bits earlier.' Oliver's trying to get me to engage, but I'm not biting.

'Oh. Right.' I continue on up the stairs, scowling like a sulky teenager but unable to help myself.

'I'll do us some pasta, okay?' he calls after me.

I mumble something incoherent.

Once I've showered and changed, I begin to feel a little more human. At least Oliver's home and sober for a change. I should give him a chance to make it up to me. I need him right now. We need each other. But I'm still so furious that I don't know how to forgive him. I reluctantly head back downstairs to the delicious garlicky aroma of something cooking.

It's already dark outside, the kitchen illuminated by the bright overhead lights. Oliver stands at the stove, steam swirling around him. The table is laid. There's fresh, green salad in a bowl and a jug of iced water on the table.

Ollie turns around with a hesitant smile on his lips. 'Do you feel any better? Want a glass of wine? I'm not going to drink in case we need to drive to the station.'

He's trying to impress me. To win back my affection with his offer of a nice meal and staying sober. 'No thanks. I want a clear head in case… of anything.' I sit and pour myself a glass of water, ice cubes clinking into my glass.

'Pasta's ready. Shall I dish up?'

'Sure. Thanks.' My words are clipped, emotionless.

He offers me black pepper and shaved parmesan. He's really gone all out, but it's going to take more than a bowl of pasta to erase his actions. Oliver sits and we start to eat. The food is good and I realise that I'm absolutely starving. I don't think I've eaten a proper meal in days. But I also feel guilty for enjoying it. How can I enjoy anything while Beatrice is missing?

After a couple of minutes of us eating in silence, Oliver puts his fork down. 'Claire, I need to explain something to you.' He cracks his knuckles and cricks his neck from side to side like he's a fighter about to get into the ring.

My food starts to stick in my throat. I sip some water to try to wash it down. 'Explain what?'

'Okay, so these past few days… I haven't been completely honest with you.' He pushes his dark-brown hair off his face and fixes me with those green eyes; the ones that usually make me forget why I'm mad at him. *Not this time.* He clears his throat. 'I've been getting anonymous messages.' He pauses. 'From Beatrice's abductor.'

I stare at him, trying to absorb what he's telling me. 'You've been *what?*' The room suddenly feels too small, too hot, too bright. I get to my feet and then sit back down again.

'Claire, I have absolutely hated leaving you on your own this week. It's been making me sick to my stomach. But these messages said that I had to stay away from you and Mum and the house. And that if I didn't stay away, they would harm Beatrice.'

'*What!* Show me. Let me see these messages.'

Ollie comes around the table, drags a chair next to me and sits. He takes his phone from his pocket and scrolls back to the beginning of the messages which we read together in silence. They're short and to the point, making it clear that Oliver has to do as they say or Beatrice will suffer. This explains everything! His disappearances, his lack of support, all his strange and out-of-character behaviour. I suddenly understand how truly awful this week must have been for my husband. How *terrifying*. I realise, with a rush of relief, that he hadn't given up after all.

This time I get up and remain on my feet, pulling at my damp hair and stumbling over to the back door, throwing it wide open and gulping down breaths of the – only marginally – cooler night air. My mind is a jumble of emotions. Shock at this new information, relief that there's some kind of explanation for Oliver's behaviour, terror that our daughter is with the person sending these messages, but also a sharp surge of anger that Oliver hadn't confided in me sooner. I turn back to face my husband who's now standing at the table watching me carefully.

'Why didn't you tell me?' I cry. 'Why did you let me think you'd given up? That you didn't care?'

'Because I wasn't allowed to. You saw the messages. They said they'd know if I told you or the police. I don't know how true that is, but I couldn't risk it. I'm really sorry about getting drunk though – that was on me. I felt so trapped in the situation. *Useless.* When I saw what my behaviour was doing to you, I thought our marriage was going to fall apart as well as us losing Bea.'

'How do you even know the messages are from the abductor? It could have been any nutcase sending them.'

'I asked for proof.' Oliver looks as if he's about to break down. His voice hitches as he whispers, 'They sent me a photo.'

'Of *Beatrice*?' I almost scream her name. The blood is whooshing in my ears and I stagger back to the table, sitting down heavily. Everything looks alien – the food, the glasses, my husband's face. It's all distorted and blurry.

'Breathe, Claire.' Oliver's crouched by my side holding my hand. 'Just breathe.'

'What was the photo?' I pant. 'Don't tell me if it's bad. I can't… I don't…'

'It's not bad,' Oliver soothes. 'Bea was sitting on the grass holding out a copy of the *Argus* – the one with my mum on the front page.'

'On the grass? Was there anything in the background? Show me the photo.'

Oliver pulls his phone from his pocket and spends a moment getting the message up on the screen. This one was sent to his WhatsApp account.

I take it from him greedily. Eager to see my baby. 'Oh!' There she is. *Beatrice*. She's wearing an unfamiliar outfit – a green-and-white sundress. Her dark hair falls around her face in tangled waves.

She's staring at the camera unsmiling, but she doesn't look scared either. There's nothing around her but grass; nothing to identify the landscape. I breathe in the image of my daughter. Fill my lungs with the knowledge that she's safe. Then I turn to snarl at my husband. '*She's alive!* She's alive and you didn't tell me! How could you not tell me?'

He straightens and takes a step back, momentarily shocked by my outburst. 'I'm sorry.'

'*Sorry?* Do you know all the things I've been thinking? Do you know how terrified I've been? How I've been desperately trying not to imagine the worst? You could have stopped those fears in an instant!'

'I know. Believe me, I know. But I couldn't tell you. What if I *had* told you and they harmed her? I would never have forgiven myself. And *you* wouldn't either. It was a terrible choice between letting you suffer and worry, and risking them harming our daughter. What would you have done, Claire? In my position?'

I set Ollie's phone on the table, splay my fingers and close my eyes for a second, trying to halt my shuddering breaths.

Oliver continues, 'I wanted to tell you so badly. In a way it was good that I wasn't "allowed" to stay in the house, because if I had, I think I would have cracked and told you everything. While I was out all day, I was trying to figure out a way to identify the person responsible. Trying to work out how to find Beatrice, but I couldn't do it. I couldn't think straight.'

'Do you think the photo's real?' I snatch up his phone again and swipe the screen to stare at the image of my daughter.

Oliver's eyes widen. 'Real? I didn't... oh no, I didn't even consider the possibility that...' His words trail off and he bends to look at the photo again. 'It looks real enough.'

I scan the photo. That's her body, the way she sits – the mole on her arm. And that's definitely her face and hair. I snap my head around to stare at him. 'Why are you telling me all this now, if you were so dead set against telling me before?'

My husband picks up his phone, takes a sip of water. 'The police have got Laurel, right? She's the one sending the anonymous texts. They said they'd brought her in for questioning. Surely it's only a matter of time before she tells them where she's moved Beatrice.'

'That's if it really is Laurel who's behind this.'

'What do you mean?' Oliver's eyes narrow. 'Her scarf was there. Bea's shoes. The sandwich wrappers. Pretty conclusive.'

'I hope so. No, I'm sure it is.'

'I haven't received any new messages since she's been taken to the station. I would normally have received one by now. I always got one in the morning and another in the evening.'

We sit in silence for a short while as my brain ratchets through all this new and shocking information, trying to take everything in.

Eventually, Oliver breaks the silence. 'So do you see why I did it? Why I had to leave you alone each day?'

I nod. 'I do. I really do.' I should be happy that my husband wasn't being the terrible, selfish bastard I had thought. That he was putting Bea's safety before everything. But I'm so exhausted I can't think straight. 'Where is she, Oll? If the police have got Laurel, then where's our daughter?'

'They'll find her,' he replies, grim-faced. 'Hopefully, they'll bring her home this evening.'

I shake my head slowly. 'It actually makes sense that it's Laurel.'

'Why do you say that?' Ollie gets up and starts clearing away our half-eaten meal, scraping the congealed pasta into the bin.

'Because she's obviously still in love with you.'

Oliver stops and turns. '*What?* No she's not.' His face screws up in disbelief.

'Yes she is. She still sees your mum every week, for a start. What's that about?'

'They're friends.'

'Right. Friends, because Jill is so on Laurel's wavelength.'

Doubt creeps into Oliver's voice. 'She is, kind of.'

'Okay, so if it's not about you, then what's her motive?' I smear a stray blob of pasta sauce across the table with my fingertip.

'Fine.' Oliver's shoulder's sag.

'I'm not saying it's your fault, Oll. I'm just saying that it makes sense that it's her. Think about it. The phone call to your mum at the fair, her in next door's shed with Philip – that's just weird. Do you think he's been helping her?'

Oliver's face darkens. 'If he's touched our daughter, I'll kill him.'

My mind jumps to Ollie's recent revelation. 'We have to show the police the messages she sent you. And the photo of Bea.' I scrape my chair back and get to my feet. 'Come on, let's go to the station. We can also find out what's going on with Laurel and Philip at the same time. See if either of them has confessed yet.'

'Okay. Do you think it's safe to show them the messages?' Oliver stands. 'I mean, I know we're pretty sure Laurel's behind it, but if she isn't…'

'You've already told *me*.'

'Yes, but I doubt they'll find that out, it's easier to keep that quiet. We can't keep it quiet if we tell the police.'

'Oh, Ollie, I don't know…' I'm suddenly starting to doubt my conviction that Laurel's guilty. 'I'd really like to show them the photo though, get them to check whether it's real or fake.'

'Tell you what,' he says, 'let's go to the station and see if they've managed to get a confession out of Laurel. If they have, then it won't matter.'

'Good idea.' My phone buzzes and I see that it's a voicemail from Stephen Lang replying to my message. I'd almost forgotten about him and my visit to the fair, but I guess that's all irrelevant now. I put the phone to my ear and listen.

'*Uh, hello, Claire. I, uh, got your message. We can meet for a drink if you like. I can be free any time this evening. Uh, let me know. Thanks.*'

I can't deal with Lang right now. He's obviously got a bit of a crush and has taken my message the wrong way.

'Who was that?' Oliver looks at me closely.

'Just a client – Stephen Lang.'

'Shall we go?'

'Yep, coming. Just let me lock the back door. I'll drive.' As I fumble with the key, my nerves are jangling. But overriding everything is the tentative hope that I might be reunited with my daughter very soon.

DAY SEVEN

I didn't send Oliver a message last night or this morning. He thinks he's off the hook. They all do.
    They're not.

CHAPTER FORTY

JILL

I sit at Oliver and Claire's kitchen table, sipping a tall glass of iced coffee as morning sunlight warms the room, and strangely I feel more a part of my family than I ever have before. When I arrived forty minutes ago, Ollie and Claire were both solicitous and thoughtful, asking how I am after yesterday when it had all been so overwhelming, discovering the boat and Bea's sandals.

They tell me that, although they don't know where Beatrice is, apparently she's safe. The abductor sent them a photograph of her as proof that she's unharmed. So, as we're now 99 per cent sure that the abductor is Laurel, we're hoping she'll be found and brought home today. I can hardly dare to hope that this nightmare might all soon be a distant memory.

I still can't believe that Laurel is behind it. She was my daughter-in-law and, even after she and Oliver split, I still thought of her as family. I now can't help looking back at our whole relationship through this new horrific lens. That she could be capable of doing this, of putting my family through so much grief... it's shocking. Could she really have set me up with that phone call at the fairground? Taken Beatrice? Pretended to be helping, when in reality she's behind the whole thing?

Oliver keeps squeezing my shoulder and Claire has been genuinely kind, asking if I managed to get enough sleep last night, and telling me to stay for lunch. I'm glad to see that things seem better between them than they were yesterday; they're easier with one another and with me. If my granddaughter were here safe and well, I would be truly happy right now.

'Are you sure I can't make you any breakfast, Mum?' Oliver gets a knife out of the drawer as his toast pops out of the toaster.

'I'm fine, darling. This coffee's lovely, Claire.' I'm trying to stay calm and act normally for the sake of Oliver and Claire, but inside my stomach churns with tense anticipation while we wait for news.

Claire brings her glass over to the table and sits next to me.

I shift in my seat and smooth my dress. 'I can't understand why the police still haven't located Beatrice. Surely after questioning Laurel, they should know where she is.'

'I know.' Claire frowns. 'I was sure we'd hear something last night. We even went to the station to see if there was any news, but they just sent us home saying they'd be in touch with any updates. The waiting's painful. I feel sick with nerves. I don't think I can stomach this coffee.' She pushes it away and brings her hands up to her cheeks.

The doorbell rings and Claire and I both freeze and stare at one another.

'I'll get it.'

Oliver strides out of the kitchen while Claire and I rise from the table. We're both wondering if this might be the good news we're waiting for. I hear a woman's voice. Claire leaves the kitchen but I stay where I am, hovering beside the table. They return to the kitchen seconds later in the company of a neat brunette in her thirties. The woman is wearing smartish grey trousers and a short-sleeve lemon blouse, small gold studs in her ears.

'Mum, this is DS Gayle Hobart. I don't think you've met. Gayle, this is my mother, Jill Nolan.'

'Hello, DS... Hobart,' I say awkwardly, not sure how to address her.

We shake hands.

'Hello, please call me Gayle.'

Claire edges back around the table. 'Would you like a drink, Gayle? Is there any news?'

Gayle smiles. 'I'll have a tea please.'

'I'll make it,' Oliver says to Claire. 'You sit and finish your coffee.'

Claire touches his forearm and retakes her seat.

Gayle sits, encompassing us all in her gaze. 'I'm here to update you, but before I do, I think it's best to say up front there's still no news on where Beatrice is.'

The room deflates. You can hear it, the sudden shrinking of sound, the shrivelling of hope.

'I'm sorry,' Gayle continues. 'This doesn't mean anything bad. It's just that we're not there yet. At least we know she's out there somewhere unharmed if that photograph is anything to go by.'

'So it's a real photo?' Oliver asks. 'Not a fake?'

'It's real,' Gayle confirms.

Oliver, Claire and I let out a collective sigh.

Gayle carries on. 'Laurel Palmer and Philip Aintree are still answering questions, but they both deny having anything to do with Beatrice's disappearance. Ms Palmer says she doesn't know how her scarf ended up in the barge. Apparently, she misplaced it during the search party last week, which she says you can confirm, Jill.' Gayle turns her attention solely onto me, and I feel heat flood my cheeks.

'Oh. Well, she did mention something about misplacing her scarf, but I can't confirm that she did. Only that she *said* she did, if that makes sense?'

Gayle gives me a non-committal nod. 'Ms Palmer suggested that someone could have planted her scarf on the boat.'

'What about the sandwich wrappers and water bottles?' Claire asks. 'Did you do a DNA test?'

Gayle tucks a strand of hair behind her ear. 'We tested for prints, and they do have both Ms Palmer's and Beatrice's fingerprints on them.'

Claire shakes her head and clamps her teeth together in fury. 'That bitch,' she hisses.

'Wow!' Oliver slumps back against the counter. 'So it really was Laurel.'

Gayle keeps going. 'We can't jump to conclusions. Ms Palmer says she has no idea how her prints got on there.' Gayle pauses. 'There is one strange thing... they also found *Jill's* prints on the egg mayo sandwich and on one of the water bottles.' She directs her gaze to me.

'What?' My hand flies to my throat. 'That's impossible. I'm sure I didn't touch anything while I was on the boat. I remember when I followed you in there I was thinking that we shouldn't touch anything. In fact, I'm sure I told you the same thing.'

'That's right.' Claire nods. 'You did.'

I screw up my face, trying to remember. 'Although... my mind was all over the place, so I guess it *is* possible.' I scratch the top of my head. 'Maybe I did inadvertently touch them. I really don't remember.'

The police took all our prints and DNA samples at the start of the investigation – I suppose situations like this are the reason why. Gayle is staring at me without any kind of expression on her face. Oliver and Claire are darting glances from her to me. There's a lump in my throat. They surely can't think that I had anything to do with this.

I turn to my daughter-in-law. 'Did I touch the wrapper, Claire?'

She shakes her head. 'To be honest, Jill, I really can't remember. We were both in such a state.'

Gayle nods and turns her focus back on me. 'The DI might want to talk to you at some point, Jill. But I'll let her know what you said, okay?'

'Okay.' I've suddenly gone all jittery again. The warm, hopeful feeling I had earlier has evaporated to be replaced by genuine fear that they might actually believe I'm guilty of having something to do with my granddaughter's disappearance. No. It's nonsense.

Gayle continues her update. 'Although we were unable to get the specific location, we discovered that the message Jill received yesterday originated from the Christchurch area. So we're confident the person responsible is still local.'

I nod. 'Okay. The other thing I was wondering is how could Laurel have sent me the message, when I was with her at the time I received it?'

'She could still have sent it,' Claire says. 'All it takes is a tap of her finger.'

'True.' Oliver's jaw tightens. 'Or it could have been Phil who sent it.'

'Speaking of which…' Gayle pulls something out of her bag and passes it to me. 'Here's your phone back.'

'Oh, thank you.'

'We found the boat's owner by contacting Bournemouth Water Leisure about the mooring. It's owned by a gentleman who's been living in Portugal for the past two and a half years. He hasn't been back to the UK in almost a year, and was upset to hear that his boat had been broken into.'

'And you believe him?' Oliver asks, his shoulders tensing.

'We're checking out his story.'

'You've been working hard,' I say. 'Thank you.'

She nods at me with half a raised eyebrow and I somehow feel as though my words came across as patronising. Or like I'm trying to be the teacher's pet by praising her. I didn't mean it that way. I only meant to be appreciative.

A noise from the hall has us all turning our heads.

'Was that the front door?' Claire stands.

I suddenly feel quite shaky. 'Has someone just let themselves in?'

CHAPTER FORTY-ONE

JILL

'Hello!' A female voice drifts down the hall. 'Claire? Are you in? Your front door was unlocked.' Freya walks into the kitchen with a cautious expression.

We all relax when we see who it is, but there's also a wave of disappointment that it's not Beatrice, the one person we're all desperate to see.

Freya must see something in our expressions because her face falls. 'Hi, oh, I'm sorry, I didn't realise you had company. I'll come back another time.'

'Don't be silly, come in.' Claire gives her a hug and makes the introductions. But Gayle gets up from her seat. 'I'll get going.'

'You don't have to go,' Claire says.

'Sorry,' Freya says again. 'I've obviously come at a busy time. Honestly, I'll leave you guys to get on with…'

But Gayle is already on her way out. 'I'll call if there's any more news.'

'Sorry,' Oliver calls after her, 'I forgot to make your tea.'

'It's fine.' Gayle turns and gives him a rueful smile before turning to my daughter-in-law. 'Don't worry, Claire. You look after your guest. I'll see myself out.'

Freya looks a bit flustered. 'Sorry, I just stopped by to see how you're all doing and if there's been any news. I brought a loaf of

Mum's bread and some jam. They send their love, by the way.'
Freya plonks a paper bag on the counter and sits opposite me.
'Nice to see you, Jill. How are you doing?'

'A bit shaken if you must know. This whole business is just—'

'It's terrible, I know. I can't even imagine what you're all going
through.' Freya shakes her head and blows air out through her mouth,
her blue eyes filling with emotion. 'I just wish I could do something
more. Has there been any progress? Was that woman here about…?'

'She's a detective, our family liaison officer.' Oliver leans against
the counter, filling Freya in on the past twenty-four hours while
I sit quietly, trying not to fly into another almighty panic. Why
were my prints on that sandwich packet? Did I really touch it? I
honestly don't think I did, because I remember being quite forceful
with Claire that she should not touch anything. So why would
I then go and do the very thing that I was telling her not to? I
wasn't exactly thinking straight, so who knows? I certainly can't
remember clearly enough to know for sure.

Once Freya has been caught up on what's been happening,
Claire starts speaking. 'I know this is probably nothing, but there
is something else that's been playing on my mind…'

We wait for her to continue, but her cheeks are flaming and
she looks reluctant to continue.

'Well?' Freya nudges.

Claire shifts in her seat. 'Actually don't worry, it's really not
important.'

'You have to tell us now,' Freya says.

'Honestly, it's nothing.'

'Freya's right,' Oliver says. 'You can't leave us hanging, Claire.'

She sighs. 'I'm only telling you this because it happened, not
because I think it's relevant to anything.'

I stay silent, but I have to admit to being intrigued by what's
got my daughter-in-law so flustered.

Claire tuts and flicks her hair behind one shoulder. 'Okay. So yesterday, before I followed Jill to the river, I went to the fair.'

Ollie frowns. 'I thought the fair had gone already?'

'Yeah, it has,' Claire replies. 'To Wimborne.'

'You went to Wimborne?' Oliver's frown deepens.

'Yes. But I didn't find anything there.' She scratches her ear and clears her throat. 'Anyway, as I was leaving, I saw one of my clients parked opposite the showground. Stephen Lang. He's the one who brought round flowers after Bea disappeared, and he offered to help, if we needed it.'

'The white lilies,' I say.

Claire turns to look at me. 'Yes.'

'White lilies?' Freya repeats.

'He brought round white lilies,' I clarify. 'I told Claire at the time those flowers are symbolic of death. I don't know why I said that, though. It was quite an insensitive thing to say.'

Freya raises an eyebrow. 'Well that's not creepy at all.'

'I think Lang has a crush on me, that's all.' Claire pulls a face and shrugs.

'*What?* Why didn't you tell me this before?' Oliver cries, his expression darkening. 'We should definitely tell Gayle.'

'Really? But it's just a crush.' Claire doesn't sound enthusiastic.

'I'm not happy about some weirdo stalker bringing you death-flowers and following you all over the county.'

'That's a bit dramatic,' Claire replies.

'I agree with Oliver. You should tell the police.' I stare at my daughter-in-law until she finally nods heavily.

'Fine,' she replies.

'It can't hurt,' Freya adds.

Claire sighs. 'If we tell the police about that, then I'm going to have to tell them the rest – about me going to the fair and, well, technically I was trespassing.'

'Don't worry about that,' I soothe. 'It's understandable, in the circumstances.'

'Hmm.' She looks doubtful.

The doorbell rings, taking our attention, and Claire seems relieved by the distraction. All this coming and going is making me dizzy. But maybe it's Gayle back with good news about Beatrice. Oliver goes to answer it and comes back a few moments later with a bulky grey-haired woman who looks maybe a decade older than me. I vaguely recognise her face, even though it's pulled into a grimace and her whole body is bristling with anger.

'Sue!' Claire stands while Freya raises her eyebrows in my direction.

Oliver shifts awkwardly, shrugging apologetically to Claire. 'Sue wants to have a word.'

I try to think where I know her from, and then I remember – this is Philip's mother, from next door. I've spoken to her a handful of times before, usually on Oliver's doorstep where we've commented on the weather.

'Who are these other people?' Sue's normally soft west-country drawl is clipped and harsh today. Seems like she hasn't recognised me either.

Oliver swallows. 'This is my mother, Jill, and our friend Freya.'

Sue harumphs. 'Well I don't suppose it matters if they hear what I have to say.'

'How can we help?' Oliver asks.

She folds her arms across her chest. 'My Philip… has been at the police station… since *yesterday*.' As she talks, she tilts her head first one way, then the other like a seesaw, as she emphasises each phrase. I'm almost hypnotised by the movement. 'How could you think that Philip has anything to do with what's happened to your little girl? I know you're going through a lot right now, but this is just…' She throws her hands up in the air. 'It's just unbelievable, is what it is. As if it isn't enough that my house has been searched twice, top-to-bottom, my Philip then had to spend all last night in a police cell.'

No one says anything for a moment. Eventually Freya clears her throat. 'I know it must be hard, but the police are just doing their job. They have to interview everyone, and they've got evidence they have to follow up.'

Sue huffs. 'Well, I understand that, but we've been neighbours for years.' She turns to Claire. 'I never thought you'd turn on us like this. It's pretty obvious you're just looking for someone to blame and you're using my Philip as a scapegoat.'

'Now hang on a minute...' Claire's expression clouds over.

'I think Freya's right,' Oliver interjects. 'Let's all stay calm and wait for the police to do their job, okay?'

But Sue isn't stopping or calming down. 'And that woman my Philip's taken up with, Laurel, do you know her?'

'She's my ex-wife,' Oliver says quietly.

'*What?*' Sue almost screeches. 'Your ex-wife is trying to get in with my Philip? This is all very strange.' She shakes her head. 'Once this is over and my Philip comes home, I'm putting the house on the market and getting as far away from you people as possible. I was already thinking about moving somewhere with fewer steps, and you... well, you're not the nice family I thought you were, so this has made up my mind. There's something dodgy going on here.'

'Okay, Sue, I think that's enough.' Oliver guides his neighbour back out the way she came, but she continues to rant even as she's stepping outside. The front door closes loudly, cutting her off mid-flow.

'What a dreadful woman,' Freya mutters under her breath.

'She's worried about her son,' I reply. 'I'd be the same if it were Oliver at the police station. I'm sure she'll calm down.'

'Unless he's arrested and found guilty,' Claire adds. 'In which case, I'll call the estate agents for her.'

The uneasy feeling in my chest has hardened into a knot of anxiety and I suddenly realise why. 'There's something that's really worrying me,' I announce, looking up at Claire and Oliver.

'What?' Freya asks, concern etched across her face.

'If Laurel and Philip really are guilty of taking Beatrice, then who is she with now?'

CHAPTER FORTY-TWO

CLAIRE

'What's wrong?' Freya's making us each a sandwich while I stare at the message on my phone. Reading it has sent my pulse rocketing. This is the last thing I expected. What on earth can it mean? I'm already unravelling over Beatrice. Jill was right to worry about who's looking after her. If Philip and Laurel are being kept in for questioning by the police, then Bea could be locked up all alone. She'll be scared, hungry, thirsty. We need to find her as quickly as possible.

Right now, it's just Freya and I here at the house. Oliver's dropping his mum back home. Poor Jill has been quite overwhelmed with all this morning's activity. First Gayle coming over with an update, Freya showing up, and our incensed neighbour, Sue Aintree, barging in. Jill had been growing paler by the second. Then she quite rightly brought up her worries about who currently has our daughter. The same worries that are tearing me apart right now. If Laurel and Philip are guilty, but refuse to admit it, then they're obviously not going to give up Beatrice's location. But if they're not guilty, then we're back to square one and no nearer to finding her…

And now I get this text message.

'Claire?' Freya nudges me from my thoughts. 'You okay?'

'Uh, yeah, fine.' I get up from the table. 'I've just got to make a quick call. Back in a mo, okay?'

'Course. Do you want Cheddar or cream cheese in your sarnie?'

'Either's great. Thanks, Frey.'

'No worries.'

I step outside onto the searing-hot terrace, close the back door behind me and walk a little way up the garden. Already sweating under the midday sun, I find a shady spot beneath an overhanging buddleia, sharing the space with a thousand bees and butterflies.

The text message appears to be from Kai, the boy from the fair. He's asking me to call him ASAP. He must have got my number from Sam, the woman I gave my card to. This is weird. I'd already written off the fair as a dead end, my suspicions unfounded after scaring that little child and her mother half to death in their camper.

I call him and wait. Kai answers after a couple of rings. At first, all I hear is loud music and all the shouts and screams of the fair. But then he speaks. 'Hello.' His voice is gruffer than I remember.

'Kai? It's Claire. What's this about? I just got your message.'

There's a pause and I make out a faint muffled conversation. 'Hang on. Just gotta find somewhere a bit quieter.' I hear his breath as he walks, and the thud of his footsteps. The background noise grows fainter. 'That's better.'

I wish I'd brought a drink out into the garden with me; my throat is dry and tickly. I swallow and lick my lips.

'Claire, you still there?'

'I'm here.'

'Okay, so here's the deal. I'm going to tell you this thing, but you're not going to tell anyone you heard it from me, okay? My old man will kill me if he knows I've been speaking to you.'

'Your old man?'

'My dad.'

'Who's your dad?'

'Monty, the fairground manager. You met him, remember?'

'Yeah, I know who Monty is. I just didn't realise he was your dad.'

'Well he is, and he wouldn't want me blabbing to you. So you have to swear you won't say anything.'

'Um, yes, fine.'

'Swear it then.'

'Okay, I swear I won't tell anyone you spoke to me.'

'Good. So, last week, on our way to set up the Christchurch site, one of our small caravans was stolen. We sometimes leave a couple of them in lay-bys and have to come back for them – not enough towing vehicles. We do it all the time. Anyway, before the Christchurch set-up, one of them was gone when Tanner went back for it. The old man was proper pissed off.'

'That's… not good, I guess. But why are you telling me this?' I'm confused and disappointed by his story about the caravan. I thought he'd messaged me to tell me he knew where Beatrice might be, or that one of the workers had seen her.

'Think about it. It seems like a bit of a coincidence, don't you think?'

'Sorry, I don't get it.'

I can hear the exasperation in his voice. 'You know… what better place to hide a stolen kid? A caravan that you can park pretty much anywhere. And if she's found, who do you think's gonna get the blame?'

I inhale sharply. Could Kai be right? Is that what's happened? Is someone using the fairground caravan to hide Beatrice?

'Did you report it as stolen?'

'No, we usually sort these things out ourselves.'

'Surely it would help to report it.'

'If we reported it missing and then they found your girl inside, we'd be suspects, wouldn't we?'

I think about what he's saying, but have to disagree. 'I don't think you would. Does that mean you're looking for it yourselves?'

'No. After your daughter went missing, the old man called a stop to the search.'

'What! *Why?*'

'People like to blame us for everything. As soon as the fair arrives, anything goes missing in town, it has to be our fault – electronic gear, jewellery, cars, kids… you name it, we get the blame. If we found the caravan with your daughter inside, we'd be caught up in the police investigation.'

'But if you reported the caravan missing to the police, then surely it would be obvious that it wasn't you who took Beatrice if she's found in it! Plus, if you'd reported it at the time, we might have got her back by now.'

'Yeah, well, that's not the way we do things.'

I try to tamp down my anger as he carries on talking.

'Look, Claire, I know it might be hard for people like you to understand—'

'People like me?'

'Rich, middle-class…'

'I'm hardly rich!'

'You know what I mean. Anyway, things like that can put us out of business. Even if it's not our fault. You have another newspaper story with "missing child" and "travelling fair" in the headline, and the damage is already done. We've had one lot of headlines this week, we don't need any more.'

Kai's doing me a favour by telling me about this. I don't want to piss him off, so I try to calm down. 'Now that you've told me, will you at least help me look for the caravan?'

'Nah, mate. I'm already regretting telling you.' He's annoyed with me for having a go at him, and I can't really blame him. 'So, like we said, you're not going to mention my name, right?'

'No. I'll just say I had an anonymous tip-off.'

'Okay, because you swore, right?'

'Yes. I promise, your name won't leave my lips.'

'Okay.'

'Thanks, Kai. I really appreciate it.'

He sighs. 'Yeah, well, I've been thinking about your kid. I didn't want to be the one responsible, you know.'

'I do know. Thank you.' Something else occurs to me. 'What does the caravan actually look like?'

'It's just a white caravan. Oh, and it's got two blue waves going down the side and maybe two on the front, can't remember exactly.'

'Okay, thanks. Do you know the make or model?'

'Uh, yeah, it's a Rio Coaster.'

'What about a number plate?'

Kai pauses. 'Sorry – that changes depending on who's towing it.'

'Okay. At least I have the make and model.'

Once the call is over, I stay where I am for a moment, beneath the canopy of soft green leaves, thinking about what Kai has just told me. My heart is still pounding in my ears, my mind racing. Could he be right? Could Laurel, or Philip, or whoever took Beatrice have stolen the fairground caravan? I'm impressed with Kai at having reached that conclusion on his own. Unless... maybe all the fairground workers are thinking the same thing. It could be common knowledge among them, but they've decided to turn a blind eye. In fact, the more I think about it, the more I realise that's probably the case. I shake my head over and over at the thought that none of them were willing to go out on a limb for my daughter. Thank goodness for Kai and his conscience.

I sink down onto the paving stones and sit cross-legged for a moment. My brain is in overdrive thinking about what might come next. I guess the police could deploy one of their search helicopters to locate the caravan. But what if it's hidden beneath the cover of trees or under something else? Could they use thermal imaging? Would that even work? I don't know. I need to stop this speculation. The police will know what to do for the best. They're trained in this stuff.

Still sitting in the garden, I phone my husband, swearing aloud when the call goes to voicemail. I call Jill next. If Oliver's still driving her home, she can relay the message. I grunt in frustration as her phone also goes to voicemail, but I decide to leave her a message anyway. She can tell him when she gets it.

After ending the call, I clutch my phone, head spinning with all this new information. Could this be the breakthrough we've been waiting for? Does this mean I'll be reunited with my daughter soon?

CHAPTER FORTY-THREE

Although I love being with my son, I'm relieved to finally be home alone. It's been such a stressful time I can barely think straight. I'll make a cup of tea and try to read a few chapters of my novel, switch my brain off, just for an hour or so. Because if I don't, I honestly think I might end up having a nervous breakdown. I already feel on the edge.

I'm ashamed to admit it, but I never used to believe in such things as nervous breakdowns, nervous exhaustion, depression and all those other 'wishy-washy' terms. Then, after Bob died, I realised that the reason I never believed in those things was because I'd never experienced them. Trauma and grief opened my eyes to a whole new way of looking at the world – more compassionately, I suppose.

I turn on the kettle and rinse out my favourite mug. It's actually Bob's mug. On it are the words: *World's Best Dad*. Oliver bought it for Bob years ago when he went to London on a school trip. He bought me one that said *World's Best Mum*, but it broke some time ago. I only ever drink out of Bob's mug when I'm alone. It brings me comfort.

My phone buzzes from the kitchen counter where it's charging after running out of battery from its night at the police station. I glance over to see that I have a voicemail from Claire. As I listen to it, I pace the kitchen, my heart rate increasing with every word:

'*Jill, listen, I've just found out that someone stole a fairground caravan before the fair set up in Christchurch last week. I think the thief could be the same person who took Beatrice – maybe it was Laurel, maybe not, we don't know. So if we can find that caravan, we might find Beatrice. If you're with Oliver, can you tell him? Also let him know that I'm heading to the police station right now, okay? They need to locate that caravan as soon as possible. It's white with a blue wave design down the side. Thanks, Jill.*'

Oh my goodness. I'm in a right old dither now. I walk across the kitchen and sink into the armchair, thinking about what Claire's message might mean. My heart lifts for the first time in days and I get to my feet again as adrenaline floods my veins. If Beatrice is in that caravan then we really and truly might have a chance of getting her back today.

I'd better get down to the police station ASAP. I'll meet Claire there.

Thankfully, I still have my driving licence for a few more days, so I unplug my phone – which is only seven per cent charged – and hurry down the road to where my Nissan Micra is parked. My earlier exhaustion and anxiety have vanished, to be replaced with a cautious optimism. Just imagine if I get to hug my precious grand-daughter today. That will surely be the best moment of my life.

CHAPTER FORTY-FOUR

CLAIRE

'Claire!' It's Freya calling through the back door. 'Claire? Are you still out here? Lunch is ready when you are.'

I heave myself to my feet just as she's coming up the steps.

'There you are!' She smiles and shakes her head. 'I thought you'd disappeared. Everything okay?'

Back inside the house, I relay everything I've just learned to Freya – minus Kai's actual name; I did swear an oath to him after all. Freya listens with a growing expression of shock on her face.

'So obviously,' I continue, 'I'm going to have to go straight to the police station to tell them about the caravan.'

'Of course! Did you tell Ollie yet?'

I shake my head. 'I think he must still be driving Jill home. I left her a message to tell him I'm going to the police station.'

'Do you want to bolt down some lunch first?'

'No thanks. I need to get the police on the case.' I close and lock the back door and swig some water. 'Sorry to run. You stay here and finish your sandwich.'

Freya grabs her bag from the counter. 'Don't be daft, I'll drive. You can eat on the way. You need to have something to keep you going.'

'You sure?'

'Totally.'

I grab a couple of Tupperware boxes from the cupboard and dump our sandwiches inside, trying to go as quickly as I can. Then I hug my friend, relieved that she's offered to drive. I'm so jittery, I'm afraid I'll have an accident if I get behind the wheel. I realise that I could simply call Gayle with the information, but I want to tell them face to face. I need them to act on this straight away, and I want to be there while they do it. This information is too important to relay over the phone.

Freya and I leave the house. I climb up into the passenger seat of her Land Rover and fasten the seatbelt.

'Sorry there's no air con,' she says. 'We'll open the windows, get a breeze going.'

'No worries.' I open up the sandwich box and take a bite of my Cheddar and cucumber sandwich, knowing I need to keep my energy up. 'Thanks, Frey. I don't know what I'd have done without you this past week. Honestly, you really find out who your friends are when bad things happen.'

She nods, her eyes on the road ahead. 'Any time, Claire.' She has a distracted look on her face.

'What's wrong?' I ask.

'Would you mind if we just swing by the farm before we go to the station? It's not too far out of the way. I forgot to drop off a tyre pump for my dad.'

My heart sinks. I know she's doing me a favour by driving, but I'd rather have driven myself than waste time going to her farm first.

She senses my reluctance. 'I promise it'll be really quick. I'll drive fast. I know how important this new information is.'

Sure enough, she has her foot hard on the accelerator, driving almost recklessly.

'Careful!' I cry as she almost takes out a cyclist.

'Oops.' Freya winces. 'Don't worry, he's fine.' As Freya takes the turning towards Hurn, she navigates the narrow lanes with ease.

I take a few more reluctant bites of my cheese sandwich before giving up altogether. This delay has made me lose my appetite.

She puts a hand out to squeeze my arm. 'You okay? Honestly, this won't take long, I promise. Dad'll kill me if I forget – he needs it for one of the tractors. Why don't you just call the police now?' Freya suggests. 'That way, we won't be wasting any time.'

I perk up a little at the suggestion. 'I'd rather tell them in person, but you're probably right. I think I will.'

She turns to me with a sympathetic smile. 'It'll be okay. You'll soon find out where Beatrice is and then things can go back to how they should be. This will all turn out to have just been a terrible blip.'

'I hope you're right.' I reach into my bag for my phone but, annoyingly, it's not in the little pocket where I normally keep it. It must have slipped down to the bottom. I rummage through the contents of my bag, but it's not there. 'Damn.'

'What's wrong?' Freya's eyebrows quirk up in the middle.

'I think I've left my phone at home. Ugh, I don't believe this.'

'I hate it when I do that. Feels like a limb's missing.'

'I know. Can I use yours?'

'Well, you could have, but the battery's dead. Sorry. I should have charged it up at yours.' She screws up her face. 'We'll be at the farm in a minute. You can use the landline.'

'Okay, thanks.' I try to loosen my shoulders, but my whole body is tense and quivering with impatience. I'll be glad once I've told the police, at least then they can start the search. I notice that we've now bypassed the main farm and are travelling alongside one of the fields. 'Can I quickly stop off at the house and make the call?'

'Don't worry, there's a phone in the barn you can use.'

'Okay, cool, thanks.' Luckily, I have Gayle's card in my bag, otherwise I'd have to dial 999 and wait while they put me through to the right department.

Freya turns into one of the field entrances, hops out, unlocks the gate and hops back in again. The field is massive but empty, the patchy, dry grass suggesting it's not being used for anything at the moment. We clatter over a cattle grid and then bump along a dirt track towards a dilapidated stone barn at the top of the field. Freya pulls up outside the barn and gets out of the Land Rover. She grabs a heavy-looking cardboard box from the rear of the vehicle.

'Come on, this won't take long.'

CHAPTER FORTY-FIVE

JILL

I slip into the driver's seat and call Oliver to let him know what's happening. But my call goes straight to his messaging service. I wait impatiently for the beep.

'Ollie, darling, it's Mum. Not much battery left in my phone. Just to say I'm en route to the police station. Claire's discovered something about a stolen caravan. So head to the police station and we'll see you there and fill you in. See you soon, lots of love.'

I start up the car, my hands shaking with the anticipation of finally finding Beatrice. I know I should temper my excitement, but I can't help it. We have to keep positive, don't we? How else would we get through days like this?

I pull out of my parking space and drive carefully along the road towards Soper's Lane, the site of the fair where all this began. I'd rather not drive past it, but it's on the way to the police station, so I don't have a choice. I turn right out of my road and cruise along the lane which, thankfully, isn't too congested right now. To my left, the green grass of the park is filled with people all the way to the border of dark trees in the distance. Patches of yellowed turf are the only trace that the fair was ever here.

I continue on my way to the station, trying not to let my mind wander, concentrating on the road and the traffic because I can't afford to have an accident right now. Not when we're on the verge of such a huge breakthrough. I'm about to take the turning towards the police station when my attention is taken by a blue Land Rover up ahead almost knocking over a cyclist. The man on the bike manages to avoid being hit by mounting the pavement at the last minute. He yells something rude at the Land Rover, and I can't say I blame him. Poor man must be shaken up.

I consider pulling over to see if he's all right, but then I realise that it's Freya's Land Rover. Silly girl seems to be driving quite recklessly. She's not alone in the vehicle either. I speed up a little until I'm close enough to see that her passenger has straight black hair. It's Claire. Freya must be driving her to the police station. That's kind of her, and must be why she's driving so fast. I hope they don't get into an accident.

To my confusion, instead of heading towards the station, Freya takes the turning towards Hurn. If I remember correctly, that's where her family farm is situated. Why would she be going there with Claire? I slow down. Should I continue on towards the station, or should I follow Claire? Maybe there's been a new development. What should I do?

CHAPTER FORTY-SIX

CLAIRE

I peel myself reluctantly out of the vehicle and follow Freya across the scrubby grass towards the old stone barn. I'm still slightly annoyed with her for wasting precious time instead of heading straight to the police station. But at least I'm nearly at a phone now.

Freya sets down the cardboard box while she fumbles with the huge padlock on the solid wooden door to the barn, cursing before she finally manages to insert the key and turn it. She heaves open the door, picks up the box and inclines her head, urging me to follow her inside.

The interior of the barn is dark, with shadowy corners and a damp feel, despite the heat outside. A thin rectangle of light spills in from outside and onto the dusty stone floor, but it's not enough to illuminate the vast space. The scents of diesel and dry grass tickle my nostrils. As my eyes gradually adjust, I make out a jumble of old farm equipment in the far corner. I follow my friend as she crosses the stone floor and deposits the box next to a large metal storage bin. She stoops over the bin and starts poking around. Freya uses her free hand to point at the nearby wall. 'The phone's just there. Help yourself, I won't be a minute.'

I look across to where she's pointing at a grubby-looking olive-green phone fixed to the wall, complete with a circular dialling pad. It looks like it started out life in the seventies.

Freya laughs at my doubtful expression. 'Don't worry, it's old but it works. Mobile signal's patchy up here, so it's handy to have a landline sometimes.'

'Okay, thanks.' I march over to the phone and pick up the dusty receiver, cradling it between my ear and my shoulder while I squint down at the phone number on Gayle's card, trying to make out the tiny digits in the gloom. I quickly realise with a beat of annoyance that there's no point deciphering the number because the phone at my ear is dead. There's no dial tone. Nothing whatsoever. I press the phone cradle several times, exhaling in frustration.

I'm about to tell Freya about the dead phone, when I feel a sharp and sudden pain on the back of my head followed by nausea, dizziness and then… nothing.

CHAPTER FORTY-SEVEN

CLAIRE

I try to open my eyes, but they're sticky and heavy, as though they've been glued together. My chin is pressed into my chest, my arms ache terribly and I feel sick and groggy. I try to bring a hand up to rub my eyes, but I can't seem to move it. I try the other hand, but it too appears to be restricted somehow. Eventually, I manage to open my eyes.

Wherever I am, it's gloomy. My head is slumped onto my chest and as I attempt to lift it, a violently sharp pain rips through me, making me so dizzy that I almost throw up. I make myself stay very still for a few moments until the spinning stops, my chin no further up off my chest than before.

Fragments of memory come back to me. I'm in the Collins's barn… Freya brought me here… why am I here…?

I suddenly realise that my hands are tied together in front of me with white nylon rope. My feet are also tied, but I can't see what they're tied to. I'm sitting on some kind of box. Maybe a packing crate. I remember Freya, and a green phone. I was about to call the police. Is Freya still here? Is she hurt too?

'Freya?' My voice comes out as a whisper. I swallow, trying to get some saliva to lubricate my throat. There's a metallic taste in my mouth. I think it might be blood. 'Freya, are you okay?' This time it comes out as a croak.

'You're awake then?'

I recognise that voice.

A pair of feet appear in front of me. Small feet wearing grey trainers.

I recognise those feet.

I force my chin up off my chest, wincing through the pain in my skull and neck. I see green cargo shorts, a strappy black vest top, shiny chestnut hair framing a tanned freckled face.

I recognise that face.

'Freya,' I say, clearly this time.

'Hey, Claire. Wasn't sure if I might have killed you. Gave you a pretty hefty clomp to the head.' Her voice is trying to be light and friendly, but I can hear the tight note of tension behind it. Her jaw is taut and her eyes are glittering strangely.

'You,' I breathe. 'You… hit me?' A weak light is filtering in from somewhere and my eyes are growing accustomed to the gloom, despite the strange stickiness in my eyelashes. The air is thick and humid. I'm so thirsty. 'What's going on?' I ask.

'Ah, okay. So I guess we're going to do this now.'

'Do *what*? Freya, what's happening? You brought me here, you knocked me out?' I feel like I'm in some alternate reality.

'Hang on a sec.' Freya moves out of my field of vision. I daren't turn to see where she's gone – I can just about cope with the throbbing ache in my head, but I am absolutely not ready to face the other skull-searing pain triggered when I move my neck. She returns seconds later with another packing crate that she places directly opposite me and uses as a seat.

'Freya. What's all this about?' As soon as I ask the question, my daughter's face flashes into my mind and a stab of terror replaces the pain in my head. '*Beatrice!* Do you have her? Is she here? You didn't… you didn't do anything bad, did you?'

'Shh, calm down, Claire. Not that anyone can hear you all the way up here, but I need you to be quiet and let me explain the whole thing so that you can understand it properly, okay?'

I feel like screaming, yelling, cursing, crying. But there's no telling what this new version of Freya will do. She might just knock me out again and I can't afford for that to happen, so I'm going to have to play this her way while I think about how to get free. 'Okay,' I force myself to say through gritted teeth.

Freya gives me an appraising look. 'First of all, you can stop looking at me in that judgemental way, because you have absolutely no fucking idea what it's been like for me. No idea whatsoever.'

I gulp, unsure whether to comment. I think it's safer to stay silent for the moment.

'You know that Ollie and I had a thing when we were at school, right?'

I nod. I did know this, but according to both of them it was no big deal. There had been a big group of friends and, to hear them talk about it, they all went out with one another at different times while they were teenagers.

'Well, Ollie and I were in love, and we were each other's firsts, if you know what I mean? You never forget your first time, right?' She gives a bitter laugh.

This is news to me. Oliver never mentioned it. We've never been bothered about each other's previous relationships. But the thought of Freya and Oliver together like that makes my stomach lurch uncomfortably.

Freya grimaces. 'What Ollie never knew back then was that I got pregnant. And I...' she swallows. 'I got rid of it.'

I can't help a gasp escaping my lips.

'I know, right?' She gives me a sarcastic smile, but I don't buy her unemotional act.

'You didn't tell him?' I ask.

'No. Because that's how much I loved him. I didn't want to ruin our relationship with the drama of a teen pregnancy and having to make a big choice and all that crap. So I spared him the pain and went through it by myself.' Freya's voice is light, as though what she's telling me is no big deal, but her jaw is tense and her eyes are shot through with pain.

'What about your mum and dad? Did they know?'

'Nope. I arranged it all on my own. Didn't want anyone finding out and spreading rumours. I know that once you tell one person, you don't have a hope in hell of keeping it quiet. I debated about whether or not to tell my parents, but I was too scared of their reactions. They were pretty strict with me back then, being the only girl. My brothers were even worse, completely overprotective. So I got it done and assumed Ollie and I would carry on where we left off. But then – spoiler alert – he finished with me anyway.' She curls her lip at the memory. 'Said that he loved me but we were better off as friends. That we were too young to settle down.'

No matter what Freya's become now, I still feel sorry for the teenager she was back then. For what it must have been like to go through something like that alone. 'So he really had no idea about the pregnancy?'

'I already told you, no.' She shoots me an exasperated glare.

I'm desperate to ask about Beatrice, but I daren't make her angry. It takes all my willpower to let her continue without interruption.

'At first I was gutted. But then I realised that if I wanted this to work, I needed to give him space. Ollie and I were in love, we were amazing together. Perfect. We made each other laugh and we loved all the same things – the same bands, same films, all that stuff that was so important back then. The stuff that bonds you. That *binds* you. It's just that the timing was off. We were too young. I think he noticed a change in me after the pregnancy. I was probably a bit withdrawn for a while. So I thought I'd give us both a few years to play the field, have fun, sow our wild oats, all that stuff. Then, we could find one another again. Pick up where we left off. Only I left it too long because then he met Laurel Palmer.' Freya's voice curdles over her name.

'She was this supposed free spirit, this incredible artist, blah, blah, blah. Ollie confided in me about *everything*. We'd stayed friends – I made sure of that because I was waiting for the right moment for our friendship to turn into something more. And then this fucking hippy bitch steals him from right under my nose. You can see how that's pretty unfair, right?' Freya fixes me with a look that demands an acknowledgement, so I give a half nod and a shrug.

'Right. So I thought I'd have to wait it out. That after a while they'd break up, and then I'd be able to be the one to comfort him. I thought it could actually work out better than I'd originally planned. But then he went and proposed to her, and I had to pretend to be happy for them. I almost gave up on Oliver after that. But when you're someone's soulmate, it's not that easy to walk away… I did split them up eventually – planted so many seeds of doubt in Ollie's mind about Laurel cheating on him that he just couldn't trust her. Their arguments were legendary – so much smashed crockery, you wouldn't believe it.'

While Freya's telling me about her sick games and plans, all I can think about is my daughter. Surely Freya wouldn't harm a child to get what she wants? Would she? Looking at her crazed expression, and hearing these insane justifications for her actions, I'm not so sure. This is not the Freya I know. I don't recognise this woman at all.

I pull at my wrists and try to angle my fingers to tug at the rope, but without getting a look at what I'm doing, it's impossible. Besides, Freya is sitting right in front of me. There's no opportunity for me to do anything without her seeing. How did I let myself end up in this situation? How did I not see what Freya's really like? Am I that stupid? That gullible?

Freya's still talking, and everything she's saying sounds like fiction. But there's a saying, isn't there, that truth is stranger than fiction. She stares at a spot past my head, lost in her recollections.

'Once Laurel and Oliver's divorce came through, I felt so much lighter. Like I could finally breathe again. Ollie leaned on me heavily after that. We were almost inseparable. I saw him through all those dark times when he was sick with jealousy over Laurel's imagined lovers, and desperate with grief at his failed marriage.

'Once he started coming out of the fog, I arranged a few days away at a festival to cheer him up, inviting all his friends, but planning to finally make my move. I'd been getting really strong signals from him that he was falling for me again, but I wanted to play a little hard to get. Wanted him to do all the running.' Freya sighs and her eyes go glassy at the memory. 'So we went to the festival. It was at the Larmer Tree. You remember that, don't you, Claire?' Freya refocuses her eyes and stares directly at me.

My stomach drops. That's where I met Ollie for the first time. Where we fell for one another. Hard. 'Freya, I had no idea you were even interested in him. If I'd known…'

Freya wrinkles her nose. 'You'd have *what*? Stepped aside? I doubt that very much. I could see you were besotted.'

She's right. Of course I wouldn't have stepped aside. I'd seen Oliver Nolan and it had been electric from the start. Nothing would have stood in my way. Or his. Freya and I weren't even friends at the time.

As I listen to Freya pour out her deepest darkest secrets, I feel a strange mixture of pity and revulsion. She's had all these feelings for my husband that she hasn't allowed out for years. She's been nurturing them all this time and I had no clue. Nor did Oliver by the sound of it.

Freya sighs. 'I gave up on Ollie after that. Not completely, I still harboured a hope that maybe one day something might happen. But I stopped actively planning to get back with him. I decided that I needed to move on. To meet someone new. I tried. I had lots of relationships, as you know, being my best friend and all that.'

Freya gives me a smile that chills the marrow in my bones. How could I ever have thought I knew this woman? She's a complete stranger to me. Was it all an act? Has she been playing a role all these years, secretly mocking me while trying to stifle her jealousy? The thought makes me shudder.

If Freya had truly given up on Oliver, then why did she choose to befriend me? Surely, if she was trying to get over him, the last thing she would have wanted was to be best friends with his new wife. And yet that's what she chose to do. Our friendship has meant that she's been able to stay close to Ollie. To hear everything about his life through me. I've confided almost everything – our celebrations, bad patches, everyday arguments... she's had a front-row seat to all of it.

So if she's lying about having given up on the two of them ever getting together... what happens next?

CHAPTER FORTY-EIGHT

JILL

I park in a shallow lay-by further up the road and walk back towards the field's entrance, curious yet unsettled by Freya and Claire's decision to come here rather than go to the police station, where Claire assured me in her voicemail that she was headed. Has something happened to change her plan? Has she got some new evidence? Another tip-off from someone? Or could this be something to do with the caravan in Clare's message?

Another reason I decided to follow Freya and Claire towards Hurn rather than go to the police station like I'd planned was to keep an eye on Freya's erratic driving. I was worried they were going to have a crash. Freya tore up the lanes as though there was a forest fire chasing them.

She passed by her farmhouse and sped alongside field after field. By the time I caught up to them, I glimpsed the rear of her Land Rover disappearing through a field gate. They didn't spot me behind them but, to be fair, I could barely keep up. I'm not confident driving along these narrow country lanes. I didn't want to beep my horn or flash my lights at them to let them know I was there, in case Freya braked suddenly or I caused her to swerve. She already had one near miss with that cyclist.

As I walk back towards the field's entrance, the road is quiet, thank goodness, as I'm not sure there's room for a car to squeeze past without squashing me into one of the bramble-covered hedges. The air is heavy and still. I make out the distant hum of traffic from the main road and the sound of a crow cawing in a nearby field. Unfortunately, the hedge is too thick to peer through to see what Freya and Claire are up to, but I reach the metal gate soon enough.

It's closed and I wonder how easy it's going to be to climb over, but when I give it a little push, it swings open silently. I edge through the gap, picking my way over the cattle grid, and push the gate closed behind me. I hope Claire's not going to mind me showing up like this. Maybe I shouldn't have come. But a wild voice in my head is telling me to keep going.

I shield my eyes against the glare of the sun as I gaze around the sloping field. There's a large stone barn at the top end and I make out the blue smudge of Freya's Land Rover parked out front. The field is huge and the heat is merciless. I wish I'd worn a hat. No good wishing.

I trudge across the patchy grass. The field looks smooth from a distance, a soft, swelling rise, but up close it's pitted with humps and dips, hillocks and rabbit holes, as well as being rock-solid after weeks of no rain and hot sun. The walk uphill is making my legs ache and I'm paranoid about twisting an ankle. At least I'm reasonably fit and I also have a small bottle of water in my handbag which I'm looking forward to opening.

Finally, I reach the barn, and it's heaven to stand in its cool shade. The wooden door is partially open and I can hear voices inside. Or rather, I can hear *Freya's* voice. She sounds agitated. I remain outside the door for a moment, wondering whether or not to interrupt. If they're having an argument, they might not take kindly to me barging in. Especially as Claire specifically asked me to go to the police station. I pluck my water bottle from my handbag and take a few refreshing swigs, hoping the cool liquid will clear my head and help me decide what to do.

CHAPTER FORTY-NINE

CLAIRE

Freya eases herself up off her packing crate and prowls around the barn, stretching her arms out in front of her, something I wish I could do. My feet are cramping and my arms ache so badly.

'I thought I might have actually found happiness again with Joe.' She's talking about her most recent boyfriend. He ended his relationship with her last May, after two years together, but Freya never gave me a reason for it. She just said that Joe had fallen out of love with her. I'd been angry with him on her behalf, wanting to confront him and ask him what the hell he was playing at. But Freya had forbidden me from doing it. Made me promise that I'd leave him alone. I couldn't understand it. They'd seemed so happy together.

'I was sorry about that,' I offer. 'I was furious with him.'

Freya's eyes soften. 'I know you were. But you never knew the real reason we split.' She pauses and comes and perches back on the edge of the crate. 'Ugh, this thing is so uncomfortable.' Freya grimaces and then gives me a spiteful look, knowing full well that I must be ten times more uncomfortable than she is.

'Joe always wanted a family,' she says, 'so we decided to start trying.'

'I never knew that.'

'That's because I didn't tell you.' She tosses her hair. 'I wanted to get pregnant and then announce it to everyone. But of course, this is me and my shitty luck we're talking about. After eight months of trying, I went to see a fertility specialist who informed me that – *surprise!* – I'm now infertile.'

'Oh, *Freya*.' Even knowing all the despicable acts she's carried out over the past decade or so, I still somehow feel sorry for her.

'Yeah, I know. Tragic, right?' She flashes me a cold smile. 'My doctor couldn't tell me whether it was because of the termination I'd had when I was younger or not, but I'm sure it didn't help. After all, I wasn't always infertile. I told Joe that he didn't have to stay with me. That he should find someone who can give him a family. He acted all noble and said that he still loved me and wanted us to stay together and maybe we could try surrogacy or adopt or something. But I wasn't about to let him stay with me out of pity. That's not what I wanted at all.'

'It wouldn't have been pity,' I offer. 'Joe loved you.'

'Shut up, Claire. You can be so patronising sometimes; you know that, right?'

I flush and bite my tongue.

'Anyway,' Freya says airily, 'after Joe left, I got to thinking. Why the hell did I let you and Oliver get away with stealing my happiness? I gave up far too soon. I handed both of you my friendship and you took it so easily, like it cost me nothing. Like it was your right to have it. You both used me horribly. Not only that, but Oliver took away my chance to have children, to have a family with a good man.'

I want to stick up for my husband. To tell Freya that it wasn't exactly Oliver's fault that she couldn't have children. He'd had no choice in the matter. He hadn't even known she was pregnant. Hadn't known about the termination. I know it must have been a tough decision for her. It's not my place to pass judgement on what she did back then, but I do have to stop her doing something terrible right now.

That bump on the head has made me really woozy, but Freya's still talking so I'm trying my hardest to take it all in.

She shakes her head regretfully. 'Joe and I could have been really happy. We could have built a good life together. Maybe not as good as the one Ollie and I should have had, but good enough. I spent the last year or so thinking about what I could do to make things right. To balance the scales back in my favour. Because life doesn't do that for us. We have to do it ourselves. It's not true that when one door closes another door opens. In my case, all the fucking doors slam shut in my face, and it's just not fair!'

I let out a slow breath. Freya's face is twisted into a snarl that doesn't even look human. I'm starting to worry about what her endgame might be. She's seriously not right in the head. Something is very broken inside and I'm fearful for my daughter's as well as my own life. Because it's pretty bloody obvious now that Freya Collins is behind Beatrice's abduction and I have no idea what she's planning.

Freya folds her arms across her chest and leans forward, staring intensely at me. I stare back for a moment, but can't hold her gaze. She laughs when I look away.

'It was a shock,' Freya says. 'No, not a shock, more of a *surprise* when I saw *Jill* with the girls at the fair rather than Oliver. I'd been looking forward to seeing him there. To imagining his reaction after he realised he'd "lost" his daughter.' Freya does little air quotes that make me want to vomit. Hearing her admit to taking Beatrice is like being punched in the stomach. Only much, much worse.

Freya continues talking, ignoring the fact that I've started shaking and sweating, that I can barely breathe. 'My plan didn't change when I saw it was Jill at the fair instead. That only made my task easier, because' – Freya gives a little smile – 'we all know how scatty Jill can be.

'I planned our girls' night out after you told me that you and Oliver were taking Bea and her friend to the fair. Firstly, I thought the night out would be a good alibi – because how could I have snatched Beatrice when I'd been on my way to meet you at a restaurant? Thankfully, it didn't even come to that. Secondly, it would have been impossible for me to take Beatrice if you and Ollie had both been there at the fair. I had to get one of you out of the way.'

'What have you done with her?' I pant. 'Just tell me where she is! You better not have harmed my little girl. If you've done anything, I'll—'

'You'll what? You can't do anything, Claire. You're tied to a packing crate, in case you forgot.' She smirks and I want to claw her face off.

I know it's not a good idea to antagonise Freya right now, but I'm not thinking straight. My supposed best friend has just admitted to this heinous act and I can't do anything about it. Heedless of the agony sparking through my brain, I strain at my wrist ties and try to yank my feet free, but Freya has done too good a job of restraining me. I'm not getting free of these ties without help.

'She's just a little girl, Freya, that's all.' My voice breaks. 'Beatrice has never harmed anyone. Least of all you. She loves you. How could you do anything to scare her? To hurt her?'

'Oh calm down, Claire. As if I'd hurt Bea. What sort of person do you think I am?'

I exhale, hoping and praying that what Freya says is true. 'Do you *promise* she's okay? That she's *safe*?'

'I'll admit it,' Freya continues, ignoring my question. 'I did take Beatrice out of anger, without any real idea of what I was going to do next. Once I had her, I realised I wouldn't be able to let her go without incriminating myself. Because, of course, she's seen me now. She's been spending a few fun days with Aunty Freya. She thinks she's having a nice holiday.'

'Thank God,' I mutter. All these dark thoughts I've been having, imagining the very worst things. And all this time she's been fine. Happy, even, with one of her favourite people. Freya has always indulged Beatrice. 'Where is she?' I snap. 'Is she in that caravan you stole?'

Freya glares at me. 'I'm telling you what happened. Be patient, okay? As I was saying, I was worried about being incriminated. So, the best way to avoid that was to set someone else up. It was pretty easy actually. I managed to find Laurel's scarf on the ground during last weekend's search party. I stuffed it into my bag without touching it, using one of Beatrice's "lost" signs to pick it up so it didn't get contaminated with my fingerprints. I also fished Laurel's sandwich wrapper and water bottle out of the bin. Planted all of them in that abandoned boat for Jill to find. Pretty good, hey?

'So now Laurel and her boyfriend are in custody, and there are all sorts of other suspects floating around. I thought Gavin Holloway was a particularly good one.'

I realise I'd almost forgotten about the choirmaster, since the discovery of Laurel's scarf on the boat and then Kai's subsequent tip-off about the caravan theft. So much had been going on. Holloway must be innocent.

Freya confirms my deduction. 'I started the rumour about Holloway being at the fair myself, by having a little gossip with a couple of the farm labourers. Dad helped me out nicely with that one.'

My mouth drops in horror. 'Your *dad*? Don't tell me he knows about this too.' The thought of Trevor Collins helping with Beatrice's abduction is somehow even worse than Freya's betrayal. My skin grows cold and bile rises in the back of my throat as my fear escalates. I can't believe Freya's father is part of this madness. Trevor and Lynn are good people, *surely*.

Freya rolls her eyes at my question. '*As if.* No. Dad just happened to conveniently repeat the rumour about Holloway while you were at the house. My parents don't know anything. They wouldn't understand what I've done. They met young, married young, never had to go through what I did. They don't have a clue what my life's been like.' She shakes her head in exasperation. 'They were so lucky. That's all I wanted for myself. Someone to love. A family.'

'You can still have a family.' I'm desperate to get through to her. 'Why don't you get back in touch with Joe? Tell him you've changed your mind. You can still have it all. You don't need to do this.'

'He's married to someone else,' Freya says flatly.

'*What?*'

'After we split, Joe went travelling. Met a Kiwi girl and they got married. I saw the wedding photos on Instagram.'

I clamp my jaw shut, not wanting to say something that might make this even worse.

'Anyway, I'm not talking about Joe any more. I don't even want to think about him. Don't mention his name, okay?' Freya glares at me and I give a single nod that sends flares of pain across my skull. 'So, I wanted to end this whole abduction charade. I was going to figure out a way to do it. I've already told Bea to tell the police that it was Laurel who took her. Told her it would be our special secret.'

'You said *what?*'

Freya ignores my question, continuing with her confession. 'So my plans were all on track until that bloody fairground boy tipped you off about the caravan.'

I exhale. 'So Beatrice is in there? You stole the caravan and then stole my daughter, and you hid her in that caravan?'

'I did. Which is why I couldn't let you go to the police station and tell them about it. Which is also why I took your phone out of your bag before we left your house. It's currently lurking in one of your kitchen drawers.'

I blink furiously, stunned at the endless deceptions of the woman I thought was my best friend. I am, however, massively relieved that in my haste to tell the police, I omitted to tell Freya that I left a voice message for Jill, explaining about the stolen caravan. So, even if something bad happens to me, at least Jill will make sure the police find Beatrice. Please, God, let her have listened to my message already and be on the case.

Freya stands up again and stares down at me with contempt in her eyes. 'Now that Laurel's out of the way, in police custody, soon to be imprisoned for abduction, all that's left is to remove you from the equation and then maybe I can finally have my chance with Oliver. And with Bea of course. We can be the family we were always supposed to be.'

I let out a disbelieving snort. 'You know you don't stand a chance of getting away with this. What you're suggesting is ludicrous. I thought you were more intelligent than this, Freya.'

She stiffens and then immediately relaxes. 'I already told you, Bea's agreed to say she's been with Laurel – the lady with red hair. She was excited about keeping her fun holiday with Aunty Freya a secret.'

My blood seethes and boils at the thought of Freya making my daughter lie. 'You haven't got a clue,' I scoff. 'Beatrice will never be able to keep quiet about it. You obviously don't know how lousy kids are at keeping secrets.'

Freya's face tightens, but suddenly she grows thoughtful and starts pacing the dusty floor of the barn. After a moment, she stops and narrows her eyes. 'Okay. Thanks for your input, *Claire*. So now I'm in a dilemma, aren't I? If Beatrice won't keep our holiday a secret, then what will I have to do to shut her up?'

Too late, I realise my mistake. Fear oozes from every pore in my body. 'No,' I plead. 'You were right,' I add, trying to make myself sound less desperate, more casual. 'Of course Bea will listen to you. She'll think it's a game. What I said before… I was wrong, I was just trying to piss you off. Of course Beatrice will keep your secret. You know that. We all will.'

But Freya isn't stupid. She knows I'm lying to save my family. 'Too late, Claire. I don't believe you. Looks like you and Bea will *both* have to have an accident.'

CHAPTER FIFTY

JILL

The interior of the barn is cool and dark, but I wish I'd stayed outside, because what I'm hearing right now is making me nauseous.

When I arrived, I waited outside for a few minutes in the hope that Freya's angry rant would stop at some point, giving me an opportunity, a pause in the conversation to walk in and find out what was going on. Maybe even try to mediate. But there was no gap; her voice just went on and on. So eventually I chanced it and snuck in through the crack in the open door, stepping out of the light and pressing myself back against the barn wall where Freya's monologue suddenly became clear as a ringing bell.

I've been in here for a while now, creeping along in the shadows of the cool stone walls. The content of Freya's conversation is so crazy that I almost wonder if I might be hallucinating. The biggest shock is seeing the terrible state of my poor daughter-in-law. She's tied to a crate and there's dried blood in her hair and all down her face. I'm surprised she can even see, because it looks like there's blood stuck to her eyelids.

'Don't think I can't see you there, Jill, skulking about in the shadows. Who do you think you are? Special Forces?'

I freeze, my heart clattering against my ribcage as Freya turns around and skewers me with her gaze. Should I try to run? There's no way I could get away from her. She looks lithe and strong. Tough. She's a farmer used to dealing with heavy machinery and livestock. A pensioner like myself would stand no chance, even with the benefit of my Pilates classes. I cast around for something heavy. Maybe I could thwack her over the head. Who am I kidding? She'd use whatever I had against me. My shoulders go limp as I realise it's hopeless.

'Jill!' Claire cries. '*Run!*'

I stare over at my daughter-in-law, trying to convey an apology in my eyes.

Freya walks towards me. 'That's right, Jill. No point running or fighting. You'll only get hurt. Although it looks like that might be an inevitable outcome anyway.' Her tone suddenly changes. 'Where's your phone?' she barks. 'Did you call anyone?'

'My phone's dead, Freya.'

She holds out a hand and I drop my lifeless mobile into her palm. She examines it for a moment before nodding, satisfied, and slipping it into her pocket.

Claire looks up at me with sorrow in her eyes. 'Jill! Why did you come here?'

'I saw you in Freya's Land Rover and I followed you.'

'But why? I left you a message. I asked you to go to the police station.'

'Oh dear.' Freya gives Claire a sarcastic frown. 'What a surprise, renegade Jill didn't do as she was told.' Freya turns to face me with an insincere smile. 'You've made quite a few mistakes this week, haven't you, Jill? She grips my upper arm and drags me across the barn towards Claire, who shoots me a look loaded with frustration and desperation.

'Jill, I thought I made it clear you were supposed to tell the police about the caravan! I can't believe you came here! Now it's *hopeless*.'

Freya's eyes widen as she looks from me to Claire. 'Oh.' She shakes her head at Claire. 'So you *did* message Jill about the caravan. Well played, Claire. You kept that hidden nicely from me. It's a shame scatty Jill didn't listen to you. Well, a shame for *you* anyway. Lucky for me though.' Freya pushes me down on to the hard stone floor. I land on my bottom and the impact judders through my body, my teeth clamping together painfully.

Did that hurt?' Freya sneers. 'Looks like old age is catching up with you, Jill. Never mind, maybe I'll put you out of your misery.'

I flush. But this time it's not with embarrassment or shame or fear, it's with anger at this horrible woman who's put my family through such an ordeal. I'd really like to give her a piece of my mind, but perhaps now isn't the best time. Then again... 'What happened to you, Freya? I always thought you were such a nice girl. Your mother and father will be heartbroken by what you've done.'

'Stay there and don't move.' She turns away for a moment to reach for something behind her.

'Run,' Claire hisses down at me.

'No, she'll catch me,' I whisper back.

Claire grimaces and inhales. 'I know, but isn't it worth a try?'

I shake my head. 'How are you feeling?' I murmur. 'You don't look good, Claire.' I take a closer look at the dried blood. 'Did she hit you?'

'*Why* did you come here?' Claire groans and tosses me another look of disappointment.

Freya turns back to face us. She's holding a ball of nylon twine and some kind of multitool. She flicks out a blade and slices off a long length of the twine, using it to tie my wrists and ankles together so that I'm bent forwards at an uncomfortable angle. I can tell this is going to become very painful very quickly.

'I'm going out for a short while to check on my little guest,' Freya says briskly. 'Make the most of your time, you don't have much left.'

We both watch as she strides away across the barn towards the open door.

Once I gauge that she's out of earshot, I whisper to my daughter-in-law. 'Don't worry, Claire.'

'How can you even say that!' she hisses back. 'You heard her. She's got Bea. She's going to get rid of us. You've screwed this up! We both have.'

I don't take offence at her tone. She's got every right to be angry and terrified. 'Claire, listen. While I was "skulking" in here, I found a few bars of phone signal and used my last four per cent of battery to text the police inspector. I told her exactly where we were, and that Freya Collins was holding you captive. I told them Freya's blue Land Rover is parked outside. I wasn't sure if the message had got through, but just before my screen went dead, I got a text back saying: *Hold tight. We're on the way.* They're on their way, Claire. The police know we're here.'

Claire's jaw falls open before her whole face crumples with emotion and relief. 'Oh, Jill, I can't believe it. I honestly thought… I just…'

'I know, I know.' I wish I weren't tied up so I could give her a hug. I've never seen anyone more in need of one. 'I sent the same message to Ollie.'

I realise Claire is sobbing and I wish I could put my arms around her. She gazes down at me, her tears making tracks down bloodstained cheeks, dripping off her chin. 'I can't believe you did that. Jill, you're an absolute bloody hero.'

I gaze towards the open barn door just as Freya comes back into view and pulls it closed behind her, plunging us both into darkness.

For a moment, there's nothing but the sound of our jagged breathing and Claire's soft sobs of relief. Thankfully, it's not completely dark in here; a few patches of light filter in through chinks in the roof and walls, and my eyes slowly adjust to the gloom.

An engine starts up. Freya's Land Rover.

'I hope the police get here soon,' Claire stammers.

'Don't worry. I'm sure they will.'

A few minutes later, a juddering noise makes us both look up.

'Is that…?' Claire's voice trails off.

'A helicopter,' I finish her sentence.

'Do you think it's the police?'

I can now hear the sound of a siren getting louder. And another.

'Oh, I'm certain of it,' I reply.

CHAPTER FIFTY-ONE

FREYA

I bump across the top field in my Land Rover, away from Claire and Jill tied up in the barn. 'Bloody Jill and her bloody sleuthing,' I mutter to myself.

I'd only just got used to the idea that I was going to have to get rid of Claire and Bea, and now I'm going to have to deal with Jill too. I didn't want to do any of that, but they've forced my hand. I reach the gate, hop out and yank it open. The lane is deserted, thank goodness. I edge out of the field and take the time to close the gate behind me before climbing back into the Land Rover and heading up the lane.

I'll have to arrange an accident of some kind... something believable. At least the police don't know about the caravan. I still have time to think of something – something that I can pin on Laurel. But I'd better do it fast.

A distant sound settles on the edge of my hearing, but I don't have the bandwidth to pay it any attention. I need to think of a plan. 'Bloody Jill,' I mutter again. Her arrival has made everything ten times harder. I can't let her ruin my goal of being with Oliver again.

I know I'd decided that it was too risky to let Beatrice live, but I wonder if there's any way I can keep her. When all is said and done, I do have a soft spot for the girl. My plan was for the three of us to be a family – me, Ollie and Bea. But without Beatrice, how will that happen? I shake my head to clear it, to stop the crowd of thoughts and emotions taking over. What I need is some calm, quiet time to think.

What IS that noise? I glance behind me to see a small dark shape in the sky, growing bigger, getting closer. I swallow and blink, my stomach grinding. No. It's just a coincidence. That helicopter is nothing to do with me.

Nevertheless, I speed up a little and take the next left turn. Hopefully, the helicopter will keep going straight ahead to wherever it's headed. I glance in my rear-view mirror to see it veering left towards me, drawing closer, the juddering of its blades now almost deafening. I spot the words POLICE emblazoned across the side. 'Shit, shit, shit! No!'

I need to stay calm. I mustn't panic. This could be nothing but an outrageous coincidence. Maybe they're simply looking in this area for Beatrice, or maybe they're after someone else entirely. If that's the case, then why are my hands trembling and why is my left leg shaking uncontrollably? Sweat prickles on my forehead and under my arms. I grip the steering wheel tighter, unsure whether to continue driving at this same pace so as not to appear guilty, or to put my foot to the floor and try to outrun them.

Blue flashing lights coming up the lane behind me help to make up my mind. I take a breath, put the Land Rover into third gear and press down on the accelerator, taking a sharp right turn down the next lane. I know these narrow country roads and farm fields like the back of my hand, but will that knowledge be enough to lose a helicopter? Don't think about that, just concentrate on driving. I also need to draw them away from Bea's caravan.

As I increase my speed, a wail of sirens start up behind me and I almost veer into the hedge in shock as I'm instructed to pull over by an obscenely loud police megaphone.

'Yeah, right. That's not happening.' As I race and brake and swerve along the deserted lanes, I shoot glances left and right at the field entrances. All I need is for one gate to be open. Just one. On these

*tarmac surfaces, the police vehicles are gaining all too easily, but my
4x4 will outpace a police car cross-country.*

*Finally, up ahead at the T-junction, I see what I'm looking for —
Davey Lyndhurst's lower field has both gates wide open. He, or one of
his farmhands, must be in there, but I don't care about that. I come
up to the 'Give Way' sign at the end of the lane, ignore it, and almost
fly across the road, praying there are no cars coming. My luck holds,
and I find myself jolting across the cattle grid into Davey's twenty-acre
field, which just so happens to back onto woodland.*

*The helicopter is right above me now like a giant spider, the
moving shadows of its whirring blades passing across my windscreen
and bonnet. Behind me, three police vehicles have followed me into
the field, the distance between us increasing with every metre. If I can
just make it to the woodland, I can slip away through the trees and
hide from the helicopter beneath the thick summer foliage.*

*A dull thud in my chest tells me that my dream of being with Ollie
is over. That the best I can hope for now is to evade capture. A small,
panicked voice tells me that even that is impossible. That it's too late.
Even if I manage to get away from my pursuers today, where would
I go? How would I live? I'll deal with that later. Right now, I need
to lose the police.*

*I floor it to the end of the field, by which time I've managed to
accrue a healthy distance between me and the police cars. Right now
it's the helicopter I'm most worried about. My heart rate increases as
I reach the edge of the woods and drive alongside the trees, casting
desperate glances into the undergrowth, looking for a path of some kind.*

*Yes! Finally, I see what looks like a gravel track up ahead and I
nose my vehicle beneath the trees, plunging into the dappled gloom of
the woods. It's rough going, but that's great because it means the police
cars will have an even harder time on this uneven, flinty terrain.*

*I gun the engine along the track, which is barely wide enough for
the Land Rover, but at least that means the tree canopy stretches right
across the path. So why then can I still hear the helicopter directly above*

me? How can it see me through the trees? If I can't lose the helicopter then how will I escape?

The police cars have already made it onto the track and the path is narrowing, slowing my progress. I need to get out, to try to slip away on foot. No time to lose. I grab my bag, ditch my phone and fling open the Land Rover door, jumping out and hurling myself into the deepest section of woodland I can see.

I stagger a good way before risking a glance over my shoulder. It's not good. I spot at least two uniformed male pursuers. A panicked sob escapes my lips. Surely there must be a way out of this. A brilliant plan I can conjure up. Something. Anything. All I can do is run, paying close attention to the ridged tree roots and clawing branches – the last thing I need is to trip and fall.

The harsh sounds of police-radio chatter follow me through the gloom, the intermittent shouts from the officers telling me to stop running, that I'm under arrest. I can't stop now. I have to at least try to get away. How can the helicopter still be overhead? There's no way it can see me.

My breathing is so loud, my lungs ready to explode. I'm fit and healthy. I can normally run for miles. But not like this. Not with pursuers at my back and fear in my chest squeezing the breath out of me. This is agony. I want to fall to my knees and sob at the injustice of it all.

Only when I hear the bark and whine of dogs approaching do I finally realise that it's truly hopeless. That the chase is finished. That I'm finished. My dream of being with Ollie is over.

I slow my desperate run to a walk, raise my hands in the air and turn around.

CHAPTER FIFTY-TWO

CLAIRE

Gayle drops me and Jill at the entrance to the field where the stolen caravan was hidden. So now here we are, striding shakily across the grass, every nerve ending in my body lit up with anticipation. The paramedic did a decent job cleaning all the dried blood from my head and face, although she warned that there's still some caked in my hair that won't shift without a proper wash.

Checking me over, they said I have a mild concussion and insisted on taking me to hospital. Of course I refused. I'm not delaying my reunion with my daughter by going where they'll probably only tell me to rest. I can do that at home with my family. At least I don't need stitches. I didn't tell them about the mother of all headaches that's zigzagging across my skull. I'll deal with that later and go to the hospital tomorrow if I really need to.

After placating the paramedics, I then had to deal with Gayle, who said that it wasn't advisable for me to greet my daughter straight away, looking like I did in my bloodstained clothes. But there was no chance I was agreeing to that either. Not when every cell in my body is screaming to go to her. In the end, the paramedic kindly lent me a spare shirt and Gayle relented.

Once they had the information about the stolen caravan, the officers located it almost straight away. It had been sitting in a disused field not far from the Collins's farm. Oliver went straight there when he arrived. I spoke to him ten minutes ago on Gayle's phone.

Oliver tried to reassure me that Beatrice is absolutely fine. Wonderful, in fact. Seemingly unharmed and unaware that she'd been kidnapped; she thought she'd simply been staying with Aunty Freya for a few days. I'd known she wouldn't be able to keep that information to herself. Apparently, according to Beatrice, it had been boring and hot in the caravan, and she'd had to spend ages all by herself, and she can't wait to come home to see Mummy and Granny.

Once the police discovered who was behind the abduction, Freya didn't get very far in her Land Rover. According to Gayle, Freya saw the police helicopter hovering above her vehicle and realised she was in trouble. There was quite the police chase around the lanes and into a neighbouring farmer's woodland where the helicopter tracked her using thermal imaging. I'd have paid good money to see all that, after what she's put us through.

So now Jill and I are half-running, half-walking across the patchy grass towards a caravan hidden from view of the road by a dense stand of trees. Emergency vehicles litter the site. Lights flashing, security tape flapping, and people in uniforms talking into radios, along with the busy-looking white-clad CSI team.

I turn to Jill. We inhale in unison. Her eyes are bright with nervous, excited emotion. My heart jumps a beat and my shoulders tingle. I won't be able to truly relax until I see Beatrice with my own eyes. Until I'm reassured that she's whole and unharmed.

I suddenly grit my teeth in fury at the thought of our daughter locked up on her own for hours at a time. The blood begins to roar through my veins again. Freya better hope I don't run into her on a dark night. She better pray she gets locked up where I can't reach her. I take another deep breath, trying to banish my ex-friend from my thoughts. This is finally the moment I've been waiting for. I should be thinking good things, not getting sucked back into a vortex of rage.

'You okay?' Jill puts a hand on my arm and we slow down for a millisecond.

'Just trying not to think about Freya.' I narrow my eyes and start striding once more.

Jill sighs and catches me up. 'She's a very troubled girl. Let's concentrate on our darling Bea instead.'

'Good idea.' I exhale and my blood cools a little.

Now everything is moving in slow motion as we approach the trees, and the large white caravan comes into full view, early evening sunlight glinting off the windows. A man steps out from behind it.

It's Oliver. In his arms he's carrying a dark-haired child in a red dress. I let out a gasping sob. Jill and I stare at one another with what can only be described as unfettered joy, our hearts swelling, no more words needed.

Oliver sets Beatrice down onto the grass, crouches and points in our direction. I forget about my throbbing head, about where I am and what's happened as I stagger into a makeshift run.

Bea's face breaks into a radiant smile. '*Mummy!*' She races towards me, arms outstretched, and I can't speak, can't even see as the tears fall down my cheeks and I sink to my knees. She almost knocks me to the ground as she flings her little arms around me and I breathe in the scent of my daughter. Kiss her all over and squeeze her tight.

My daughter is finally safe.

ONE MONTH LATER

The folding chair in my cell is uncomfortable, its back slopes at the wrong angle. At least it makes a change from lying on that hard, narrow bed. I like to alternate between the two. I'm not used to staying in one place. Before this, my days consisted of striding through fields, driving farm vehicles, seeing to animals and fences, manual labour. I'm not sure how I ended up here. How things spiralled so badly. And I can't work out whether I'm at fault, or whether it's everyone else who's to blame. Whatever the reason, none of it's fair. Why do some people get their happy ever after and others end up trapped in a small room with dirty walls and no fresh air?

I pick at the skin around my fingernails, taking pleasure in the raw flaky mess surrounding the nail beds. Each nail is a work of art in itself, a sore little canvas of blood and skin. The thing I don't understand about any of this, is why I placed so much importance on Oliver. If I think about it – and I do – we were together for such a short time. Granted, it was a wonderful time. The best months of my life. But since then, I realise he's actually caused me nothing but pain. The pain of getting pregnant, of losing a child, of yearning for our lost love, of jealousy over his new loves, of hatred, of bitterness, of rage. And for what? So I could end up in this room?

I can't have ended up here because of him, *can I? I try to push out the crowding thoughts of all the things I've done. The years of gaslighting and manipulation. Of lies and schemes. The abduction of a child. Of Beatrice. I inhale and blink back tears. It was justified.*

She should have been mine. Mine and Ollie's. I shake my head at the blurred carousel of thoughts that won't stop wheeling around my head. If only they would settle on a real answer. But they never do. They just keep spinning...

CHAPTER FIFTY-THREE

JILL

'Granny, are you going to come to the harvest festival next week?' Beatrice holds my hand as we wait for the bus up the road from her school, which sits midway between her house and mine.

'I most certainly am. Do we need to get some donations together for it? Tins of food and packets of soup?'

'Um, yes, I think so. Mummy said she'd buy some stuff at the weekend.'

'We can have a look in my cupboard too, if you like. See if we can find a few bits for you to take home this evening.'

'Yes!' Beatrice smiles up at me, excitement spilling over.

I lean down and kiss the side of her head, stroking the wispy dark strands of hair that have come loose from her ponytail. It's at moments like this when last month comes rushing back to me. The horror of almost losing her forever. I shouldn't dwell on it, but it's sometimes hard to put aside. The fear of what might have happened.

One positive that's come out of such an awful situation is that I now get to play an active role in looking after my granddaughter once more. I collect her from school twice a week, and she comes back for tea. As well as spending quality time with my granddaughter, I also get to see more of Oliver as he picks her up from mine after work and always makes time for a chat and a cuppa before they both head home.

I realise that part of the reason I barely saw Oliver before was that I placed too much responsibility on him to care for me after Bob died. I wanted him to take charge and be 'the man'. I'm ashamed to remember that I played up to the image of being the frail old grandmother, when I'm actually not. My rescue of Claire and Beatrice showed me that I've still got plenty of fire left in my belly. So, now I've decided that I'm leaving it up to Oliver to see me whenever he's free, rather than pressuring him to come over all the time. Funnily enough, I see an awful lot more of him now than I did before.

Along with these unexpected pleasures, my relationship with Claire has blossomed into something wonderful. Yes, she's my daughter-in-law, but she's also becoming a cherished friend. I realise that my continued friendship with Laurel didn't help my relationship with Claire at all. Not that Oliver and Claire knew an awful lot about mine and Laurel's ongoing friendship, but listening to Laurel's woes was bound to make me more biased against Claire. I don't think I ever gave Claire a proper chance to be part of my family, and for that I'm sorry.

In addition to our improving relationship, Claire and Ollie now know all about my financial mess and, far from being judgemental, they've both been really sympathetic and helpful. We've decided that the best thing will be for me to sell the cottage. Apparently, because of its town-centre location, it's actually worth quite a lot. At first, I was resistant to the idea, nervous of leaving my house – the last home I shared with Bob – but Oliver explained that I could then buy a lovely apartment and still have a small lump sum to live off, which will mean less scrimping and saving. No more sleepless nights stressing about money worries. There might even be a bit left over for a holiday.

I've already accepted an asking-price offer on the house, and I've found a pretty, characterful ground-floor garden flat on the other side of town which is walking distance to the shops. Walking distance was an important factor, because I've now had my driving licence revoked for eighteen months. I've sold my car and I don't miss it at all. Maybe I won't bother buying another one when my suspension's over. It would certainly make better financial sense. I can't believe I'm thinking about saving money in this way. Claire has taught me well.

'Here's the bus, Granny!' Beatrice startles me out of my reverie.

'Put your hand out then. Wave it down.'

Beatrice plants herself squarely on the pavement and sticks one skinny arm out into the road. The bus driver smiles, gives her a thumbs up and pulls over while everyone else at the bus stop coos over how cute Bea is. Pride and love swell in my chest and I want to proclaim loudly that she's my granddaughter. Of course I don't, I simply take her hand as we step up onto the bus, the two of us, ready to take on the world.

CHAPTER FIFTY-FOUR

CLAIRE

Oliver and I walk up the sandy path as sunlight glints through the pines, willows and birches of St Catherine's Hill. Despite the heat of the day, faint signs of autumn catch my eye – leaves tinged with orange and yellow, and brown curling heather that carpets the earth around the trees.

Ahead of us, Beatrice darts and weaves through the bracken with that energetic blonde bundle of craziness who's recently become the fourth member of our household – Winnie the golden retriever.

Oliver and I had decided that we were going to wait until next spring to get Beatrice a puppy, but one of Jill's Pilates friends runs a dog rescue centre and, according to Jill, two-year-old Winnie was just perfect for Beatrice and we just had to come and see her. Of course, as soon as we clapped eyes on the pup, it was love at first sight, and I already can't imagine life without her. Beatrice is besotted. We all are.

That first night our daughter came home was both wonderful and unsettling; Ollie and I didn't want to let her out of our sight. We hugged her, kissed her, let her play with whatever she wanted, ordered her favourite Domino's pizza, with rocky road ice cream for dessert. But, although we were in raptures over her return, she was so at ease that it felt strange. We'd thought we would be comforting her and soothing her tears, or worse. Instead, it just felt... normal.

That night, we tucked Beatrice up in bed with all her cuddly toys arranged around her. We sat on the edge of the bed and read her stories until she fell asleep. Even then, we couldn't bear to leave the room. We sat for ages just gazing at our daughter, throwing each another occasional grateful glances. Eventually, Ollie and I tiptoed downstairs where we talked about how we'd have to be careful not to change how we interacted with our daughter. We had to get back to normal, for her sake. At least Freya hadn't traumatised her in any way that we could see. It was just me, Ollie and Jill who had gone through hell.

'Beatrice!' Ollie calls out. 'Stay where we can see you!'

'We're right here!' Bea replies, charging back onto the path, Winnie panting at her heels.

This is our new after-supper routine – a family walk up the hill. It's great while the weather's good. I only hope we can keep it going in the cold and rain. Oliver's already bought us some wellies and thick socks in anticipation of winter.

The fallout from Beatrice's abduction has been varied. Laurel and Philip were released from police custody without charge. Both Philip and his mother, Sue, have avoided all communication and eye contact with us. Sue's been as good as her word and has planted a large 'For Sale' sign in her front garden. Laurel hasn't been in touch with either me or Oliver, although Jill's met up with her a few times and says she seems to have taken it all very personally. I don't suppose I can blame her. We did accuse her and her boyfriend of child abduction, after all.

Gavin Holloway the choirmaster had been nothing but a red herring planted by Freya to send us all looking in the wrong direction. The police informed him that he was no longer a suspect.

My client, Stephen Lang, had simply been an overenthusiastic amateur sleuth. I suspect he did have a little crush on me and wanted to help out. He had a similar thought to me that perhaps Beatrice had been taken by a fairground worker, and so he decided to stake out the Wimborne showground with a packed lunch and a pair of binoculars. But he panicked when he saw me there, and drove off, worried I would think he'd been overstepping his bounds. Together, Oliver and I reassured him that we were grateful for his concern.

Monty Burridge got his caravan back and I never once mentioned Kai's name to anyone. He did, after all, contribute to getting my daughter back safely. I messaged Kai afterwards and said if he ever needed me to return the favour, I'd be happy to help him however I could. I received a brief text back saying thanks, and that he was glad we'd got our daughter back.

'You okay?' I ask my husband.

He smiles and slings an arm around my shoulder, pulling me close. Oliver's found it harder to recover from the ordeal than I have. He's scarred from that week when he had to deal with those threatening anonymous messages alone. When he was terrified that one wrong move would result in the abductor harming our daughter. He was trembling with rage when he discovered that it had been our so-called friend who had put him through the wringer.

After he calmed down and heard the whole sordid story of why she'd done it, Oliver was devastated to learn that Freya had gone through an abortion back when she was only seventeen. That she'd done it alone, and hadn't felt that she could confide in him about it. That he wasn't able to help her at the time. Jill was also upset, especially as she knows Freya's parents and is sure that they would have been supportive if only they'd known.

It's hard not to imagine that if Freya *had* chosen to confide in her parents, perhaps all our lives would have followed very different paths. What if she'd told Oliver at the time, or kept the baby...? But I don't suppose there's any point in thinking along those lines. Things happened the way they did, and that's that.

Along with the rest of us, Oliver had no idea that Freya had been secretly wreaking havoc in his life for over a decade. I've persuaded Ollie to get some counselling about everything and he's got his first session next week, so we'll see how it goes.

And, of course, we still have the whole court case ahead of us. DS Gayle Hobart remains a fixture in our lives, keeping us informed of how everything's progressing, and of what's still needed from us. So I guess we won't be able to properly relax until Freya's been found guilty and sentenced, and this whole sorry mess is tied up. Right now, Freya's locked up, awaiting trial. Gayle says the case is cut and dried. That the evidence is overwhelming, so there's no doubt. Gayle confirmed that Freya will be pleading guilty to child abduction.

As for me, this whole episode has made me take a good look at myself and my relationships. I realise that I've treated Jill, Oliver and even Laurel unfairly. They were all victims of Freya Collins. If I'd trusted them more, I might have found Beatrice sooner. My biggest regret is the way I've treated Jill these past few years. She's only ever been kind to me. I think, if I'm honest with myself, I was jealous that she clicked more with Laurel than with me. But that's probably because I never really gave her a chance to get close. I had a chip on my shoulder and gave *myself* the role of inferior second wife – Jill never did.

So I'm making up for lost time, starting with trusting my mother-in-law to look after her granddaughter again. Jill has now started picking Beatrice up from school twice a week and taking her back home on the bus for tea. I'm also going to make sure that I see Jill at least a few times a month, either for lunch, or coffee, or a dog walk. We need to look after one another. We're family. And she did save my life after all.

It also dawned on me that Oliver and Laurel's marriage might never have ended if Freya hadn't sabotaged it. This gave me a few sleepless nights, but Oliver reassured me that he and Laurel were a mistake, that their relationship was too rocky and unpredictable. He said that of course he had loved her at one time, but they were completely incompatible as a couple. He told me that I'm the real love of his life. No one else.

The four of us finally reach the summit of the hill. No matter how many times we climb to the top, this view of the Avon Valley always takes my breath away. Especially on an evening like this where the sun spreads orange and golden across a pale mauve sky. We sit on what has now become *our* bench. Me, Oliver and Beatrice, with Winnie snuffling around the vicinity for rabbits.

Oliver takes a packet of mini Jammy Dodgers from his pocket and Beatrice squeals her approval. Even Winnie is tempted away from her rabbit-chasing to sit prettily in front of us in the hope that we'll share.

'Can we bring Granny up the hill with us tomorrow?' Beatrice asks. 'I think she'd like to throw sticks for Winnie, and see the view too.'

I bend to kiss my daughter's warm cheek. 'That's a lovely idea. We'll ring her when we get home, see if she'd like to come for tea first.'

We lean into one another, the three of us, quietly munching our biscuits and watching the fiery sky. These are the moments we have to cherish, I think to myself, trying to inhale every second, every molecule, every breath. To truly savour the here and now.

Because we never know how long this fragile happiness of ours will last.

EPILOGUE

The weather has finally turned. I sit in my favourite seat, in my favourite café on Bridge Street, nursing a caramel latte while the rain pummels the pavement, along with any poor pedestrian who happens to be out in it right now. The café is only a quarter full today. There are too few people willing to brave the storm. Not me. I don't mind a bit of rain. I revel in it. It's good for the soul.

I'm not one to moan, but actually this whole situation is grossly unfair. Claire and Oliver get their happily ever after with Beatrice, Jill gets to be the heroine of the day and Freya gets her well-deserved punishment.

But what about *me*?

According to Claire, Freya confessed that she tricked Oliver into believing I was unfaithful to him. That's the reason my husband lost trust in me and why we always ended up fighting. Why ultimately he wanted a divorce, due to 'irreconcilable differences'.

Freya Collins ruined my life in her quest to get Oliver. But instead of making him fall for her, the stupid bitch cleared the way for Claire to steal him. Where's the justice in that? Nobody seems to care that Freya broke up my marriage. That I'm left with my emotions still in tatters, without the love of my life. Instead I'm making do with Philip Aintree and his bloody mother who, it would seem, loathes me for putting her son through a police investigation that wasn't even my fault!

Dark thoughts plague me as I sip my coffee, while outside, sheets of rain bounce off the road and deep thunder rolls through the town. The café's staff and customers murmur and exclaim as a jag of lightning illuminates the dark sky. Even this dramatic display of nature isn't enough to distract me from my worries.

The only reason I set my sights on Phil in the first place is because he's Oliver's neighbour. It gave me a way to get close to Ollie again. To see Claire Nolan close up. You get a pretty good view from Phil's shed into Oliver and Claire's kitchen… not to mention their bedroom. But it was hard to watch them together. Torturous. Some people might question why I put myself through it, but you don't get what you want by sitting around wishing for it. You have to put a little work in. Suffer, even.

It wounds me to think of Claire with the surname that should have remained mine. I've hated being Laurel Palmer again, but I knew it would be weird if I kept his name after the divorce. Jill wouldn't have liked that either. And I had to keep her on side. Jill always preferred me to Claire. If it were down to her, Ollie and I would never have parted. Although lately she's grown cooler towards me, which is annoying.

It's just not fair. None of it. I'm the only innocent person who's lost out here. I tried to tell Jill how I'm feeling, but she didn't understand at all. She's grown closer to Claire these past few weeks. All that stress and drama had the unfortunate effect of bonding them.

Jill was sympathetic towards me to a degree – she always is – but I could tell by her pinched lips and the way she shifted her shoulders that she'd rather I hadn't spoken about my feelings. Well, tough shit. Because I'm not going to step aside and compromise my happiness just because someone else has crapped all over my dreams.

Why should I have to make way for everyone else's happiness, while I live a shadow life, watching them have their time in the sun? I always felt that events beyond my control split us up back then. So now that I know for a fact it was Freya – and Freya is out of the way – I can finally concentrate on living the life I deserve. On getting my husband back.

I call the waitress over and order another caramel latte along with one of their sugary apple turnovers. I'm going to need the energy. I have a lot of planning to do…

A LETTER FROM SHALINI

Thank you for reading my twelfth psychological thriller, *My Little Girl*. I do hope you enjoyed reading it.

If you'd like to keep up to date with my latest releases, just sign up here and I'll let you know when I have a new novel coming out.

www.bookouture.com/shalini-boland

I love getting feedback on my books, so if you have a few moments, I'd be really grateful if you'd post a review online or tell your friends about it. A good review absolutely makes my day and I appreciate each and every one.

When I'm not writing or spending time with my family, I adore hearing from readers, so please feel free to get in touch via my social media pages.

Shalini x

 ShaliniBolandAuthor

 @ShaliniBoland

 @shaboland

 4727364.Shalini_Boland

 www.shaliniboland.co.uk

ACKNOWLEDGEMENTS

Thank you to my sensational publisher Natasha Harding. It's always such an absolute joy to work with you. Long may it continue! Thank you also to the wonderful Ruth Tross for your early guidance and feedback; it was a real privilege.

Endless thanks to the talented and super hard-working team at Bookouture: Jenny Geras, Kim Nash, Noelle Holten, Sarah Hardy, Alexandra Holmes, Mark Alder, Natalie Butlin, Alex Crow, Peta Nightingale, Hamzah Hussain, Saidah Graham and everyone else who makes up the dream team.

Thanks to my brilliant copy editor Fraser Crichton for your honest comments and insightful suggestions. To my talented proofreader Lauren Finger. And to my fantastic cover designer Lisa Horton.

I also need to bow down at the feet of Katie Villa who has narrated all my Bookouture books, under the superb production of the Audio Factory. You guys always do such an incredible job of bringing my characters to life. Thank you!

I feel very lucky to have such loyal and thorough beta readers. Thank you Terry Harden and Julie Carey. I always value your feedback and opinions.

Thank you once again to author and police officer Sammy H. K. Smith for advising on the police procedure. As always, any mistakes and embellishments are my own.

To all my loyal and lovely readers who take the time to read, review or recommend my books, without you, I wouldn't get to write the stories I love. So thank you, thank you, thank you!

Thank you times a million to Pete Boland, who is the most handsome and supportive husband ever. To Jess, my woolly writing companion. And finally, thank you to my children. You manage to stay kind, funny and upbeat, despite the obstacles you've already had to face. The world is a better place with you in it. You make me proud to be your mum.